TIME AND HEALING

Time Trilogy - Book Two

Colleen Reimer

COPYRIGHT PAGE

Published by Colleen Reimer at Smashwords, 2017.
Copyright 2015 Colleen Reimer.

Smashwords Edition, License Notes
Thank you for purchasing this book. This book remains the copyrighted property of the author, and may not be redistributed to others for commercial or non-commercial purposes. If you enjoyed this book, please encourage your friends to purchase their own copy from their favorite authorized retailer. Thank you for your support.

All scripture quotations in this publication are from the Holy Bible, NEW INTERNATIONAL VERSION®.
Copyright © 1973, 1978, 1984, 2011 by Biblica, Inc. All rights reserved worldwide.
Used by permission. NEW INTERNATIONAL VERSION® and NIV® are registered trademarks of Biblica, Inc. Use of either trademark for the offering of goods or services requires the prior written consent of Biblica US, Inc.

ISBN: 978-0-9953219-3-9

This is a work of fiction. Names, characters, businesses, places, events and incidents are either the products of the author's imagination or used in a fictitious manner. Any resemblance to actual persons, living or dead, or actual events is purely coincidental.

Front cover art created by Kurtis Molvik and Matthew Reimer.

Dedication

I dedicate this novel to all those who are searching for healing in their lives.
Sometimes the healing of our hearts can come in unorthodox ways.
Far be it from God to stick to conventional methods although he is allowed to work in whatever way he chooses.
Out-of-the-box methods are not beyond his litany of choices.
Be prepared!
After all, he is God!

Acknowledgment

I wrote the second book of this trilogy many years ago, 2004 to be exact, and recently decided to dust it off and get it going again. This novel also needed a great deal of reworking to make it ready for publishing.

There are a few I would like to thank for bringing Time and Healing to the printed page. My daughter, Felisha, proofread it and marked corrections for me. My friend Jenn Kononoff also read the manuscript and marked corrections.

I want to thank my editor, Julene Schroeder, for the awesome work she has done on my manuscript. She gave suggestions on which parts/chapters were unnecessary information. Her assistance helped to condense the book, kept the story line moving and make for a better reading experience for my readers.

My husband and our four children have been a huge support as I write. Jerrie, my husband, has been my greatest advocate, allowing me to explore my creative side. He is such a blessing to me!

I also thank God for the gift of writing. Without him this book would not exist.

My readers also deserve a huge thank you for following my work and reading what I write.

CHAPTER 1

June 1988

Rain poured down in heavy sheets and pounded the windshield in a rhythmic staccato as the traffic slowed to a snail's pace on the crowded interstate. Sally Windsor tensed at the wheel and flicked her windshield wipers to high as she maneuvered through the rush hour traffic. The wipers worked feverishly to keep up as the dark clouds above dumped their heavy load on the overtaxed freeway.

A few reckless drivers paid no heed to the dangerous driving conditions, swerving between other motorists, eager to get an advantage. The roads were much too treacherous for such reckless moves. It was difficult to see the highway lines, covered in a layer of scurrying water, and the spray from the careless few made the driving conditions even more perilous. Releasing a seething sound between her teeth, Sally shook her head. It took all her focus to stay in her lane of traffic.

Her thumb tapped out an impatient cadence on her steering wheel as the traffic repeatedly slowed and picked up again. The announcer on the radio described the gridlock on the highway and the dangerous driving conditions but there was no information on what was causing the slowdown except for what she already knew. It was raining cats and dogs.

A turn of the knob filled the space with light jazz, so much more soothing than a highway report. Her mind felt tired after a long week. The weekend stretched before her and for once she wasn't working and glad of it. She stifled a yawn. The overtime hours she'd put in lately were taking their toll.

The rain slowly let up and vehicles began to pick up their pace. After a few yards (at least that's how it felt to her), a sea of red tail lights beamed ahead as everything slowed again. Sally stayed in that snail-like pace for a few minutes when traffic came to a complete standstill.

A few minutes later, in her rear-view mirror, she noticed flashing lights approaching from behind, along the shoulder. First a police cruiser swooshed by. A short while later a fire truck and an ambulance followed. They all stopped about a half a mile up. It was hard to tell from where she sat because other vehicles blocked her view.

Every workday she made this trip and, after a hectic day, she was longing to get home and put her feet up. It was about an hour's commute from her office to her apartment in Markham, Ontario but this rain and whatever was happening up ahead was slowing things to an unbearable crawl.

A few more police cars whizzed by on the right shoulder. She put her car into park, placed her head on the backrest, closed her eyes and sighed with exasperation.

When she opened her eyes again, she noticed people up ahead begin to exit their vehicles and gather on the highway. Brightly-colored umbrellas bobbed up and down along the usually busy 401. It was an odd sight. Maybe she should get out too and find out what was going on. It would beat sitting here not knowing. Sally switched off her car, grabbed her umbrella and purse, locked the door and stepped outside. The clouds above were still emitting a steady drizzle.

She looked down at her ensemble. She was in no mood to ruin her Armani suit or new Gucci shoes but curiosity pushed her to investigate. Stepping to the shoulder, she strained to get a better view of the trouble ahead. From this vantage point she could vaguely make out something blocking the road. Moving farther toward the hold-up was her only option. Others began doing the same. It was a longer walk than she had bargained on.

As she neared the cruisers with their flashing lights, confusion and frustration buzzed through the crowd gathering on the highway. Police officers up ahead were corralling a group of curious commuters back from an accident scene. As the crowd grew exponentially in size, people leaving their vehicles to join the mob, the officers were having difficulty keeping the mass under control. One police officer managed to quiet the group and explain the situation. Everyone grew unusually still. Sally pushed forward to listen.

"There's been an accident," said the officer, his black uniform already soaked. "A tanker is banked on its side and fuel is spilling all over the road. The situation is volatile and everyone is being asked to leave their vehicles and stand back as far as possible. Now, all of you get back."

Someone in the crowd asked if there were any other vehicles involved in the accident.

The officer answered, "Yes. There was also a car involved."

"Did anyone get hurt?"

He nodded. "The car didn't stand a chance. The tanker truck completely mangled it. A lady and child were thrown on impact. It doesn't look like they made it. The guy in the truck is pinned inside but still alive. Rescue workers are trying to dislodge him. It's an extremely hazardous situation and the fuel all over the road is making it a treacherous mission. We're asking for your cooperation in staying back to a safe location."

A burly man close to Sally said, "Sounds like you all need some prayer."

Sally stared at him and felt sorry for the deluded man.

The officer nodded and said, "It wouldn't hurt."

But it won't help either. Sally shook her head.

The officer turned to direct another group away from the danger.

All around her people were doing as told, moving away from the potentially explosive situation. But there were only two police officers manning the operation. Sally stayed where she was, watching. Something urged her to move closer to the accident scene instead of farther away. An uncanny desire to see who the lady and child were pricked at her curiosity. Not that she had any propensity for blood and gore. No. Normally the very sight of it made her queasy. Merely cleaning up a bad cut made her gag. And yet the longing to know more was becoming intense and impossible to ignore. She slipped over to the shoulder and headed in the direction of the overturned tanker truck, feeling conspicuous already.

What the burly man had suggested crossed her mind. Prayer? When had that ever helped anyone? It certainly wouldn't aid that lady and her child. It had never helped her parents either. She had put any childlike faith behind her years ago.

As she came to the edge of the bridge, she stopped. She could clearly see the overturned tanker now, lying prone just past the bridge, emergency workers frantically scrambling to contain the disaster. The traffic had been stopped just before the bridge, an overpass over another busy highway. Police cruisers on the road below, their flashers blazing through the drizzle, had stopped traffic there as well. The fuel spilling from the tanker was making the entire area perilous.

Past the bridge, on the grassy incline to the right, Sally could see a small, mangled red car and it caused her heartbeat to quicken. It looked just like a friend's car. She chided herself for jumping to conclusions. It was impossible to make out the model from here, maybe not possible at all from its rearrangement by the tanker. By the look of things, no one in that vehicle could possibly have survived the collision.

She swallowed and placed a hand on her heart, which was pounding furiously beneath her Cole Haan coat. Through the drizzle, she was sure she could make out two still, covered forms lying on the green turf. They appeared motionless and abandoned.

All effort was focused on containing the fuel spilling over the freeway and dislodging the truck driver from his potentially explosive prison. Firemen were busy spraying some kind of coating over the fuel. There was a lot of shouting back and forth. Emergency workers crawled over the overturned rig like ants on an anthill. People were running here and there. It looked completely chaotic but she was sure there was some kind of order to the apparent mayhem. All focus was on the truck, spilled fuel and saving the driver.

Sally glanced back to the two lying prone on the grass. All she could deduce was that emergency workers had given up hope on them. Otherwise, why weren't they frantically trying to save them?

She took tentative steps across the bridge. If she was caught and sent back to wait with the others, so be it. Just maybe the workers were too engrossed in the emergency on the bridge to bother with her. The odor of fuel was overpowering as she drew closer to the rig. She covered her mouth and nose with one hand and kept walking. At the other end of the bridge she turned to look back. Surprisingly, no one had seen her cross.

Hurriedly, she spanned the distance to where the grass sloped down to meet the road below. Fear hammered against her ribs as she studied the crumpled car and its spilled contents. Looking over, she could see that the two sheet-covered bumps on the grass had been thrown a good hundred yards from the vehicle and quite a distance from each other.

After setting her purse down close to the mangled car, she headed to the largest covered form first. The grass was soaked and Sally stopped for a minute to look down at her expensive Gucci leather shoes. They were already wet from her walk in the rain. The damage had been done. She inhaled, released a ragged breath and cautiously continued.

As she reached the bundle on the ground, she nervously glanced back once more to the feverish work on the overpass. No one bothered to look her way. Hopefully they'd remain engrossed in their work for some time.

Clinging tightly to her umbrella, she lowered to her haunches. A thought invaded her mind. *If Jesus were here, he would raise them up and heal them right on the spot.*

Where in the world did that come from? I gave up religion a long time ago!

She shook her head and ignored the peculiar, unexpected thought.

Cautiously she lifted a corner of the sheet and looked. The woman lay face up, her rearranged face white as a ghost, blood spilling from her nose, mouth and ears, with a pool of blood gathering beneath her head. Pulling the sheet back further, Sally noticed the woman's right leg bent in a strange position with a bone exposed and jutting out at an unusual angle. The awful, gut-wrenching sight caused Sally's stomach to turn in revulsion and she quickly lowered the cloth again. Her middle heaved but she managed to force it down. The temptation to abandon the woman was strong but she couldn't leave yet. Sally had to know. The woman's face, even with the disfigurement, looked familiar. A wave of chills ran down her spine as the realization sunk in. The red car belonged to her friend after all.

This was Emma Flare. They'd gone to high school together and frequented many of the same parties. Emma was vivacious, always the life of the party, but she'd had her close calls, drinking and driving, drug overdoses – and yet she seemed invincible. Emma was the lucky one, never got caught and seemed to breeze through unscathed.

Not anymore!

It was a huge blow. To see Emma here, lying lifeless in a pool of her own blood, shook her to the core. Sally stood in stunned grief and left the sheet lying on Emma's chest, leaving her face exposed. Although they'd never been terribly close, they'd known each other for a long time. They hung out with the same crowd.

Emma got herself pregnant in twelfth grade. It probably happened at one of the parties; she was never quite sure. The father still remained a mystery. She'd kept the baby, abandoned her dreams of college and became a mother and provider, despite the huge protests from her parents.

She gave birth to a beautiful baby girl. Tiffany was gorgeous even as an infant, with a head full of dark hair just like her mother. At her birth, Sally had gone to see mother and baby in the hospital and brought a gift.

Wiping away a stray tear, Sally turned from Emma's broken frame. The small bundle lying a stone's-throw away choked her up and tears gathered in her eyes. She walked over and knelt down beside the second white sheet. After lifting it down to the girl's knees, she was surprised at the lack of damage to her body. There was no immediate sign of trauma at all.

Sally stroked Tiffany's arm affectionately. She'd held this girl in her arms a few times. After some mental calculation, Sally estimated that Tiffany was five now, ready to start kindergarten in the fall. Her long, dark hair caressed the grass beside her. Her usually bright, inquisitive eyes were closed in death, her face a pasty white. A sob escaped Sally's lips and grief filled her chest.

"How could this…have…happened?" It was hard to voice the sorrow gathered inside. "It's not fair! It's too soon…for you to go, Tiffany." Tears rolled down her cheeks as she stroked the girl's arm.

She remembered what a lovable little girl Tiffany was, with her mischievous smile and stunning looks. It was all so terribly tragic.

Sally let the tears flow and whispered. "This world needs you, Tiffany. You can't be gone yet. It's too soon!"

Another thought flashed across her consciousness: *The power of Jesus' name can raise Tiffany up.*

Where are these weird thoughts coming from?

Anxiety threatened at the bizarre words infiltrating her mind. As she gazed at Tiffany's lifeless body, the idea refused to leave. The more she pondered it, the more courage she felt.

It certainly couldn't hurt, right? I mean, what other chance do they have?

Sally took a ragged breath as fear tap danced across her ribs at the sheer absurdity of what she was about to say. "Okay, here goes!" She stared at the beautiful girl's pasty face and said, "In Jesus' name, come back, Tiffany."

She felt absolutely foolish. She no longer believed in any of this hocus-pocus. Reaching over, she stroked Tiffany's arm a while longer. How peaceful she looked as she lay in a death sleep. Sally gently moved a tendril of dark hair away from Tiffany's face to get a better look. In shock, she let the hair drop. There was now slight color in her cheeks. Sally stared for a full minute and yet the girl stayed immobile.

As Sally reached for Tiffany's wrist to check for a pulse she was sure she saw movement and locked her eyes on Tiffany's face again. After a few moments, with no sign of life, she again focused on finding a possible pulse. Where her life blood should be beating, it was silent. She allowed her gaze to find Tiffany's face again. Maybe she had only imagined the color. Repositioning her fingers on Tiffany's wrist, she waited. There! She did feel something! Maybe it was only her own heart pounding in her chest that caused her to imagine the sign of life.

It was then she saw Tiffany's lips move! She dropped the girl's wrist as though it were live with electricity, moved back a step and watched to see what would happen, her heart pounding in shock. Tiffany's head began to move slightly, back and forth. Then her eyes opened.

Sally screamed and fell over, her backside hitting the soaked grass.

Tiffany's big eyes locked on hers. Sally stared at her in terror.

"Where am I?" she said in a shaky little voice. "Where's my mommy?"

Taking quick, shallow breaths, Sally tried to regain her calm. She lifted herself off the grass and knelt down close to the girl. Running away as fast as she could was what she should do, but she couldn't abandon the girl now.

"Hi there, Tiffany. Are you okay? Do you hurt anywhere?" Concern flooded Sally with the words. There was still a possibility of internal injuries.

Tiffany's forehead scrunched before answering. "No, I don't think so. Why am I lying down outside? I'm all wet!"

Sally repositioned the umbrella to shield Tiffany's face. "It's raining out here. You and your mommy were in an accident. I think your mommy is hurt bad and you might be hurt too, so don't move, okay?"

"Okay."

"I'm going to check on your mommy and I'll be right back, but you have to promise me that you won't move." Sally didn't want her seeing Emma in the state she was in. After a moment of silence, she repeated herself. "Will you promise?"

"I promise. I won't move."

"Good girl. I'll be right back." She covered Tiffany, to just under her chin, with the wet sheet to protect her a little from the rain

Walking away on legs that threatened to give way, Sally had no desire to go see Emma again but she had promised Tiffany. Coming to where Emma lay, she knew it was hopeless. There was too much damage, too much spilled blood. At least little Tiffany was okay. It was one sliver of hope, at least for now. There had been no sign of injury on her small body.

What would Tiffany do without a mother? It all seemed so wrong. There were grandparents who could raise her but life wouldn't be the same without her mother. Sally couldn't keep the tears from starting again as she felt overcome by the injustice of it all. Emma hadn't lived a perfect life by far but she didn't deserve this.

Emma was gone, that much was clear. Her half-open eyelids, pasty white complexion and twisted limbs told it all.

A thought weaseled in. *If Jesus had power to raise the dead when he walked the earth, then his name must have the same power now.*

Stop already! What is wrong with me?

She hadn't given Jesus the time of day in so long. Why now? It confused her but more than that, it terrified her. Lowering to her haunches, she held her umbrella over them both to ward off the new barrage of rain. After staring at Emma for a long time, striving to keep her panic at bay, she reached over and placed a hand on her belly. It was the one spot clear of blood.

Tiffany's voice floated toward her. "How's my mommy?"

Sally ignored her and tried to focus. "I'm so sorry, Emma. I never thought you'd end up like this. Your daughter needs you. You can't be dead. It's just not time for you to go. Would you mind if I pray?" *What am I doing? Of course Emma wouldn't mind! She can't hear a thing! I don't even know how to pray.*

She felt completely helpless as tears dripped from her eyelids and slipped down onto Emma's still frame. "Well, here goes. God...um Jesus.... What am I doing?" Confusion slammed into her. This was ridiculous! A sob erupted and squeaked from her lips. She couldn't let Tiffany hear her. After gaining a small measure of composure, she ventured, "Okay, Emma, come back in Jesus' name."

Sally instinctively scooted back, watched and waited. Nothing happened. What did she expect? Tiffany's resurrection was most likely a recovery. She probably hadn't died at all. She'd probably hit her head hard when thrown from the vehicle and it put her out for a bit. It was only coincidence that her prayer preceded Tiffany's wakeful state.

Emma looked so twisted and bloody. Forcing the tide of furry and sorrow down, she willed herself not to groan and make a scene. She didn't want to frighten Tiffany. Covering her face with her right hand, she struggled to rein in her emotions. Slowly she lowered her hand and stared at her friend. Terror ripped through her in that moment.

When had Emma's face turned a fleshy pink? As Sally watched, Emma's features slowly transitioned from a peaceful, relaxed, sleeping state to a tense and horrified expression. Suddenly her eyes sprang open, she sat straight up and screamed.

"Ahhhhhh...... I'm out, I'm out! I'm really out! Oh thank you, God!" Emma placed her bloody face into her hands and shrieked as if in absolute terror.

Sally stood quickly, backed up a few steps and gazed in frozen shock. The horror etched on Emma's face was traumatizing. With tormented eyes, Emma glanced at Sally then buried her face in her hands again. She rocked back and forth as if she were trying to forget some horrific experience, groaning as though she were about to lose control.

"Oh, God, please forgive me! I never knew! I never knew! Please take my life. I give it to you." Her desperate, agonized sobs gradually changed to cries of relief.

Emma was a mess. Tears streamed down her cut cheeks, her broken nose ran profusely, mixed with blood. The blood from her ears had stopped flowing but even so, she looked ghastly.

No words came. Sally stared at her with a mixture of confusion and terror. She wasn't quite sure what had happened. It all seemed utterly surreal.

Emma's shaky voice broke the silence. "I heard your voice telling me to come back. It really was you. How did you know I was in that awful place?" She wrapped her arms tightly around herself and shivered. Rain from above was dousing her.

Having jumped back from Emma's position, Sally's umbrella offered no relief to the woman but moving closer wasn't an option yet. Sally was shaking uncontrollably. "What place?" she asked with a trembling voice.

"I was in the worst describable, pitch-black place!" Emma's eyes were glazed with fear. "There were terrible creatures there and they were torturing me! They kept mocking and ridiculing me about rejecting Christ! The heat was unbearable! My skin was on fire and it wouldn't stop! I kept begging God to get me out of there! I begged over and over again! I'd never felt such desperation. Finally, I saw a bright light and I knew it was Jesus. I just knew!"

Sally took one more petrified step back.

"He showed me my life, all the chances I'd had. I'd rejected him again and again. He told me that now it was too late. I begged him to give me another chance. He asked me if I'd live any differently if he did. I promised him the moon! I've never felt so anxious and been in so much pain in my entire life! And then I heard your voice, telling me to come back." She stared hard. "And here I am. Thank you, oh Sally, thank you with all my heart!

Sally's whole body quaked at the outlandish tale. This couldn't be happening! With a shaky voice she said, "I'm glad you're back, Emma. But I didn't do anything."

"But you called me back, didn't you?"

"I did but I didn't know it would work."

"I heard you call me back in the name of Jesus. Do you know him?"

Sally shrugged and felt like an imbecile. "I did once but I don't know him anymore."

"Well, whatever you said worked and I'll never forget it, not ever! He got me out of that horrible place and I owe him my life." Peace shone through the gore on her face.

It was completely disconcerting. Emma's transformation was astounding.

How did this happen? By a few simple words? How was this even possible?

Emma began to search the surrounding area frantically. "Where's Tiffany? Where's my baby? Tiffany?"

Sally's insides felt like jello, unsteady and wobbly, but she needed to answer. Releasing a deep, wavering breath, she said, "Tiffany's fine. She's lying over there." Her finger pointed the direction. "I told her I was going to check on you and asked her to stay still. I didn't see any injuries but we won't know about any internal stuff until the paramedics get here."

"I want to go see her. Could you help me up?"

"You shouldn't move till the paramedics check you." But then again, she had sat up on her own without trouble. She took a look at Emma's leg beneath the sheet. No, she definitely shouldn't stand. She pointed to it and said, "I don't think you could walk on that leg if you tried."

Emma glanced down at her twisted leg and said, "Oh!" Concern clouded her eyes. "It looks bad, doesn't it? Where are the paramedics anyway?"

"I think they'd given up hope on you two."

Understanding lit Emma's eyes. "I see."

"I thought you were a goner. I never had a good look at Tiffany, though, before she regained consciousness."

With her heartbeat slowly returning to normal, Sally looked back toward the overpass. Ambulance lights flashed, ricocheting off the water on the road, cascading the light farther than normal. Two ambulances stood a few hundred feet from the overturned tanker – for safety reasons, she supposed. The emergency workers stood around, at the ready. Police officers and some firemen also stood guard, watching as the man in the truck was being cut out of his prison. No one looked her way or made any move to assist Emma or Tiffany. But they had no idea circumstances had changed.

"I'll go and check on Tiffany. I'll be right back."

"Please do, Sally. Let her know I'm okay. That I love her."

Sally nodded and, with umbrella in one hand, walked over to where Tiffany lay. She wished she had an extra umbrella to leave with Emma. It was a relief to escape the myriad of conflicting emotions she'd felt around Emma. She still didn't understand what happened back there, didn't know if she ever would. Her whole body shook and she knew it was not because of the cool rain. Her legs felt like play dough, ready to buckle at any moment. As she reached Tiffany's side, she hunkered down beside her, shielding both of them from the rain with her umbrella.

"Tiffany, honey, your mommy is doing well. She loves you. So don't worry, okay?"

"Okay, I won't."

Child-like trust. Sally could hardly remember ever feeling that way. She glanced up the incline and noticed a man standing beside Emma's mangled car with his eyes fixed on her. He looked relaxed in his blue jeans, white t-shirt and running shoes. A slight smile curled the edges of his mouth. His shoulder length hair seemed light and airy as it blew in the breeze. He had no umbrella and yet his hair appeared unaffected by the rain. Sally stood slowly, confusion crowding her senses.

His head moved, a nod of approval. At least that's what it looked like. Light began to emanate from him, glowing outward as though he were lit from within. The light grew gradually brighter until suddenly he was gone. He simply vanished! Sally blinked her eyes furiously and looked again but he had completely disappeared.

I hope my mind isn't going on me! This sure is weird.

She tore her eyes from the spot and turned back to Tiffany. Repositioning her umbrella to shield the girl, she kneeled down beside her again. Hearing loud voices, shouting and running feet, she jerked her head up to look. She knew immediately she'd been spotted, as police officers, firemen and ambulance workers rushed toward her, all yelling at the same time.

"Now I'm in trouble."

"What did you do to get you in trouble, Miss Sally?" asked Tiffany. She looked anxious.

"Don't worry. I think it'll be okay." She gave the girl a weak smile and stood to prepare for the onslaught she knew was coming.

The questions came fast and furiously.

A police officer took a go first as he reached her. "What are you doing here? Weren't you told to stay back with the others?" He looked angry and flustered simultaneously.

"I know this lady and her child. I'd like to stay if I could."

"No, that's totally out of the question. They're both dead and there are professionals who will take over now. It's too treacherous here and you need to move away from this situation with the others."

A paramedic asked, "What happened here? These two were pronounced dead by the head paramedic." He stared dumbstruck at Tiffany.

The police officer turned his attention to the little girl on the grass. Incredulity replaced his angry expression.

"I'm not exactly sure, sir," Sally offered.

Another paramedic, with an imposing presence, came to stand with them. His composure was shattered by what he saw.

The first paramedic turned to the other man and asked, "You pronounced both the mother and child dead, didn't you?"

The head honcho knelt down beside Tiffany and checked her. "They were both deceased," he said in confusion. "There was no pulse. This little girl's neck was clearly broken." He looked completely perplexed as he studied her neck.

Tiffany giggled and said, "That tickles."

The man looked at her with a baffled expression. After finding no apparent injuries, he turned to look in Emma's direction and stood. "The lady also had no pulse and was bleeding profusely from her extremities. It was very clear to the men that were with me and to me that there was no hope for them. I don't know what happened here."

"They're obviously very alive," said Sally, feeling some amusement over their bewilderment.

"It's totally unexplainable." He headed over to Emma, scratching his head in confusion.

A team of others followed closely behind, all mirroring each other's puzzlement. Questions murmured through the group, but no clear answers were forthcoming. Soon they let the queries go and busily attended to Emma's injuries and monitored Tiffany's vital signs. Soon all the workers were consumed with the task at hand.

An ambulance from the bridge made its way toward them, parking just above the grassy decline. It seemed they'd forgotten all about Sally's presence. She didn't mind watching. She'd seen the worst anyway. A voice behind her made her jump.

"I suggest you move back from the action here and let the professionals do their work." A police officer pointed toward the crowd a few hundred feet away.

She nodded and reluctantly ascended the embankment. Inching her way up the incline, the wet grass making it difficult, she stopped to stand beside the mangled red car. Emma's sobs filtered toward her but, through the tears, her thanks to God echoed through the falling rain.

Sally struggled to know what to make of it all. Maybe Emma had simply hallucinated in her unconscious state. To admit that Emma had gone to a place called hell would require too much soul-searching. She avoided that subject like the plague. Explaining away religion and God was her way of life. She never allowed her mind to wander there.

So why did I allow this to happen? How did my guard slip?

"What are you doing here?"

The fireman's question made her jump for the second time.

He gave her a sympathetic smile. "You need to stay back with everyone else. This is still a very perilous situation."

"She's my friend," was all she could think to say.

"I'm sorry, but you're too close to the spilled fuel. You'll have to move back with the others."

Nodding numbly, she picked up her purse from beside the mangled red car. While the fireman watched, she made her way to join the crowd gathered on the side of the bridge. As soon as she reached them, the questions began. Reluctantly, she revealed just enough to satisfy them.

Separating herself from the group, she stood apart and tried to process all she'd witnessed.

Emma and Tiffany would be okay. It was one bright note after years of losing those she loved. Saying goodbye to another friend was, for now, postponed. There had been too many funerals, some from drug overdoses and some caused by drinking and driving. It had taken its toll on her emotions. Somehow she managed to block out the pain each time and go on.

She'd been taught differently, at least by one parent. Her mother had been diligent to take her and her brother, Robert, to church for years. Sunday mornings were her dad's time to get over his hangovers. Yes, her family had some dysfunction but what family didn't?

When she became a teenager she'd rebelled and refused to placate her mother any longer. She vowed never to enter church doors again. It didn't take Robert long to follow her lead.

It disappointed their mother terribly but it didn't stop Sally from abandoning church. To Sally's thinking, church was her mother's lifeline and a crutch to get through her difficult marriage. The anger, fights and tension were constant facts of the Windsor household. Strife had moved in as a permanent resident and refused to leave, squeezing peace out for good.

Sally had moved out on her own as soon as she could manage it financially and never looked back again.

Her view of religion had been tainted. Although her father confessed to be a Christian, his lifestyle was less than admirable. The hypocrisy was too blatant and any love far too distant. Nothing about it fit right in her mind

Emma and Tiffany were being lifted into the waiting ambulance. Soon the flashers and sirens were in full swing and the vehicles tore down the shoulder toward the hospital. A few minutes later, the man from the tanker truck was extracted, placed on a stretcher and lifted into another ambulance. The crowd erupted with claps and cheers. Sally looked on straight-faced, feeling nothing like celebrating. The ambulance also left with a barrage of lights and noise.

It took some time, but eventually the emergency workers allowed people to head back to their vehicles. The tanker had been set erect and moved by a few large tow trucks. Firemen were cleaning up the last of the fuel spillage.

After her walk back to her car, Sally sank into her driver's seat, feeling utterly drained. Tears threatened and her emotions felt raw, taut and overtaxed. Traffic finally started moving. She couldn't wait to get home!

CHAPTER 2

August 2003

Tessa Fields finished balancing the books, printed off some email attachments that needed to be filed then began to tidy up her office. For the most part, the week had been fairly quiet at the Mansion of Hope.

The Mansion of Hope was one of the elaborate mansions on Young Street in Chelsey, Minnesota. It had been refurbished to house a women's rehabilitation center. It looked radically different now than when she'd first visited this place a few years ago. It had been abandoned by its previous owner and left to the elements until it was a sorry sight to behold, and was left in that debilitated state for many years. It still surprised Tessa that the city of Chelsey didn't intervene, allowing the formerly exquisite mansion to deteriorate to that degree. There were rumors back then of the place being haunted. She'd come to believe differently after visiting it.

The city eventually condemned the house and scheduled it for demolition. But after some extraordinary circumstances, they reversed their decision. Church on the Move, the church she attended with her husband, Cody, purchased the mansion for next to nothing and renovated it. That's when the home began to take on its former grandeur. It took some time, but gradually the past beauty of the place replaced the decay, despair and hopelessness of its abandonment.

Tessa's office was located in the former sitting room, although they'd divided the room with a wall, allowing for two offices close to the foyer. Her side didn't include the fireplace but she was okay with that. Her desk was situated so that she could look out the large bay window to her left and enjoy whatever the weather offered her. A large oak tree was visible from where she sat and brought back myriad memories.

Working at the mansion allowed her the privilege of enjoying its magnificence. She never tired of its elaborate entrance, the two curved stairways leading to the top floor, where a balcony overlooked the expansive foyer. The massive chandelier, which hung from the two-story ceiling, had been refurbished and sparkled like she remembered from times gone by.

The home was massive, with plenty of room for its present use. Every part of the home was elaborate, each room large and impressive and the vintage feel retained with the renovation, in keeping with the time period of its original build. Everyone who entered the large double doors was spellbound by the beauty of the entrance. The rest of the place was no less impressive.

Many of the women they presently housed had been in the program for a few months and were almost through with their detoxification treatments and training. There were two new women who had arrived within the last few days. They seemed to be handling the process fairly well.

Deborah was staying with the women tonight, to assist them through any difficult stages. She was well-experienced to handle it. And yet, for no explainable reason, Tessa felt edgy.

She decided to check on Deborah and the condition of the other two women before leaving. Exiting her office, she entered into the expansive lobby at the front of the building, where grand curved staircases led upstairs on either side. At the top, she walked toward the left side hallway where a secured door blocked the entrance to the hall and punched in her code. The door clicked and she walked through to the women's detoxification units. At the first room on her right, she glanced through the small window in the door and noticed Deborah sitting quietly beside the bed. The woman, Lily, lying prone on her mattress, appeared peaceful, under control.

Why was she feeling so apprehensive, then? Tessa reached for the doorknob and opened the door.

Deborah's head shot up in surprise. "What are you doing here? I thought you'd already left."

Tessa stepped inside. "I just finished up in the office. I thought I'd check on you first and see how things are going. Is everything okay?"

"The two new women are doing fine. Lily here has had some difficult moments today. She was struggling earlier but she's settled now."

Tessa glanced over at the white-faced woman on the bed. Lily was soaked with sweat and her breathing came labored.

"Have you given her any medication to help calm her?"

"No. They are far better off, in my opinion, if they can get rid of the toxins without more toxins being pumped into them. She's been hallucinating the last two days and that's been her greatest struggle. It's created a great deal of fear and panic but she seems to be over that, at least for now."

"And what about the other one? Veronica Billings? How's she doing?"

"She seems to be breezing through the detox. There've been some rough moments for her but she's doing great. I should check on her now." Deborah stood and started for the door.

Tessa followed her to the hall. "Do you think you'll manage tonight with two new women to work with?" The unease wouldn't leave.

Deborah stopped and punched in the security code to lock the door before heading to the next room. "It wasn't a problem last night with the two of them and I don't foresee any difficulties. Bill will be downstairs if I need him." Bill was the security guard on site. Deb stopped at the next door over, punched in her code and walked in.

Tessa entered and closed the door behind her.

Deborah took a seat beside Veronica, who was curled into a tight ball on top of her blankets. She wore the customary garb for the home, light green pants, with long sleeved, v-necked top in the same shade, and white slippers for her feet. Lying on her side, her arms hugged her knees, her eyes were shut tightly and soft whimpers escaped her lips.

After watching Veronica for a few moments, Tessa found her emotions filling with deep compassion. She'd seen many in this same condition and yet each time she did, her heart went out to them. So many lives were torn apart and ruined by substance and drug abuse. None of those who came here wanted to continue the life they had. For a myriad of reasons, they all came desperate for help, their lives spinning out of control.

Hope. That's what was offered here – a new chance at life – and that's why they kept coming.

Over the past two years, Tessa had seen many women beat their addictions. Hope for them had returned. She prayed silently for these two new women.

Deborah said, "They're both settled."

"Yes. It looks like everything's under control. I'll go then, but call if there's any change, okay?"

"Thanks, Tessa. I appreciate the offer."

She left the room, locked the security door at the end of the hall and made her way down the stairway. Peace is what she should have been feeling and yet a nagging sense of peril tugged at her. Halfway down, she stopped and prayed once more, making sure she covered everything she could think of. Shrugging off the feeling of uncertainty, she made her way to her office to grab her purse and coat.

This office had been home to her for two years now and quite the adventure it had been. She smiled at the thought. God had used such a dramatic way of averting her plans to set her on the path he'd destined for her. She was thankful that she'd listened to his guidance and obeyed. Working at the Mansion of Hope gave her tremendous satisfaction. Going to work was something she now enjoyed. It sure beat working as a waitress at The Eating Place. No more disgruntled Martha to deal with, one of the managers there. It also topped working with numbers as an accountant for the law firm.

Her husband, Cody Fields, had been very instrumental in directing her to help those less fortunate than she. He'd also, at one time, been addicted to drugs and alcohol. That was before they met and he'd been miraculously delivered by the power of God. He fell in love with God from that time forward and his great zeal had a definite impact on her life.

Cody also worked at a home similar to this one, but for men, named Manor of Peace. Church on the Move bought both facilities and renovated them into suitable homes for those overcoming addictions.

Cody loved the work he did with the men. His work was more direct, counseling and teaching them new skills. He often worked weekends but this weekend he was off. It was something Tessa was looking forward to – a few quiet days together.

Thoughts of her husband brought a wave of warmth. Their two and a half years of marriage were, to date, the best years of her life. She closed her office door, draped a sweater over her shoulders, walked through the large foyer and on to one of the hallways that led to the back door and parking lot.

As Tessa started down the hallway, an unusual sound stopped her in her tracks. She turned and strained to hear. The hush of the expansive lobby was all that echoed back. Shaking off the uncertainty, she turned again to leave. The phone in her office was ringing now and she could hear someone's voice from somewhere in the building. That wasn't so unusual. The home was nearly at capacity.

She would have ignored it if not for the strangeness of the sounds. There was something in that voice, tension maybe, that made her stay. Even with it muffled by the walls and floor, the voice sounded frantic. Pounding feet from the top floor made her pause.

Her cell phone chirped from her purse. She dug it out quickly and flipped it open. It was the number from the upstairs phone. She placed the phone to her ear and said, "Yes?"

"Tessa, Tessa are you still here!" Deborah sounded beside herself.

"Yes, Deb, I'm still here. What's wrong?"

"Please, get up here as fast as you can. I have an emergency! I've already called Bill Quincy and he'll be here as soon as he can. He left on an errand. Please, come help!" The phone went dead.

Tessa ran toward the stairs, slipping her cell phone back into her purse and taking the stairs two at a time. At the top of the steps, through the glass insert on the hall door, she saw Deborah standing outside of Veronica Billings' room, peering through the small window. Her phone was attached to her ear and she was frantically relaying information to someone. Adrenaline flowing, Tessa unlocked the hall door, turned and locked it behind her, and raced toward Deb.

Deborah flicked her phone shut and turned uneasy eyes to her.

"You're hurt," Tessa said.

"Yeah. I got creamed good!"

"What happened in there?"

"I didn't expect her to respond like that. Veronica was fairly settled when you left but shortly after, she sprang out of bed as though something threw her out. She came after me with swinging fists. It took me totally off guard."

"You have a cut above your eye."

"Yeah. She got a few hard punches in before I could get my thoughts together enough to get out of there. I threw a chair between us or else she'd have exited the room right behind me. The chair made her trip and fall." Guilt washed over her features. "I hope I didn't hurt her. She must be hallucinating big time to become this violent."

The noise from the room was appalling. Tessa moved to take a look. Deborah shifted out of the way.

"I locked her in. She's been throwing stuff around since I left the room."

The carnage Veronica had managed to create within a few minutes was astounding. The room was a total disaster and she was still raging out of control. Her metal bed had been overturned, the mattress and bedding strewn from one end of the room to the other. The small nightstand was smashed badly. From here it looked as though only two of its legs remained attached. Splinters of wood stuck out where the other two legs should be. Books and personal effects were scattered around the room. A cup lay on its side, spilling water around its periphery.

Veronica stormed the door and Tessa flinched when she connected. There were numerous cuts on her face and arms. She held a piece of broken pottery from the plant that had previously decorated her nightstand. Veronica had insisted on a potted yellow mum for her room, her favorite. It now lay shredded and stomped so fine it was hard to recognize. Veronica attempted to slice through the metal door with the broken pottery piece, the glass insert – anything to get out.

When that failed to work, the woman wandered around the room, picked up random items and flung them wildly around, ranting and screaming at the top of her lungs. It was a frightening vision to watch. How could someone, so calm one minute, turn into a raging lunatic the next?

Tessa's heart sank watching the tortured woman fighting an unseen adversary, an enemy of her own making. It seemed bent on her total destruction.

"She's hurting herself."

"I know." Deborah's eyes clouded with worry.

"Who did you call?"

"I called Charlie Kendal. If anyone can help, I know Charlie can."

"I think you'll need more than one man to contain her rage."

"I'm hoping that with Bill coming and now Charlie that we'll be able to handle her and get her secured for the night."

"She really hit you hard, Deb! How do you feel?"

There was a deep cut just above her eyebrow. Blood trickled down her cheek and one eye was beginning to swell shut. It would soon start to discolor.

"Not the greatest. She also punched me in the gut. It took my breath away for a few seconds. I had a hard time reacting quickly. She hit me a few more times but I barely remember where because I was so frantic to get out of there."

They both turned at the sound of feet pounding up the stairs. Bill Quincy appeared and hurried toward them.

"How's she doing, Deborah?" He was clearly out of breath from his hurried flight up the stairs. Possessing a middle-aged extra tire around his middle, there was no way he was in good enough shape to handle the out-of-control woman on the other side of the door. He said, "Whoa, look at your face!"

After filling him in on the details, they both decided it prudent to wait for Charlie's arrival before attempting anything.

Charlie Kendal also worked at the Manor of Peace, Cody's right hand man. He was accustomed to dealing with severe cases of detox. He was a big man with a muscular build, well able to strong-arm patients into submission, securing them to their beds with straps and brackets. Tessa hated seeing women bound and contained that way but in this case, there was no other option.

Veronica would only end up hurting herself if left in this condition. Tessa peered nervously through the window again, impatient for Charlie to arrive. The woman had settled some, although she still looked agitated as she paced the room. She kicked things out of her way and stomped her feet but she was no longer heaving objects around. Her previously furious gaze had given way to a pained expression.

Bill scooted closer and Tessa moved to let him take a look. An idea struck her.

She turned to Deborah and asked. "Should I call Cody to come help? I know he'd come right away if he knew we needed him."

"That might be a good idea. We'll need all the support we can get." Deborah leaned up against the wall and tenderly touched her face with one hand as her other hand held her traumatized stomach.

Tessa made the call.

Cody answered. "Hey, darling! Are you on your way home?" The sound of his voice still thrilled her, especially after a long day apart.

"No. I'm still at The Mansion of Hope. We've got a situation here. It's Veronica. She's out of control. Could you come over and help out? Charlie's on his way but we need another strong guy."

"I'll be right there."

Within ten minutes Charlie Kendal arrived and Cody was right behind him. Cody sidled up beside Tessa and placed a quick kiss on her lips. After the three men discussed their strategy, Deborah punched in her code and opened the door. The three men entered and she secured the door after them.

Deborah and Tessa watched from the little glass window.

The three approached Veronica cautiously. Her gaze was diverted to the mangled objects of her now reined-in fury. She paced and kicked items out of her way with a grunt and cry of frustration. Slowly, she turned in the men's direction. The gaze of solitude and self-infliction gradually shifted to offence and rage. Growling as though she were a cornered wild animal, she flung herself recklessly toward them, her arms swinging madly. The pupils of her eyes disappeared as a deep darkness overtook her.

The situation had quickly become volatile again. Tessa and Deborah prayed frantically for protection for the three brave men. As Veronica barreled toward them, Charlie leaned back, stuck out his foot and sent her flying face-first onto the floor. She struck hard, turned quickly, grabbed Charlie's leg and bit him as hard as she could, causing him to cry out in pain.

Charlie being incapacitated for a moment, Veronica sprang to her feet and with superhuman strength jumped high into the air, kicked out her feet to connect squarely with Bill's chest, sending him flying backward onto the floor. Her crazed eyes then focused on Cody who looked taken off guard by the sudden upper hand she'd taken. A flustered look filled his face at suddenly being exposed.

Tessa felt a rush of fear over his safety. "God, please give Cody wisdom to know what to do!"

"Amen!" Deborah quickly agreed.

Their eyes were peeled on the unbelievable fight between the petite woman and three strong men.

Veronica stopped for a moment, glared menacingly at Cody then sneered in contempt. Cody's face shifted from one of fear to determination. Courage emanated from him as he pointed a finger straight at her. It made her stop and take note.

Cody's voice echoed through the room and could be heard through the door. "In Jesus' name, I speak peace over you, Veronica. Stop this now and be quiet! You will not harm anyone, anymore, and you will calm down now."

His words were spoken to a greater audience than just the frail woman staring at him. Slowly, her countenance began to change. Instead of the dark blackness staring out from her eyes, light began to return, her pupils emerged and an emotional meltdown ensued.

Veronica folded into herself and fell into a heap on the floor, the fight finally out of her. The superhuman strength was gone and in its place remained a broken, suffering individual desperately in need of help. Curling into a ball, Veronica wrapped her arms tightly around her knees and wept.

The three men approached, cautiously this time. Charlie took her arms, wrestling them from her tight hold about her knees and secured them behind her back. Bill lifted the bed from its side and righted it. He quickly threw the mattress, pillow and bedding back on in a haphazard manner.

Deborah went to unlock the door.

Tessa placed a hand on her arm. "Not yet. Wait till they have her firmly secured."

Deborah sighed. "The bedding's a mess." Order was important to Deb.

Tessa allowed a small smile to curve her lips. It was easier now, knowing Cody was out of danger.

Cody prepared and attached the straps and buckles to the bed that would keep Veronica safe. All three lifted Veronica, her form limp and weak, and placed her on the bed. After lacing and buckling her tightly, it was clear she wouldn't be going anywhere tonight.

Then Deb unlocked the door and the two entered. Standing at the bed rail, seeing Veronica in this state, filled Tessa with an overwhelming sorrow. Never had she seen such a frantic display before. It broke her heart to see a woman so bound by addiction, so controlled by the demons it invoked. It was a vivid reminder that addictions came with a price.

They all helped to clean the room, setting things back in their rightful place. Charlie removed the broken nightstand and came back with an intact one. Bill found a broom and swept up the destroyed plant and pot. Deborah returned to the righted seat beside Veronica, sat down and opened her Bible. With a clear, determined voice she began to read scripture verses out loud. It was something they did on a regular basis at this home. The founders of this detoxification center believed the best medicine was the word of God and Tessa had seen it work miracles in too many women's lives to argue with the method.

Charlie left the room and returned shortly with some medication and a needle. Deborah stood immediately and put her hand out to object.

"I don't think that'll be necessary, Charlie. Veronica has settled and I don't want her to have unnecessary chemicals in her bloodstream."

"Deb, are you nuts? Have you looked at your face lately? We need to do this."

"No! And that's my final answer!" Deborah was well-seasoned for her job. She'd been doing this kind of work for many years before she started at the Mansion of Hope and everyone respected her opinion.

"Okay, Deb. I hope you know what you're doing." Charlie reluctantly retreated with his tray of medication but he didn't look pleased.

"I can stay the night," offered Tessa. "You need to rest your injured body." Although apprehensive, she knew it was the right thing to do.

Cody stepped forward. "That's right. Tessa and I will stay and you can go recuperate. We'll manage fine."

A torn look filled Deb's eyes. She took her responsibility seriously but was clearly in pain. Finally, she asked, "Are you sure the two of you want to stay here?"

"Definitely," said Cody.

"But I remember Tessa telling me that you haven't had a weekend to yourselves in a long time. It's hardly fair to do that to you."

Tessa shook her head. "Don't you worry about what's fair, Deborah. You need to take care of yourself tonight and rest. Cody and I will be fine and we'll still be together." She slipped her hand into Cody's.

Deborah nodded. "All right then." She rose slowly and left the room with a limp.

"She's feeling every step," whispered Tessa in concern.

"She should see a doctor and make sure there's no injury."

Charlie stepped forward. "I'll help her down the stairs and suggest she go to emerg."

Bill nodded and said, "Well, that added some interest to the evening. I'll be downstairs if you two need me. Just give me a buzz."

They nodded and Bill left. The room fell silent.

Cody turned to Tessa then, held her close and kissed her with desire.

Pulling away, she said, "I'm sorry about tonight. I had planned to make Italian creamed chicken breasts, rice pilaf and steamed carrots for dinner. With lit candles, it would have been a very romantic evening."

Cody gazed at her lovingly. "We could do it tomorrow night."

"That would work." She smiled and leaned into him.

He held her close and placed kisses on her forehead.

It felt wonderful to be held like that in his arms.

They finally pulled apart. Cody went to get a second chair and they settled in for the night. Veronica, their assignment, was already sleeping, her soft snores filling the small room. All her activity had plumb worn her out.

CHAPTER 3

June 1989

Sally Windsor walked into her small kitchen and headed toward the refrigerator. A picture on the top right corner, held by a pineapple magnet, caught her eye. It was barely visible, crowded out by numerous notes and pictures cluttered around it, all held in place by gaudy magnets. It was the only way she could remember her appointments.

I should get rid of half this stuff. A bunch of junk is what it is!

Reaching for the half-hidden picture, she took it from the fridge. Emma and Tiffany stared at her from the glossy finish, their arms around each other in close embrace. Their happy smiles brought a twist to her insides. The picture had been taken a few weeks after the accident. Emma gave it to her as a gift when she'd dropped in to visit.

The memory of that visit came like an unwelcome guest. Sally had tried to be civil and sympathetic at first but Emma would not stop talking about God. The extreme discomfort it had created still troubled her. Her words and prayers had brought Emma back to life so why did talking about God bother her so much?

She'd cut Emma short, made some excuse of having some appointment and asked her to leave. Avoidance was the best policy in dealing with this sort of thing. That was eleven months ago and she hadn't seen Emma since. Emma didn't come around to the parties anymore since she latched onto religion. That was fine with Sally. Keeping out of Emma's way suited her well. Having this picture here, staring at her from the fridge, was tiresome.

After opening the kitchen drawer, filled with bills, pens, pads of paper, paper clips, batteries and various useless objects, she threw the picture in, adding to the growing stack. She breathed a sigh of relief, turned back to the refrigerator, opened the door, grabbed two cans of beer and took them to the living room.

She couldn't help feel a tinge of disdain for the man sitting on the couch. Felix grabbed the beer she held out for him and she took a seat beside him. They'd been living together for six months and it had been a rocky relationship from the start. They'd met at a dance in one of the clubs she frequented. He seemed amiable enough at the start, showed interest in her life and things progressed from there. After a month, she'd agreed to let him move in. It helped curb her loneliness.

The mistake she'd made became clear with time. Blunders were commonplace for her when it came to relationships. They never lasted long. If only she had the guts to kick Felix out, but she hated confrontation. Enduring a slip-up seemed easier than fixing it.

He didn't have a job and showed little interest in getting one. Her career supported his laziness. Felix had no complaints about the arrangement but she was miserable. All the bills were her responsibility. She'd once suggested they split the cost but Felix responded violently. He'd stormed to the back bedroom, came back with a gun and waved it in her face, yelling and screaming some nonsense about treating him with respect.

That's when she knew he had to go but she was scared. His little escapade taught her to keep her mouth shut. She didn't really believe he'd ever do her any harm. To endure Felix wasn't really that difficult and having him around made her feel less lonely. At least there was someone to talk to, smoke up together with and they both loved to party. Maybe those were poor excuses to let him stay but she didn't have the courage or the heart to kick him out.

More often than not, when she arrived home from work, she'd find Felix high on drugs. Where he purchased them, she didn't know. Where he found the money was also a mystery. On weekends she wasn't a saint, but during the week, while she worked, she stayed clean.

Her career was her great love and she wouldn't risk it for the world. Fashion design was her passion and she had dreams of one day opening her own business. Going to work was never a chore. It excited her, fueled her.

Felix was the only difficult issue in her life at the moment. She highly suspected he was involved in drug sales. How else could he afford them without a job? He'd never asked her for money. His pride prevented it. She didn't question him about his life; she didn't want him questioning her so she likewise left him alone.

He chuckled beside her over some stupid joke on the sitcom. To stomach the junk he watched on TV was a challenge. Maybe it was her dissatisfaction with Felix that made her so cynical. She used to enjoy watching evening shows.

Her mind wandered. She was twenty-four and didn't have much to show for her two years of work except for a wide array of designer clothes and shoes filling her closet. Clothes and shoes were her two great loves and her closet attested to it. Her bills were paid punctually every month but her partying habits made it difficult to save much.

She considered herself pretty, average in height, with shoulder-length, brunette hair, styled perfectly at all times. Being in the fashion industry encouraged the best in her – make-up worn meticulously, nails polished and the latest of styles framing her form. These qualities kept the male species looking.

Thinking about it made her wonder why she'd ever settled for Felix. Looking sideways at him, the sight of him depressed her, so she turned her eyes to settle on the TV again but her mind couldn't focus.

Taylor Fashion Design Company was located downtown Toronto. Living in Markham gave her fairly reasonable access to the office. It took her around forty-five minutes to an hour to drive there with traffic, sometimes longer. Downtown Toronto was a zoo but she'd gladly brave the traffic to work. Designing clothes was a lifelong dream fulfilled.

The sitcom ended, Felix switched off the TV and turned to face her. "Hey, do you want to go the party at Jake's tonight?"

"No! Jake's nuts. His parties are too much for me."

"What? Are you turning chicken on me?" he asked with contempt.

She stared at him, feeling like telling him to mind his own business. "You know what happened last time. He was higher than a kite and almost raped me! I don't feel comfortable going back!"

"You're going, woman, and that's final! I'm not going without you."

"I don't want to go! You can't make me!" she insisted.

In anger, Felix stood quickly and lifted his arm above her.

She was sure he'd strike so she shut her eyes and cringed. The hit never came. With her heart beating crazily, she glanced up to see him pacing the floor in front of her.

He'd been especially agitated lately, depressed even. She never asked him why, didn't really want to know.

Slowly her heart slowed. A wisp of compassion eased in. "What's wrong, Felix? Why are you so upset?"

He stopped by the window, parted the drapes and looked out. Finally, he let the fabric fall back into place and brought his hands to cover his face. Eventually he dropped his arms to hang limp at his side. Inhaling deeply and releasing heavily, he turned to face her.

"It's bigger than you and I put together, baby. I can't tell you because they might just kill you too."

Sally stared at him, fear filling her chest. "What are you talking about? Why would anyone want to kill you?"

"Like I said, it's better if you don't know." He took a step into the room. "I have to go. I'll see you later." He rounded the couch and headed to the front door. After grabbing his jacket, where he'd flung it on the kitchen table, he opened the door and walked out without a backward glance.

She was too stunned to stop him or to ask questions. He was in trouble – that much was clear. If someone was truly trying to kill him, then her life might be in danger too. It all depended on what he'd gotten himself into.

Maybe calling a friend would help. Amber was quite level-headed. Amber was one of the closest friends she had. If anyone could be of support, she could. She might give some good advice and she knew how to keep a secret.

Sally picked up the phone and dialed the familiar number. It rang six times.

"Hi." The voice was weak, almost indiscernible.

"Amber, is that you?"

"Yeah."

"Are you okay?'

"Yeah.... yeah, who is this?" she mumbled sleepily

"What are you up to?"

"Oh, I had a hard day at the bank. I came home and shot up."

It was Friday night. She should have known. A shuffling noise in the background gave her pause.

"Are you okay? Did you want me to come over?" Sally asked.

Silence stretched before Amber answered. "Ah…. no. Bobby's here…and…he'll take care…of me."

"Okay. I'll talk to you soon."

"Yeah…bye." The phone clicked on the other end.

Sally stared at the phone piece resting in her hand. Amber Woods wouldn't be much support tonight. She was a good friend but had problems of her own. Depression dogged her life, relieved only by her weekend binges. Bobby was good for her, understood her needs and made sure she never had to do without. Despair tormented her. Amber blamed it all on her mother – the two abortions she'd forced her into had plunged her into a deep hole.

The last thing Sally needed was Amber's mood rubbing off on her. She had other things to focus on at the moment.

Felix was turning out to be a complete screw-up. She set the phone piece back on its base. There were no feelings of love toward the louse; tolerating him was hard enough. But still, she did care about him. Knowing his life was in danger worried her. If only he'd tell her what type of trouble he was in, maybe she could help. But now he was gone and she had no clue where to look for him. If he'd gone to Jake's party she wouldn't follow. After a few minutes, she decided that there was no use in wasting a perfectly good Friday night.

Sally went to the kitchen and opened a drawer where she kept a stash. After taking it to the table, she sat down, pulled out a small package of marijuana and rolled a joint. With shaky hands, she lit it and took a long puff. Almost immediately she could feel her body relax. She took a few more long draws, enjoying the taste and the edge it took off her nerves.

The buzzer sounded lazily in the background. For once it didn't make her jump. Few visitors ever bothered to buzz from the lobby. They'd call first, making sure she was home. She wasn't expecting anyone. Apprehension returned as she wandered slowly to the intercom and pressed the button.

"Who is it?"

"It's your mother, dear."

Sally groaned in dread. Her fingers reached for her forehead and massaged as though a headache were already beginning. *Not my mother. I can't talk to her right now.* Sally took another puff and shook her head despondently.

The buzzer sounded again. After holding the button, she said, "Mom, this is not a good time for me."

"Sally, I'm your mother. I haven't seen you in ages. I'm here and I want to come up. I promise I won't stay long."

Releasing a heavy sigh, Sally depressed the button that would open the security door in the lobby. She cleaned up the marijuana package, stuffing it back into the drawer, and extinguished her cigarette in the ashtray. She placed it in the drawer to smoke later. Setting the ashtray out of view on top of the fridge, she waved her arms to disperse the odor lingering in the air. She hurried to the stove and switched on the fan. That should help clear out the smoke.

With her back against the kitchen counter, she waited nervously for the knock on the door. Three flights of stairs would take her mother some time.

The kitchen was small and homey and she liked it that way. The apartment suited her just fine. More room would be nice to give her some space from Felix but maybe she could get rid of him soon.

The inevitable knock came. Pushing off from the counter, Sally headed to the door and opened it wide. There stood her mother, breathing heavily and holding a hand to her heart.

"Those steps wear me out every time."

"Hi, Mom."

"Hi Sally." Sally went over to the table, pulled out a chair and pointed to it. Her mother came over and sat down. "Thank you, dear!"

Sally took a seat across from her mother. Silence stretched between them as her mother recuperated from her climb. Being in her mid-fifties hadn't diminished her good looks. Her brown hair was tinted with white but she wore it stylishly. Daily walking kept her fit, her classy clothes accentuating her good figure. Climbing stairs, though, was never part of her exercise regimen. Sally was proud of her mother's looks and hoped she'd look as good at that age. Her mother's constant criticism was her only complaint.

Soon the familiar, accusatory glare appeared.

Here goes!

"What is that smell again? Have you been smoking?"

She didn't say a word. What was the point?

"You need to stop, Sally. It's terrible for your health. I can't stand that smell and it's hard to breathe around it. Why don't you stop smoking? I don't understand you at all. Don't you care about yourself? It's not the way I taught you, dear. You know better. Please promise me you'll stop."

Sally stared at her but didn't answer. Letting her mother talk herself out seemed wise and then maybe she'd leave.

"And look at this place; it's a total mess. There are dishes in the sink!" She placed a hand over her chest to show her shock. "You need to look after yourself, Sally. Did I fail completely? Did I not teach you how to keep house?" She fanned her face with her hand as though she anticipated a faint. "And look," she pointed to the floor, "I see dust bunnies."

"I've been working all week. I'm tired, Mom!" *Why do I even bother?*

Her mother's eyes looked disappointed, as usual. "If you'd clean up your life it would make me so happy. And that Felix guy you live with, you need to get rid of him."

"I thought you said, last time you were here, that I should marry him."

"Well, if you're living with him, you should get married. You're living like you're married."

Sally rolled her eyes.

"He's no good for you. You look unhappy." On and on she went, voicing her uninvited opinions.

Sally let her eyes drop to her knees while her mother rambled on. It was never ending. Finally, after she'd had enough, Sally looked up, locked eyes with her mother and said, "If you'll do something about your life then maybe I'll clean up mine."

"What's that supposed to mean? We were talking about you, not me."

"The last time I checked, you and dad still can't stand each other. You're at each other's throats constantly. Why don't you fix your own problems before barging in here, pointing a finger at me?"

Regret replaced the accusation in her mother's eyes. "Sally, I didn't come here to fight with you. I want to know how you're doing."

Sally raised her arms in frustration. "I'm great, Mom! Everything's wonderful!" She dropped her arms to her lap and stared in defiance.

"It doesn't look wonderful."

"What, Mother?" she said in exasperation, her back bristling in anger.

"You look miserable. Do you want to talk about it?"

"There's nothing to talk about."

"Please, Sally, I wish you'd talk to me. I pray for you every day. How can I pray for you more effectively?" She reached out to touch her hand but Sally pulled it back before her mother had the chance.

Felix's situation played over in her mind. The temptation to shock her mother's sheltered little world was strong. But it would only give her one more thing to criticize. "I'm sorry, I can't talk about it."

"Something's bothering you. I can see it. I wish you'd let me be a part of your life, dear."

Sally smiled miserably and shook her head. "You don't want to be a part of my life."

"Yes I do. I don't know why you say things like that."

"If you knew what my life was like you'd run and never come back."

"Sally, all you have to do is come back to God. That's the answer you're looking for."

"Mom, stop! I don't want to hear about God. If God is so wonderful and so powerful then why is your marriage still such a mess? God is always your answer to my life and I don't want to hear it anymore!" She had yelled and felt bad.

Her mother's eyes misted and a single tear slid down her cheek.

Sally released a frustrated breath. "I'm sorry. I'm sorry for yelling." Her mother's pat answers weren't enough. They never had been.

Mrs. Windsor stood and pushed her chair in toward the table. "Well, I can see that you're not in the mood for a civil discussion so I'll come back when you're in a better frame of mind."

Sally could feel her mother's eyes on her but kept her gaze diverted. Seeing the pain on her face would only send her over the edge. She had too much on her plate already.

"God has never let me down, young lady. I'm not perfect and your father has not lived right. All I know is that without God I would have had a nervous breakdown with the marriage we've had. God has taken care of me and I don't care what your opinion is; God has seen me through more than you know." With that, she walked to the door and opened it.

Sally still refused to look at her even though she knew her mother was staring at her. Studying her hands in her lap seemed safer.

"I love you, Sally. I always will. You're my daughter and I'll stick by you. It doesn't matter to me what you're going through. If you ever want to talk, you know where you can find me. Good-bye, Sally."

At that she looked up to meet her mother's gaze. "I love you too, Mom."

The door closed and Sally's tears came. She wept for some time as the tension slowly dissipated from her body. Their tense and difficult relationship was hard to understand. There were numerous things that contributed to their stormy connection but she was at a loss as to how to fix things. Did she even want to?

Rebellion had become a way of life for her; aggravating her mother was actually a pleasure. Her father was drunk most of the time. He had never been there for her and it had driven Sally to find love and acceptance in the arms of too many men. And with a mother who wouldn't stop hounding her, home was the last place she desired to be.

All the losers she'd been with had left her longing for love and yet still she craved it. She knew her desperate search for acceptance wasn't producing it, but she was hopeful. Surely there was a man out there who would love her, truly love her. She had this uncanny feeling from time to time that she was trapped on a Ferris wheel with no way to get off. Dwelling on that realization too long only made her miserable and panicky.

After high school her goal was to get as far away from her mother as possible. For her post-secondary education, she chose a university in Vancouver, British Columbia. After four years of university, she moved back to Markham, rented an apartment and kept her distance from her parents. Her mother's disapproval was constant and unbearable. It was easier to stay away than endure her unending criticism. Sally knew it hurt her mother but she didn't know how else to deal with the tension in their relationship.

Now, here she was, stuck in another difficult relationship and she wanted out. Sally looked at her apartment and realized that her mother was right; it was a real mess. A clean apartment was preferable but by the end of the workweek she didn't have the energy to clean.

A knock at the door made her jump. She walked over cautiously and peeked through the little view hole. Rena, her downstairs neighbor, stood on the other side. Sally opened the door.

"Hi, Rena. What are you doing here?"

"I saw your mother on the stairs. I thought you might need some cheering up."

"It was okay, really. A bit stressful but I'm doing fine. Come on in."

"Is Felix here?"

"No, he left. Went to a party, I think."

Rena looked relieved. "When are you getting rid of him?"

"I don't know. I wish he'd just leave on his own. It would be a lot easier that way."

"You're welcome to come stay with me anytime, Sally. If he becomes abusive, just run down and knock on my door. Promise me you'll do that?"

"I promise."

"Why didn't you go to the party with him?"

"I wasn't in the mood."

Sally took down her ashtray, opened the drawer, relit her joint and they both sat at the kitchen table. She offered Rena some but she declined as she patted her growing stomach. Sally felt jittery as she took a draft of her joint.

"Your hand is shaking," Rena said in concern. "What's wrong?"

She didn't know if Rena could be trusted but she couldn't keep it in any longer. "I think Felix is in trouble. He's scared for his life for some reason." Her shaking grew worse with the telling and fear clutched her throat.

"What's he into? Something illegal?"

A question plagued her mind. She had to ask. "Do you ever see any activity here during the day that would be questionable?"

Rena's face turned pinkish. "I try not to be a snoop but I do see strange people coming and going. Felix sometimes leaves with some bigwigs in fancy cars. They look like drug dealers to me but I'm not too familiar with that kind of thing. I guess I watch too many movies." She shrugged. "I can't say anything for sure. Do you think he's in any real trouble?"

"He might be and he won't let me help him. I don't know what to do."

"If I were you, I'd kick him out before those thugs come after you."

"I don't know if the trouble is with drug dealers. Rena, please keep this quiet, okay? Felix would be furious if he found out I talked to you."

"My lips are sealed, Sally. I won't say a word. If you ever need me, you know where I am. You do know, though, that if he's in trouble with drug dealers, then you could be in real danger?"

"That's what has me so worried. He's putting me right in the middle of whatever he's into. I'm angry with him and scared for him all at the same time."

"Just remember I'm here for you. I have to run." She stood awkwardly. "Sid is with the kids and Lorena was screaming her head off when I left. He hates it when I leave him when the kids are acting up. Timmy bit Lorena after she took his toy away. I tried to bring some peace to the situation but I was ready for a break. I've been dealing with their fights all week and I was glad to get away. Call me, Sally, okay?"

She nodded as Rena exited the apartment. Rena had enough on her own plate with three little ones to raise and another on the way but she still made time for Sally and others. It was hard to imagine how she managed it all. Perhaps snooping in on neighbors' lives kept her socially connected. Sally couldn't imagine being cooped up with three kids all day, every day. Keeping her single life in order was enough of a struggle. But Rena exuded a composed personality and it was calming just to be around her.

After finishing her joint, Sally went to change into a mini-skirt and skin-tight t-shirt. She couldn't handle the confines of her small apartment another minute. A local club would help take her mind off her questions and fears.

CHAPTER 4

The irresponsible, impulsive louse had been missing for a week and Sally was extremely agitated. A visit to the police precinct the day before, to report a missing person, had only managed to fritter away her time. Since Felix was an adult, they weren't concerned. They asked if it was a penchant of his, disappearing for a few days. Well, actually yes. Felix would come and go as he wished. Communication was a skill he direly lacked.

The precinct dismissed her concerns rather abruptly after that. It didn't stop the unease crimping in her gut. Just below her usually calm exterior, anger broiled. She was furious with him for putting her through this.

After a busy week of work, she walked into her apartment, her mind racked once again by troubled thoughts. She shed her coat and shoes by the door, walked into the kitchen and flicked on the light. Tiger, her cat, meowed loudly at his food bowl. It was empty. Moving to the cupboard where she kept the cat's food, out of the corner of her eye, she noticed a dark shadow against the wall. Spinning in that direction, she screamed when she saw him there.

"What are you doing?" she hollered.

"Surprise, baby, I'm back." Felix lounged in a kitchen chair, tilted back to rest against the wall, a casual grin curling his smug face.

Taking a deep breath to calm the fury she felt, her frazzled emotions streaked to the surface and the questions came all at once. "Where have you been all week? Did you leave the city? Where did you hide? I've been so worried! Why didn't you let me know you were okay? And then you just show up and scare me half to death? What's wrong with you?"

He stared at her in surprise "Whoa, whoa! One question at a time, sweetheart. I've been busy making arrangements. I think things are going to be okay now. I conjured up a few deals and laid low for a while. Everything is back on track." He looked relaxed enough.

A lilt in his voice made her question. Something felt askew.

"What kind of arrangements? I'm entitled to know. We live together. I deserve respect. If you're in some kind of trouble, I want to know exactly what we're dealing with." Leaning against the kitchen counter, she crossed her arms and glared at him. Felix's nonchalant attitude to the hellish week he'd put her through made her more incensed than relieved.

Felix stood, came toward her, placed his arms around her waist and held her close. "I need you, Sally. I need you so desperately."

His breath was sweet and warm and showered down over her face. The tip of his nose brushed her forehead. Being needed felt wonderful. She never could resist that. It was better than nothing. Slowly she unfolded her arms and wrapped them around his middle. He felt like a scared child under her touch. That's when she realized. Trouble was still brewing and he wasn't as calm as he'd let on.

She looked into his eyes. "Tell me what's going on."

He released his hold and stood before her, crossing his arms. "I got in deeper than I should have and I found myself in a jam."

"Have you been selling drugs?"

He shrugged. "It's one way to make a living."

So it was true! "Do you think both of our lives are in danger?"

"They were after me, baby. You don't have anything to worry about now. I think I smoothed things out."

"I hope so." She didn't believe him but to accuse him of lying would arouse his darker side. Finally he was back and she didn't want to fight.

Felix grinned crookedly. He looked adorable, the way she remembered him when they first met. "Why don't you put on one of those fancy designer dresses and I'll take you out for dinner?"

She released an anxious sigh. "Sure, as long as you promise to change too. Your ratty jeans won't go with the dress I'll be wearing."

"All right, baby, let's go change."

In the middle of the night, Sally awoke with a start. She sat up with a feeling of terrible dread. Reaching over to where Felix should be, his spot was empty and cold. The thick comforter had been pulled down.

One glance told her that Tiger was in his usual spot, at the foot of her bed. She slipped her legs out carefully, without disturbing him and pulled on her fuzzy slippers before making contact with the chilly floor. It was May, slowly warming up, but the floor still felt cool in the middle of the night.

The living room was empty. Light filtered in from the kitchen so she shuffled to the door, rubbing her tired eyes. Felix sat at the table shooting up. She quietly walked toward him and sat down, waiting for him to finish.

When he was done, he turned his tear-streaked face to her, his eyes a mixture of fear and torment. With his elbows resting on the table, he placed his face in his hands and sobbed for a while. Sally placed a gentle hand on his back. Trying to appease his dilemma with mere words seemed trite. He looked truly worried.

Felix finally raised his face and spoke with trembling voice. "I'm so sorry, baby! I never meant for things to get so out of hand. I've gone and messed up so royally I'll never get out." He lowered his face into his hands again and sobbed.

"We'll manage somehow. Don't worry. It'll work out. If you need some money, then tell me."

He bolted upright as if poked with a red-hot iron and spoke with pained voice. "One hundred and twenty thousand dollars! Do you have that much money lying around?"

The amount shocked her. "That's a lot of money!" How could he have been so reckless? How did he ever manage to get so deeply in debt? "You told me last night that you had made arrangements. Did you get some money to pay them back?"

"I lied, Sally. I missed you so much. I just wanted to be with you and have one last good night together."

Dumbstruck at his honesty, despair filled her.

"I spent my time hiding. There is no money." His eyes could not hide his terror.

A thought formulated. "What about your family? They're rich. Why don't you ask them to help you?"

"They'd kick me out of their big fancy house in a heartbeat if they knew what I was into."

"It couldn't hurt to try, Felix."

He shook his head. "Go back to bed. I need time to think and be alone."

"I can stay with you if you want."

"Go, go, go!" he said with impatience, shooing her away with his hands.

She went to him and placed a kiss on his bowed head. He grabbed her hand, turned it palm up, kissed it and held it to his cheek a moment.

"I love you, Sally."

"I love you too." She didn't mean it but knew it would make him feel better. She left the room wondering if he'd be there in the morning.

Back in bed, she tossed and turned. He really was in immense danger but she knew there was nothing she could do. Run, that's what he should do. Maybe if she loved him, she'd suggest moving to another city, hiding till the danger passed. Her insides twisted at the thought. It's the last thing she wanted. Her career meant the world to her and he loved living here. He'd never move. His parents lived in Markham and he hoped one day to inherit their grand home. He was too attached to this city. Agitated thoughts raged through her mind all night, robbing her of sleep.

Toward morning, she finally dozed. A few hours later, her eyes opened and she rolled over to check the clock. It was just before noon. Felix hadn't come back to bed. The sheets on his side looked the same. She slipped out of bed and went to wash up. With her hair piled into a clip, no makeup and wearing a pair of sweats and a loose t-shirt, she went in search of Felix.

There was no sign of him in the apartment and his jacket was missing from the hook. Wandering back into the kitchen, she noticed a note lying on the table. She picked it up and read.

'I'm sorry I've been such a burden to you, Sally. I'm leaving and don't know when I'll be back. Don't worry about me. I'll be fine. Love always, Felix.'

With heaviness of heart, she sat down. This summed up their relationship – unpredictable and unstable. Felix was a sporadic soul, often acting on impulse without contemplating the consequences. Staying in the apartment seemed oppressive so she ate quickly, put on some makeup, changed her clothes and headed out the door.

~~~~

An aimless drive around the city didn't help to curb her restlessness. Shopping didn't appeal; she didn't need groceries and it was too cool to walk in the park. She stopped in front of her brother Robert's apartment building.

The building's prodigious appearance was abnormal for the area and looked more like a motel. The two-story apartment complex had outdoor stairwells ascending to the second floor from both sides. The top hallway was open to the elements, a slated fence and rail running along the outer edge. All the doors, on both levels, opened to the outside.

Robert's apartment was on the second floor. After hiking the stairs, she stopped at his door and knocked. Finally, she heard the dead bolt turn and the door opened.

"Oh, it's you, sis! Come on in."

"Hi." She stayed outside. "I thought we could go for lunch. Do you have time?"

"Uhh… I guess we could do that. I'd planned to go golfing this afternoon. I'll call Russ and let him know I'll be there a bit later than planned."

"I'd appreciate that."

Robert turned and walked away. She stepped inside to wait as he made the call. Clutter filled the small apartment. Newspapers were scattered about, empty pop cans littering every available counter, scrunched-up chip bags, boxes of crackers and dirty plates everywhere. Popcorn debris was strewn all over the carpet, the remnants of a few movie sessions. She didn't even want to imagine what his kitchen looked like.

I wonder what Mother says about this place!

Robert appeared from his bedroom and grabbed his keys from the coffee table. It was a miracle he found them so quickly. "Okay I'm ready," he said.

"Mom hasn't been here in a while, has she?"

He grinned impishly. "I've kinda let things slide."

"Does she still come clean for you?"

"Not as often as she used to. I think she's given up."

Sally nodded. "I don't blame her."

He grabbed his jacket. "I'll get to cleaning eventually."

"What you need is a girlfriend. That would give you some motivation."

"Nah!"

At the restaurant she ordered a burger and fries. She was hungry and, in her state of mind, she didn't care how unhealthy the meal was. The tension with Felix needed to be drowned by a plateful of grease. Being in Robert's company, after weeks of not seeing him, called for a sort of celebration. Their times together were too infrequent.

Robert was two years younger, only twenty-two, and was already doing well in business. After two years of Business College, during which he worked part-time for a realtor, he started his own real estate business in the city. It was a time-consuming venture but he was doing exceptionally well, better than his initial predictions. Sally was very proud of him.

"So what's up, sis?" He pushed his plate away and wiped his mouth with a napkin.

Her plateful wasn't nearly finished so she nibbled at it while they talked. After swallowing, she said, "It's Felix again."

"He's still around? What's he up to now?"

"He's in big trouble. I don't know what to do."

"And you came to your little brother for help? I'm surprised."

"I'm not here for help. I just need someone to talk to. I'm worried about him. I think his life might be in danger."

Robert shook his head, disdain in his eyes. It was no secret that he'd never liked Felix much. "The jerk's been selling drugs, hasn't he?"

"Why does everyone jump to that conclusion?"

"I knew it the first time I saw him. He has that classic look."

"He's not all bad, you know."

"Maybe that's true but I always suspected that guy was trouble. Why have you let him stay this long?"

"I don't know. I guess I feel sorry for him."

"What do you want me to do?"

"Nothing. It just feels good to talk about it. It's been like a dead weight. I had to get it off my chest. You won't tell Mom, will you?"

"You think she'll use it against you?"

"She always does. Picking at my mistakes has always been her favorite pastime."

Robert grinned. "You have to admit, Felix was definitely a mistake."

Sally grabbed a French fry, chewed and swallowed. "Why can't I pick a decent guy?" A swig on her Diet Coke felt refreshing.

"You have to be choosier. The right one will come along one day. Be patient." He really did have a million-dollar smile. No wonder he did so well in sales. He was more of a friend than a brother. When no one else understood her, Robert always had her back. He even tried to smooth the way for her and Mother. It seldom worked but his heart was in the right place.

"I wish I could help him somehow."

"Do you have any idea how much he owes?"

Apprehension gnawed at her. What would Robert think? But then again, what did it matter. "Felix told me."

"And...how much?"

"One hundred and twenty thousand."

His mouth gaped. Slowly he closed it, his eyes relaying the contempt he held for the man. "Does he have a plan of how to come up with the money?"

She shook her head. "He's terrified of what'll happen."

"The jerk!" He shook his head in disbelief. "Where is he now?"

"I don't know. He was gone when I got up. He left me a note saying he didn't know when he'd be back."

"So he's running?"

She shrugged. "That's what it looks like. I don't think he'll run far, though. He'd never leave Markham."

"So he's leaving you to deal with it?"

"I don't think so. I've never met these guys he's involved with and I don't think they'd really be interested in me."

Robert's eyes darkened. "Don't fool yourself, sis. If they're after Felix and they can't find him, they'll show up at your apartment."

"Do you really think so?"

"Absolutely!"

"Felix believes his life is in danger."

Robert swore. "Well then yours is too. I can't believe he'd pull you down with him! If he were here, I'd deck him! How dare he mess up your life like this?"

"What should I do?"

"Move out of the apartment, leave no forwarding address and disappear. That's the only way you'll be safe and be able to get rid of Felix at the same time."

"I don't know, Robert." She couldn't imagine doing that, leaving Felix with no place to come home to. "He wouldn't know where to find me."

"That's the point, Sally!" Robert seemed almost like a parent at times, so reasonable and dogmatic about his views. "Move out now or you'll be sorry."

"I don't know. I don't feel like it's the right time."

His eyes flashed with frustration. "When will it be the right time? When they carry you out in a bag?"

"I just can't, Rob! Not right now!"

He lifted his hands as if to wash his hands of the whole thing. "Okay, but don't say I didn't warn you." He placed his elbows on the table and leaned in close. "Look Sally, if you ever need somewhere to go, give me a call. You can always come and hang out with me. Okay?"

"Thanks, bro. I hope it won't come to that."

"What? My place not clean enough for you?"

"Mom wouldn't think so. She thinks my place is a pig pen."

He grinned sadly, for her, no doubt, paid the bill and they left.

It was one of the most atrocious Mondays she'd had. Three cups of coffee had made their way into her system, she was on her fourth and still couldn't focus. All the caffeine accomplished was to make her edgy, her hands shaky.

Her office, more like a mid-size cubicle, consisted of a drafting table, a desk containing her computer, pens and pencils in a holder, a drafting book resting on the right side and a cork board hung at eye level. A picture of Felix and another one of Tiger, her cat, were posted there. The pictures were held in place by thumbtacks. Sally removed the picture of Felix, studied it then slipped it into the bottom drawer of her desk. She hadn't accomplished anything in the few hours she'd been here. The picture of him was the culprit of her misery. Distraction she could do without.

Sally was attempting to design new ideas for Taylor's dress line. Normally she loved her work but today was a test in perseverance. Concepts usually came unhindered and her creative juices flowed copiously. Generating progressive fashion was what she was known for.

Sometimes she told people she was born with a needle and thread in her hand. Her mother taught her to sew when she was quite young but it was only in her teens that her talent began to blossom. Studying fashion magazines gave her the ideas she needed. In middle school, during her teen years, she began to design and sew her own clothes but it wasn't till high school that she knew it would be her lifelong obsession. Her flare for fashion ensured she always wore the latest styles, the envy of high school friends. Designing clothes had become second nature.

Some of the outfits she'd designed for Taylor Fashion had brought the company much-wanted acclaim and attention. Within only two years of employment, their confidence in her ability had garnered her status. Maybe one day she'd start her own company but the experience here was well worth it. To venture out on her own frightened her. She didn't know if she'd ever have the confidence or business skills to succeed.

Thankfully her co-workers, ten in all, didn't meddle in her personal life. Getting along with them wasn't too hard. They were all busy with their own tasks. No one liked being interrupted when working on an idea. Mutual respect flowed here.

Taylor Fashion Design had two fashion design offices in Canada and one in the United States. Gregory Taylor, in his late fifties, owned them all but personally managed the one in Toronto. His communication skills were excellent and he had no trouble describing what he wanted from a particular clothing line. As he explained what he envisioned, Sally easily created mental blueprints.

Although she was the youngest employee, everyone held her in high regard. It only made her more determined to restrict her partying for weekends. Concentrating on her career was her top priority and she'd do anything to protect it.

Jennifer, the receptionist, was in her fifties and mothered everyone. Cookies or loaves would find their way into the office and she'd share them with the entire staff. Recipes were generously given out if asked for. Janice, a girl in her twenties, had been hired recently to help Jennifer with the books.

Marie, one of the experienced designers, was also in her fifties. Her austere exterior, however, made most people keep their distance. Her staid manner hadn't intimidated Sally in the least. Marie was a well of experience and information and Sally had learned a great deal from just watching the maverick at work and listening to her words of wisdom. Marie had been with the company since the beginning and had been instrumental in making Taylor Fashion Design a respected name in this industry.

Tony, Ralph and Milton seemed to be permanent fixtures in the company. Tony and Ralph were also designers and Milton organized the fashion shows.

Tony, in his thirties, had been with the company for thirteen years. He was still trying to make a name for himself. His designs often needed reworking; what he envisioned and what was practical became opposing forces. Frustration often creased his brow. He'd had success early on with a unique swimwear line and Gregory never forgot what his people had given to him.

Ralph, in his early forties, had experienced a measure of success with his suit designs for both men and women, his sphere of excellence.

Milton was in a class all of his own. Sally still didn't quite know what to think of him. The forty-five-year-old didn't look a day over thirty. No hint of gray sprinkled his hair and his body was trim and muscled. It was reported that the gym was his second home. He really was a good-looking man. His bragging grated on the other men in the office but it didn't deter him. His expertise was in administration and planning design shows. Deadlines made him emotionally intense. At those times, it was best to leave him to his work without any distraction. During show time, his usual jovial nature was replaced by an imposter, a bear in disguise.

The accessory girl, Mary, was in her early thirties and had worked here for seven years. She accessorized all the designs. Gregory allowed her to go as outlandish as she fancied but he insisted on approving each item before a show. He seldom refused her eccentric whims and creative ideas.

Jason was only two years older than Sally and he'd already experienced success with the casual career line. He'd been here only a year longer than she. At times his designs mimicked or closely compared to hers, causing tension and competition between them.

Sally was deep in thought when a sound alerted her. Turning, she saw Milton's head inside her cubicle, a huge, spurious smile on his face and his hand waving at her. He looked ridiculous! She couldn't help but grin at his antics and found herself responding with a wave of her own.

"So what's Miss Sally working on this beautiful Monday morning?" He walked into the tight cubicle, took the empty seat in the corner and crossed one leg over the other. The miniscule area suddenly felt claustrophobic with his bigger-than-life persona taking up space. He looked as dashing and well-dressed as ever. Taking advantage of his youthful looks to hit on the young women in the office was a favorite pastime.

"I'm working on emptying the coffee pot. Can't you tell?" She held out one shaky hand.

Milton quickly stood, grabbed her hand and held it to his lips, brushing it with a kiss.

Sally broke out laughing. She should have known the temptation her hand would cause. "You know how to take advantage of any situation, don't you, Milton?"

"I couldn't pass that up, my beauty. You're not taken yet, are you?" He stood over her drafting table, still holding her hand in a tight grip.

She tried to pull it free but he wouldn't allow it. "How could I be taken with someone as handsome as you around?" Boosting his already inflated ego was a risk.

"Ah, you're playing with me, aren't you? You're trying to make a middle-aged man feel young again. Well, I have to let you know that I still catch the eye of many young women. I actually manage to get a lot of young beauties out on dates. How about it, Sally." He lifted his eyebrows a few times. "What are you doing tonight?" He finally released her hand but waited patiently for her reply.

"I'm very flattered with your attention, Milton, but I'm busy tonight."

"So you are taken!"

"I've made it a practice not to discuss my private life at work." She hoped he'd catch on and stop prying her for answers.

"One of these days I'm going to take you out on the town and we're going to have a blast. I know this awesome place; it's called Chuck E Cheese. Have you ever heard of it? It's a rocking place!"

She burst out laughing.

He sat back down, his eyes dancing as he watched her. "Oh, you found that funny, did you? I bet you've never been there; that's why you're laughing. It has these tunnels you can climb in and there are great hiding places and this ball pit that's a blast. And the games! Did I tell you about the games?"

"Okay, stop Milton, my side is hurting." Getting the words out through her laughter was difficult. "Do you actually take your dates there?"

"I do, but for some reason I can't get them to go for round two. I don't know what I'm doing wrong. I try to be the perfect gentleman, show them a fun time. What else can a guy do?" He held out his hands in mock surrender. When Gregory's voice echoed from down the hall, Milton leaned sideways out of the cubicle and looked.

Why doesn't he just leave already! I'm struggling to get anything done as it is!

Gregory momentarily popped into Sally's cubicle and looked back and forth between the two of them. "What's going on here? Are we swapping ideas?"

"Oh yeah, we're swapping ideas all right, but not about designs." Milton said mischievously as he walked back to his work area.

Gregory shook his head then glanced at Sally's empty drafting paper. "Rough morning?"

"It's not my most productive day, to put it mildly."

"Well, just remember, we need the designs finished in two weeks to get them fitted and adjusted in time for the show."

"I know, Mr. Taylor. I'll try to concentrate and get something done."

"I know you will. You've never disappointed me yet. Keep up the good work." With that, Gregory left her cubicle to check on the other designers, his custom every Monday morning. His hands-on approach made him so likable and everyone felt supported by his encouraging attitude.

Sally was about to draw out the image she was envisioning when Janice stuck her head in and asked, "Would you like a coffee?"

Her cheerful smile and bubbly personality were too much this morning.

"I've had enough coffee, thanks. But I'd love a glass of water to calm down the effects of the four cups of coffee I've already downed."

"Sure, I'll be right back."

Janice left and Sally managed a few tentative strokes of her pencil. It didn't take long for Janice to return with a glass of water.

"Thank you," Sally said, reaching for it.

A minute later Jennifer stopped by with a tray of chocolate chip cookies. "I baked these last night. Would you like one, dear?"

"Sure, why not." Sally reached for one and placed it beside her drafting paper.

It was a relief finally to be alone with her thoughts and duties. Images of Felix invaded from time to time but she forced herself to focus. Her ideas slowly took form on paper.

CHAPTER 5

2003
Tessa dropped the armload of groceries on the kitchen counter and started unpacking the bags, putting everything away. Once done, she started on dinner. Tonight would be a quiet evening with her husband. Maybe she should light some of those new vanilla votives she bought and make it romantic. She smiled as she prepared a sauce for the chicken breasts.

Baked sweet potatoes and creamed corn would finish off the dinner menu. She'd picked up fresh rye bread at the corner bakery. Her stomach was growling. Grabbing a few carrot sticks from the fridge, she munched while she worked.

Tessa loved their small house. With her mother's help she'd made valances that hung over the windows. Artwork decorated most of the walls. Cody had a flare for art and many of his paintings were framed and hung in their small home. Oil painting was his specialty, a hobby he loved and was very good at.

Thinking of his talents made her heart swell with pride. He was a wonderful husband, very good to her, but besides that, he was also a terrific youth leader at their church, strong support at the Manor of Peace and a good friend to so many.

The front door opened and closed. Cody was home. She smiled in anticipation. His feet shuffled into the kitchen. He walked up behind her, wrapped his arms around her waist and kissed her neck tenderly.

"Mmmm... I've been looking forward to this all day."

She giggled, turned around and wrapped her arms around his neck. They kissed again. It quickly turned more passionate, heat rising between them. She pulled away and looked at him. His arms were still around her waist possessively. "I'm in the middle of making dinner."

"It could wait."

"It could..." She smiled up at him. "I've missed you."

"You have no idea," Cody said with a wink.

It made her giggle. "Too much work and not enough play."

"Yeah. We've both been working too much."

"We have tonight," reminded Tessa.

He kissed her again and then let her go.

As she prepared the creamed corn she said, "This weekend should be more settled at The Mansion of Hope."

Cody took off his tie, laid it on the table, pulled out a kitchen chair and sat down. "How's Veronica Billings doing?"

"Much better! They transferred her to a room in the east wing this week. Lily James, the other girl we kept an eye on that night, was moved to the east wing too. Eventually, when they're both ready, they'll probably be placed together in an apartment in the west wing."

"I'm sure that'll be a while yet."

Tessa nodded.

Cody smiled. "It doesn't get old, does it?"

Tessa nodded. "It's very fulfilling."

Cody went to the cupboard, took out plates and set the table. He filled two cups with ice water and set those.

"Maybe we should go see a movie tomorrow night," suggested Tessa.

He turned to her. "We're taking the youth roller skating. Did you forget?"

She stifled a sigh. "Oh, yeah, I forgot." It shouldn't bother her. Leading the youth was his passion and she should be pleased to support him.

"We always have fun with the youth."

"Yeah, I know. At least I have you to myself tonight."

Cody stepped beside her and gave her a quick peck. "I love you."

It made her smile.

"Can I help with dinner?"

"No. The chicken and potatoes are baking and the corn just needs to heat."

"Okay." Cody wandered into the living room and switched on the television to watch the news.

After dinner they relaxed on the couch with cups of coffee. When the news finished, Cody reached for the remote and switched it off. Standing, coffee mug in hand, he asked, "Do you want more coffee?"

"No thanks."

"Stay here, Tessa. I'll be right back. We need to talk." With that he headed to the kitchen.

It wasn't like him to look so serious. Curiosity nudged her to know what was on his mind.

Soon he returned, sat beside her, set his steaming mug down on the end table and took her hand in his.

Staring into his eyes, she asked, "So, what's up?"

"Something's been on my mind for some time. I'd like us to make some plans for the future."

"Sounds pretty serious."

"Yeah, I guess it is."

His evasiveness was making her feel edgy. "Well, don't keep me in suspense. What is it?"

"We've been married for over two years now and I feel we have a very solid, loving relationship."

She raised her eyebrows and waited.

Taking a deep breath, he relaxed his shoulders.

"You're nervous."

"It's an important discussion."

"Okay, blaze on." Encouragement might make him relax.

"I think a deep love and solid friendship are valuable qualities to have for a strong future together." He reached for his coffee cup and took another sip.

Tessa wished he'd just get on with, get it out.

Slowly he set his cup down and turned back to her.

Squeezing his hand, she said, "So, what are you trying to say?"

"Patience, patience, my beautiful wife!" he said, patting her hand. He could be infuriatingly slow when he chose to be. "What I'm trying to say is that I think it's time we started a family. I know you love your work just like I love mine and I'm not saying you have to quit, unless that's what you'd like to do. You could still work weekends and some evenings if you want." He was rambling. "I'm ready for a baby and I want to know your thoughts on it."

She was shocked at the unexpected subject. They had talked of starting a family on rare occasions but it was always in the future. They were both so involved in work, their careers and ministry that planning for a family had never been a priority. She'd assumed he was leaving the timing to her. His seeming disinterest in the subject hadn't prepared her for this request. When she realized she was staring at him with her mouth ajar, she closed it and took a deep breath.

He stared at her, watching, waiting for her answer.

How can I respond without offending him? "I don't know what to say, Cody. Starting a family so soon wasn't in my plans. You're right when you said that I love my work. I can't imagine giving that up even for a short time."

"You mean you haven't thought at all about being a mother and having our child?"

"Yes, eventually but not this soon."

"Oh." He tried to hide his disappointment.

"You caught me completely off guard. I don't know what to say."

"That's fairly obvious." He turned to his cup of coffee and took a sip.

She'd hurt him and she felt horrible. "I'm sorry, Cody. It's just that we've never talked seriously before about starting a family."

"So, you're completely opposed to it right now?"

"I need time to digest all this."

His eyes pleaded with her.

She wished she could say yes but she had to be honest. "My gut response is to say 'Forget it, I'm not ready for a baby and the responsibility of that.' But, I promise I'll think it over."

"And pray about it. See what God wants us to do."

"I'll pray." Not that she felt like it. If it was God's plan for her to have a baby now, wouldn't she have some desire for it?

Cody took her hands again and said, "Why don't we pray about it together right now?"

She didn't want to but she said, "Sure."

They bowed their heads and Cody asked for God's will in their lives.

With full knowledge of how God could rearrange plans, Tessa didn't feel completely comfortable with the prayer.

TIME AND HEALING

~~~~~

Tessa unlocked her office door and settled into her chair behind the massive mahogany desk. There was a pile of filing stacked in the basket she'd left for this Monday morning. Now she wished she'd completed more of it on Friday.

The tension that had lingered between her and Cody this weekend was hard to unravel. She knew he wanted an answer quickly but she was still waffling on the issue. Her mind was a tangle of excuses, arguments and fearful wonderings. A baby would change so many things. She didn't think she was ready for that.

After filing a few sheets, she realized she made a mistake so pulled them from the incorrect folders and filed them correctly. Distractedly, she glanced out the front window. The leaves on the trees still boasted their summer green but soon fall would turn them a myriad of bright colors. If she got pregnant now, when would the baby come? She did some finger calculus. May. She'd have a baby in May.

A weary sigh escaped her lips. Did she want a baby? That was still the question. That she'd hurt Cody bothered her. But why had he never mentioned his desire to start a family this soon? Why pop it on her with no warning? Why the sudden pressure to start right now? It was unfair of him. Guilt and anger vied back and forth.

She pushed the baby thoughts away and tried to focus on the forms to be filed. The phone rang a few times during the next hour but she still managed to get the rest of the papers sorted and organized.

A knock at the door brought her head around. Deborah Elliot opened it and walked in. Her black eye was fading. Now only an ugly blue tinge remained.

"Hi, Deb! How are you doing?"

"Hi, Tessa. I'm okay but tired." Her shift finished an hour ago. She should be home by now and sleeping. She took a seat across from Tessa. "This eye looks terrible, doesn't it?" Tenderly she touched the skin around it.

"Does it still hurt?"

"No, there's no more pain but it looks horrible. I'm embarrassed to go out anywhere. Make-up hardly covers it. Veronica feels so badly about what happened and she's apologized over and over."

Tessa nodded. "How's Veronica doing now?"

"It's been two weeks and she still struggles with her anger. Her body craves drugs and it makes her edgy. Both Veronica and Lily were very addicted and it's taken its toll." Deb looked spent and Tessa wished she could do something to help.

"You're done your shift?"

"Yes, thank God!"

"When are you scheduled next?"

"Tonight at 10:00 but Reg and Janet Mendel offered to take it for me."

Reg and Janet were members of their church, Church on the Move, who volunteered their time to help at the two detox homes the church operated. They were willing to assist in whatever area or time they were needed, which made them a great asset to this ministry.

"Patricia just got here so she'll take over. I need to go home and get some rest."

Tessa nodded. She felt such admiration for this woman sitting before her. Deborah Elliot was a woman of the Word. Scriptures literally rolled off her tongue effortlessly, word for word. Physically and spiritually she was a woman of great strength. Maybe one day Tessa would know the Bible as well as Deb did. For now she was thrilled to keep company with such a strong woman of faith.

A concern pricked her. "Deb, will Patricia be able to handle Veronica's anger issues?"

"You know, I've finally given in to sedating her. I discussed it at length with her during one of her more rational moments and she agreed to it for a time. She's very determined to beat this thing. She was horrified to learn what she'd done that one night. I hate using medication but I think in Veronica's situation it's a good decision."

"It sounds that way."

"I'll make sure I leave instructions to have her sedated when Reg and Janet Mendel come. That way they can focus on praying and declaring scripture over her. I'm so thankful for those two warriors of God. They are such a blessing to me!"

Tessa nodded. "I'm relieved that you have some extra help. It'll help you cope with the intense responsibilities you carry here."

"I'm not afraid of hard work."

Tessa smiled. Everyone knew that. Deb was a workhorse.

"Well, enough about me. How was your weekend with Cody?"

Even though Deborah was old enough to be her mother, she was more like a friend.

"Good, but difficult."

"Okay, out with it!"

Tessa shook her head. She should have known her answer wouldn't be enough. The woman was a sergeant in disguise. Nothing got past her.

"He wants to start a family."

Deb paused. Finally, she said, "We can't lose you."

Tessa knew it too.

Then Deb said, "Wait! Let's pray right now."

"Okay," Tessa answered with some surprise.

Deborah came around the desk and they held hands. She prayed a long, ardent and heartfelt prayer, asking for God's will to be done. When she finished, she squeezed Tessa's hands and smiled. "We'll just trust God."

"Thanks, Deb."

"I'll get out of your hair and go get some sleep." She smiled and left and the room fell silent.

Having a baby and leaving this place was unthinkable. What would she ever do without these wonderful people she had come to know here? It was the most peaceful and supportive environment she'd ever worked in.

After her training at Chelsey College, she'd worked for a law firm as their secretary for six months. The job there had been exceptional in pay and in opportunity. But God had urged her to get involved here. They were looking for an accountant and secretary to help at this women's facility and she'd come fully qualified. The law firm begrudgingly let her go. That was the only difficult part of the transition. She felt terrible letting them down after they'd trained her.

Her gaze settled on the framed picture on her desk. It was from her honeymoon in Palm Beach, Florida. They'd asked someone to take the picture. She and Cody stood on the beach, the background a combination of rolling waves lashing the beach and palm trees extending out over the horizon. It never failed to cheer her. They looked so happy and carefree. This baby business was making it hard to feel that way today.

The morning flew by quickly as Tessa finished her filing, sorted through the mail and paid some bills. Her stomach grumbled for lunch. One look at the time on her computer screen confirmed that it was after 1:00 p.m. She grabbed her lunch bag and headed toward the staff room.

She downed her sandwich and apple quickly. The diet cola went down easily. Caffeine would give her a boost for the afternoon.

As she stood and stuffed the garbage into her lunch bag, a shadow appeared in the doorway.

"Richelle!"

Richelle grinned and walked into the room. They'd become friends in high school and their friendship continued till this day. She was as stylishly dressed as ever with her blond hair grown out long and her make-up done meticulously. Beautiful – that's how Tessa would describe her – maybe even a stunning beauty. Richelle used to flaunt it openly but now she wore her gorgeousness with an air of confidence and grace. Her greatest asset was her generous spirit, at least to those who knew her.

"What are you doing here on a Monday afternoon?" Tessa asked.

"What kind of a greeting is that?" With hands on her hips and her brow furrowed, she looked downright offended.

"You don't usually work on Mondays, that's all."

"I know." Richelle stepped forward and placed her hands on the back of a chair.

Tessa decided her work could wait for a while and sat back down.

Richelle stayed standing. "Some of the women have been begging me to come in twice a week. I finally worked it out with the salon. I'll be coming Monday and Friday afternoons from now on."

"I didn't know you were thinking of increasing your hours here. Did Bristol Boutique give you a hard time about it?"

"They did at first. I have a lot of clientele there and the manager thought I'd be short-changing them by working fewer hours. I finally convinced him I'd be able to handle both of these jobs, so instead of losing me altogether, they agreed to this arrangement." She pointed to the door. "I'm heading to work. Why don't you walk with me?"

Tessa followed her to a small room farther up the hallway. The sign on the door read simply, "Hair Salon."

Richelle unlocked the door, switched on the light and sat down in the hydraulic chair to wait for her first client.

"What did Charlie think of you working more hours here?"

"You know Charlie! He supports anything I decide to do. With him working at the Manor of Peace, he's always encouraging me to get more involved here at the women's facility." She smiled and it made her look even prettier, if that were possible.

Richelle and Charlie were married six months after Tessa and Cody. Since she and Tessa had always been close friends, they spent a lot of time together as couples.

At first, Charlie and Richelle had their share of ups and downs but their marriage was settling as they adjusted to each other. Both were very strong-willed, wanting control. It certainly did cause some upheaval their first year. Richelle even moved out for a time but that didn't last long. Her love for Charlie won out.

Tessa and Richelle had shared many common experiences, one of them being the time travel a few years before that rocked both their worlds. It was through that time travel, orchestrated by an angel, that God redirected Tessa's life and expanded her heart for the disenfranchised and hurting. It was through that same time travel that Charlie's heart was convicted and changed. He accepted Christ as his Savior. He was the last person Tessa ever expected to change. He was more brash and uncouth than any man she'd ever met.

Richelle resisted for quite a while but her heart finally softened to accept Christ. Six months later the two were wed. Although Richelle had changed phenomenally, there were still areas that needed work. It surprised Tessa, but Charlie had matured quickly as a Christian. His understanding of scripture was impressive and his former brash exterior was being replaced by a gentleness that was astonishing.

It was the biggest answer to prayer Tessa had ever experienced. That Richelle finally gave her life to God was exhilarating and celebratory. Richelle had been a major item on her prayer list for years.

"Did Charlie tell you what happed here with Veronica?"

"Oh yes, I heard about it! Veronica bit Charlie hard enough to break the skin. He bled. Did you know he had to have it stitched up?"

"No way!"

"Yeah! It's shocking how strong these women get when they're going through withdrawal."

Tessa nodded. "Is Charlie okay, though?"

"Yeah, it hasn't bothered him much. He was back at work the next day. My tough guy!"

"Have you heard from Luke?"

"Is he around?" Richelle asked, her eyes big.

"I heard from his girlfriend, Janaye, and she told me he'd be around this week. I don't know where he's staying so I'm not sure where to call to get in touch with him."

"Wow, I haven't seen him for a long time! I'd love to get together with him. I wonder why he doesn't call and make an effort."

"He apparently arrived yesterday. Maybe he hasn't had the chance to call. I'm sure he'll be spending the majority of his time with his mother and Janaye."

"Tessa, stop defending him! We should have been the first people he called! After all, we were like this in high school." Richelle held up three fingers with one hand and wrapped the fingers of her other hand around them.

It was true. The three of them had been extremely close in high school and had experienced the time travel together. It had been Luke who started it all. He was the one who talked them into going into the abandoned mansion with him, where they were whisked back in time, to their total astonishment.

"How things have changed, huh? Who would have thought Luke would renew his relationship with Janaye?" It truly did surprise Tessa.

"Especially with Janaye being a Christian."

Tessa nodded.

"I wonder if he's made any sort of decision in that area?"

"I haven't heard, but I have to admit I'm extremely curious. Janaye waited for two years before Luke finally pursued her again. I'd call that patience. I can't wait to see him and get the scoop first hand."

"Let me know if he calls you. I want to make sure I see him before he heads back to U of M. Do you know how long he's planning to stay?"

"Janaye didn't say, so if Luke doesn't call me, I'll try to find out where he's staying and arrange something." Tessa heard a noise at the door and turned to see a woman nervously enter the room.

"Are you ready for me?"

Tessa gave Leslie a smile. Leslie had been with them for nearly four months but still acted awkward and uncertain. She was a young thing, sixteen or so, but drugs didn't care whom they touched nor how damaged they left an individual.

Richelle said, "I'm ready." She pointed to the sink. "I'll wash your hair first."

Tessa said, "I'll talk to you later, Richelle."

"Sure."

Tessa headed back to her office. She thought about her two good friends, Richelle and Luke. The three of them had been inseparable in high school. It was Luke's fault the time travel ever started. He was the one who encouraged the two of them to visit the abandoned mansion on Young Street, the home she now worked in, this very place. He was the one who nagged at them both to go back with him for the second time. It really was his fault that Tessa had been moved to pursue God's highest call for her life. Through the mansion experience, her life and direction had been dramatically shifted.

They'd all been deeply affected by the angel-directed time travel. Tessa knew Luke had been challenged to rethink his eternity. It was through those events that Charlie had accepted Christ, and later Richelle. Luke was the only one who had resisted the pull toward salvation. The very one who had pushed for the time travel, was the only one still resisting God.

After four years of university in Minneapolis, at the U of M Twin Cities, Luke decided to take a position there for an architectural firm. They hadn't seen much of him the past few years and Tessa was anxious to touch base with him again. She'd always hoped he'd return to Chelsey to work locally but his plans had gone in a different direction. Richelle missed him too. Even Cody missed him. There was good reason.

The phone jingled, bringing her out of her distraction and back into focus.

CHAPTER 6

July 1989

Sally fidgeted with file folder clasps until she had them positioned to insert her latest designs. In her opinion, the spring/summer creations were exceptional. Once these last ones were approved, work would begin with pattern layout, fabric choices, colors and embellishments. Most of her spring/summer collection had already been tested and Gregory loved them. The fashion show for the spring collection was in September, so there was a mountain of work to be completed before then. Everyone was starting to feel the tension building. Deadlines were fast approaching.

A few clicks on her computer brought up the design cover she'd created to finish off her portfolio. Wiping the sheen of perspiration from her forehead, she stared at her computer screen and waited for the printer to spit out the sheet. The stifling summer heat was permeating the office complex. The building was having problems with its air conditioning unit again, an infuriating issue this time of year.

A small fan sat on the corner of her desk, one she'd brought from home. It helped cool things slightly. The printer finally did its thing and she retrieved the cover sheet and inserted it forefront on her portfolio.

With her designs ready, she leaned into her chair, resting her head on the tall back. If she relaxed at all, she knew she'd fall asleep. The last month had been relentless. Her work schedule had been extremely taxing and the season was just getting revved up. There was still a pile of work to be completed in the next few months. Just thinking about it made her weary.

As for Felix, he still hadn't shown his face or called since his disappearance. Although she felt frustrated at his insensitivity, her life had taken on an organized and conventional pace, which she rather enjoyed. Felix's unpredictable behavior and lifestyle were too disruptive. To have him gone gave her some stability. A sliver of guilt pressed her but not enough to keep her from enjoying her serene apartment.

If only he'd call and let her know he was okay. That's all she really needed. To know he was alive and well would ease her worry. Their relationship had been chaotic and was even now messing with her mind.

"Felix," she said in frustration, "why have you messed up my life like this?"

"For one thing, my name's not Felix and I don't recall messing up your life!"

It made her jump. Her hand went to her heart. "Milton Blake! You scared me! Don't do that to me!"

"First I get yelled at for messing up your life and now I'm in the doghouse for scaring you! I can't seem to do much right today, can I?"

She chuckled at his absurdity and could feel her tension dissipate because of it. "Shut up, get in here and take a seat!"

"Oh, now you think you can boss me around?" He crossed his arms but obediently walked toward the empty chair and lowered himself into it. He was unrepentantly and stylishly dressed in black leather pants and a white silk shirt that hugged his muscular frame.

Sally had to admit he looked pretty good for his age. His hair was jet black, short, gelled and stylish. Working out at the gym was important to him. He often mentioned heading there after work. Although his appearance was debonair and handsome, his conceit knew no bounds. Otherwise, he was actually quite charming.

"So what's happening, my beauty? Who's Felix and why has he ruined your life? I have ways of dealing with guys like him. If you need him taken care of, I want you to know that I have friends." His sudden Italian accent made her smile.

"No, no, no, Milton. I don't need him taken care of and you weren't supposed to hear me talk about him in the first place."

"Why all the secrecy?" He stared at her intently so that his eyebrows drew together.

"I don't know. I suppose I like keeping my dirty laundry to myself."

"Oh! That's the best kind to share. You can trust me, Sally! I won't tell a soul."

"Milton, I can't. I'm sorry." She could feel the tension returning.

"Let me change the subject then. How's your layout going?"

"I just finished it." She pointed to the completed folder lying on her desk and gave him a smug smile.

He clasped his hands in delight. "Wonderful! May I take a peek?"

"No! Not until Gregory Taylor sees my presentation." She placed a protective hand over her folder.

Disappointed, he said, "I don't see the reason to wait since I'll see it right after your presentation anyway. Jason showed me his designs."

"Well, good for him! I'm not Jason and my designs will far outweigh any of his anyway so I'm not falling for your bait." How dare he pitch her against Jason? He knew their rivalry. It infuriated her.

"Hey, I thought that tactic might work."

"Well, it didn't!"

"Okay, my beauty, I won't bother you another moment but what about going out for a drink after work? It might take your mind off of this Felix character. What do you say?"

"I don't know. I have an early morning. I'll need to go over my final presentation. I don't want to be out late."

"Hey, I said one drink, not an all-night party."

She didn't have the heart to turn him down and it might get her mind off her problems. "All right, I'll go," she sighed reluctantly.

"Wonderful!" Milton clapped his hands together in triumph. "With my dashing good looks and your unrivalled beauty we'll turn heads everywhere we go."

"Okay, Milton, try to control yourself. We're going out for a drink, not walking down the aisle!"

"My dear Sally. Always the sensible one. I'll come around at 5:00, okay?"

"That'll work for me."

He left and Sally started on her PowerPoint and audio presentation.

They ended up at the Kangaroo Club, a few blocks from their office building. Milton chose a table in the corner where soft lighting enveloped them and pop music played cheerfully. The corner gave them some anonymity. Hopefully no one would see her out with Milton. He was much too old for her. It made her nervous being here with him.

After ordering drinks and appetizers, Sally loosened up and started enjoying the evening. It surprised her a little, knowing how aggravating Milton could be at times. The relaxed setting brought out his more comical and entertaining qualities.

"Do you want anything else? I'm paying, you know."

Sally shrugged. She was still hungry.

"I'll order." He waved down a waitress, ordered Caesar salads, chicken entrees and another round of drinks.

Sally listened with open jaw. That was a lot of food, especially after appetizers.

"I don't think I can possibly eat that much."

"You look famished and you're much too thin."

She shook her head. "And you supposed I'd want the chicken?"

"You look to me like a chicken-loving woman." He shrugged. "We have the same tastes."

He was taking way too many liberties. "What do you mean by that?"

The waitress returned and placed a basket of fresh biscuits between them.

After she left, Milton said, "I'll let you figure that out on your own." His eyebrows raised and lowered a few times. "I'll just say this: 'Felix, eat your heart out.'" He reached for a biscuit, buttered it and took a large bite.

Sally wasn't sure what he was up to. Answering might just egg him on. Temporary silence seemed preferable.

The meal was delicious, better than what she ever cooked for herself, but she only managed to eat half. Milton helped himself to her leftovers. After the meal they both ordered coffee. Sally studied Milton while he prepared his coffee with sugar and cream.

She realized that even though they'd worked together for over two years, she knew very little about him. He was conceited, a comedian and had his bouts of anger and frustration before a show but that's all she really knew. As Milton lay his spoon down and picked up his mug, she decided to do some digging.

"Milton, have you ever been married?"

His eyes danced up to meet hers. "Oh, now who's getting nosy?"

"I just realized I don't know much about you."

"So, you want to get to know me." He grinned. "That's a good sign, I'd say."

"Control," is all she said.

His smile faded somewhat. "You don't want to know about my past. It's not a pretty picture."

"Hey, I don't know too many with a pretty past."

"That's loaded!" He stared at her intensely. "I have a feeling there's more to you than just a pretty face."

"Milton, we were talking about your past, remember?"

"See, there's something you're trying to hide. You have some skeletons in your closet and I'm going to dig them out!"

She tried to remain calm at the threat. She asked again, "So, were you married?"

"Oh, Sally, do you really want to know?" A look of dread glazed his eyes.

"Yes, I do!"

His shoulders raised and then lowered. "All right. I was married once to a beautiful model. We were both young and stupid and didn't know love from lust, if you know what I mean. It was a mistake right from the start. We only dated a month when I proposed to her and we were married within the week. It was a spur of the moment thing and I sure lived to regret it. We honestly couldn't stand each other, weren't compatible at all! I'm amazed we didn't end up killing each other."

"How long were you married?"

"Three horrible, long years!"

"How did it eventually end?"

"I found her in our bed with one of my best friends."

"Oh, no!"

"Oh, yes. Well, to say the least, that didn't go over so well."

"I'm so sorry, Milton!"

"Don't feel too sorry for me. I didn't stay faithful to her either."

"Milton!"

"I had to do something to survive."

"You should never have married her in the first place."

"Well, that's easy to say in hindsight, isn't it?"

"Did you ever marry again?"

"Never. I've never been interested in walking down the aisle again, until now of course." He reached for her hand and lifted it to his lips to kiss it.

Sally pulled away. "Milton, stop it!"

"Got you!" He pointed at her and grinned, but his eyes sent mixed messages.

"Your marriage must have hurt you a lot."

"Naw, I never get hurt. Men are tough like nails. They don't get hurt that easy."

"I don't believe that for a second." She stared at him, trying to figure him out. "Do you think you'll ever marry again?"

"Love, you must be blind!" He reached for her hand again but this time she pulled it back in time.

"Just answer the question."

"You're getting bossy again. I don't like my women bossy."

"Oh, how do you like them? Subservient?" Talk about chauvinistic!

"Maybe." He looked like he was losing interest in the topic.

She was determined to get an answer. "Have you ever fallen in love with anyone after your divorce?"

"Oh, yes. I've fallen in love with my work."

"That's not what I meant." His evasive manner was exasperating her.

Milton sighed heavily, crossed his arms on the table and gave her a resigned look. "There are women who have captured my heart but I don't know if I could call it love. I don't believe I'm a very good judge of 'love.' I'm happy with the direction of my life and I don't see any reason to change it. I would adore meeting someone I could truly connect with, emotionally, socially, spiritually and in every other way. I haven't found anyone like that in my whole lifetime so I'm thinking that marriage just isn't for me. If it happens, great! If it doesn't then I'm okay with that too."

"That's so sad. You're making me cry." She faked it and dabbed at her eyes with her napkin.

He gazed at her curiously. "Please don't make a scene over me. I couldn't handle it."

"Why do my feelings make you uncomfortable? I really do feel sorry for you."

"I'm touched that you feel that way but I don't need your pity." He took another sip of his coffee.

"Then what do you need, Milton Blake?"

He gave her a mischievous grin. "Why don't you come to my place and we can discuss it there."

"No. I'm flattered by your attention but my life is too complicated right now." *What am I saying? Maybe later I'd give it consideration?* She could kick herself! "There's no way it would work. There are too many years between us."

"How old are you?" he asked.

"I'm young enough to be your daughter. I must be a good twenty years younger than you."

"That's not too bad." He rubbed his chin thoughtfully.

"Please, this will not work for me. We're friends; let's just leave it at that."

"Where's your sense of adventure? You've never been with an older man so how do you know it wouldn't work?"

Sally stood to emphasize that her decision was final. She slipped her sweater over her shoulders.

Milton stood and was about to protest when her cell phone rang. Digging it out of her purse, she opened it and placed it to her ear.

"Hello. Calm down, calm down. I can't make out a word you're saying. Now, who is this? ... Rena, is that you? ... What? ... What? ... When? ... Oh no! ... Where? ... Have the police arrived? ... I'm on my way!"

Her heart thundered in her ears as she turned and asked Milton for a ride to her apartment. She didn't know what else to do. There was no way she could drive. Not now.

Milton's red sports car pulled close to Sally's apartment building and parked by the curb, a short way down. The parking lot was jammed full of police cruisers and emergency vehicles. Flashing lights permeated the general area. Yellow tape had cordoned off a crime scene and police officers kept the crowd back.

Sally jumped out and ran toward the scene. There was a crowd of spectators standing by the yellow tape and she caught a glimpse of a man lying on the ground. As she pushed her way closer, she noticed blood coating the pavement beneath him.

A hand on her arm brought her face around abruptly.

"Rena!"

"Sally, I'm so sorry!" With a look of compassion, Rena reached out to hug her.

Sally let Rena's arms enfold her but Rena's protruding tummy got in the way.

Pulling back, with her heart beating crazily, she asked, "He's gone?" All the way here she'd tried to get a hold of Rena for more information but she never answered her phone.

"Is he dead?" asked Milton beside her. Sally had filled him in on the way.

Rena nodded.

"No!" Sally's chest seized, making it hard to breathe. "I have to go see him." She turned away and walked as far as she could. The yellow tape straddled her waist, mocking her inability to approach. Felix was lying in a pool of blood, the police asking anyone within eyesight for information. Sally choked back her tears, hoping for a small sign of life. His still frame didn't give much hope. No one was attending him. A gurney stood to one side, ready to haul him away once the police gave the okay. After bolstering her courage, she slipped under the yellow tape and hurried toward Felix.

Someone was yelling but she ignored them, ran to him and bent down on one knee. Studying him, she could see clear bullet wounds on his neck and chest. Regret and sorrow raged through her. With a shaky hand, she covered her mouth. This wasn't supposed to happen. She never loved him but she never wished this on him.

A hand grabbed her arm but she determinedly pulled back.

"Felix!" she screamed. "Why did you come back here? You knew you were in danger! Why didn't you run?" Sobs came then, deep and powerful. The tension of the past weeks combined with this new tragedy overwhelmed her.

The hand grabbed her harder this time and yanked. She flew to her feet, her eyes matching the anger on the police officer's face, and was promptly escorted back behind the yellow line. Tears blurred her vision. The police officer released her but other arms gathered her up – Milton's. He held her firmly but gently. Her legs felt weak and her emotions raw.

She heard someone say, "We'll question you soon. Don't go anywhere."

"Give her some time, for crying out loud!" said Milton. "Can't you see she's broken up?" His arms held her up, keeping her from collapsing.

Then it grew silent all around her except for her hysterical sobs.

"Are you okay?" she heard Rena ask, her hand rubbing her back.

She couldn't answer.

"Do you know this girl and the dead man?" a police officer asked Rena.

"Yes. This is Sally Windsor. The man over there is Felix Billings."

"What's your name?"

"Rena Salvos."

"Did Felix live here?"

"No, yes. I don't know. You'll have to ask Sally that question."

Things grew quiet again, except for the hum of emergency activity. Still the sobs came. There was no way she could answer anything sensibly right now.

Then, "It looks like I'll have to ask her later. Does Sally live here?"

"Yes, sir."

"And you don't know if Felix lived here?"

"Off and on, but not steady."

"Do you live in this apartment complex?"

"Yes."

The questions continued. It was exhausting hearing it all. Milton must have known because he led her away and sat her down on a curb in the parking lot.

He held her, rubbed her hair, handed her tissues and stayed close through the harrowing, emotional upheaval. She didn't know why she was crying like she was. She didn't even care for Felix that much. But he was gone and the shock was devastating. She'd even prayed and asked God to keep him safe. Much good that did!

Bits and pieces of the interrogation drifted toward her. She wished Milton had taken her even farther away. To hear all the details of what happened didn't help. But the investigators didn't give up until they had all Rena knew.

Her voice sounded edgy and nervous as she answered them.

From Rena's answers, Sally learned that Rena had heard gunshots and looked out her window to see a white car with tinted windows. One window was rolled down, the end of a gun protruding from it. Another shot went off and that's when she noticed Felix crumple to the sidewalk in front of the building. She told them that she'd noticed the car here before, a limo, noted the license plate and admitted it had been here numerous times.

That surprised Sally. Rena had never told her.

The police were curious. Why had Rena paid so much attention to it? Because she'd been suspicious. Something about it didn't seem right. Had she seen the faces? Her answer was no.

Relief flooded Sally as they finally finished interrogating Rena. As long as they didn't come hunting for her. Being wrapped in Milton's arms felt safe and it surprised her. It also suddenly made her feel uncomfortable. She pulled away and sat up, drying her cheeks one more time. A wad of wet tissues was collecting in her hand.

Rena walked up to her and crouched down on her haunches before her. "How are you doing?"

Sally shrugged. "I want to go to my apartment. I can't stand being here." She was sure her makeup was a mess; her mascara was all over the tissue. What did Milton think of her now?

"Sally, I need to tell you something."

She turned her puffy eyes in Rena's direction. "What?"

"Those goons who did Felix in, they must have gotten into your apartment before they killed him."

"What did they do?"

"Your place is completely trashed. I heard a lot of noise coming from your floor. I was worried but couldn't go check. I was busy with the little ones. After calling the police, I waited till the clamor died down and when my husband got home, I went to check. Your door was unlocked so I looked in. It's a total mess. I don't know what they were looking for."

"No!" Sally shook her head in disbelief. "They were looking for money. Felix owed some guys money." Suddenly she thought of her cat. "Where's Tiger?"

Rena said, "I found him hiding under your bed. I brought him to our apartment. We'll take care of him. Don't worry."

Sally nodded, relieved that he was okay.

"You can't stay here, Sally," Milton said. "You're coming home with me tonight." There was such authority in his voice.

It was calming to have him take charge but reason won out. "I can't, Milton."

Rena said, "You can stay with us, Sally. Our place is full but you're welcome. The couch is available."

"I don't know. I just don't know what to do." She didn't have the wherewithal, nor the emotional stamina to make an enlightened decision. With shock and sorrow weighing heavily on her, she felt about ready to collapse.

Milton suddenly picked her up in his arms and gave instructions for Rena to open his car door for him. Sally protested but he ignored her. He carried her over and placed her gingerly onto the passenger seat. As he stood, the same investigator who had interrogated Rena approached and took out his notepad.

"Where are you taking her? I need to ask her some questions. Move out of the way."

"Sir, she's in no state of mind to be answering questions now. She's beside herself with grief. It was her boyfriend who was shot and killed. She needs some time to grieve."

"Do you want to be charged with obstructing justice?"

"I'll bring her to the precinct tomorrow!" Milton said testily. "Right now she needs time to process this!"

The man studied him, his jaw twitching tersely. Finally he said, "All right, but I need your name."

Milton told him and he jotted it down. The police officer then went to the back of the vehicle and wrote down the license plate number. They weren't taking any chances. He gave Milton the address of the precinct and finally left, returning to the action by the building.

Milton turned concerned eyes back to Sally and she gave him a weak but grateful smile.

He leaned down close and asked, "Where do you want to stay tonight? Your apartment's out of the question."

She placed a hand on his cheek and said, "Thank you, Milton, for being here and taking care of me. You don't know how much that means to me." She choked back some tears. "Would you call my brother Robert for me and ask him to pick me up?"

"No!" He suddenly looked offended. His eyes took on a gentler hue. "But I can give you a ride to his place. Tell me where he lives and I'll take you there right now."

Sally nodded. Milton stepped back and Rena came to give her a hug.

"Take care, Sally."

She nodded but the knot in her throat kept her from answering. Rena stepped away and closed the door. Milton slipped behind the wheel and the engine roared to life. Rena stood on the sidewalk and waved. Behind her, Sally could see men lifting Felix onto a stretcher, covering him with a white sheet. She tore her eyes away as Milton's car veered into traffic.

CHAPTER 7

August 2003

Tessa surveyed her appearance in the full length mirror. The new cream-colored pantsuit set off the bright blue tank top underneath. Her makeup looked good, accenting her outfit well. She'd shadowed her eyes with a light blue shade, pale pink on her cheeks and finished it off with a dusty rose gloss for her lips.

Cody entered the room and whistled in appreciation. He stepped behind her and wrapped his arms around her middle.

"You're not jealous, are you?" she asked.

"Why would I be? Luke already has a girlfriend. There's no need for me to feel jealous."

"You're absolutely right because I'm married to the most wonderful man on earth."

He nuzzled her neck, placing light kisses there.

It tickled and her shoulder puckered. With a smile she said, "I hope you don't feel too left out."

He locked eyes with her in the mirror. "I understand the situation. Luke's back in town and you three high school buddies want to get together for old time's sake. I'm okay with that. I'll miss you but I'll survive. After all, he is my brother."

"Half-brother," reminded Tessa.

It still was hard to believe after all this time. Cody only found out he had a half-brother a few years ago, during their time travel experience at the abandoned mansion. So many things had been revealed. During the adventure Cody also discovered he had a cousin he'd never known about. Their encounter with the past had garnered him two new family members.

"You're just going out with your brother-in-law. It's no big deal. I can take care of myself."

She gazed at him affectionately and smiled. "You're being really big about this."

He turned her around and kissed her soundly on the lips. Pulling away, he said, "I have my own plans."

"Oh really!" She picked up her purse from the bed and slung it over her shoulder. "What plans?"

"Oh, wouldn't you like to know?" he said teasingly.

"Yes, I deserve to know."

"I have a party planned."

"With who?"

"A friend's coming over." He smirked impishly.

"And …… who is it?"

With a shrug he said, "Charlie."

She nodded. "That's good. What's the plan?" she asked as she headed to the front door.

"We'll watch the baseball game, order pizza and pig out. I bought tortilla chips, salsa and a pack of coke. We should be set for the evening. We're going to be a couple of couch potatoes tonight."

"Sounds like it." She smiled. "It'll keep Charlie busy tonight too."

"Our women are both playing hooky. It seemed like a good idea to hang out."

At the door she looked out the side window and noticed Luke waiting on the curb for her. His gleaming, white corvette was impressive and quite the upgrade from his previous old green beater.

She slipped into her new, cream flats and stepped toward Cody for another kiss. With his arms wrapped around her and his intense kisses leaving her breathless, it was clear he wasn't willing to let her go just yet.

"I'll miss you," she said, gazing into his eyes.

"I'll miss you more." One more kiss on the tip of her nose and he let her go.

~~~~~

Luke picked up Richelle next and they headed to The Eating Place, the restaurant where Tessa had once worked. There was no sign of Martha, one of the shift managers Tessa dealt with years ago – a memory best forgotten. That woman never did like her very much.

The hostess seated them at a round table in a private and cozy corner. All the staff were unfamiliar. It surprised Tessa. She did notice Les, the owner, talking to someone close to the kitchen. At least the ownership hadn't changed. Seeing the crowd beginning to fill the place, she was happy the food hadn't lost its great reputation either.

The warm colors and plants trailing their leaves from beams from above gave the place a nostalgic feel. Being with her longtime friends again felt wonderful. It happened so seldom. She and Richelle were both married and busy working. Luke lived in Minneapolis and rarely came to visit in Chelsey. Perhaps now, with him seeing Janaye again, he'd stop by more often.

Tessa studied Luke's handsome face and said, "It's wonderful having you around again. It's been too long!"

"Thank you, Tessa! It has been a long time."

Richelle said, "Far too long! What do you think you're doing, leaving us here in Chelsey and going off to work in Minneapolis? Whatever happened to your promise? I thought you were going to come back here after university. How about that company you worked for here during the summers while you were attending university? I thought they were going to hire you after you were done your training."

"Yeah, I know. It did look good for a while but then this other company in Minneapolis started pursuing me and I decided to try them out. They're a huge architectural engineering firm and I thought I'd have a better chance at advancement with them than the small one here in Chelsey. It was a matter of bettering my career."

"So you gave us up for a job? That's pathetic!"

"Hey, Richelle, don't be so hard on me. I came back to visit."

"That doesn't count, buddy! No one walks out on friends like that and gets away with it."

"And, what are you planning to do about it?" Pure enjoyment showed in his eyes. It was obvious he'd missed this verbal jousting with Richelle. They were both known for their quick, smart remarks.

"Oh, just wait. I'll think of a way to pay you back for your insensitive ways."

He made a grunting sound. "You're just a bunch of wind. An empty threat is all you can manage."

Richelle turned toward Tessa. "Do you remember him being this cocky?" She glanced back at Luke. "You had better behave yourself tonight. Remember, it's the two of us against you."

He shook his head and chuckled. "So how's the hairdressing business, Richelle?"

"Changing the subject, huh?"

"I thought it might be wise."

"Ah, you've matured some."

Luke ignored her. Tessa was surprised. He always had the last word; at least he tried hard. With Richelle it was nearly an impossible feat.

"I love what I do," said Richelle. "I'm still enjoying the work and my clientele is booming. Fitting everyone in is difficult some weeks. I've thought of starting a place of my own but, after some serious consideration, I decided against it."

Luke said, "I don't see why you wouldn't since you have such a great clientele base. They'd move with you and you could start making some real money. Why not do it? Is Charlie holding you back?"

"No! Charlie is not holding me back! He's a wonderful husband and supports me in whatever I want to do. Don't start with your comments about Charlie, Luke. I don't appreciate it."

He held up his hands in surrender then held one out to her in offering. "All right, I'll leave Charlie alone. Truce?"

Richelle stared at his hand hanging in mid air and grimaced. Reluctantly she reached over and they shook on it.

Luke exhaled and said, "I heard from Cody that Charlie's working at the men's detox shelter."

"I thought you were going to leave Charlie alone?" asked Richelle.

"I meant I'd stop downing him. Do I have to stop talking about him completely?"

"We can talk about my sweet man as long as you behave yourself. And to answer your question, yes, Charlie's working at the Manor of Peace. After some courses, he's started counseling the men. He's doing an amazing job. I'm very proud of him."

"How in the world did he go from wood working and helping his dad with mechanics to counseling men hooked on drugs? It's seems like a bit of a stretch to me." Luke crossed his arms, rested them on top of the table and waited for her reply.

"You just don't know Charlie very well."

"You mean he's not crass, crude and obnoxious anymore?"

"Luke!"

Tessa sighed. She'd forgotten how aggravated those two could get with each other. Would she never stop having to play referee? Oh well, at least it would bring back some high school memories.

Richelle said, "Charlie's always had a soft, caring heart despite his tough exterior. He's also changed a lot since he's become a Christian. All he wants to do now is help people."

At the mention of Christianity, Luke's interest faded. He turned to Tessa. "How's your work at the Mansion of Hope? It must be somewhat depressing being surrounded by women who've messed up their lives."

"Well, you're right in a way. These women have made decisions that have turned out badly, although I don't believe one of them set out to do that intentionally. Every one of them has hopes and dreams. Mansion of Hope is actively helping to restore those."

"Yeah, but do you enjoy the work?"

Tessa smiled. "Yes, I do. I find it extremely fulfilling to see these women change before my very eyes. They arrive in desperate situations and are able to leave changed, with a renewed sense of hope for the future. It's never become boring yet and it never ceases to amaze me how God can turn a person's life around."

"And to think that old mansion is now an addiction rehabilitation place is crazy!" Luke said.

"It's a beautiful place. You should check it out," Richelle said.

Luke nodded. "Maybe I should."

Tessa said, "Every time I think of how that house went from holding so much despair to offering hope now makes me smile inside."

"It's been quite the turnaround." Luke fell silent, his expression hard to read as he studied his ice water.

"So what about you, Luke? What's new in your life?" asked Richelle.

After a moment of silence, he finally said, "There's not much to tell. My job is going great and I'm making some good money. What else can I say? Life is good."

Tessa asked, "What about Janaye Howard? We heard you're seeing her again. Is that true?"

"You two don't want to hear about that."

"Oh yes, we do!" insisted Richelle.

"What do I say?"

"Tell us the truth."

"Are you sure you want to hear the truth?"

"Yes we do." The two girls answered simultaneously.

"The truth is it's none of your business." He grinned at them mischievously.

"Oh, come on, Luke, out with it!" demanded Richelle.

"You two are shocking me with such a display of unabashed curiosity." Luke shook his index finger back and forth, only to prolong their agony.

Tessa sighed in frustration and said, "Come on, Luke, please tell us about Janaye."

"I guess I won't be able to get off the hook this time." He took a sip of water, leaned back and said, "Well, where do I start?"

"At the beginning," suggested Richelle.

"I was born in…"

"Not that beginning!"

He chuckled. "Okay." After one more sip of water he said, "Well, I couldn't forget about Janaye. During my last two years in university, while I was dating other women, I would always compare them to her and none of them measured up. There's something about that girl that's always intrigued me. I could never place my finger on it but I couldn't ignore it anymore so I called her a few months ago. I didn't even know if she was seeing someone else because I hadn't talked to her for so long."

"And, then what happened? Was she dating someone else?" asked Richelle.

With annoyance, he stared at her. "Richelle, be patient. You're like a testy kid! I should prolong this just to teach you a lesson."

She released a puff of air, making her lips pout. "Just tell us what happened."

"Did you know that patience is a virtue? But I haven't found too many people who actually possess it."

"You're getting under my skin! Would you just spill the beans?"

He turned to Tessa. "Hey, do you think I should tell Miss Barbie, the prying one, what happened?"

Miss Barbie was Luke's favorite nickname for Richelle. The name started in high school when Richelle began to fill out and her looks amazed everyone. It still suited her. She was as gorgeous as ever. Although he'd always admired her looks, their characters were like sandpaper to each other. It was quite fascinating to observe, but not always enjoyable.

Tessa was growing tired of the friction. She said, "Well, if you don't want to tell us about Janaye, then I'll take the floor and talk about my Cody and our great marriage."

That was enough threat for him. Luke gave her a wink and said, "Okay, we don't want to be bored to death, so here goes. I called her a few months ago and boy was I ever nervous. For all I knew she was married and had a few ankle biters around."

"Wouldn't that have been embarrassing?" Richelle chuckled.

"Would you be quiet and let me talk? Do you want to hear the story or not?" He was looking to start a fight.

Tessa was in no mood for it. She could see Richelle revving up with a reply.

Quickly Tessa asked, "So what happened when you called her?"

Richelle's mouth shut in mid retort.

"I kept our talk on surface stuff at first. I asked where she was working and how she'd been. Her answers were all short and no-nonsense. It made me even more nervous. I kept thinking that maybe she had a husband listening in on another line or something. I talked about myself mostly, which I didn't really enjoy doing, but, hey, it filled in the dead spots and kept me from revealing why I'd really called."

"So how did you find out she was available?" asked Tessa.

"I finally came out with it. I asked her if she was seeing anyone and she said yes."

"No! So you're not seeing her?" Richelle asked in surprise.

"Well, she did say the relationship was a bit rocky and she wasn't sure if it would continue. She asked for my number and said she'd call if anything changed. I gave the okay. Within a month I got the call and we started communicating via phone. I came out one weekend to see her and she's been to Minneapolis once to see me. We tested the water at first to see if this was something that could work. This is my second time coming back here to see her and I decided to make it a more extended visit this time."

Richelle's brows furrowed in anger. "You were here once before and didn't call us? How dare you?"

"Chill out, Barbie! I only had two days and I wasn't going to spend it pursuing you, a married woman. I was here to spend time with Janaye so cut me some slack."

"I can see your point," said Tessa. She turned to Richelle. "He's right. Why would he spend his time with us on such a short visit?" She turned back to him. "You're exonerated, Luke."

"Well, thank you. You're so kind to give me some space and breathing room here." He gave Richelle a smug look and pulled at his shirt collar as if he needed more air.

Richelle shook her head indifferently but her curiosity won out. "And, how is it going? Do you two get along well?"

"Wouldn't you like to know?"

"As a matter of fact, yes."

"All right you two, especially Richelle, who can't seem to get enough juicy morsels of information." He gave her a mock disapproving look.

"You pegged me right. You may as well just get on with it."

Luke shook his head, shrugged his shoulders and said, "I like her. She's probably too sweet for me but we get along great and she's as wonderful as I remember." He fell silent, a pleased expression on his face.

Tessa couldn't resist commenting, "This is quite a change for you, especially knowing that she's a Christian."

"She is and that's the only drawback for me. I know she's concerned about the fact that I'm not and also that I'm not interested in becoming one. I know it's very important to her. I've been upfront and told her I won't accept Christianity just because of her. In other words, I won't fake it for her sake. If it can't be real to me then I'm not interested. I'm not very good at acting. She agrees with that. The decision has to be mine entirely."

"So, is she still willing to date you with the way things are?" asked Tessa. A tug of hope pulled at her. For Luke to become a Christian would be an answer to a long-breathed prayer.

"She insisted that as long as we're dating, I accompany her to church every Sunday – as long as I'm around, that is."

"Wow! She's a tough woman." Tessa felt immediate respect for her.

"Are you going to let a woman boss you around like that? I can't believe my ears!" Richelle looked dumbfounded. "I wouldn't let my significant other call the shots like that." She shook her head. "You sure have changed!"

Luke looked stupefied. While Richelle and Charlie dated, Luke had often used that rationale on Richelle. Charlie had been far too dominating where Richelle was concerned and enjoyed ruling their relationship. Luke had often highlighted this weakness in her man. Now, with Richelle offering some of his own advice back to him, he quipped, "Don't get too excited now, Richelle. Try to control yourself."

"You used to be so independent and bragged about how you'd never let yourself be hemmed in by anyone. What happened?" Richelle was laying it on thick so Tessa decided to rescue him.

"It's called love. Luke has fallen in love. Don't you remember, Richelle, how you used to tell him that once he fell in love his views would change?"

"That's right. Now look at him – a blubbering fool."

Luke shook his finger at her threateningly. "You're asking for it, Barbie Doll."

She grinned wickedly at him from across the table.

Tessa asked, "So, did you agree to Janaye's ultimatum?"

"Well, she's the girl I've been looking for all these years so what choice did I have. I had to agree."

"So you're going to church with her tomorrow?" Richelle asked with a smug smile.

"Yes, Miss I-Told-You-So-Smarty-Pants. I'm going to church tomorrow. To tell you the truth, I'm dreading it. I haven't been in a church since your wedding, Barbie Doll."

"You never know; you might come to enjoy it. It can happen, you know."

He shook his head. "I can't imagine that. All I know is that I don't want to lose Janaye again."

"Ahhhh... That's so sweet," Richelle said sarcastically.

Exasperation clouded his eyes. "You deserve a good thrashing."

She howled with laughter. When she finally settled, she said, "You'd be thrashing two if you did that."

"What?" The insinuation was clear enough but Tessa had to know for sure.

Luke looked as clued out as most males on the subject. He stared at her blankly. Finally, he held up both hands, palms up, his face clouded in confusion. "What are you talking about? Are you turning kinky on me?"

"You're pregnant?" asked Tessa.

"Well, why don't you let the whole world know while you're at it? Sheesh! You said it loud enough for the entire restaurant to hear!"

"Sorry." Tessa clamped a hand over her mouth but the excitement she felt made her giggle.

Luke asked, "You're pregnant?" The news was obviously still settling in.

Tessa said, "This is so exciting, Richelle! When did you find out?" Haw far along are you?"

"I just did a home test a few days ago and it turned out positive."

"Wow!"

Luke's silence was unusual.

Richelle turned to him and asked, "So, Luke, what do you think of me becoming a mother?"

He shook his head slowly and said, "Poor baby, is all I can say."

"Luke!" Her bright smile vanished quickly, replaced by a look of aggravation.

His eyes became serious. "Why would you want to start a family so soon? What were you thinking? Charlie and you have had your issues. Now you want to throw a baby into the picture? It seems completely negligent! It just proves my point about Charlie."

Anger flashed in Richelle's eyes. "And what is that?"

"He's an irresponsible oaf who can't think through the consequences of his actions."

Tessa felt shock at his cruel words. How could he say such things to Richelle?

"How dare you?" Richelle said angrily. Tears suddenly sprang to her eyes. "What do you know about responsibility, Luke? You're single and only look out for number one. I don't see you taking care of anyone but yourself. You have no right to come here and tear my husband apart and judge my life." She swiped the tears away before she continued. "I can't remember you being so cruel. What's happened to you? I don't want to spend my evening like this." She stood and reached for her things.

Luke quickly rose, skirted the table and approached her. He reached for her hand and knelt down on one knee. Richelle tried to yank it free but he held tight.

Tessa was grateful he had the sense to right his wrongs.

"I'm sorry, Richelle. Please forgive me. The things I said were uncalled for. I take them back. If Charlie has been able to live with you for this long, supporting you, I'm sure he'll be able to handle supporting a baby."

"That's supposed to be an apology?" Her tears still showed and anger laced her voice now.

"I said that wrong. Why can't I say anything right today? I didn't mean it that way. I guess I don't know Charlie very well and I'm not a very good judge of his character. If you love him and you've stayed with him this long, then I'm sure it will be a stable environment for a baby. Please, Richelle, I'm sorry I hurt you. I never wanted to make you cry." He handed her a paper napkin from the table.

She wiped her eyes slowly and stared at Luke on bended knee. Her tears finally stopped flowing. She no longer looked ready to bolt for the door. Luke gazed up beseechingly, as though begging for her forgiveness.

"Get up, Luke! You look stupid down there."

He let go of her hand and she sat down. He slowly returned to his chair.

"So, does that mean you forgive me?" He asked tentatively.

"Yes, for now. I hope you can behave yourself. It's not much fun when you act like such a jerk."

"Again, I am so sorry, Richelle."

"Just be aware, a pregnant woman has hormones that are raging out of control and emotions are very volatile. I used to take much worse from you, but lately I can't handle much. You'll have to go easy."

"You're going to be a mommy, huh? How does that make you feel?"

Richelle released a shaky breath. "Honestly, I'm absolutely thrilled. Charlie and I have been trying for a few months. When we found out I was pregnant we had a celebration. We took pictures of the two of us with the positive strip card."

Luke groaned at that.

"We went out for dinner and then went for a walk at the park. We talked and dreamed of what it will be like to be parents and who our child will look like." Richelle beamed with enthusiasm.

"Now, doesn't that concern you just a little?" Luke asked cautiously, a small smile lighting his eyes.

Richelle puckered her lips in disapproval. Luke raised his hands in surrender.

"Sorry, sorry."

Tessa said, "I'm still trying to get over the shock! How do you feel? Do you get morning sickness?"

"No sickness. I've been feeling great so far except for the emotional roller coaster ride. Charlie doesn't know what to do with me some days. He says I've become a different person and he feels like he has to tiptoe through the tulips. I feel bad about that but I can't seem to control my mood swings."

"So what about your career?" asked Luke. "Will you throw that out the window now that you'll be a mommy? That would sure seem like a waste to me."

"I haven't quite decided what I'll do." Richelle bothered her bottom lip. "Charlie would prefer I stay home with the baby and then only continue doing hair at the Mansion of Hope on weekends. That way we wouldn't have to leave the baby with a caregiver too much. I'm not sure if I'm willing to give up on my career completely, though. That's one area we're not quite agreed upon."

"Would you take a few months off when the baby comes?" asked Tessa.

"Yes. I would definitely take a few months off to recuperate. Right now I'm just looking forward to finally showing so I can go buy maternity clothes. I want people to be able to see that I'm pregnant."

"Barbie wanting a tummy? That's a switch!" Luke chuckled. "What will you do if you stay fat after the baby?"

"I won't! If I gain some extra pounds, I'll shake them fast."

He said, "Have you seen some of the young mothers out there? Some still look like they're pregnant."

Tessa said, "Well, I can't imagine Richelle letting that happen. As long as we've known her, she's been super keen on watching her weight. Her eating habits are pretty strict."

"If I'm still big after the baby I'll starve myself till I'm thin again and I'll exercise too. Luke, you can't depress me about having a baby no matter how hard you try."

"Is that what I'm trying to do?"

"It sure sounds like it." She smiled at him sweetly, choosing not to let him get to her this time.

Tessa said, "Oh, I don't think Luke wants to depress you. He just loves to tease you. It's his way of showing you he loves you."

Luke frowned. "Is that what I've been doing? Showing her I love her?"

Tessa shrugged.

He chuckled. "I'll have to do it more often then."

Richelle groaned. "I don't think I can handle much more of your love. I'd much rather have you say it instead of tease."

Luke couldn't resist the challenge. He stood and scooted over to her chair, bent down on one knee, took her hand and raised it to his lips and kissed it.

She snickered in amusement.

Lowering her hand, he looked into her eyes. "My dear, Richelle, dost thou not know how I love thee? My heart beateth loudly for thee and I cantst barely breath for thy awesome beauty and magnificence. Wilt thou accept my humble praise and adoration?"

"Luke, knock it off. You're embarrassing me." She wiggled her hand to pry it free but Luke's hold held firm.

Tessa cracked up at the ridiculous display. Those two could still put on a show. Very little ever embarrassed them. They never cared who was watching.

He finally got up and returned to his seat. The tension was broken and their easy camaraderie continued.

After hours of conversation they finally headed to the main doors. Luke paid the bill, left a hefty tip and they exited the restaurant together.

Luke's swanky new car was parked in front of the restaurant, a little number he'd bought since his employment in Minneapolis. He used to drive an old wreck of a thing that made a lot of noise. Financial success brought some incentives. Tessa was proud of him.

"So, Richelle, do you trust this car a little better than my old one?"

"At least I'll end up at the other end with the same hairstyle that I started out with. That old heap you had jumped and bumped down the road like a big old toad. I have to admit you've moved up a few notches. It's very impressive."

He looked thrilled. "Get in, and I'll show you what this baby can do." He slipped into the driver's seat and started the engine.

"Just remember that you have delicate cargo aboard," Richelle cautioned him as she took her seat.

The car roared as he stepped on the gas and pulled out into the street.

Richelle said, "Oh Luke, I forgot to mention that you can drop me off at Tessa's place. Charlie's there with Cody and he'll take me home from there."

"Sounds good to me."

The old mansion was coming up on the left, the one that had been transformed into the Mansion of Hope, where both girls worked.

Tessa said, "Luke, look. That's the old mansion our church renovated. What do you think?"

He slowed. "Wow, it looks a lot different now than it did a few years ago. It's amazing!" The car veered to the curb and he stepped on the brake to take a better look.

That was where the time travel had happened, except the house was abandoned and completely dilapidated back then. All three of them were together that first time. They had gone back numerous times as the lives of the family from the past were revealed. It had changed all of them.

Now the large mansion was restored to its former beauty and majesty. Large pillars in front held up the roof, jutting over the expansive porch at the front. The windows glistened in the evening sunlight.

"They've done a beautiful job of restoring it," stated Luke.

"You should stop in sometime and I'll take you on a tour. They've done a great job inside too."

"I might just do that."

Luke turned back into the road and sped like a racecar driver toward Tessa's house and screeched to a stop at the curb.

Richelle speedily exited the vehicle and turned to Luke. "Whew, we made it. You better slow down if you don't want to get a ticket."

"Yes, Mommy Barbie. I'll be sure to do that."

Richelle glared menacingly.

Tessa turned to him and said, "Thanks for the ride. Do you want to come in for a while and visit with the guys?"

"Thanks, but no. I need to get going. It was a fun evening, girls."

With that his Corvette sped off once again.

CHAPTER 8

August 1989

Sally's head was pounding as Milton led her from the interrogation room, out the front doors of the precinct to his car sitting in the parking lot. The Advil she'd taken in the morning before coming hadn't helped a bit. The drumbeat inside her head intensified with the bright sun glaring at her from above.

The forceful interrogation had left her drained and longing for bed. Arthur Tilley had been thorough and severe, questioning her whereabouts, the issue of drugs in her apartment, consorting with a felon, etc, etc. He'd even interrogated Milton. Poor man. She felt sorry for him. His only fault was taking care of her and being her pillar of strength.

Arthur questioned Milton thoroughly to see if their stories agreed. They were accused of being lovers, planning Felix's murder. Their innocent date had turned into a nightmare.

This was Sally's second interrogation. She'd been a basket case the first time – crying, blubbering and not making much sense. So they gave her time to regroup. Today Arthur Tilley accused her of not caring, not reporting Felix's absence. Not until they questioned her about drug money did she finally reveal the truth. The amount he owed stunned Arthur Tilley. Had she ever seen the men Felix consorted with? No. What about Rena Salvos? Would she have seen them? Sally was sure she had.

Only after this bit of information did Arthur finally regress from his relentless questioning and eventually released them. His next victim would be Rena. Sally felt sorry for Rena already. The sentiment was lessened by her relief at finally escaping Arthur.

Now, walking to Milton's car, she couldn't wait to slip into the seat and close her eyes. She'd do about anything to shut out the unforgiving sunlight that exacerbated the pounding in her head.

Milton helped her inside and asked, "Where should I take you?"

She squinted up at him. "Back to my brother's place."

He closed the door, hurried to his side, slid behind the wheel and soon the precinct was behind them. Closing her eyes, she leaned back and rested her aching head.

It was Thursday afternoon and Milton took the day off to be with her and help her through the day. It was kind of him to give her the emotional support she needed. She took a peek at him, gratitude swelling within her for his tender attention. She closed her eyes again and dozed lightly.

Felix's passing was over a week ago and the funeral still hadn't taken place. Hubert and Marjorie Billings, his parents, insisted on an autopsy to find out more details. The crime unit had agreed to it, although the evidence was quite clear. His parents, wealthy pillars of the community, had insisted their son would never have been involved in a drug deal. There must be some other explanation. So the investigation continued. Hopefully it would wrap up soon.

The police obtained a search warrant for her apartment and also Milton's home. Milton had been furious over it but there was nothing he could do to stop it. Nothing had shown up at either place except for a small amount of marijuana Sally kept stashed in her kitchen drawer. They were frantically trying to bring some connection of her small amount of narcotics to Felix's involvement in selling drugs. Sally knew they wouldn't be able to make that stick. No weapon had shown up that would match the bullets taken from Felix's body. Milton did have a handgun but it didn't have bullets that matched the ones they found in Felix.

The car rolled to a stop and Sally opened her eyes. Surprised, she sat up and stared in confusion. They were outside a hotel lobby. She looked over at Milton who gazed at her with an innocent smile.

"Don't worry. I won't be staying. I need to get back to work and get ready for our next show. I am so behind with my work schedule, it's ridiculous. You need some peace of mind and this will be the perfect place to get it."

"I don't have any of my things."

He ignored her, jumped out and helped her from the passenger side.

"Milton, I need stuff."

"Don't worry, beautiful, I'll bring some things by later. I don't want you to fret about anything. Just relax and do whatever you want - cry, scream, sleep, take a long bath, whatever."

Sally felt like a child as Milton led her into the hotel, paid for her room and walked her to the door. She didn't know what to say as she gazed into his eyes. Tears threatened once again and she felt stupid and weak for not being able to control her emotions.

"Hey, don't worry about it." He rubbed her cheek tenderly. "You don't have to say anything, okay? And don't worry about work. Gregory Taylor is giving you as much time as you need. Your designs are done and approved and they are going into production as I speak. You deserve a break."

"Does everyone in the office know about Felix?" Her voice shook with emotion. She couldn't bear to have everyone know all the details of her sordid life.

"They know your boyfriend was shot and killed. That's all they know so far. Let's hope the newspapers don't air all the dirty laundry. I know how important your privacy is to you. I promise you that I won't spill the dirt."

"Thank you, Milton. You don't know how much that means to me!" With watery eyes she gazed at him, overcome by gratitude and willing herself not to cry.

He embraced her, held her tightly for a moment, then let go and walked down the hall. She watched till he disappeared around the corner.

Entering the room, she closed the door and, as she did, exhaustion hit her full force. Heading to the bed, she let herself fall onto it and her tears erupted with a vengeance. Sobs tore at her frame, shaking her to the core. Her life had been a roller coaster ride for so many weeks that it had now taken its toll. This last week was the last straw. She cried long and hard. Finally, she fell asleep, the sweet relief blanketing out her grief.

~~~~~

Sally unlocked the door to Robert's apartment and stepped inside. Relief washed over her as she kicked her high heels off and placed her Yves Saint Laurent handbag on the entrance table. Peace, that's what she wanted more than anything. Why was it such an elusive thing? Maybe a long, hot bath would coax some her way. She sat down on the couch to regroup her thoughts first.

The funeral had been taxing, too much for her frazzled nerves. To cope with another loss, another friend gone, was crushing. His mother had looked at her accusingly. Felix's brother had approached her and asked her why she hadn't let them know he'd been missing for so long or that he'd needed money. She'd explained the best she could but it wasn't enough. They still blamed her for his death. The look in their eyes, the disdain and bitterness she saw there, was proof.

Chapel Ridge Funeral Home, where the funeral was held, was located on Woodbine Avenue and was grand enough for a Billings funeral. The solid brick structure with pleasant greenery all around gave it a peaceful feel. Nothing but the best would do for a family steeped in money. That Felix hadn't had the courage to ask his parents for the amount he owed still angered Sally when she allowed her thoughts to go there.

The lid of Felix Billings' casket had been open when she first arrived, his body displayed for viewing. He'd looked so serene and plastic. When she touched his arm she'd been shocked at how cold it was. No absurd thoughts came to her this time, no suggestion of bringing him back. Now, as she pondered that, she wondered if she should have tried anyway. Not that she wanted him back but neither did she want him dead.

Her outfit, the black A-line dress, a Donna Karan design, fit in well with today's mood. Her heels were also by Donna Karan. She wore a Philip Treacy hat, black with a funky white swirl at the front. Maybe it was a bit over the top but it went well with the plain dress. Pulling at her hat now, she removed it and set it beside her on the couch.

Noise from the kitchen alerted her. She turned her head and listened, sitting upright in case she needed to run. Who was here? Robert was out for the evening so who was in the apartment with her?

Suddenly the door from the kitchen opened and out stepped her mother.

"Mom! What are you doing here?"

"Come into the kitchen. The water's hot and I'll make some tea. We need to talk." She disappeared back through the door.

Sally rubbed her forehead and released a frustrated breath. This was the very last thing she needed right now. Her muscles were so tight they were ready to snap and she could feel the onset of another headache. Inhaling deeply, she released air slowly between her teeth and headed to the kitchen, dreading their talk already.

On the table stood a full arrangement of flowers, bright daisies, pink roses, carnations, greenery and Baby's Breath. It was beautiful and she could smell the scent from the doorway.

"Those are for you, dear. I thought you might need some cheering up today." Mrs. Windsor picked up the card leaning up against the vase and handed it to her.

"I don't know what to say."

"You don't have to say anything." With a compassionate smile, she said, "Go on, open the card."

After opening it and reading the kind words, she could feel the familiar trickle of tears on her cheeks. The gesture really touched her. Her mother did care. It was hard to tell with all the criticism she usually pointed her way.

Her mother came and wrapped her arms around her. Sally rested her head on her shoulder and cried once again.

"My life is such a mess."

Her mother stroked her hair for a few minutes in silence. "I know it doesn't look good right now but it doesn't have to stay that way, Sally. God loves you and he wants to help you."

"God doesn't want me, Mom," she mumbled from her mother's shoulder.

"Of course he wants you!" She pulled away and held Sally by the shoulders. "Why wouldn't he want you?"

"It's too late."

"What do you mean 'It's too late'?"

"I don't know. I just don't think God would want me. I've messed up too bad." She pulled away and dropped into a kitchen chair.

Mrs. Windsor sat down next to her and eyed her curiously. "God does want you and he is waiting for you. All you need to do is say yes to him."

She doesn't know how wrong she is. My life is such a pathetic mess and she has no clue.

Mrs. Windsor patted her hand and said, "There's always another chance with God." She stood. "I'll fix the tea."

Sally folded her arms on the table and lowered her head to rest there. She closed her eyes and wondered whether her mother was right. Was there really another chance with God? Did she even want to believe?

She felt utterly hopeless. How would she ever function normally again? Going back to work would be so difficult. Enjoying life again seemed impossible. If only she could crawl into a dark, deep pit and be left alone for weeks, maybe months. Perhaps then she'd get over this darkness she felt.

She felt a small stirring deep inside, a knowing that, though life was horrible now, one day things would get brighter again. Glancing at her mother at the counter, filling cups with steaming water, the thought wouldn't budge.

I wonder if she's praying for me. Maybe that's where the sliver of hope's coming from.

CHAPTER 9

2003

It was Monday morning and Tessa couldn't focus. Staring out the large bay window in her office, at the huge oak tree in the yard, she thought of the conversation she'd had with Cody at the restaurant after church yesterday. The message Pastor Chad Casey delivered had impacted her and encouraged her decision. Submission to one another had been his emphasis and it had helped solidify her previous tentative decision on Cody's request.

After a meal at their favorite Italian restaurant, while sipping their coffees, she'd told him. He'd been ecstatic. She'd made his day. They'd discussed at length the decision to start a family. Cody had pressed her to make sure it wasn't something she'd live to regret, something she might resent him for if she felt forced into it. She'd told him that she was quite sure it was the right choice and the right time. The peace she felt in her heart was her answer.

Turning back to her desk, Tessa couldn't help but smile, remembering Cody's exuberance. But she had to redirect her focus so she picked up her agenda and got busy.

The day flew by, with phone calls of interested inquiries for their facility, forms to be filled out, a backlog of filing and updates on the women currently enrolled, documenting their progress on the computer. With the unusual amount of interest in the home, she was just finishing the last of the forms as her day was ending. It needed to be printed and filed and then she'd be done.

In a few days she'd contact each potential client to see if she was still interested and wanted to proceed with the application process. Many inquired but never followed through. A little encouragement often gave them the impetus to take the step toward their own freedom.

Her cell phone rang beside her, so she picked it up and answered. "Hello."

"Hey there, beautiful! I'm parked outside Mansion of Hope by the curb and is it ever bringing back memories!"

"Luke! You came." Tessa felt thrilled. "Come to the front door. I'll let you in."

Hurrying to the door, she opened it and waited for him to span the distance from the curb.

He took the steps of the landing two at a time and closed the space to her quickly. His arms opened wide and he wrapped them around her, lifting her off her feet and swinging her around. She giggled girlishly. Finally, he set her down and grinned.

"Now, that's quite the greeting," she said.

"I couldn't leave the city without coming to see what you do every day."

She led the way into the large facility, excited to show Luke the transformation of the old mansion.

"Wow!" he said, stopping just inside the doorway and staring. "It's amazing! It looks so much like it did when we went back in time here. It's uncanny!"

"I know. And I get to work here every day."

Luke stared at the expansive entrance, the design so similar to when they'd seen it in its prime. Tessa watched him as he gazed around.

The foyer was massive, with a large open area and high ceiling. The spectacular chandelier hung from above. Farther back, the curved stairway on either side led to the top floor where the balcony overlooked the grand entrance area. The entrance was big enough to host a party and dance.

A round, decorative table stood in the center of the foyer, a massive dried flower arrangement arranged on it. Real flowers were out of the question, too expensive and too much work. One of the members of their church was gifted in crafts and she'd made it for the home. If one didn't know, it would be hard to tell that the flowers weren't real.

Tessa said, "So many days I walk into this place and just stop and stare. Memories flood back every time. Sometimes I almost expect Mary or her parents to show up."

"That must feel so freaky. I don't think I'd want to work here."

"I love it. To know what happened here in the past gives me great perspective."

Luke looked at her and his eyebrows reached for each other. "In what way?"

"The past doesn't have to dictate the future. The family that once lived here dealt with difficult situations. There was a lot of sorrow. Now," Tessa waved her hand outwards, "this home is turning sorrow into hope for so many."

"It is quite the turnaround."

Tessa nodded and said, "Come, I'll show you my office." She led the way to the right and opened a door.

"Hey, this room has been changed!"

"Yeah. It used to be the large sitting room where we spent a lot of time during the time travel. We've renovated it into two rooms, an office at the front of the house and a small sitting room in the next room over, where the fireplace is."

"Is the fireplace still there?"

"Yep. I'll show you later."

"I'd love to see it."

Tessa walked into her office and Luke followed her.

"So this is where they have you slaving your days away? It's such a shame to have such a beauty hidden away in an office."

"You're a shameless flirt," she said, shaking a finger at him.

After studying her desk, filing cabinet and bay window overlooking the grassy yard, he said, "Isn't it stifling being stuck in this room day after day?"

"I love it here! This work feeds me."

He nodded. "I guess it's like the thrill I get from my work. Some don't understand."

Nodding, she said, "I can't show you much here at the Mansion of Hope. Visitors are restricted. It is a women's facility so males aren't really allowed."

With a nod, he said, "I'd like to see whatever I can, though."

"Okay, let's go." Tessa showed him the small sitting room and some of the counseling and training rooms. She also showed him the expansive and impressive dining room on the opposite side of the house. They'd kept it close to the original design. It was the room where their last time travel had taken place and brought back memories every time Tessa entered it.

Luke stood just inside the door and shook his head. "Being in this room makes me feel hungry."

Tessa chuckled. During their time travel they'd had to watch people eating a leisurely meal which lasted well over an hour but couldn't ever take a bite themselves. It was a painful experience for Luke.

The room was huge and, although the large dining room table was no longer there, the room was put to good use. This is where they held many grand celebrations for those who'd successfully made it through their program and were ready to graduate. It stood empty now but they had numerous collapsible, circular tables and chairs in storage that could be set up for festivities.

They left the room and Tessa showed him a few other areas of the home that were not being used. Luke looked overcome at being back there again.

"I'm amazed at this place. It's like we're back in the past again."

"We're very much in the present." Tessa couldn't keep from smiling.

"I can tell you love it here."

"I do. I wouldn't want to be anywhere else."

Hey, would I be able to see the Manor of Peace, the men's place? Would Cody give me a tour?"

"I'm sure he would. I'm just finishing up for the day. Why don't we drive over there together?"

"So, I'm not allowed to tour the women's facility but you're allowed to enter the men's one?"

"I might have to wait for you in the foyer."

"Oh, I see how it is. Cody doesn't have enough pull there to get you in?"

"Maybe," she said, with raised eyebrows.

Luke waited in the foyer while she finished a few last-minute things in her office; then they left together.

At the Manor of Peace, Luke parked his car in the lot behind the facility, beside Cody's truck. She'd called him earlier, letting him know they were coming.

Church on the Move had purchased an older, two-story office building and renovated it to accommodate a men's rehabilitation center. The upgrade to transform the Manor of Peace was significantly less than what the Mansion of Hope required, allowing the men's facility to open much sooner than the women's home.

Luke and Tessa took the sidewalk that skirted the building and headed to the door at the front.

Inside, in the foyer area, a desk took up the focal point before them. On the wall directly behind it were the words in silver motif, "Manor of Peace."

Tessa gave the reason for her visit and Ben offered to page Cody.

It wasn't long till Cody appeared, walked up to Luke with outstretched hand and said, "I'm glad you came, Luke."

Luke said, "Yeah, I was curious about this place."

Tessa asked, "Am I allowed to tag along?"

Cody looked at her and grinned. "Of course. I told a bunch of guys that I'm bringing my wife through on a tour. They'd be disappointed if you didn't show up." He led them through an iron gate, which separated the foyer and office area from the rooms beyond.

Once through, Luke turned to Cody and said, "I don't get the gate. It makes me feel like I'm entering a prison."

"Actually, it's a place where men get a chance to escape their prisons," laughed Cody.

Luke didn't answer.

Cody locked the gate behind them and led the way upstairs. The second floor had a large sitting area at the top of the steps with couches and chairs placed in clusters and a few end tables centered between them. Magazines and books were stacked neatly on each table and floor lamps provided light.

They passed a few rooms, each door with a small window at eye level.

"Are all the doors locked?" asked Luke.

Cody said, "Not all. It depends how far along the men are in the drying out process." He pointed to one and Luke scooted over to take a look. "The man in this room is in the beginning stages of detox and, as you can see, there's a caregiver in there with him, closely monitoring his progress."

After peeking into a few more rooms, Luke said, "Wow! There's something to be said for staying clean!"

Cody said, "That's for sure! Many are at the end of their ropes when they finally contact us."

"How long does it take for them to get free of the craving?" asked Luke.

"For some it's a lifelong battle and for others they seem to overcome the cravings quicker and live quite normally."

Luke looked dumbfounded. "You're kidding about the lifelong thing, right?"

"No, an addiction is sometimes a lifelong addiction. Total abstinence is the only solution."

"So what's the program like? What do you actually do for these guys?"

"The initial detox is different for each man, depending on his addiction level. The long-term, in-patient program can last anywhere from five weeks to one year. We offer counseling sessions, re-training sessions, chapel, spiritual training, therapy, occupational training and a variety of different group sessions to teach them to cope once they're back in the real world."

"Well, I think it's pretty amazing what you're doing here. I couldn't do this – work with men like this." He shuddered. "I'll keep my engineering job and my secretary, thank you very much."

"Spoiled, that's what you are," said Tessa.

"And that's the way it's going to stay."

"You sound a bit too comfortable," said Cody.

"I like comfortable."

Tessa couldn't resist. "Was it comfortable going to church with Janaye on Sunday?"

"I don't think that deserves an answer." But Luke's lips did twitch into a hint of a smile.

"Come on, how was it?"

"It was like, church. It's definitely not in my comfort zone but hey, maybe I'll adjust."

"You might come to like it," she suggested.

Luke said, "Don't count on it."

Tessa hoped Luke would find some peace in his life through a relationship with God. Shortly after his birth, Luke's father had abandoned both him and his mother and he had always struggled with resentment and anger toward him. She knew that this was the first time Luke had ever attended church.

Cody unlocked another door and led them down another hallway. "I could have taken you down this hall first but I first wanted to show you where the guys start when they come to us. We can get to this other hall from the sitting room we walked through."

Most of the doors down the hall stood open.

Luke asked, "Who stays in this wing?"

Cody said, "The men on this side have finished the initial stage of the program and don't have the severe urge to bolt and run. They're well on their way to recovery. We allow them more freedom. We offer classes for them that will help in their complete recuperation. Some are mandatory and others are optional, depending on the issues in each man's life."

Bedrooms ran the gamut of the hall, simply decorated with single beds, a desk, chair, nightstand and lamp. A single, wing-backed chair and armoire in the corner finished off the décor.

Cody turned into another short hall. Near the end, to the right, was a common room which offered snacks, coffee, tea and pop. Cupboards lined one wall and a fridge, stove and microwave lined the opposite one. Two rectangular tables filled the space between, surrounded by folding chairs.

The end of the hall opened into a large sitting area with windows overlooking a small yard. A wide screen television was mounted on the wall and couches surrounded it. To one side stood a large pool table, a bookcase against the wall behind it. Magazines, books and games filled an oversized bookcase. A pop machine hugged the corner.

Everyone turned to look as the three entered the room. Charlie and a few other men were on the couches laughing at some joke. He waved, got up and came over.

Tessa could feel numerous, admiring eyes on her. A woman in the facility was actually forbidden but there were exceptions to the rule.

"Hey there! Luke, you came," said Charlie.

"Yeah. So this is what you do every day, is it?" He waved a hand toward the room. "You spend your time socializing?"

"I wish my job was that easy," he said with a grin.

"So what is it you do around here?"

"Socializing is definitely part of my job. These guys don't just want to be preached at. They want to know that we really care about them. I can't do that sitting in an office all day."

Luke nodded but looked uncomfortable.

"But I also do a bunch of other stuff. I counsel a lot of these guys and help them through the initial detox period. I teach some occupational classes like construction basics and mechanical skills and whatever else the manager needs me to do."

"You're a jack of all trades, huh?" A hint of disdain crept into Luke's voice.

"Just call me Jack." Charlie grinned wide again.

Tessa felt amazed at his ability to let Luke's snide comments slide off like water. He sure had changed. A few years ago, Charlie would have fought to defend his honor. A swift upper cut would have laid Luke out flat. But that was the old Charlie.

"If Charlie's a jack of all trades, he's the best and most productive one I've ever known," declared Cody. "He's amazing with the men here and has this ability to talk them into stuff I can't imagine."

Charlie shrugged. "I don't do much." He looked embarrassed and studied the tile on the floor.

A man in his thirties approached.

"Hi, Lane," said Cody, reaching out to shake his hand.

Lane nodded and introduced himself to Luke. "I'm Lane Wheaton. You?"

"Luke Owens." The two men shook hands.

Cody said, "Lane's been with us for four months now. He's almost through the program and has experienced great success here. He's almost ready to head back to his job."

"I don't know about that," said Lane. "I'm nervous about leaving; don't know if I'll be able to cope."

Charlie said, "We'll always be here for you if you need us."

Lane nodded. "I know but it still makes me feel nervous. This is a safe place. It can be pretty unforgiving out there."

"When you leave this home God is going with you. You can call on Him day or night," reminded Cody

Lane looked over at Tessa and said, "So this is your wife, Cody?"

"Oh! Sorry! Yes, this is Tessa."

Lane extended his hand. His grip was solid. "Nice to meet you."

Tessa smiled and said, "It's nice meeting you too."

He nodded, stepped past them and headed toward the doorway. Cody slapped him on the back as he left.

During the tour of the lower level, devoted mostly to teaching rooms, offices, kitchen and dining room, numerous men stopped to chat and Cody introduced them to Luke and Tessa.

Looking at Luke, Tessa realized he was ready to go. She supposed he'd heard enough testimonies and accounts of God's grace to last him for a while.

At the door Luke said, "Thanks for the tour. It was nice to finally see the place. You've done a great job with it."

"Thanks. We're very proud of it."

Cody turned to Tessa and said, "I have to stay a bit longer. I'm meeting with one of the men in a few minutes."

"Luke can give me a ride back to the Mansion of Hope. I left my car there."

"Sure," offered Luke.

Cody nodded, leaned over and gave her a kiss. "I'll see you later then." He looked at Luke, smiled and punched him affectionately on the arm. "Thanks for coming, brother."

Luke and Tessa left and headed to the women's facility. The ride was uncharacteristically quiet. He looked deep in thought and she wished she could read his mind.

CHAPTER 10

February 1990

Sally glanced outside her childhood, bedroom window. Outside, lazy snowflakes wafted to the ground from a heavy, gray sky. The yard was already coated with a new layer of white and the clouds promised more of the same. Bare trees and bushes were draped with snow, a winter wonderland scene. She'd checked the forecast earlier. Hopefully the roads would be passable and the day would proceed without a snag.

Her wedding dress, reflected in the full length mirror attached to the closet door, looked fabulous, simple but elegant. She'd designed it with an A-line skirt, and it suited her figure well. A small amount of beadwork ornamented the bodice, which scooped low. The lace sleeves were form fitting, ending in a slight point which extended onto her hand in an elegant drop.

Glancing at her face brought a smile. Her makeup was well-defined but not ostentatious. She was pleased with it and knew Milton would like it.

Her veil hung over a chair beside the mirror. Milton had designed that. He'd insisted on contributing to her look for their special day. It was a little over the top with its feathery crown and layers of tulle. Sally took a deep breath. Was she ready for this? She wasn't sure. It was a big step, the biggest she'd ever taken.

Milton's tender care since Felix's demise had softened her heart and she could honestly say she loved him. He'd been extremely attentive and persistent. It had been impossible to ignore his perpetual advances, especially with her heart needing so much tending.

But she was scared. What if all his attentiveness vanished after the vows were said? What if Robert was right? He'd warned her. Something about Milton's character caused him concern. She'd taken her brother's apprehensions seriously and looked for warning signs but hadn't found any. Milton's desire to woo and please had overshadowed anything her brother said.

Being here in her parents' home, surrounded by familiar childhood objects brought a feeling of nostalgia. Her mother had insisted she prepare here. This place also bombarded her with difficult memories: her parents' fights, her father's unpredictable ways after drinking and her mother's constant nagging. Perhaps she should have simply prepared with Milton and shucked superstition to the wind.

A knock at the door brought her head around. Her mother opened the door and walked in.

"Oh Sally, you look beautiful!" She wore a light coral chiffon dress. It fit her well, made her look as stylish and beautiful as usual.

"Thanks, Mom."

Mrs. Windsor stopped before her with a look of admiration. Slowly, the look faded, replaced with deep concern. "Are you sure, Sally?"

Immediately irritation flooded her at what she anticipated her mother would say. Her muscles stiffened.

"I've told you my concerns before but I have to say what's on my heart. I love you, Sally, and I don't want you making a mistake. Your father, Robert and I have talked. We're not certain that Milton is the right man for you. He's old enough to be your father and his eyes roam too much. We're concerned about his ability to commit."

"Mother, stop!"

"No, hear me out. He might be enjoying the attention he's getting now from marrying a woman half his age but I don't believe he has staying power. For crying out loud, he's nearly your father's age! And he's a flirt."

Sally turned away, anger boiling beneath her controlled exterior. Her mother always had the ability to aggravate and infuriate. She refused to allow her to ruin her special day.

"What if he won't stay faithful? Have you thought of that?"

Sally glared at her mother. "This is my wedding day!" She shook her head in despair. "Your words are hurting me! I love Milton and all you can do is tear him apart? What gives you the right to come in here and say such things? I need your blessing on this day, not your awful predictions!"

"If I believed he truly loved you and was committed to you, I would support this wholeheartedly. Sally, I love you and want the best for you."

"He does love me. And how can you judge what is best?" She didn't have to say more. Her mother knew. She looked hurt.

Well, at least they were even.

"This conversation is not about me. This is your future we're talking about. All I want is for you to be happy."

"I was happy until you walked through that door and tore me apart. I've made my decision and I'd appreciate it if you'd try to support me." Tears threatened but Sally determined not to cry. She didn't want to destroy her carefully-applied makeup.

Mrs. Windsor took Sally by the hand and patted it. "I'm sorry I've upset you. If this is your final decision, I'll try to be happy for you. I'll accept Milton as my son-in-law even though he is almost my age." She shook her head. "And I'll be praying for you. I want you to be fulfilled."

"Is that your blessing?" She felt incredulous. This conversation should not have happened.

"It's my prayer for you, Sally. After Felix, you deserve to be happy." She probed her daughter's eyes but Sally pulled her hand away and looked into the mirror.

Mrs. Windsor turned to the door. "By the way, Robert is looking for you. Should I tell him to come in?"

Sally nodded and between clenched teeth said, "Yes."

Her mother left the door open and Sally sank into the Victorian chair in front of her makeup table. She felt exhausted already and the day had barely begun. Why did a conversation with her mother always leave her feeling beat up? A pleasant relationship seemed utterly unattainable. Sally buried her face in her hands, her mother's words of doom echoing through her mind.

A hand on her shoulder made her jump. Robert's reflection in her makeup mirror smiled at her. She gave him an accusing look.

"Oh-oh! What did I do now?"

"You think I'm making a mistake," she said matter-of-factly.

A look of understanding crossed his face. "You were talking to Mom."

She didn't answer, only continued to stare, her arms crossed.

"You look beautiful, by the way."

She scowled.

"Okay. I'm only concerned about your future, Sally. I want you to be happy."

"You don't think Milton can make me happy?"

"No I don't, but I do believe that if you work at this marriage together, you could be content."

Sally felt confused.

"There's something about him I don't like. If he could control his urge to flirt with every short-skirted, pretty girl that crossed his path, just maybe he'd be a good husband."

"It doesn't bother me," she said, defensively. "Milton is Milton. I know who he is. But he says he loves me and I believe him."

Robert shook his head, disbelief in his eyes. "Being engaged to you hasn't deterred him from chasing other girls."

"Can you prove it?"

"No."

"Then this conversation is over."

"Sally, I just wish you'd think this through carefully."

"You don't think I have? You think I'd agree to marriage without careful consideration?"

He shrugged noncommittally.

"Milton treats me like a princess and he takes care of me. When Felix was murdered he stood by me the whole time. He did more for me than any of my family did."

"We couldn't get close to you. He dominated the situation."

"That's not true! He was loving and attentive. I believe he'll be good to me. I wouldn't marry him if I thought differently. Please, trust me on this, Robert. I can't bear my family tearing apart the man I love on my wedding day." A tear slid from her eyelid and rolled down her cheek. It angered her even more. Now her makeup would be a mess.

Robert reached for a tissue and handed it to her. She took it and swiped at her face angrily.

He got down on her level and said, "I'm sorry, Sally! Will you forgive me for being so thoughtless?"

"I don't know if you deserve it. My whole family is acting like a bunch of ogres!"

"I'm very sorry. Please forgive me! If you're happy, I'll be happy."

She stared at him with a mixture of contempt, yet gratitude for his unending loyalty and love. "All right, I forgive you."

His eyes grew stern. "I promise, though, if Milton ever hurts you or does you wrong, he'll feel some pain."

"Is that a threat or a promise?" His protectiveness warmed her heart.

"Both." Robert stood, bent over her and placed a kiss on her cheek. "Thanks for asking Emily to be a bridesmaid. It means a lot to her."

Emily and Robert had dated for four months now. She was a sweet girl, good for Robert and was becoming a fast friend.

"Of course. I couldn't think of anyone else I'd rather have as a bridesmaid. Having the two of you together in the wedding party is perfect."

He nodded. "Fix up that makeup of yours. We can't have a sloppy bride walking down the aisle. Good luck!" With a thumb up and an encouraging smile, he exited the room.

After dabbing at the moisture still glistening on her cheeks, she reapplied some foundation and powder. Self-doubt nagged her. Why had they insisted on dumping their fears on her on her wedding day? They didn't trust her judgment at all. Was she really that undependable in making wise decisions?

Another knock at the door brought her head around. Amber Woods, her maid of honor, entered with a smile. "Wow! You look gorgeous, Sally!"

"Thanks." She fell silent and studied her morose face in the mirror. Do you think I'm doing the right thing?"

"Marrying Milton?"

She spun her chair to face Amber. "Yes,"

"Do you love him?"

"I believe I do. He treats me better than Felix ever did."

"It wouldn't take much to beat that."

"Well, that's true. I hope I'm not jumping into this too fast. Felix has only been gone for six months. Do you think I'm on the rebound?"

"Sally, I have to ask again. Do you love Milton?"

After releasing a weary sigh, she said, "Yes. I love him and don't want to live without him."

"Well, then there's your answer." Amber smiled reassuringly.

It brought some calm to her frazzled emotions.

For Amber to bring peace in the midst of her stormy feelings must be a sign. Amber struggled with depression quite frequently, the past month having been particularly severe. She'd even contemplated suicide. For her even to agree to be in the wedding party had been something. To have her bring a waft of calm now was a talisman.

Amber said, "You do look uptight!"

"You have no idea – but I feel a lot better now."

"Turn around. I'm going to give you a neck and shoulder rub."

Sally willingly cooperated. Amber's fingers worked magic and soon her tense muscles started to relax.

The wedding ceremony took place in a small chapel in Toronto. It was elegant but simple, just the way Sally had envisioned it. Her mother's pastor performed the ceremony.

The bridesmaids wore simply-cut dresses, similar in style to Sally's dress, in a pale peach shade. Bouquets of fresh white lilies, peach-colored mums, white roses and sprays of baby's breath accentuated the color of the dresses. Sally's bouquet was a medium-sized arrangement with mostly white roses, a few light peach roses, with sprays of baby's breath throughout. White ribbons extended from her bouquet and trailed down to rest against the flowing skirt of her dress.

Milton's suit was a classic black, with a crisp white shirt and a peach bow tie. Ralph from the office was Milton's best man and Robert was the other attendant. They were dressed in black suits, white shirts and black bow ties.

Candles around the small chapel gave off a soft glow and brought a peaceful aura to the small group gathered.

Family and close friends were in attendance. All their co-workers from Taylor Fashion Design were there with their spouses. Sally's uncle and aunt, Tommy and Clara Parker, and her cousin, Benny had come. Milton's father had passed away eight years ago but his mother was here, on the front row, opposite Sally's parents. Milton had two brothers who came: Tim, who was recently divorced and came alone, and Eric, just younger than Milton, with a new young wife on his arm.

Rena Salvos and her husband from her former apartment complex had come. Some friends from Sally's party days were there as well.

Her father walked her down the aisle, Milton gazing at her with desire the whole way. It made her skin tingle. Her father handed her off and went to join her mother on the front row. She draped her arm through Milton's and stood before the preacher, her heart beating nervously.

The ceremony was short with an aura of serenity as if the whole congregation were holding their breath. After the vows were said, Milton lifted the veil from her face and kissed her with passion. Yes, she loved him!

The small crowd clapped and cheered. Sally felt a surge of joy at that moment. They turned and walked to the back, her hand holding onto the arm of her new husband.

She was married! She finally did it! Nothing could erase the euphoric feeling she felt.

The rest of the day was a blur of activity as they hurried off for wedding pictures, a reception at a local hall, then set off for their honeymoon.

CHAPTER 11

May 1993

Sally stared at her empty work sheet for a half hour but not a single idea emerged. Trying to form any kind of creative thought seemed completely elusive. Work the last few weeks had been nearly impossible; she'd accomplished very little.

It was a busy time of the year when all the designers were expected to finish up their designs for the following fall/winter season. Gregory Taylor was keeping a vigilant eye on her and it only increased the tension she felt. Sally knew she wasn't performing as expected but her personal issues were overwhelming her. Focusing had become a daily challenge.

After a look at the clock on the wall, she slammed her pencil down, cleaned up her station and gathered her things. There was no point in staying. She wasn't executing anything and it was time to call it quits.

Jason Johnson appeared around the corner and stared at her. "Why are you leaving so early?"

His accusing glare only fueled her frustration. "I'm done."

Her biggest rival looked smug. "You're done all your designs," he said cynically.

Did she have to respond? She exhaled in annoyance and said, "No."

"I only have three more designs to perfect and I'll be finished my fall line. How about you, Sally? How many do you have left to go?"

"Don't you worry about me. I have a handle on it." She straightened up her desk.

"You sure are touchy, hey?"

She turned and glared at him. Why did he always have to brag? Competition should be his second name. "I'll get my designs done in time and they'll far outweigh yours as usual." To be harassed by Jason grated more than usual today. Being cordial was out of the question. She grabbed her purse and coat and walked toward him.

He blocked her escape. Jason gave her a funny smile; it disappeared and his gaze grew serious. "How are you handling the divorce, Sally?"

"Why would you care?" She was in no mood to discuss it.

The concern in his eyes jogged her memory. Jason had gone through a difficult divorce the year before, but she'd hardly taken note of it or given any emotional support. It made her feel awkward now.

Their working relationship had been mostly competitive. She'd actually relished that time during his personal issues. It had given her an edge while he grieved. It now embarrassed her and she lowered her eyes.

"I've been where you are," he said.

"I remember," she said quietly.

"If you ever need to talk, I'm here." His eyes held compassion, which surprised her. "You've had your share of difficult situations."

He was referring to Felix as well as to the fiasco with Milton. It brought on a feeling of claustrophobia. "Jason, I really have to get out of here, okay?" She wasn't used to him looking at her this way. His concern would make her cry.

"Can I take you out for dinner some time?"

My greatest rival wants to take me out for dinner? That's rich!

"I don't think that's such a good idea."

"Why not? I think we'd have a lot to talk about."

That's how the whole thing with Milton started. I don't dare take the risk.

"The divorce is still too fresh, I'd end up a basket case and you would end up regretting it. Besides that, we're like cat and dog; we've never gotten along so we'd probably end up in a fight."

Jason said, "I can see that you're hurting, Sally, and I want you to know that there is hope after divorce. After Melanie left, I thought I'd die, that life would never be good again. I turned to God for help. He brought me peace and healed my broken heart. I know He'd do the same for you."

Beneath her ribs, her heart beat out a frantic rhythm. She didn't do religion. Hadn't she made that clear? And yet Jason's openness was surprising. It was the last thing she'd expected from him.

Jason said, "I know Milton was an absolute jerk. You didn't deserve to be treated like that. I just want you to know that God can heal your broken heart. He's the only one who can."

Sally refused to melt down in front of Jason. She blinked rapidly and said, "Look, I appreciate your concern but I really have to go now."

"Alright." He stepped aside.

Jason's words echoed through her mind. He was right. Milton really was a jerk and she'd royally messed up in her judgment of him.

Her family had been right but there was no way she'd ever admit it to them. The facts of her life were dire. She was twenty-eight years old with a boyfriend who had been murdered and a husband who had lost interest in her. Her track record was the pits and her self-esteem was in shambles.

She unlocked the door and walked into the large apartment she'd formerly shared with Milton. A wave of sorrow hit her. She still loved Milton and longed for things to be different. He'd moved in with his new girlfriend so there was no hope for that.

Moving back to Markham held no appeal. The convenience of living close to her job was significant and almost deleted the need for a vehicle. She still owned a car but seldom used it except to visit her parents and Robert and Emily, but even that had become sporadic the last few months.

The first year of their marriage had been good. Milton was sweet and considerate most of the time, in spite of his spurts of anger but as she became settled and stronger emotionally, Milton's interest waned.

He became engrossed in his dream to start his own design business and pursued it will all his energy. As his business grew, their times together became more and more limited. His once tender affection became increased distraction. Eventually, her suspicions began.

When she finally found the courage to confront him, he didn't even try to deny it. He admitted he no longer loved her, came clean about his affair with his young secretary and insisted on a speedy divorce. Just like that. Their short, three-year marriage was done.

She was devastated, crushed and crippled. She'd become an absolute hermit, a recluse. That was the only way she knew how to cope right now. Her apartment brought hurtful memories but for now it was her haven, a place to get away.

After pouring herself a drink, she sat down to watch the news. Drinking had become a habit the last few weeks. It helped calm her nerves and still the overwhelming hopelessness she felt. She ate little and knew she was wasting away. Her stylish designer clothes were beginning to hang off her thin body. She didn't care.

The phone rang out cheerfully and she groaned. She let it ring a few more times before reluctantly picking it up.

"Hello."

"Hi, Sally. How are you?" It was Robert.

"Not great."

"Why don't you go out for dinner with Emily and me? We'll pick you up and treat you to a night out."

"No. I appreciate your concern but I'd rather stay home."

"You've been hiding away in that apartment of yours too long."

"A month isn't that long."

"For you it is. You're an extrovert. You love people. Please let us take you out, okay?"

"I don't want to. Just leave me alone. I'm not in the mood to pretend I'm okay."

"You don't have to pretend."

"You don't want to be with me then."

"Why?"

"Because I'm hurt, angry, disillusioned and feel like committing murder at the moment!"

"You're not serious are you? I mean you wouldn't actually kill Milton, would you?"

"I thought you promised to take care of that for me."

"I'd love to but I don't want to sit in jail for the rest of my life. The creep's not worth it."

"Why didn't I see through his masquerade? Why was I so gullible?"

"You were going through a very difficult emotional time and he made sure he was your hero. He took advantage of you, used you as his showpiece. What older man wouldn't want a young, beautiful woman on his arm?"

"He used me."

"You're better off without him."

"Everyone says that! But I still love him and it hurts like crazy!"

"I'm sorry."

"It's not your fault." She rubbed her aching head. "If he'd leave this other girl, I'd take him back in a heartbeat."

"Have you been drinking?"

"That's a side issue. I don't know how I'll ever be happy again."

"Well, you certainly wouldn't be happy with that idiot. I wouldn't let you go back to him, Sally. In fact, I'd break every bone in his body if he came crawling back to you. You'll be happy again, sis. Look, once you're over Milton, Emily and I will set up a double date and we'll introduce you to a decent guy."

"Not right now, Robert. I can't even think straight. I'm struggling big time with my designs for the next season. I'm a complete mess."

"Don't be too hard on yourself. If your job is too much for you right now, then quit. I'd hire you in a flash. You could do my bookkeeping."

"It would bore me to tears and you know it."

"Yeah, I know."

"Look, I've got to go." She couldn't handle any more conversation.

"Just remember that I'm here for you, sis. You don't have to handle this alone."

"Thanks, Robert." She gratefully switched the off button and set the phone down.

After grabbing the remote, she switched off the T.V. and sat in silence. The tinkling of the ice in her drink was the only noise in the expansive place.

This apartment was much too big for her and she really couldn't afford it. She'd have to start searching for a more inexpensive place but she had little motivation to do anything.

CHAPTER 12

March 1995

The freakish March snowfall made the streets of Markham hard to navigate. Robert had given her directions to a restaurant she was unfamiliar with and she struggled to see the signs in the nearly-dark streets. Her nerves were taut.

Why had she ever agreed to this dinner? Robert was much too persuasive and persistent. He absolutely had not left her alone till she agreed to his stupid plan. Now, driving the treacherous streets, her anger resurfaced and she was tempted to leave him and his wife high and dry.

They'd set her up with a mystery date, a double date. Robert and Emily were waiting for her at this hard-to-find place.

This part of the city was unfamiliar to her, the shadowed darkness and heavy snowfall making it hard to see the signs. She finally pulled over at the next intersection, scooted over to the passenger side, rolled down her window and took a good look. After glancing at the map on the dash, she realized the street she was looking for was one block over. She moved back into the driver's seat and drove on.

There it was. She turned and spotted the restaurant immediately. The sign read, Will's Grill.

What a dim-witted name!

After parking her car, she sat quietly for a while. Her nerves were jumping like hot cakes on a skillet. She hadn't dated since the divorce. It was over two years now but seemed like yesterday. For her even to have agreed to this ridiculous double date was completely out of character.

Guilt. That's what it was. Robert's incessant begging had finally broken through. She couldn't bring herself to say no again. Maybe finally giving in, going for his sake, would get him off her back. It was sure to be an uncomfortable and wearing evening.

With a grunt of frustration, she opened the car door and stepped out into the winter white.

"I may as well get this over with," she said, slamming her car door shut and heading to the restaurant entrance.

She stepped inside and the hostess smiled. Before she could say a word, Robert appeared and waved her in.

"Hi, Sally. I'm glad you came."

"Whatever." She didn't bother hiding her lack of enthusiasm.

He grabbed her by the elbow and led her to the table.

She gave him a sideways glance. "So where's this wonderful, mystery man you insisted I meet?"

"Walter is running a little late but he just called and said he'd be here in a few minutes. Man, I thought Emily and I would have to eat alone when the two of you weren't showing up."

"Walter? You had me come all this way to meet a guy named Walter? His name sounds ancient!"

"No more ancient than Milton."

She shrugged.

"Don't judge him before you meet him, Sally. His name's Walter Tassey. I really think the two of you will hit it off, so please give him a chance." Robert stopped at a booth for four.

Emily stood and gave Sally a hug.

"Hi, Emily."

"Hi, Sally. It's been a while since we've seen you. I'm so glad you made it tonight."

"Well, don't count on me staying long." She sat down dejectedly, not at all comfortable with the circumstances.

Emily sat down next to her. At least she wouldn't have to share a bench with Walter. To face him was better than have him making advances beside her.

Robert said, "You need to snap out of this self pity. Tonight might just be the thing to help you."

"I don't remember asking for your help, Robert, or for a report on my state of mind."

"Oh, just chill! You'll like him. He works for me. He's an assertive real estate agent; he's motivated and fun to be around."

"He sounds like the perfect person if I ever need to buy some property."

Robert ignored her and continued. "Around women he's a perfect gentleman and I have a strong hunch that you two will be a good match. Give him a chance. If you can't stand him, then that's that. I won't try hooking you up with anyone else. Okay?"

"Is that a promise?" Sally leveled him a stern look.

"Yes, that's a promise." He grinned mischievously.

"I'll hold you to it."

"You mentioned maybe giving religion a try. This guy's religious."

"I said that?"

"Yes."

Yes, she had. Nothing else seemed to work. Her life was still empty and depressing. Maybe if she gave God another try, her life would improve. To attempt it might be worth it. She thought of something. "He's not part of some weird cult, is he?"

Robert broke out in laughter. "No!" he finally said. "He reminds me of Mom in some ways. He's not pushy or preachy like her but he does seem like a sincere Christian. I thought that might be what you're looking for."

She nodded, not that Robert would really know. He stayed away from all religion. "After Milton and his unfaithfulness, I thought maybe a Christian man might be more dependable husband material."

"Have you picked up religion?" asked Emily.

Sally shrugged. "No, but I could try it, I suppose."

Robert raised his brows and smiled.

Fear suddenly overwhelmed her. "Why am I doing this? I don't even want another man. I'm not ready."

Robert leaned forward and said, "You're doing this because you don't want to be alone the rest of your life and you need to move on with your future."

It was true. She didn't want to spend the rest of her life alone. The thought of that was depressing.

"Look, here he comes so behave yourself." Robert stood to shake Walter's hand.

Sally turned to look at him. He stood a few inches taller than Robert and was amazingly handsome, with dark hair and stylish clothes. His most outstanding feature was his eyes. They were large, beautiful blue eyes that seemed to look through her with intensity. That was one plus for him.

She judged he was close to her age. Another check. But no good-looking man would take her for a ride again. She swallowed a lump in her throat and willed herself to act polite.

Robert made introductions all around. When Walter took her hand in his and shook, she felt nothing. She simply nodded in acknowledgement. That's all he deserved. Walter took a seat across from her, next to Robert.

Sally braced herself for the evening. It felt too long already.

His eyes locked with hers. "I'm very pleased to meet you, Sally. I've heard so much about you and you're as lovely as your brother insisted you were."

"I have to admit, I haven't heard much about you at all. Robert and Emily refused to tell me anything about you until I arrived here. They only assured me that I would like you. By the end of this evening we'll know."

"Ah! A woman who is forthright and truthful. I like those qualities. The evening is starting off on a good note already." He smiled brightly.

Sally broke eye contact and studied her menu.

Emily said, "Walter, why don't you tell Sally what kind of church you attend?"

Robert and Emily had never entered a set of church doors since their wedding day. Emily's conniving annoyed Sally.

Walter looked somewhat caught off-guard, which Sally found amusing.

"Ah, yes. Well, my father started the church. It's independent and not affiliated with any main denomination. Since we're being honest and upfront right from the start, I'll let you know, Sally, that I'm a Christian and quite involved in my father's church. It's a large part of my life."

"Robert has already informed me that you're religious. I've never dated a Christian before so I'm not sure if you'll be the right dating material for me." She had no desire to play games and might as well get to the point quickly.

"Well, since this is only our first meeting and not a date, we should be safe on that account. We can get to know each other as acquaintances for now." Walter smiled sweetly.

It looked too sweet to be sincere. An 'x' went on her mental list.

"What's the church like?" she asked.

"It's very traditional. The men preach and teach and the women serve."

"Like what?" asked Emily.

"Pardon me?" asked Walter.

"The women. How do they serve?"

"Our church is different than others. Most churches abuse women's gifts, allowing them to teach most of the Sunday school classes, hosting ministries and the various help ministries. We do not misuse their great talents but only utilize those who truly desire to and are led by God to do those things. We encourage the men to take their role of leadership and responsibility that my father and I feel are lacking in many churches."

Sally felt instant respect for him. Hadn't she seen this very thing in her own home growing up? Her father had been completely deficient in responsibility, forcing her mother to take the role of leadership in the home. Spiritual direction had been left to her mother, not that Sally benefited from it, but even so, it was true. Perhaps if her father had taken his proper role, just maybe her life would have turned out differently, better.

Walter's words fell like rain on parched ground. The wisdom in them astonished her. A man like Walter, with his insight and wisdom, might be perfect for raising a family together. Suddenly it hit her; she was getting way ahead of herself.

"...Sally, Sally?" Robert stared at her. "Are you okay? You were zoning out."

She chuckled nervously. "Sorry about that. My mind was wandering. I guess I've had a long day."

Walter's big, beautiful eyes studied her. "Don't worry about it. I asked you something. I was wondering what church you attend?"

"Robert didn't tell you?"

"He told me that you've been married before and that you're divorced. You've had a difficult life and you're still hurting and a little bitter. He also told me that you're very cynical about meeting someone or ever falling in love again."

Sally turned an accusing glare at Robert. "Well, it sounds like Robert told you a lot about me." She turned back to Walter. "I don't attend any church."

"Well, I'm glad that's out in the open. This is turning out to be a productive evening, isn't it? And to think, we haven't even ordered our beverages yet."

The attentive looks and subtle interest from Walter amazed her, but that her body was responding to it angered her. She enjoyed the attention. It had been a long time since a man had looked at her this way. But she had determined not to like him. This was not how she had imagined the evening going.

"This evening is definitely progressing faster than any of us imagined." Robert waved to a waitress who seemed intent on ignoring their table.

Oh, just shut up, Robert!

The waitress finally made her way over and took their drink order.

Those mesmerizing eyes were staring at her again. "Robert tells me that you design clothes for a Toronto company. How long have you been doing that?"

At least the topic was shifting to something safe. These were her stomping grounds. "I've been designing clothes since I was a child. I've been doing it professionally for about seven years. Just recently I've been enjoying some real success with my designs. The divorce put me through a slump for a while but I'm back in business."

"That's great. You're not only a beautiful woman but also a bright and successful one. That's a wonderful combination and I like it." His eyes seemed to envelop her.

She could feel the connection between them, the pull of attraction. It frightened her, the feeling somewhat claustrophobic. She was forced to lighten the mood. "My brother tells me that you work for him. Is he as intolerable as a boss as he is as a brother?"

Walter laughed. He had a nice laugh. "Actually Robert is the best boss I've had in years. He's very easygoing, basically a pushover. I get away with almost everything."

"That doesn't sound like my brother. You must be talking about his twin."

Walter looked confused and turned to Robert. "You have a twin?"

"No, Sally's just fooling with you." Robert looked smug.

"Ah, I'll have to keep an eye on you. You're a tricky one." With folded arms resting on the table, Walter gazed at her with a little too much admiration.

Sally refused to lock eyes with him. "Not as sneaky as my brother. He's a real card and you'll see a whole lot more of him than you ever will of me." Setting that straight felt good.

Her feelings felt frazzled and confused concerning Walter but there was no way everyone here had to know. She'd keep them guessing.

Walter didn't appear fazed by her blunt words. "I believe I'll be seeing much more of you, Sally, than I'll ever see of Robert."

Her temperature rose and it wasn't anger she felt. She refused to look at him for fear he'd see the emotional attraction in her eyes. Those feelings had been dead and gone for so long that they frightened her. How could he elicit such dramatic feelings from her in such a short period of time? It was unbelievable. She felt as though she were being sucked into an emotional roller coaster ride she was completely unprepared for.

The waitress appeared with a tray of drinks and Sally exhaled a pent-up breath of air. They ordered their meals and the waitress left.

A change of subject was in order. Sally turned to Emily and asked, "How's the day care going?"

"It's busy but I enjoy the little tikes." She was a woman a few words and it seemed like pulling teeth to get anything out of her.

"How many kids do you have now?"

"Well, there are three adults and each of us is responsible for six children."

"Eighteen. That's a handful. Do you have any babies in that mix?"

"I have one baby, three two-year-olds and two that are three. They're all still little and a lot of work."

"Do you think you two will start a day care of your own soon?"

Robert leaned forward and said, "What are you implying, sis?"

"You know."

He shook his head.

Sally smiled mischievously. "I've been waiting for a niece or nephew for a while now. I was just wondering if you were in the mood to share when I could be anticipating one."

He looked incredulous. "We haven't even been married two years and you want us to have a baby?"

"It's enough time."

Robert shook his head definitively.

Walter chuckled. She liked his laugh. It tinkled like a bubbling stream.

"So, would you like a family someday, Sally?" asked Walter.

She hated being put on the spot by him. "Not really. I can't even manage my own life most of the time so I can't imagine being responsible for another human being."

"Well, I'd like to have children some day. I don't believe life would be worth living without children to raise and love."

His open selflessness only made her like him more. She swore in her mind. Why couldn't she hate him? She wanted to hate him. It wasn't working out as she'd planned.

Maybe a selfish answer would turn those eyes, deep pools of blue, away. "I don't think I could handle more than one or two at the most. I can't imagine running after a bunch of snotty-nosed kids and them messing up my neat and orderly life."

His immediate, impish grin caught her off guard.

She giggled without thinking.

Robert's nod to Emily didn't go unnoticed. Sally gave him a kick under the table.

"Ouch! What did you do that for?" He stared at her in frustration and reached down to rub his leg.

"Sorry, I wasn't planning to kick quite that hard. You deserved it, though! You two are impossible with all the looks you're giving each other."

"Sis, you are too much! This evening is going like clockwork and you're mad about it. I don't get it!" He looked upset and pleased all at the same time.

"You're rubbing it in. It's ticking me off!"

"Do you want Emily and me to go? Leave you two alone?"

"Maybe!" She could feel Walter's intense gaze riveted on her. She finally turned to meet his eyes. "What do you make of their matchmaking and secret smug looks?"

"I think their matchmaking has been a tremendous success and I believe the two of us will be alone together before long. I think we owe it to Robert and Emily to let them stay. After all, if it weren't for them I never would have met you." He reached over and grabbed her hand before she had the chance to pull it out of reach.

His touch sent waves of electricity shooting up her arm. She was astounded by the unexpected sensation and stared at him. With some determination, she pulled her hand from his. She swallowed and said, "All right, the two of you can stay. But no more secret looks or winks or else this evening will come to a sudden close. Promise?"

Robert grinned. "We'll try to behave ourselves."

"You'd better!"

Their food arrived and everyone dove in, except for Walter. He lowered his head to pray first. The other three stopped uncomfortably while he finished. He started eating, not drawing attention to the fact that his prayer had stopped all action.

Her mother had taught her to pray when she was a child. She hadn't prayed over a meal since the last time she'd been to her parents' place. Now Sally wondered if prayer was something she could become accustomed to once again.

Walter was a surprise. That she'd responded to him the way she did amazed her. She pondered the fact that her blunt, honest statements hadn't scared him off. It impressed her. Her tactic to turn him off had backfired. She was finding him completely charming and attentive.

It didn't matter what she said or how she said it, her words seemed to completely fascinate Walter. His focus was directed toward her the entire night. It left her feeling heady.

Their time together ended too soon. Robert and Emily said goodbye and Walter walked her to her car.

She turned and held out a hand to shake his. He smiled in that way of his, making her heart speed up. Stepping forward, he took her hand but then gave her a kiss on the cheek. His breath on her face felt like fire.

"I thoroughly enjoyed this evening, Sally. I want to see you again. Would that be all right with you?"

Sally felt at a loss for words. Was she really ready for this?

"You did enjoy my company, didn't you?" He looked nervous for the first time.

"Yes. I did enjoy your company and I would like to see you again."

He breathed a sigh of relief and smiled brightly. "You had me worried there for a minute. Can I see you tomorrow?"

"Tomorrow? Tomorrow's Sunday."

"Yes, I know it's Sunday. Can I see you tomorrow?"

Things were moving way too quickly. His mesmerizing eyes were winning over her good sense. "All right. Tomorrow would work."

"Would you give me your phone number so I can contact you?"

Sally found a piece of paper in her purse, scribbled the number down and handed it to him.

After another kiss on her cheek he said, "I'll call you in the afternoon."

"That'll be fine."

He turned and headed to his car. She felt breathless at the speed things had moved. She opened her car door and slipped behind the wheel. Without another look in his direction, she started her car and drove away. Her life was heading in a track that scared her; yet she didn't have the desire to change it.

CHAPTER 13

Before heading back to Toronto, Sally decided to check on Amber Woods. It might get her mind off of the man she'd just met, clear her thoughts of him.

Amber lived on the sixth floor of the apartment complex. Sally rode the elevator up, her nerves a jumbled mass. She couldn't remember the last time she'd seen Amber. Since she was in Markham, it seemed a good time to check on her. Her voice had sounded angry on the foyer intercom.

It had probably been a year since she'd had any contact and she felt ashamed of herself. Amber needed a reliable friend, someone to lean on. Sally hadn't been that lately. The last year she'd been focused on getting her job back on track, forgetting about Milton and moving on. She had been so single-minded that she'd completely neglected Amber and really had no idea what her friend's life was like right now.

The elevator door dinged open; she walked to the apartment door and knocked. It took some time but eventually it swung open and a foul smell wafted from the apartment.

Amber looked terrible. Her wrinkled, dirty white t-shirt and gray sweat pants looked well-worn and her hair was a tangled mass. Sally was shocked to see her so disheveled. What could have happened to make her deteriorate to this extent?

"Amber? How are you?"

With a cynical smile, she asked, "As if you care?"

"I'm here. I was in the city and thought I'd drop by. It's been a while."

She scoffed. "Like what? A year?"

Sally knew she deserved it. Amber had called numerous times during her divorce, but Sally had always cut her short.

"I'm sorry. I truly am. There's no excuse for me not calling or making an effort."

Amber's eyes looked hollow, empty. Sally sensed a warning, which alarmed her.

"Well, you may as well come in since you're here." Amber walked back into her apartment, leaving the door wide open for her.

Sally came in and closed the door. The place smelled musty and closed in. Everywhere she looked, she saw dirt, things lying around, clothes strewn about, magazines in disarray, end table and coffee table littered with dirty plates, pop cans and empty food containers. A glance into the kitchen told her it didn't fare much better. The sink was full of dirty dishes and pots. The table was cluttered and the floor looked in need of a major scrubbing. The apartment was a disaster.

What really caught her eye was the cradle in the corner and the pink baby blanket Amber grabbed as she sat down on the soiled couch.

She knew Amber struggled with depression and was borderline manic, but to go to such lengths seemed odd. Or had she had a baby? Sally hadn't heard.

Gingerly she sat down at the opposite end of the couch and studied her. Tears filled Amber's eyes and slipped down her cheeks.

"Are you okay?"

Amber swiped at her face and glared at her from the corner of her eye. "No."

She felt like an absolute heel for not knowing, for not keeping in touch; but she was determined to find out. "What happened?"

Her eyes looked hopeless as she turned them to Sally. "I had a baby; did you know that?"

"No, I didn't." She felt like the worst friend imaginable. "I'm so sorry."

"My little girl only lived six hours." Her face contorted in anguish and her tears flowed.

"Oh, Amber, I'm so sorry!" Sally scooted closer and wrapped her arms around her. Amber folded into her embrace.

Sally grabbed a few tissues from a box on the loaded coffee table in front of them and handed them to her.

After drying her face, Amber straightened and said, "Bobby and I named her Elizabeth Joy. She was such a beautiful baby.

When I was holding her I thought my life was finally turning around and I could make things right." She struggled not to cry.

Sally rubbed her back and waited.

"Then they told us there was something wrong with her heart. They rushed her into the emergency room after she was born and when they brought her back she was dead." Her voice choked and new tears flowed.

"Oh, no!" Sally felt horrible, especially for not knowing. "When did you have her?"

"Two weeks ago," she said with quavering voice.

Sally didn't know what to say. This was the last thing Amber needed. Her state of mind was fragile as it was without this added heartbreak.

"I was so sure this time would be different and I would do the right thing by this baby. Bobby and I were so excited and now my whole life has fallen apart."

"Where is he?"

"I don't know! He left a week ago and I haven't seen him since."

The louse! "Why did he leave?"

"He said he thought this baby would finally bring me out of depression. He's threatened to leave before. My depression is hard on him. When Elizabeth died, it plunged me into a deep pit of blackness and I haven't been able to snap out of it. I'm on heavy anti-depressants but they don't do a thing."

"So he's gone for good?" *I could kick him for doing this to Amber.*

"He said he needed some air to breathe, time to think. I've lost both the baby and Bobby. There's nothing left to live for." The deadness in her eyes scared Sally.

Amber reached between the cushions of the couch and retrieved a revolver.

"What are you doing with that?" cried Sally.

"I don't want to die alone, Sally."

"What...what are you talking about? You don't need to die! You're young and have your whole life ahead!"

"I have nothing to live for and you know it." Amber's expression became suddenly calm and determined.

Sally was terrified. "You can't kill yourself!"

"Yes, I can."

"Wait, Amber! Bobby will come back! He loves you and he won't want to live without you. He's just shocked and heartbroken right now over the baby. He won't stay away, I'm sure of it! There are many people who love you and don't want to live without you."

"Like you, Sally? I'm lucky if lots of people love me like you do."

"I know I deserve that," Sally said.

"That's not very comforting. You didn't even know I was pregnant!" Amber cocked the gun and slowly raised it to her temple.

"Amber, no! Please, don't do this!" Tears filled Sally's eyes and dripped from her eyelashes. What she'd thought would be a long overdue visit with a dear friend was turning into a horrible nightmare and she didn't know how to stop it.

Amber actually smiled then and lowered the gun an inch.

Was it her tears that brought the response?

"Sally. Don't cry. I finally realize this is what I have to do."

"No, you don't, Amber!" Sally almost shouted.

"You need a history lesson," she said with sad eyes. "Remember how I killed my first two babies"

Yes, she'd had abortions; Sally remembered.

"And now the baby that I actually wanted died. The man I love walked out on me. Tell me one good reason why I shouldn't pull this trigger." Amber's unruffled, resolute expression was uncanny.

It was enough to make Sally come unglued emotionally but a sudden thought held her together. Hadn't she decided to try religion? Why not ask God to help? Maybe He could do something with this mess.

God please help me!

The idea came quickly. Hopefully it would work.

Sally swiped the tears from her cheek, held out a hand and touched Amber's arm. "Remember when we were both sixteen and we went to that party at Fritz Wentworth's house?"

With an incredulous look, Amber said, "What's the point? I'm holding a gun to my head, ready to blow my brains out and you want to talk about a party?"

"Work with me here, Amber, okay? Do you remember that party?"

Amber looked flustered and impatient but said, "Yes."

"Do you remember how smashed we both got?"

"Yes," she said with a roll of her eyes.

"The next morning we woke up at your sister's apartment and we didn't remember how we'd gotten there. We were both sacked out in the living room. You were on the couch, I was lying on the floor and we felt awful. I eventually got up and made us coffee and you turned on the TV. This preacher guy was on. He talked about our lifestyle and what a dead end street it was. He kept talking and describing a horrible, thorny, rocky path that was difficult to travel on. He insisted that the only way to get off of the pointless path was to turn around and get back on the main road."

"Sally, what's the point?" Amber screamed. "I should shoot you first just to shut you up!"

"I'm not through!" She tried to sound firm and make Amber listen. "The preacher said that the main road was Jesus, that he's the *only* one who could turn things around and make life worth living. Remember what you said then?"

The gun lay in her lap now. That was a good sign. Amber shook her head. "Stupid preacher! You're nuts! Turn off the TV! I don't know what I said!"

"You turned to me and said, 'I wonder why I've never given Jesus a try. I've tried everything else and it hasn't worked. Maybe He could make sense of my life.' Do you remember that, Amber?"

A cynical grin played at the corners of her mouth; then her eyes filled with sorrow. "Sally, I don't think God's big enough to get me out of this dark hole."

"Have you asked him?"

"No. And I don't want to. He's the one who took my baby."

"You don't know what's waiting for you on the other side of death. I don't know either, but it just might be worse than life. What if it's an even darker hole than this?"

"But, I have to get out of this hell I'm in, Sally! I can't take my depression anymore. It's consuming my whole life." Her calm exterior was crumbling. "What am I supposed to do?"

She shrugged. "Give God a chance with your life. Maybe He can do something." *Who am I to give this advice? It's not like I've followed it myself. Do I even believe my own words?*

"God seems like such a thin straw to hang on to." Amber held up the shiny revolver and pointed to it. "This seems so much easier and quicker."

"Yes, but only if it brought the peace you're hoping for. That's a huge unknown. The risk seems way too great."

"I don't know what to do. I feel so confused."

"Why don't you try it? Ask God to help and see what happens. It couldn't hurt."

Amber glanced at her. "Have you ever tried it?"

"No, but I've been seriously considering it. My way hasn't brought much success either. My relationships have been complete failures actually. I've been considering checking out Christian men to see if that will make a difference."

"So what do I do?"

"I don't know exactly. Have you ever prayed before?"

"No. I've yelled at him plenty, but that's it."

"Just say whatever comes to mind."

With the revolver still resting in her hands, Amber looked up at the ceiling. Her breathing slowed and her eyes blinked a few times as she began. "God...I don't know what to say. I...haven't done much of this. Sorry for cursing you, yelling at you. I guess that wasn't very nice. I ...miss my baby and ...I miss Bobby." Her voice choked and it took a few moments for her to gain control. "I need some help here. I hate being depressed. Could you please get me out of this black hole I'm in? I want Bobby to come back. Could...you arrange that? That's it."

Sally gazed at her. "That's good." She was pretty sure that qualified as a prayer. It didn't sound like the way her mother prayed but it would have to do.

"So now what? My life is supposed to improve dramatically, just like that?"

"You haven't given God much time to answer, have you?"

"I need an answer now, Sally! Not tomorrow! Now!"

"But, if the answer comes tomorrow, wouldn't it be worth waiting for?"

Amber shrugged, misery hovering like a cloud around her.

TIME AND HEALING

Sally reached an open hand toward her. "Give me the gun."

She studied the revolver in her hands.

"Amber, please give me the gun. You don't want to use it."

Slowly, she lifted it and dropped it into Sally's waiting hand. Wrapping her hands around the cold metal, she breathed a sigh of relief.

Amber's face once again contorted as a wave of melancholy overcame her.

After placing the gun on the floor, Sally reached over and grabbed both of Amber's hands in hers. "Listen, I'm going to stay here with you tonight. I'm not going anywhere until we can figure out how to get you some help. All right?"

Amber nodded, a look of relief crossing her face.

Sally took her in her arms and held her tightly. That was a close call. Too close. She was shaking with the emotional upheaval. Amber's body shook with sobs.

"I need something."

Sally knew what that meant. "Where do you keep your stuff?'

Amber told her and Sally went to get it, hiding the gun in a closet on her way. In the bottom drawer of Amber's dresser, she found a medley of supplies. She grabbed the package of pot and headed back to the living room.

As Amber rolled herself a joint, Sally made some strong coffee.

Blaming and finger-pointing were futile. Since her divorce she'd also regressed to using pot and other drugs. It helped her cope. Maybe meeting Walter would help change that. Perhaps she could stay clean if she had a man with strong principles. She smiled at the thought. It was impossible to keep him off her mind. Their conversation at dinner kept playing through her mind.

They drank coffee and Sally listened as Amber opened up and shared her story. It was late by the time they headed to bed.

The running shower woke Sally in the morning. When Amber entered the living room, where Sally had spent the night on the couch, she looked like a different woman. She wore jeans and a soft, cashmere, pale-blue sweater. Her hair was shiny, clean and pulled up into a ponytail.

After a shower, Sally joined Amber in the kitchen and they made breakfast together. It felt like old times, except for the dark circles under Amber's eyes. She'd been through the wringer! They sat down to eat scrambled eggs, toast and dark coffee. Sally smiled at Amber and she actually smiled back. That was a definite improvement.

The time on the wall clock told her she'd have to leave soon.
Suddenly the phone rang and Amber's eyes clouded with fear.
"I'll get it," offered Sally.
"Hello?"
"It's Bobby. Is Amber there?"
"Why did you leave, you jerk? You really hurt her!" She couldn't help confronting him. What he did was inexcusable.
Amber's eyes registered hope.
"Sally, just put her on."
After pulling the phone from her ear and looking at Amber, she asked, "Do you want to talk to him?"
She nodded.
Sally said, "Okay," and handed the phone over.
They talked for a while. Sally took her mug of coffee into the living room and browsed through a magazine.
When Amber entered the room a few minutes later, her eyes twinkled and a smile curled her lips.
Sally set the magazine in her lap and looked at her. "So?"
"He's coming over. He apologized and wants to come back."
She didn't know what to say.
Amber shrugged. "God answered."
"I guess he did."
"I'll be okay now. Bobby will help me through this."
"You need time alone with him," she stated.
"Yeah, that'd be nice."
She was no longer needed. She stood and Amber stepped toward her.
"Thank you for everything. I almost killed myself. Thanks for stopping me." Gratefulness flooded her eyes.
They hugged each other for a long time.
"You'll be okay?" asked Sally.
"Yeah. Now that Bobby's coming, I'll be okay."
Sally pulled away and walked to the door. After slipping into her coat and picking up her purse, she opened the door and turned.

"I'm sorry for not knowing about the pregnancy, baby and everything."

"I forgive you," Amber said quietly.

"If you ever need anything, please call me."

She nodded.

"Okay." Looking deeply into Amber's eyes she saw a calm peace. That was new.

Amber said, "Thanks again for everything."

"Anytime."

"I'll hold you to that," Amber said with a hint of a smile.

Sally nodded and left. The door closed with a click behind her. Once in her car and on the 401, heading toward Toronto, relief flooded her. The death of another friend had been narrowly avoided. She shuddered involuntarily.

CHAPTER 14

September 1995

Colorful leaves floated down from the trees lining the streets as Sally made her way to the GO train station. A brisk wind wrestled the dry leaves from the emptying branches, scattering them haphazardly around her as she walked. In the western sky, the sun was hovering well above the horizon. Soon the days would become shorter and the trip home from work would be much darker.

She loved this time of year when the array of colors made her walk home a panorama of beauty. Dry leaves crunched beneath her feet, adding to the aura of the season. The sights and sounds thrilled her; plus, walking kept her in shape and the fresh air was invigorating.

The apartment she'd moved into after the divorce was a bit farther from the office but it was close to the train, within walking distance. She hardly needed her car, which suited her just fine.

The platform at the station was teeming with people heading home. Sally squeezed in and waited. Thoughts of Walter wafted through her mind. She found him there often. Six months had passed since they first met and it had been a whirlwind from the start.

Walter was sweet and absolutely adored her. His aggressive pursuit of her had been intoxicating and at times she felt she was dreaming. Things had taken such a sudden turn that it made her head spin. To feel loved by a man boosted her self-image dramatically; although, thoughts of marriage made her anxious and succeeded in erecting a wall of objection.

The train screeched to a halt and she boarded. There were no available seats so she grabbed a pole and held on. People stood all around her. The train was packed.

Her mind wandered again. She knew she loved him. It had taken a while but, with his unending romanticism, persistent attention and words of affection, her heart had softened.

Going to church with him seemed a logical progression in their relationship. It had been a stretch for her. She wasn't used to sitting still for so long. Walter's father, Sheffield Tassey, was a big man whose very presence demanded respect. He frightened her a bit. His sermons were fiery and forceful. That she didn't understand much of what he said didn't bother her. The dynamic tone of his voice demanded that she sit up and listen. She respected his strong leadership. Everyone in the church revered him.

The music was tame but good. She knew none of the songs at first but soon learned and started singing along, regardless of her inability to keep a tune. The vibrant singing of the congregation helped hide her off-key notes.

Walter's mother, Lynne Tassey, was short, plump, quiet and submissive to her husband. She was as unimpressive as Mr. Tassey was gregarious. That he ruled the roost was dramatically clear, both at church and at home. Sally had been to their home for many meals after Sunday services. Lynne was a good cook but Sally found the strain in their conversation stifling.

Sheffield dominated the dialogue, with his point of view adamantly stated on any subject they discussed. Sally found him overbearing but she was willing to overlook that in light of her relationship with Walter. Sheffield's strong leadership skills outweighed the things she disliked about him.

Walter had made it very clear within the last month that he was interested in making their relationship permanent. He talked freely about marriage, children and settling down. She always tensed and backed away at those times – not that she didn't love him. She just wasn't ready for a firm commitment so soon. She'd suggested moving in together but he didn't approve. That was not the way their church did things.

The train came to a halt at her stop and she exited.

Her apartment was only a few blocks from this station. With the weather being so beautiful, she didn't mind the trek.

Work today had been quite interesting. Gregory Taylor had scheduled an important meeting this morning where he'd laid out the plan for a new fashion design office in New York City. He rehashed their history, the opening of the offices in Minneapolis and Chicago, their success and growth.

He outlined the plan, timing, the opportunity it offered, the designers and the step up into being real contenders in the fashion industry. To accomplish this new venture, his proposal was to move two successful designers from each of their present locations to New York. Everyone would be given equal opportunity and he'd seriously consider each request for a transfer. The board room had tittered with excitement and questions about the process. He'd answered one at a time, clearing away confusion and laying out the sacrifice required.

After the extensive meeting, there was much talk within the office about who would be going. Jason Johnson was thrilled with the opportunity and already planning how to broach Mr. Taylor about his usefulness to the New York expansion. Jason thought the two of them would be asked to go. They were both single, the move would be less complicated for them and they were both very successful with their designs. He was sure they would be pinpointed for the promotion. Sally didn't know what to think.

That it would be a promotion was clear. The opportunity was huge, the implications astounding. If only this had come six months earlier, she would have jumped at it. Now she wasn't so sure.

Some had already decided against it for varying reasons: big families, responsibilities, the hassle of paperwork required in moving to the U.S., the upheaval...and the list went on. Others were taking the opportunity seriously, weighing the options and trying to decide whether the pros outweighed the cons.

This new development filled her thoughts as she made her way into her building and up the elevator. She unlocked the door to her apartment, walked in and dumped her purse on the chair sitting in the entrance.

Walter would be there in half an hour. She had to change and get ready. She'd have to tell him tonight, explain how huge an opportunity this would be for her. To go to New York and become established as a designer was too great a chance to let slide. Surely he'd understand her desire and give it some serious thought. His plans to wed her would have to be put on hold or just maybe he'd be willing to move there with her. After slipping into a mini skirt and wrap-around halter, she studied herself in the mirror. She crossed her fingers then searched in her closet for her new Valentino heels and a shawl for the cool night air.

The doorbell rang and she hurried to open it. Walter looked dashing in an Armani suit. Her heartbeat quickened the moment she saw him. That he dressed well was one reason she'd agreed to date him in the first place. He looked utterly handsome and mesmerizing. His smile was like the warmth of the sun and the desire in his eyes quickened her heart. The man was a fine specimen and she realized she was falling head over heels for him.

"Hi there," she said.

Stepping inside, he took her in his arms. "You're a sight for sore eyes." He nuzzled his face into her neck and groaned. "How I've missed you this week."

Her heart thundered at his touch and she melted into him. He placed light kisses up her neck and then found her lips. His kiss was passionate and long. It left her breathless, wanting more. He finally pulled away, his eyes dark with desire, his arms holding her at a safe distance.

"We should get going."

"We don't have to go right away."

His look was intense. "Yes, we do."

Shrugging off her disappointment, she grabbed her wrap and purse. He was so careful to do everything according to his religious rules. She had no choice but to acquiesce.

They went out for dinner, watched a movie then stopped at a coffee shop. Sally ordered a cappuccino and honey-glazed donut. Walter got a black coffee and a piece of chocolate cheesecake.

As she finished, she knew it was time to broach the subject. "I have something I'd like to discuss with you."

He looked up in interest, his blue eyes big with curiosity.

"It has to do with my job."

"Sure! Spit it out."

"It would bring huge change and would affect us."

His temple creased. "Really? How huge is it?"

"Gregory Taylor, my boss, is opening an office in New York City and is planning to transfer two designers to that location. The possibilities for advancement and recognition are massive. He's opened it up to all designers but said there were a few he's pinpointed for this opportunity."

"You're not actually considering it, are you?"

Sally's hands began to sweat and she wiped them on her skirt. "Well, actually, yes. The opportunity is phenomenal, especially in fashion design. New York City is the place to be recognized. It's a once-in-a-lifetime chance."

He frowned in confusion. "So, where does that leave us?"

She swallowed and said, "Our relationship means a great deal to me. That's why I want you to be a part of this decision. I want to know if you'd consider moving with me." She kept her hands hidden, her fingers crossed beneath the table.

"To New York City?"

"Yes. I know it would be a major move but I believe it would be good for us. We could start over together in a new place. It would be an adventure." She smiled hopefully.

He leaned back and crossed his arms, his jaw twitching. "Sally, Markham is my home. That's where I was born, grew up and that's where I work. I don't want to move to another city. I certainly don't want to move to another country. I couldn't even work there without some kind of work permit or something. Maybe your company would take care of you but what would I do?"

She hadn't felt this nervous in a long time. "I don't know. I'm sure we could work it out. I'm actually an American citizen, dual citizen. I was born in the States and moved here with my parents when I was a toddler so I can freely work in either country."

"That's great, but you still haven't answered my question. What would I do there?"

"I don't know. We'd have to check into the process of getting you a work permit. It would take some looking into but it would be doable."

He shook his head determinedly. "No! I don't want to move away from Markham. My parents live in Markham and we have a good church here. I have no desire to change my life that drastically." His eyes looked dark. "What made you think I'd be willing to move?"

He does care for me, doesn't he? Is my career that unimportant to him? Doesn't he realize how rooted I am to my occupation?

She was angry that he answered so flippantly. She pushed down the desire to lash back. "I didn't know how you'd respond. I never fully realized how settled you are here. I've never been that attached to this place or my family. My career means more to me than all that."

He sat forward and reached toward her, the palms of his hands up.

She held back, frustration still gnawing at her.

"You're upset."

After a deep breath and exhaling slowly, she said, "Yes, I am upset."

"Give me your hands," he said.

"Why?"

"Because, I love you."

Sally slowly placed her hands on top of his waiting ones and he squeezed tightly.

Looking deeply into her eyes, he said, "I can see you're disappointed, Sally. I'm sorry to be the cause of that. I hate to let you down like this but I do need to be honest about how I feel."

"I know." It was difficult to shake off the despondency she felt.

Walter waited a moment before continuing. "If you insist on moving to New York, I would understand that. You're a businesswoman at heart and your mind is on promotion and pursuing your career. I don't want to be an obstacle standing in your way. If this is something you feel you need to do, then I will support you. But I have to let you know, I can't imagine our relationship going very far or continuing if you decide to move to the States. It would be impossible to have a meaningful relationship long distance. I want to marry you, but if you decide to move, that would change everything."

Disappointment greater than she'd ever known filled her then. "Are you sure about wanting to marry me?"

"Absolutely! You're the one for me. I'd marry you tomorrow if you were ready."

Shock hit her at his bold declaration and she didn't know what to say.

Walter looked at her in concern. "Are you okay?"

"I don't know. You seem so sure of yourself."

"I am."

She nodded. Why did she feel so uncertain then? Suddenly everything confused her. Was moving to New York the right thing? Was marrying Walter in the cards for her? Did she even want religion? It suddenly felt so restricting, limiting – stifling even. New York offered so much freedom, opportunity, adventure and career advancement. Marrying Walter was enticing and offered a new chance at love. The pull between the two was excruciating.

"I want to know how serious you are about moving to New York, Sally."

Focusing on his words was difficult. She shook her head to clear it. "I'm not sure how serious I am. I know I was very excited about the opportunity when Gregory presented it. After talking to you, I feel uncertain. Now that I know how you feel, I need time to process the information."

"So, you're still considering it. Even after I shared my opinion?" He looked incredulous.

Allowing him to control her like this was dangerous. She'd traveled that path before. With such a favorable shot in fashion design she had to make her own decision. "I have to give this offer some serious consideration, Walter. My work is too important to me."

"I see." He looked deflated and hurt as he pulled his hands from hers and set them on his lap.

She felt like a heel but she couldn't give up everything for a man, no matter how charming and sweet he was. She would not let his wishes rule her life; of that she was determined. All the options had to be weighed carefully before she made any firm decision.

He paid for the meal and took her home, the ride shrouded in silence. After dropping her in front of her apartment building, he gave her a quick peck of a kiss, then left.

Standing on the sidewalk, she watched him drive off till he disappeared from view. He was upset. He'd never acted so coldly before but she couldn't really blame him. He'd invested a lot of time into her and their relationship, had high hopes for their future. Now she'd dashed all his efforts in one evening and he was reeling from it.

Guilt assailed her but she couldn't change what she'd done. She owed it to herself, after all the years of work and effort it took to get to where she was, to consider this opportunity seriously.

That he responded so selfishly infuriated her. *All he could think about was his desires, his way, his church and his comfort. Did I matter at all? Did my dreams matter to him?*

But she loved him; she knew that now. To lose him could destroy her. Or would it? She wasn't sure. She'd lost so much already. Which would be worse, to lose the chance of a lifetime, the advancement of her career, or to lose Walter?

Her eyes misted and filled with tears. One let loose and trickled down her cheek. She swiped it away as she turned and headed into her building. Somehow she'd make a decision, based on facts and her future, not on temporary emotion.

CHAPTER 15

End of January 2004

The round tables in the dining room were covered with crisp, white tablecloths, decorated in a wintry theme. Styrofoam snowmen, decked with a blue scarf, hat and mitts, stood as a center showcase on each. Colored thumbtacks formed their facial features. They sat on snowflakes made of light blue felt and covered with silver sparkles. The place mats, napkins and cups were in different shades of blue. Baby blue tea lights were positioned in three clear holders on each of the tables. Sparkling paper snowflakes hung from the expansive ceiling throughout the room.

This elaborate dining room always brought back so many memories of when Tessa had visited the place when it was abandoned and falling apart with her two good friends, Richelle and Luke. When they entered the property, each time they passed the large oak tree in the middle of the yard, they were transported back in time. Difficulty and sorrow plagued the family that lived there then. They'd seen so much heartache take place in this very home.

Their last travel in time had been focused on this dining room. Being in this room always took her back to that moment, bringing back all its memories. The young woman they saw, Mary, had gone through so much pain and sadness, doomed to a stressful upbringing, demanding father and loveless marriage. Tessa was thankful that now this house brought hope to those who visited.

Studying the room, the two large crystal chandeliers sparkled, diffusing an elaborate pattern on the ceiling, walls and floor. They added so much sophistication to the expansive room. The snowflakes, hung from the ceiling, added to the festive look. Instead of the one massive table, which had been here during the time travel, a multitude of round tables, now decorated, filled the extra-large room. The big bay window, facing the front yard, let in natural light through the sheer curtains and added to the mesmerizing feel of the place.

Tessa adored the look. She was sure the banquet would be a hit. The ladies would love all the fuss being made over them.

Reg and June Mendel were attaching white and blue streamers across the room in an eye-pleasing pattern. The last finishing touches were being made. Tessa spent much of her day helping prepare for this evening. Exhaustion was creeping in. Being pregnant made her tired all the time. It was something to which she was constantly having to adjust.

No one here knew of her pregnancy. Her plans were to tell Richelle tonight. She was looking forward to it.

She and Cody had kept their secret fairly private so far. They'd shared their news with her parents on the weekend and the response had been thrilling. Both of her parents were beside themselves with excitement. It was fun to watch their reaction.

She'd also told them about her plans to take some extra courses in counseling women and that she still planned to work part-time at the Mansion of Hope after the baby came. They were very supportive, her mother promising to help out as much as she could.

She wondered how Cody's mother would respond to their news. Chondra, Cody's sister, would be thrilled for them. Now she was eager to tell everyone as soon as possible. Telling Richelle would be so much fun! To be pregnant at the same time would make their friendship even stronger.

Tessa needed to head home to rest and change before the evening's celebrations; she still had time. She scanned the room once more and turned to leave. Stopping by her office, she grabbed her coat, purse and boots. As she locked the door, she heard footsteps behind her. Deborah Elliot walked toward her, a file in her hands.

Deborah said, "I'm so glad I caught you. I've wanted to give you this information for some time. I'm sorry it took so long." She handed over the file. "This is the information I told you about. These cases will give you an idea of how to handle and evaluate the women who will be coming here. Look them over and then give me your input."

"Thanks, Deborah. I've been looking forward to studying these." She flipped the cover over and thumbed through the pages.

"How are you feeling about this new level of responsibility?"

"I'm a little nervous about interviewing new women; but, I've been trained so I'm sure I'll handle it."

"I know you will. You have an awesome way with the women. Honestly, when you first showed interest in taking some of the training sessions I had reservations. But, after seeing you work in some of the classes, I have to admit that the women respected you immediately and responded to your creative way of teaching."

"Thanks! That means a lot! I was starting to doubt the direction I've been heading."

"I know God will use you in a powerful way in these women's lives. And remember, if you ever need help, Patricia and I are always here. You won't be thrown into it on your own." Her smile was reassuring.

"I'm grateful. I don't think I'd be pursuing this without that support base."

"We'll be here for you when you need us."

Tessa nodded.

"I have to run. I have so much to do before the banquet tonight. Just look over those papers and ask if you have any questions."

"I will. See you tonight."

Tessa stepped out into the crisp, winter air, the snow crunching beneath her feet as she made her way to the parking lot. With every breath, little puffs of white billowed around her. Her nose and ears cooled quickly as she hurried to her vehicle. Climbing into her stiff car, she started the engine and it groaned to life. It would take a while before it produced any heat.

As she pulled away from the Mansion of Hope she thought over the two major decisions she'd made a few months earlier. She didn't know how they could be reconciled. Pregnancy and her deeper involvement in women's lives at the Mansion of Hope hardly seemed compatible. But, she'd taken courses to prepare and she was ready to launch out.

Her new direction at the home was twofold. She would now be involved in initial evaluation, deciding if the women who came to apply qualified for their program. She'd also be involved in counseling women in individual sessions. She felt inadequate, even with the training. How could she truly relate to them when she'd never been in the place they were? But Deborah had told her often that the biggest asset to the job was compassion and a longing to see them set free.

Deborah's encouragement was constant and gave her the boost to continue. She'd sat with her during her first few evaluation sessions and helped her. Deborah had also joined in with the individual sessions a few times. The one-on-one sessions still made Tessa nervous, yet there was also an undeniable peace. This was where God wanted her to be. She knew that. How a baby would fit into the plan she didn't know. Trusting God to work out the details seemed the best thing to do.

~~~~

The banquet was wonderful and the catered meal delicious. Soft music played over the intercom, serenading them through the meal.

Tessa scanned the room to see the precious ladies who were gathered. They looked like sophisticated businesswomen instead of the broken, torn women who had come to them months ago. She felt thrilled to be here with them, celebrating their success. Each one was a miracle story.

This evening was like a dream come true for many of them. Alumni members had also been invited, those who had gone through the program and successfully stayed clean. All the staff was in attendance. Conversation hummed in the full room.

Deborah stood, waited for the room to quiet then introduced Veronica Billings, asking her to say a few words.

Veronica wore a simple dress in a bright violet color, which went well with her long, black hair. A thin gold chain graced her neck. Her black heels made her appear even taller than her five-foot-eight height.

Nervousness defined her as she stepped behind the microphone, placed her notes on the podium and scanned the room. Everyone broke out in cheers and clapping. Veronica smiled shyly.

After clearing her throat, she began. "Well, you all know me. I'm Veronica Billings." The room erupted with cheers again. "I've been here six months now and the staff agreed to let me attend tonight."

A few whistles and a few exclamations of approval pierced the air.

"Many of you have seen me at the group sessions and know a lot of my shady past already. It's been a tough go for me. Coming here and admitting I needed this was hard. I had so many mixed feelings that I didn't know which way was up.

"I grew up in a dysfunctional home." Veronica went on to speak of her difficult life, failed relationships and downward spiral with drug use. "Getting so addicted to drugs was my way of attempted suicide. My friend and I decided to do it. Her life was the pits too and so we planned it out. Overdosing seemed like such a good idea at the time." Her voice cracked and a tear trickled down her face.

Someone stood to hand her a tissue.

She wiped her eyes and continued. "It's still too fresh in my mind. Anyway, my brother found the two of us in my apartment and rushed us both to the hospital. My friend didn't make it and my life hung on by a thread. I still struggle with the guilt of her death. I know God has forgiven me but it still plagues my mind at times. It took about a week in the hospital before I was well enough to be released. My brother was devastated by it all and insisted that I go for help. He couldn't handle the thought of losing his only family member and, honestly, I hadn't even considered how my suicide attempt would affect him." She wiped away a few more tears.

"I came here for him. He forced me. I didn't know how I'd be able to cope without drugs. They were my lifeline. The detox process was horrible. I'm sure Deborah can attest to that."

Deborah nodded.

"I'm so sorry about the black eye I gave you."

Chuckles rippled through the room again.

"Something happened those first few weeks I was here. Everyone who looked after me would read to me from the Bible. I thought that was so strange at first. I didn't understand how an old book like the Bible could help me. Every time they would read from it, I felt this tug of war inside. A part of me wanted to hear what they were saying; yet another part of me wanted to tear the book out of their hands, rip it to shreds and curse. It was the strangest sensation!"

Echoes of agreement rose from the women.

"The words began to get to me. They told me about Jesus and the way to be saved. I'd never heard those things before. Well, it worked. I accepted Him and things started to shift."

The crowd cheered again.

"Something inside me changed. The 'dark thing' that was ruling my life was suddenly gone. The heavy, thick cloud hanging over me, draining me of everything good, dissipated and vanished. I felt loved for the first time in my life. The process of getting clean was still hard but it became a lot easier. The staff taught me that God made me for a reason and that I wasn't just an accident. I had a purpose." Her eyes shone brightly.

"The staff asked me to share my favorite verse. It's 1 John 3:1." She looked down at her notes. "It says, 'See what great love the Father has lavished on us, that we should be called children of God.' That's what I am now and I'm so grateful!" She made eye contact with staff members scattered throughout the room. "I want to thank you for all you've done for me."

As Veronica made her way back to her seat, the women rose to their feet, shouting and clapping. The offer was made for any of the others to take the mike and share. A few took the opportunity and did just that.

When the testimonies ended, Deborah Elliot stood and walked to the front, clearly touched by the evening's proceedings. She turned watery eyes across the room and said, "I want to thank each of you for giving us the opportunity to help you. I know I'm speaking for all the staff when I say it's been an absolute adventure for all of us who work here. Getting to know each one of you has been our pleasure and to see you here tonight, free of addiction, is the greatest gift you could give us. Not only have you made it through the program but I am confident that you'll continue in the things you've learned here. Leaving the Mansion of Hope can feel daunting and overwhelming. Going back to normal life can be scary." She pointed to some of the alumni. "Many of you have been away from us for up to a year and you've stayed free. That's tremendous!"

The women clapped again; the staff joined in.

"We are so proud of each one of you. There are some here tonight that are just barely through the program and are at that crossroads of heading out to live a normal life. We will always be available to you. The evening sessions we offer will be a great benefit in staying free. This is a night of celebration for your accomplishments. It is our way of saying congratulations for your awesome achievements and also thanking God for his ability and power to set you free. Give yourselves a standing ovation."

Chairs scooted and screeched as the women stood and rocked the room with another round of raucous applause.

The meeting was adjourned and the ladies gathered in groups to talk. Most of them stayed late, drinking coffee and enjoying dessert. Tessa made her way around to congratulate each one. As the evening progressed, the room slowly emptied.

Richelle sat down with a cup of coffee and waved Tessa over to join her.

Tessa sat down opposite her and said, "Wasn't this an amazing evening?"

"Yes," she said, nodding. "Veronica sure has come a long way, hasn't she?"

"I'd say!"

"I'm tired out. It's been a long day." Richelle's belly had grown round and full.

Tessa reached over to pat her bulging tummy. "How's baby doing?"

"Growing!" Richelle rolled her eyes. "I'm getting so huge. It's embarrassing."

"You're seven months along. You're supposed to be big."

"I suppose, but I hate being so fat. When I look at you and all these slim ladies around me, my size completely irritates me."

"Another two months and you'll be done. You'll be slim before you know it."

"I try to remind myself of that." She rubbed her bulging abdomen.

"Having a baby is a big deal."

She nodded. "Big in more ways than one."

Tessa chuckled. This seemed like a good time. "In a few months I'll look just like you."

Richelle stared open-mouthed at her as understanding slowly registered. "You're pregnant?"

She nodded and signaled for her to hush. "Only Cody and my parents know so far. You can't spread this around until we've told the rest of our family and friends."

"How far along are you?" she asked with a dumbfounded look.

"Two months."

"That's so exciting. We'll have babies together!"

Tessa nodded, feeling the thrill anew. Always best friends, now they'd share having newborns within months of each other.

"I can't wait to tell Charlie. He'll be pumped!"

"Actually, Cody insisted he be the one to tell Charlie. He wanted to get together with him tonight so Charlie probably knows by now."

"Oh." Richelle pouted. "I would have loved to tell him." She came over and gave Tessa a hug. "Isn't it thrilling? We'll be mommies together."

Tessa grinned and squeezed Richelle's back. This had been fun.

CHAPTER 16

October 1995

Gregory Taylor's office was large and beautifully decorated in transitional style. A massive mahogany desk stood center, Gregory's nameplate dominating the front of the desk. An expansive, mahogany bookcase lined one wall. A black leather office chair sat behind the desk and another two chairs, also in black leather, faced the desk. Ornate black onyx statues stood on marble stands throughout the room, depicting models walking the runway. A few oil paintings hung on the walls, beautiful women in garden scene settings. One was rumored to be his wife. No one knew for sure. Gregory never mentioned her. His wife never visited the office and no one knew for sure what she looked like. He preferred to keep his private life exactly that, private. Sally understood the desire.

Hardwood flooring ran the gamut of the room. To one side sat a love seat, chair, coffee table and ottoman, with an oriental rug tucked beneath the tiny sitting area.

Sally sat down in one of the leather chairs facing the desk and waited for Gregory to arrive. Although he'd sent for her, he was presently in discussion with Ralph over the ladies' suit line and said he'd be in shortly.

A large aquarium to the left, against the wall, resting on a large mahogany table caught her eye. Gregory loved exotic fish and loved to explain them, given the time. Looking at them swim lazily back and forth brought an illusion of peace and calm. If only Sally could feel a sliver of that.

A week ago, Gregory had offered her a top position in New York. She'd be one of the elite designers there – a complete honor – and he'd given her a week to decide.

If only there were a way to be certain of the future. Would she be completely happy with Walter if she decided to pass up the move and stay here for him? To give up this opportunity, choose to take a chance on love, caused her stomach to twist into knots. What if she chose him? Would the relationship end up in disappointment? But then what if she chose promotion, rejected this newfound relationship and then never met anyone like Walter again?

Her head hurt from thinking. What should she do?

The door swung open, tearing her from her thoughts. Gregory sailed in with a smile, walked behind his desk and sat down. His hair looked tousled and his tie hung crooked beneath his Taylor-designed suit. He wasn't slim but he wasn't unfit either; his height and weight were well-suited. With his commanding presence, he filled his role well.

It was clear he was looking for an answer today but she felt so ill-prepared, so confused. She needed a magic ball, Tarot cards, anything to help her decide.

"So, here we are," he said, running a hand through his messy hair.

He needs a haircut.

"A little rushed this morning?" she asked.

"Oh my, it's been crazy and it's only 10:00 a.m.! I'm so sorry I kept you waiting. I had a breakfast meeting with some potential clients who flew in from New York and then my meeting with Ralph. There's so much to attend to that I can't do it all. My head has been spinning for a good month." Gregory grabbed his head with both hands, dropped them back down onto the chair's armrests and released a heavy sigh. "I hope you have some good news for me, Sally, because there have been too many snags in this new venture already. I don't need any more bad news this morning."

She shrugged. "Then maybe I should leave right now."

He looked incredulous. "You're not saying what I think you're saying, are you?"

Sitting forward, she said, "I know this is an awesome opportunity for me and phenomenal to my career but there are other issues at play in my life right now that conflict in a big way. I would love to be able to say 'Yes, I'm moving' in an instant and forget about everything else."

"So why don't you?"

"This has been one of the hardest decisions of my life." With a conciliatory gaze, she said, "I'm sorry, Gregory, but my answer is no."

He looked stunned and disappointed at her answer. He rested his elbows on the chair's armrests, his hands folded in his lap.

"Is it about the money? Do you want more? I can arrange that."

"No, it has nothing to do with the money. What you offered was extravagant."

"What is it then?"

She felt like a heel saying it. "It's a personal matter."

"Who's the lucky man?"

With a small smile, she shrugged. She didn't like divulging personal matters.

"You're still as mysterious as ever, aren't you?'

"That's the way I like to keep it, sir."

"Well, I'd be lying if I said I wasn't let down. This is another serious blow to the new office project. Did you know that Jason also declined?"

That news did surprise her. "No, I didn't. I knew he was vacillating but I was sure he'd go for it."

"He also had personal issues that interfered. You were the two that I had in mind for New York. It would have given us a huge edge right from the start. I have some other people that I would consider sending, but you and Jason were the cream of the crop."

Sally felt awful. "I don't know what to say, Gregory. I'm sorry. If my significant other would agree to move, I would jump at it in a heartbeat, but he's refused even to consider it."

"Just give me a name and I'll have someone take care of him. I have connections in this city." He tried to sound mob-boss tough.

She smiled at his attempt at lightheartedness.

In consternation, he rubbed his chin.

"Gregory, I'm sorrier than you know. I would have loved to move."

He looked at her. "Don't worry about it. We'll work things out somehow." With a nod, he said, "That's all for now."

She left the room feeling so badly for what she'd just done. It was really her only choice. Wasn't it?

TIME AND HEALING

Sally walked over to her answering machine and checked the calls. Walter still hadn't returned her call. Why was he waiting so long to respond?

After a shower she'd try calling him again.

She showered quickly and slipped into blue jeans and a comfortable Alexander McQueen, short-sleeved sweater. While drying her hair with the blower, a knock at the door brought her head up. She peeked outside the bathroom door and listened. There it was again.

"What bad timing! My hair isn't even done!"

She walked to the front door and peeked through the peep hole. All that filled her view was a mass of blood red flowers.

"Who is it?" she asked through the closed door.

"I have a delivery from Laura's Florist Shop for a Miss Sally Blake."

She opened the door, the chain lock still in place. "Who are they from?"

He fumbled with the large arrangement and pulled out a card. "Uh…a man named Walter Tassey." His eyes lifted to lock with hers.

After unbolting the chain, she swung the door wide. A young man handed her the bouquet and left. She closed the door with her hip and carried the large arrangement of red roses to the table. It was sprinkled with baby's breath and greenery. Its size was astounding and it was gorgeous!

If this was Walter's response to her decision, then her fears could finally be laid to rest. Relief flooded her and a smile caressed her lips at the realization. If he was happy, she was happy. It filled her with long-awaited peace – if what she felt could be called that. She knew so little of it.

Sally fixed her hair and as she finished the last of her makeup she heard her phone ring. The number displayed tempted her not to answer.

I suppose I should. Get it over with.

Lifting the phone to her ear, she said, "Hello, Mom."

"So? Have you made your decision yet? Are you moving or are you staying?"

She sure knows how to cut to the chase. "I've decided to stay here."

"Oh, thank God for that! I am so happy, Sally! Have you told Walter yet?"

"Yes."

"I'm sure he's relieved as well, isn't he?"

"I haven't actually talked to him but I left him a message. I have a feeling he's very relieved." Her eyes locked on the flowers.

"I'm sure he is. I'm just so glad you'll be staying here. I couldn't bear the thought of you moving all the way to New York. I'd have missed you terribly."

No you wouldn't, Mother! You really can't stand me!

She said, "I have to go, Mom."

"Oh, all right. I love you, dear."

"Love you too." She hung up and released a puff of air. Why did she always tense up with her mother on the other end of the phone?

Why she still bothered trying to mother her was a mystery. There was very little effort made by either of them to stay in touch. When they did see each other, it taxed both their patience.

She wandered into the kitchen and grabbed a Diet Coke from the fridge. After sitting down in the living room and flicking on the TV, her mind wandered. The news broadcast didn't begin to catch her attention.

Since their discussion over her potential relocation, Walter hadn't called or made an effort to see her and he made no attempt to hide his frustration. She'd called him a few times but their conversations had been awkward and tense. Her attempts to see him were rebutted by unbelievable excuses.

Why wasn't he more understanding? Didn't he realize how important her career was to her and what a sacrifice she'd made? But then again, she had also hurt him. He'd made his intentions completely clear concerning her, shared his heart of wanting to marry her. Then she'd pulled this stunt. Her reticence to commit to him and then vacillating over the New York move had upset him just as much. She couldn't really blame him and yet she still felt perplexed by his response.

The roses were definitely a positive sign. The agony of the last few weeks and missing him so much had made her realize that she didn't want to live without him. With a gulp, she finished the last of her soda and stood to dispose of it. A knock at the door stopped her. She set the empty can down and headed to the door.

A look through the keyhole set her heart racing. After unlocking the door, she opened it wide.

Walter immediately stepped toward her, wrapped his arms around her and lifted her off the floor. His lips molded against hers in hot desire. Slowly he set her down, cupped her face with his hands and his kisses became tender.

When they parted, Sally's heart was beating wildly in her chest and she didn't want him to stop. Wrapping her arms around his neck, she pulled him to her. The kiss was strong and needy this time and when he finally pulled away, his eyes were dark orbs of desire.

"I missed you," he said breathlessly.

She smiled. "I missed you."

He moved her inside and closed the door behind him. His eyes darted to the kitchen table. "I see you got the flowers."

"Yes! Thank you, Walter. They're absolutely beautiful!"

"Not as beautiful as you." He grabbed her again and kissed her with longing.

The release his tender touch brought was exhilarating. There had been so much strain the past few weeks and it had taken a toll on her. Her eyes filled with tears and one trickled down her cheek.

"What's wrong, Sally?" Walter took his hand and wiped the stray tear from her cheek.

"It's been terribly difficult not seeing you for so long."

"I'm sorry. I was just so scared I was going to lose you. I couldn't bear the thought of you moving away and leaving me."

She nodded and buried her head in the crook of his neck and caressed him there with light kisses.

Walter said, "I got your call this afternoon and I almost touched the ceiling in celebration. I couldn't live without you, Sally." He pulled away and reached into his jacket pocket. After lowering to one knee, he raised a small box and opened it toward her.

She gasped and raised a hand to her mouth.

With eyes full of longing, he looked up at her.

Panic overwhelmed her and she was sure she'd faint. The air seemed thick, heavy and it was hard to breathe.

He grabbed her right hand then. It helped to steady her.

It was too soon! Much too soon! Finally, with one hand over her heart, she said, "Walter, what are you doing?"

"Sally, I love you. I want us to be together. Would you please marry me?"

"But, we've only been seeing each other for six months. It's so soon!" She pulled at the neckline of her sweater to get some air.

"It's been nearly seven months now." His eyes darkened. "Sally, you chose not to move to New York. Why?"

Frantic to get some air, to get away, she said again, "It's so soon!"

Anger laced his voice this time. "Sally, why didn't you want to move?"

Feeling trapped, she said, "I didn't want to leave you."

"Do you love me?"

She looked at him then. There was love in his eyes for her. He loved her. He'd told her often enough. The tenderness in his eyes started to calm her frazzled emotions. Her breathing gradually slowed and the frenzied feeling subsided.

Weakly, she said, "Yes."

"We love each other, Sally!"

She nodded. It was true.

"I want to spend the rest of my life with you. And you don't want to leave me. If we love each other, the next step for us is marriage."

Yes, it makes sense. It should make sense. But why do I feel so afraid?

He said, "I'm not saying we have to get married in a month. All I'm asking is: do you want to marry me?"

If only there were a guarantee of happiness forever, then this decision would be so easy. She still felt so much hurt from her other relationships – so much disappointment – that she didn't know what to do. Walter's eyes showed such strength and confidence. The feelings raging inside her were exactly the opposite.

"Do you think we'll be happy together?" she asked in a shaky voice.

"I know this is hard for you, Sally. You've been hurt. But I promise you my undying devotion and love. I know we'll be happy together."

His eyes still mesmerized and dazzled her. Was it just his looks that tugged at her heart so? She broke eye contact, glanced down at the sparkling ring in its case and released a nervous sigh. She had such a longing to be loved and cherished forever. Was it only a childish wish? Did "forever" really exist? How would she know if she never took another chance? She glanced up and locked eyes with him again.

"Can you promise me that we'll have a happily-ever-after ending?"

"I'd promise you the moon if I could, Sally."

A wistful smile curled her lips. She still felt incredibly frightened but he was so handsome, she could hardly stand it.

"My dear Sally Blake, will you marry me?"

She pushed the fear down and said, "Walter Tassey, my answer is yes."

A boyish smile beamed at her. Walter released her hand, pulled the large, solitaire diamond ring from the box and slipped it onto Sally's left hand.

She lifted her hand and studied the ring. It was gorgeous! Overcome by emotion, tears filled her eyes and slid down her face.

Walter stood and gathered her into his arms. With light kisses to her forehead, he whispered words of love to her. It felt wonderful being wrapped up in his arms, so safe and protected.

The two-week separation had been hard on both of them and the emotional reunion more than she'd expected.

CHAPTER 17

November 1996

In the foyer of the church, Sally stood apprehensively with her attendants as she held her bouquet of white roses with one hand and picked at it anxiously with her other. Butterflies fluttered in the pit of her belly. Her friend, Amber, now Amber Richards, looked at her and winked. Sally had been true to her word to stay in touch and their friendship had deepened and become very special over the past year and a half. Sally breathed deeply.

It was just over a year since Walter proposed. She felt as ill-prepared now as she had then. The questions were still large in her mind. Would they truly be happy together forever? Was marriage meant to last?

Sally took a few steps toward the entrance of the sanctuary and gazed at the seated guests. She could only see the backs of their heads; yet she knew each one. Her mother was seated on the left. Her father waited in the foyer with the rest of the wedding party, resting on a chair till the procession began. A group of relatives sat behind her mother. Her cousin, Benny, facing the back, caught her eye and waved.

Sally's friends and co-workers were seated in the rows behind her family. Their support helped relieve some of the pressure and apprehension she was feeling.

Walter's parents sat to the right side on the front row. Sheffield Tassey would be conducting the ceremony but at the moment he sat next to Lynne Tassey as they waited for the wedding to begin. Walter was an only child so just his parents occupied the front row. He had a number of family members who were in attendance: aunts, uncles, cousins and grandparents. Many of their church members and friends were also there.

Walter had insisted the ceremony take place at his father's church and Sally had agreed. It seemed the appropriate course to take. The sanctuary was average-sized and tastefully decorated. It was perfect for the intimate ceremony they'd planned.

The church was simply named "Tassey's Sanctuary" and reflected Sheffield's hard work and heart's devotion. It was obvious that this place was his pride and joy. Sally only hoped she'd be an asset to this house of worship, his congregation. Her lack of experience in religious matters troubled her. She had no idea what she was doing. Hopefully she'd learn fast.

The walking-down-the-aisle music started and she jumped. Amber stepped beside her, placed a hand on her arm and squeezed.

"You'll be fine. Just relax."

Sally nodded.

Amber was her maid of honor and Emily, her sister-in-law, was her bridesmaid. She had no flower girls or ring bearers. That's how she'd wanted it, plain and uncomplicated. Emily walked in first, followed by Amber. They wore simple-cut gowns in a shade of light green, with wide, scooped necklines. A broad waistband and flaring skirt ended mid-calf. Gold chains with emerald pendants graced their necks, her gift to them.

Her wedding dress was fancier than what she'd intended. Walter had drooled over it once and pointed it out to Sally in a magazine. She decided to surprise him by purchasing it. Hopefully he'd be impressed.

The bodice was full of beautiful beads and sequins and sparkled as she moved. It had a similar neckline to the bridesmaid dresses, but her waistline scooped down into a point, center front, making her slim frame look even thinner. It then flared out toward the floor with a long train trailing behind her. Layers of lace decorated the skirt. She thought it was much too frilly. Her veil was also very ornate with beadwork and sequins. Although it was overly ostentatious for her liking, she did feel like a fairytale princess.

Her father approached and smiled. "Ready?"

She nodded.

Vern Windsor wasn't as robust and strong as he used to be. Years of alcohol abuse had taken its toll. Apparently he'd cut back on his use of whiskey for health reasons, her mother had informed her. She was relieved to hear it but the effects of years of drinking showed.

The song, "This Day I Give my Love Away," started over the speaker system. It was time. When she took her father's arm and they started toward the front, the look in Walter's eyes said it all. He loved more than the dress. He couldn't take his eyes off her as she approached and his look warmed her straight down to her toes.

His attendants stood beside him – Derek, a good friend, and Robert, her brother.

Sheffield asked who was giving the bride away and Vern said that he and Melody were. Sally stepped in beside Walter and took his hand. Amber stood to her left.

Amber and Bobby had married nearly five months ago. After seeking professional advice, she was now on an alternate medication that moderated her depression. So far it was working. Curbing her drug use and aggressively attacking her addictions had paid off. She was a different person. Sally couldn't remember seeing her this happy before.

The ceremony flew by in a blur and before Sally knew it, she and Walter were being introduced as Mr. and Mrs. Walter Tassey. That was followed by pictures and a reception and dance at a local hall.

At the reception, her mother caught up with her at the restroom. Melody looked stunning, as usual. Her light-blue dress with cream accents and matching hat suited her. She'd supported this marriage from the start. Knowing that Walter was religious was the clincher. Sally was sure that was his biggest asset in her mother's opinion.

But now there was a concerned look on her mother's face. "Sally, did you know Sheffield Tassey named the church after himself?"

"Yes. He's very proud of his accomplishments. It's an amazing church, isn't it?"

"But why would he name it after himself?"

She shrugged. "I don't know. Does it matter?"

"I think it does."

Sally couldn't think of a reason why. He'd worked hard and deserved the recognition.

"It seems odd. And the message he gave during the ceremony was strange."

Sally shook her head in disbelief. "You can't say one good thing?"

"Does Sheffield speak about salvation? Is Jesus lifted up here? Does he even speak about God?"

"Mother! Stop this!"

"I'm concerned."

"You weren't concerned when we got engaged. You actually encouraged it, nearly applauded me for my choice in a man. Now you're suddenly having some sort of cold feet syndrome?"

"Something just doesn't sit right about this church."

She couldn't believe it. Not again! How dare her mother do this again?

Sally turned on her heel and headed back to Walter. A cloud of bitterness settled over her for the rest of the proceedings.

Later, after everything was wrapped up, as they were heading to their hotel, Sally's anger subsided somewhat.

While Walter drove he glanced at her. "Are you okay?"

She looked at him. "You noticed?"

"Back at the reception you seemed to zone out on me."

With a shrug, she said, "It's my mother. Just being around her is stressful."

"Want to talk about it?"

"No. I want to focus on the next two weeks."

The Dominican Republic was where they were spending their honeymoon and she couldn't wait to get there.

"All right. We'll forget about parents, family and friends and enjoy our honeymoon. Is that a deal?" His handsome features and beautiful eyes were overwhelming.

She smiled at him in pride. He was hers now. "It's a deal!"

~~~~~

Sally walked into her apartment with an armload of groceries, closed the door awkwardly with her foot and headed for the kitchen to drop her load. She'd worked a half day, stopped at the store and came home. Working Saturdays was not her choice but it was a busy season.

Walter was out with a friend and he'd mentioned dropping in to see his dad in Markham. Sheffield had asked to see him. She wondered what that was about and was sure he'd fill her in later. Surprising him with a nice dinner should set the mood for the evening. He'd promised to be home by 5:00.

Dinner preparations occupied her attention and with the main items cooking, she hummed a tune as she set the table. Their five months of marriage had turned out to be everything she'd hoped for. Finally to have a fulfilling relationship was a dream come true. Walter was a perfect gentleman, and his tender love was a balm to her soul. She thought she'd been happy marrying Milton but that was tame compared to what she had now.

Turning down the New York opportunity seemed trivial compared to the satisfaction she experienced with Walter. She'd made the right choice. She was sure of it.

Work was as hectic and demanding as ever for her at Taylor Design. Gregory Taylor had promoted her to the prestigious women's business line, which was becoming a very successful avenue for the company. Sally was also continuing her original line of design as well. Her life was busier but she couldn't complain; it's what she loved to do.

After the wedding, Walter had moved into her apartment in Toronto, making the transition to married life smooth and easy. She loved living so close to her job. Walter drove to his job in Markham each day, but didn't seem to mind the inconvenience. He was eager to make life comfortable for her. She grinned at the thought of how well he treated her.

Her brother, Robert, insisted he deserved the credit for their happy marriage. Sally refused to give him the recognition he wanted. Their marriage was heaven-made. At least that's what Walter kept saying. She was quite sure he was right.

With dinner well on the way, she headed to the bedroom to change. The dress she'd recently designed fit her well. It was part of the casual line, which boasted layers of cream-colored, chiffon material over a slim, body-fitting dress. The sleeves stopped three quarters down her arm and the neckline sloped in a V. She grabbed a pair of cream-colored Gucci shoes from her closet. She'd have to recycle shoes soon. Her collection took up most of this closet, plus the one in the guest room.

As she entered the main living area she heard the key in the lock. She stopped and waited for him. Walter stepped inside, his arms loaded with bags. A few packages dropped when he saw her. He stood in stunned silence, his mouth ajar. He let the rest of the bags fall to his feet, kicked the door shut with his foot and hurried toward her.

Grabbing her, he kissed her hungrily. Finally coming up for air, he gazed into her eyes, aflame with desire.

"Are you hungry?"

"You bet I'm hungry."

The look in his eyes told her it wasn't food he was thinking of. She giggled but it was stilled by his lips on hers. He led her to their bedroom.

Later, after dinner was done, they sat at the table and sipped hot coffee out of large mugs.

"Why did your father want to see you today?" she asked, gazing at him, overcome with the love she felt.

An odd look crossed his face. "It was nothing, really. He talked about the church and some of his plans and that's about it."

"But on Sunday he mentioned this awesome direction he'd received. He specifically wanted to share it with you. Was it as amazing as he implied?"

Walter squirmed slightly.

What's going on?

Her instincts went on full alert. This wasn't like him.

"I don't know. The things he talked about didn't really impress me that much."

"What did he say?"

"I tried to discourage him from some of his ideas. I really don't want to talk about this, Sally." His eyes turned dark.

His reticence to open up made her uncomfortable. *Why is he so vague? What's he trying to hide?*

"Why are you brushing me off?"

"I'm not."

"Yes, you are! I'm part of this church now too and I want to know what direction it's going."

"I would like to tell you, but my father made me promise to keep it quiet for now."

She had trouble believing him. "You can't even talk about it with your wife?"

"That's what he said."

"Are we a couple or are we not? In the sight of God, we've become one so why can't you tell me?"

"I'm sorry, Sally, I made a promise." He looked uncomfortable and his jaw twitched nervously.

"You made a promise to me first. Our marriage should mean more to you. Is this what you want – us keeping secrets from each other?"

"Look, Sally, I promised my father!"

"That's the point I'm trying to make! Why did you make such a promise in the first place? I don't want any secrets between us. I want our relationship to be open and honest and this is not helping."

He stood in frustration, stalked out of the room and headed to their bedroom. She sat stunned. She couldn't believe it! How could an evening that started out so lovingly and sweetly end up in an argument?

His behavior was inexcusable. Hadn't she willingly embraced his church, his father's creation, at the exclusion of all others? There were things about the church that irritated her, but she had held her peace. She hardly understood a word Sheffield preached on and yet she was starting to feel like she belonged there. It was becoming home. Now to be excluded from the plans and intentions of the church angered and hurt her.

In frustration she cleared the table and did the dishes. Walter always helped her. His absence only made this evening seem stranger. The time cleaning would give her a chance to calm down.

What could have made Walter so nervous and unsettled? She had to admit that Sheffield Tassey's church was the most unconventional church she'd ever attended and yet she still respected the man. He ran the church with strong leadership skills and precision. The people there revered him.

After putting the last dish away, the chattering T.V. in their bedroom drew her attention. Walking in, she saw Walter on the bed resting against a pile of pillows. He noticed her without looking, picked up the remote and frantically flicked from one channel to the next.

She sat down next to him. Reaching over, she rested her hand on his leg. He ignored her. It was uncharacteristic. He usually cuddled up when she reached out, especially in bed.

"Walter, I don't want us to fight but I do want there to be open communication between us."

There was no response. He was absorbed in watching nothing in particular.

"Walter, please, we need to talk."

"I don't want to talk about it!"

"Why not?"

"You don't know my father, that's why. If I tell you what he talked about, it would hurt you. I know it would anger you so I'm not saying a word." Walter clenched his teeth.

Sally suddenly realized how difficult this meeting with his father had been. "It might help you to tell me about it."

He turned to her then, the look in his eyes sending chills through her. "It would break my heart to tell you."

This strange conversation dumbfounded her. It was completely confusing. "I don't understand, Walter. Why would what you and your father discussed break your heart?"

"It would also break yours."

She shook her head. "I don't understand."

"I can't tell you."

"Does your father hate me? Does he want you to divorce me? Come on, I want to know."

"Stop, Sally! Just stop it! My father doesn't hate you and he's totally against divorce. I'm not saying another word. Stop questioning me or else I'm leaving for the rest of the evening! I can't handle any more today!"

Something in his eyes told her to back off.

"Okay. But secrets have a way of being exposed eventually. I will find out."

"Is that a threat?" he asked.

She pulled back in surprise. "No, but it is common knowledge."

"Not if I have anything to do with it." He glared at her gravely before turning back to the television.

He seemed like a different person. His eyes relayed a darkness and hopelessness she'd never seen before. If only she'd been a fly on the wall in her father-in-law's office. Then there'd be no mystery, no wondering. Whatever could they have discussed that would have brought this on? Walter had never excluded her like this before. He had never treated her with such coldness, except when she'd considered the move to New York. But this was different.

Walter finally stopped flicking channels and decided on a show. Sally tried to focus on it but her mind felt scrambled. Something was terribly wrong. If only she knew what it was.

~~~~~

Sally walked into her parent's home without knocking.

"Hello?" she yelled, but no one answered.

The quiet of the house echoed back. That was odd. The glass door by the patio was open, the screen the only barrier. She wandered over to it and looked out. Her mother was on her knees in the garden, gloves on her hands, pulling at weeds.

Melody wore a big-brimmed straw hat, well-worn pants and baggy shirt, her typical gardening garb. Sally studied her. Even in grubby clothes her mother looked fit and stylish. Melody stood then, grabbed a hoe and hacked at the weeds with more force. She loved gardening and planted vegetables every spring, regardless of the fact she only had two to feed.

Although the yard was modest in size, every inch was well utilized. It wouldn't take long for the multitude of perennials to bloom. Daffodils and tulips were already in full bloom with well-developed stalks. Annuals would be planted in every available spot soon and add to the profusion of color.

Birds chirped cheerfully from the few trees in the yard. It sounded heavenly, the signs of spring a relief.

She loved this time of year. It always filled her with so much hope. Being married to the man of her dreams still exhilarated her. If only the dark cloud that had descended recently on their relationship would evaporate and disappear.

Watching her mother in the garden brought back peaceful memories. This is how she liked to think of her mother, a woman who was industrious and willing to give for her family. She'd tried her best to be a good mother. Sally knew Melody loved her but their relationship just wasn't amicable.

Sally slid open the screen door and stepped out onto the deck. Her mother's head came around at the noise, surprise on her face. Sally waved.

"Sally! I didn't know you were planning to visit." She dropped the hoe, pulled off her gloves and headed to the deck.

"I wanted to surprise you."

"You did that!" She walked up the steps and gave Sally a hug. "Can I get you a drink?"

"No. Sit down and rest a bit. I'll get us something." She scooted into the kitchen and poured two glasses of ice water. Stepping back onto the deck, she handed one to her mother. "Here you go."

"Thank you!" Melody looked a little tired as she reached for the glass then relaxed back into her patio seat.

"How long have you been working out here?"

She glanced at her watch. "About two hours. There's still a lot to do. I love this time of year. Everything's new and fresh and I love watching things grow. It gives me a thrill."

"I admire your gardening ability, Mom, but digging in the dirt has never been something I'd dream about."

"You don't know what you're missing, dear."

"I'll take a chance on that."

Her mother smiled. It was surprising; they'd actually begun their visit on a pleasant note. Their relationship had been stiff and rocky since the wedding. There had been little effort on either side. Her mother had tried to see her but Sally had declined every invitation. Today guilt drove Sally to drop by. It was time to let the wedding issue go.

"I'm glad you stopped by, Sally. I've missed you terribly." There was sorrow in Melody's eyes.

"I'm sorry, Mom." Sally meant it.

"And I'm sorry if I hurt you. I never meant to. I shouldn't have said what I did on your wedding day. I know it upset you and I'm sorry about that."

"I've gotten over it."

Melody nodded. "Have you seen your father?"

"No, is he home?"

"He's resting right now. He's been doing so well lately. Alcoholics Anonymous has been such a blessing to him and he's been attending church with me fairly regularly."

"Really?" That was completely uncharacteristic of him.

"He treats me differently lately and I truly believe he's accepted Christ as his Savior. He doesn't admit to it but, with the way he's been acting, our home is finally peaceful and we hardly ever fight anymore. God has answered my prayers."

"It sure took long enough," Sally said cynically.

"It did take some patience – yes, years of praying for him."

"That's great, Mom. I'm happy for you." For some reason, the news only frustrated her. She should be thrilled for the change. It just came years too late, too late to change her childhood.

Melody studied her. "You know, I've been thinking."

This sounds dangerous.

"I know I haven't been the perfect mother but now that you're attending church and have turned your life back to God, the two of us should be able to establish a new friendship with each other."

"That would be nice, wouldn't it?" Her heart wasn't in it. To tolerate each other was all she was hoping for. Also, going to church hadn't really changed her much. She didn't feel any closer to God, even though she'd hoped joining a church would accomplish that. The only difference in her life was the feeling of love and acceptance from her husband.

Prayer was a struggle. When she did try it, the ceiling above seemed made of steel. It was like talking to herself and it frustrated her.

"It's possible, Sally."

She grinned contemptuously. "You mean we could actually speak to each other without tearing each other apart?"

"Do you think we've been that bad?"

"Yes."

"Well, that's another thing I've been praying about. I long for us to have a good mother-daughter relationship. I want to be a good mother to you."

What Sally was hearing didn't make a lick of sense. "Mom, I'm thirty-two years old. I think it's time to give up and just accept our relationship for what it is. We will never be buddy-buddy and

I've come to terms with that. It's time that you do too. Let's make the best of our relationship the way it is, okay?"

"That may sound reasonable to you but with God all things are possible. He has a way of turning things around and bringing unlikely miracles."

"There's been too much water under the bridge for that."

"Now let's change the subject. How are you and Walter doing?"

"Our marriage is wonderful and perfect. Walter's a good husband. We're extremely happy together." The look in Melody's eyes told Sally she didn't believe her.

"Wonderful, perfect, extremely happy? Those are strong words."

Tact was one thing her mother lacked. Sally could feel anger making an advance and she'd determined before coming not to get angry.

"Can't you just accept the fact that maybe I've made a good decision? Why is it so hard to believe that I've finally found the man of my dreams? And for the record, we are very happy together!"

"Sally, I'm sorry, I didn't mean to get into this again. My concerns lie with Sheffield Tassey and his church. I'm sure you and Walter are very happy."

For some reason her mother's concerns didn't infuriate her this time. She felt curious instead. "What do you mean?"

"I don't know if we should get into it. I don't know if I have the energy." She did look tired, even with sitting in the shade.

"I'd like to know."

Melody took a deep breath and exhaled slowly. "Mr. Tassey spoke some things at your wedding that seemed off. It made me question his beliefs and his stance on marriage." She stopped and studied her daughter.

"What did he say that you questioned? I don't remember hearing much of anything that day."

"Well, your aunt and uncle were also concerned. Benny also mentioned later that he had a strange feeling about Sheffield Tassey."

Impatience drove her on. "You still haven't told me what he said during the ceremony."

"Well, he spoke of marriage and that how two become one. I agree with that. He also said that the one who is saved can bring salvation to the one who is not saved and that it's a ministry of mercy. He implied that this salvation technique could be used outside of marriage as well. We weren't quite sure what he was referring to but it sounded strange. He went on for a while on that tangent. It didn't line up with the Bible. After that he defined the roles of a man and woman in marriage."

"I don't remember him saying anything about salvation."

"Do you remember him explaining the roles of a wife and husband?"

"No."

Melody looked unsure of elaborating.

Sally said, "So, what did he say?"

Clearing her throat, she said, "He described a wife's role as submissive, subordinate and completely obedient in all situations." Her eyes betrayed concern as she continued. "The husband was to be god in the home, his every word as a direct word from God himself. He explained that if a wife did not obey her husband in all things, it was showing direct disobedience to God and would result in just punishment."

"He said that?" Why couldn't she remember that? It was outrageous!

"Now, I agree that a wife needs to be submissive. The Bible teaches that, but if a husband is walking in disobedience to God, then a woman should not obey a man instead of her God. Sheffield Tassey seems to have an extreme control issue and that is where my concern lies."

Shocked, Sally didn't know what to say. Walter had never insisted on obedience like that. They decided things together, discussed everything and came to a mutual decision.

"Has Walter ever expressed his views on these things?"

"No! Never! There has never been a problem regarding what you're talking about. I don't really see Sheffield as dominating or power-hungry. He's a strong leader and is respected for it. No woman is ever punished for disobeying her husband." She chuckled at the hilarity of it.

"Are woman allowed to give their opinions in church or be involved in any way?"

She answered with pride, "Men are the spiritual leaders in the church. They're very involved in every aspect, from teaching, being on various committees to leading. That's one of the things that impressed me from the start. They don't run the women ragged and allow the men to sit back and do nothing."

Melody nodded. "Like Dad and I?"

"Exactly!" She'd made her point and it felt good. "I want my husband to be the spiritual shepherd of our home. When we have children, he will be the one taking the family to church and teaching them the Bible." Sheffield often used that phrase when referring to the men of the church – "spiritual shepherds" – and she liked it.

"So women aren't allowed to get involved?"

"They are welcome to do things in the church if they have a specific gift but it isn't encouraged."

The concern in Melody's eyes deepened. "Keep your eyes and ears open, Sally. Read your Bible and judge everything that is said and done in that church by the Word of God. That will always be your guideline. You still have the Bible I gave you, don't you?"

"Sheffield Tassey has instructed the congregation not to read their Bibles privately. He said that since we are not Bible scholars, we could easily be led astray by our ignorance. Since he studies the scriptures diligently, he'll always explain it to us as he receives it from God. I trust his interpretation of the Bible more than I trust any other preacher's."

A strange, fearful look passed over Melody's face. "Sally, please promise me that you'll start reading the Bible. How do you know if he's telling you the truth if you don't know the truth?"

"Mother, don't be so scared. You should be thrilled that I'm part of a church and that I attend regularly. My husband's father is a pastor and my husband is dedicated to the church and very involved. I don't see the problem. I thought you'd be happy for me."

"I'm happy that you're happy but I see some danger in Mr. Tassey's preaching. Promise me that you'll compare his teaching to the Bible?"

"If it'll make you happy, then yes." Sally had no intention of studying her Bible. The times she had attempted to read it only made her confused and bored. She much preferred someone else studying it for her. If this promise to her mother would shut her up, she was willing to mouth the empty words.

Relief flooded her face. "Thank you, Sally."

Guilt washed over her. Sally stood and said, "I have to go."

Melody rose and came to her. After a long hug, her mother stepped back, held her at arm's length and said, "I'm glad you came. You should say hi to your dad before you leave."

"I don't want to wake him. I'll drop by again." She gave her mother a quick peck on the cheek and headed for the door.

As she started her vehicle and saw her mother wave from the doorway, she decided to find her Bible in one of the boxes she'd stacked in the storage room. It was the least she could do and would maybe erase the lie she'd told.

CHAPTER 18

February 2004

Tessa woke with a start and sat up. Her heart pounded wildly in her chest and her breaths came in short, frightened intervals. She reached for the lamp beside the bed and flicked the switch. The flood of light didn't begin to touch the darkness of dread she felt. She placed a hand on her expanding abdomen and rubbed tenderly.

Perspiration clung to her hair, making it stick to the back of her neck and her nightgown. She lifted her damp hair from her neck, then glanced over to where Cody was sleeping. He rolled over toward her and she placed a hand on his shoulder. His eyes opened a crack. When he noticed her sitting up, his eyes opened a degree further. He reached over to touch her leg with his hand.

"What's wrong, hon?"

"I had the dream again."

"Now... what dream was that again?" He asked groggily as he struggled to keep his eyes open.

Tessa felt bad about waking him but she needed some support. "I told you about it a few days ago. You don't remember?"

His eyes closed tightly. Slowly he opened them again and said, "Sorry. No, I don't."

She swung her legs out of bed.

"Where are you going?" He asked sleepily.

"I'm too terrified to sleep and you're not much help." Setting her feet into her fuzzy slippers, she turned out the light, grabbed her housecoat and exited their bedroom.

As she entered the living room, she picked up her Bible from the end table and leafed through the pages. Pacing seemed more beneficial than sitting. She was too agitated to stay still.

"God, please help me get rid of this awful feeling!"

She felt like crying. The reoccurring dream greatly disturbed her. Did it mean something? And why all this fear? She'd asked

God to take it away but still it came during the night when she was defenseless and unable to fight.

Romans was a good place to start. She turned to the eighth chapter and started reading at verse fifteen: "For ye have not received the spirit of bondage again to fear; but ye have received the Spirit of adoption, whereby we cry, Abba Father." She flicked through her Bible till she came to the second book of Timothy, the first chapter, where she had underlined the seventh verse: "For God hath not given us the spirit of fear; but of power, and of love, and of a sound mind."

Closing her Bible, she paced the room and prayed. Suddenly she saw Cody standing in the doorway and stopped.

He came over and placed a kiss on her lips. "We're going to fight this together, whatever it is, okay?"

Relief flooded her and a tear trickled down her cheek. "Thank you!"

He led her to the couch and they sat side by side. Turning to her, he said, "First of all, I need to know what this is all about. Tell me your dream again."

She was still shaking and her body began to feel cool as it dried.

Cody reached to the back of the couch where they kept a cotton throw blanket. Wrapping it around her shoulders, he placed an arm around her and squeezed. "Better?"

She nodded. Taking a deep breath, she began. "I've had this stupid dream for a few weeks now and I don't know what it means. It didn't cause me any fear at first but the more I thought about it, the more fearful I became. Now every time it comes, I wake up shaking with terror."

"Why don't you tell me the details?"

"Okay." Taking a deep, calming breath, she exhaled slowly. "In my dream, I'm giving birth to a baby. It's always a girl. I'm thrilled with her, loving on her and amazed at this miracle." She glanced at Cody, making sure he was listening this time. His eyes never strayed from her face. "As I'm holding her, this woman walks into my hospital room and takes my baby from me. She stands there for a while, cuddling my baby and smiling. It seems that she's also thrilled about the baby and she keeps saying thank you over and over again. I start asking the woman to give my baby back but she refuses. She then walks out of the room, taking my baby girl. I'm screaming after her. That's when I wake up."

Cody looked as puzzled as she felt.

"The first time I had the dream, I thought it was one of those pregnancy ones, those bizarre ones that don't really mean anything. It didn't really frighten me, but the more it comes the more afraid I become. Each time I have the dream my terror grows."

"How often have you dreamt this?"

"Four times now."

He thought for a while. "Could it be from God?"

"Would a dream from God bring me this much fear?"

"Well, remember what you said? You told me that the first time you had the dream you felt no fear. The fear only came after you thought it over. That's the clue that maybe the dream is heaven-sent. Only when you thought about the dream, and considered what it would mean to you, did the fear come in."

"That is true," she said cautiously.

"We need to ask God about this. If it's from him then he's trying to tell you something. If it's not from him then we need to take authority over this. No evil spirit is going to harass my wife while she sleeps." His gaze was stern and determined.

A rush of gratitude filled her. His desire to protect her made her feel safer already. "So, what do we do now?"

"Let's pray!" He grabbed both of her hands and began. "Dear God, I ask that you'd reveal the source of these dreams and what they mean. If these dreams are from you then I ask that your peace would flood Tessa's mind and heart right now. I ask that you'd give her peaceful nights of sleep. In Jesus' name, I take authority over the spirit of fear that is trying to harass my wife and I bind you from your assignment against her. Dear God, I know that this child in Tessa's womb is a gift from you and we thank you for it. I pray protection over this little one. Watch over it as it grows and as Tessa gives birth. Protect it from all harm. Your word says that the fruit of her womb is blessed so I thank you for that. We thank you for wisdom in this situation, in Jesus' name, Amen!"

Darkness lifted and peace settled down around her, an inexplicable feeling. The suddenness of the change shocked her. Her breathing settled and the frantic beating of her heart slowed.

She looked at him. "The fear is gone." A tentative smiled curled her lips.

"Thank you, Lord!" Cody's exuberance came and went quickly. With a serious gaze, he said, "So that means the dream is from heaven."

Tessa shook her head. "But what could it possibly mean? It doesn't seem like a good dream."

"He'll reveal it to us. We have to be patient."

"I hope he does it soon. I hate not knowing. Maybe it doesn't mean anything."

Cody looked dubious. "Well, remember how I prayed. I asked that if this was a dream from him that he'd flood your mind and heart with peace. That's exactly what just happened."

"That's true." Why did she still feel so perplexed then? "Or maybe, when you took authority over the fear, it took a hike and the peace came."

"That's possible but I still think God gave you the dream."

"You really think so?"

He nodded.

"Maybe he'll show you what it means," said Tessa

"Maybe he will."

"Then you have to tell me as soon as you know, okay?"

"I promise I will." He stood and held out his hands to help her up. "I'm ready for some shut-eye."

"Me too." She dropped the cotton throw on the couch, grabbed his hands as he pulled her to her feet. "I need a shower first. I was soaked with sweat earlier. Hopefully my side of the bed is dry by now."

"I'll change our bedding while you shower."

"Thanks, Cody!" He was so good to her. She gave him a kiss before heading to the bathroom.

CHAPTER 19

November 1997

Sally's nerves were taut as she fussed with the tiny buttons of her Anna Sui blouse. The buttons were a bother, but paired with the skirt she'd designed, the overall look pleased her. She slipped on pantyhose and a pair of Prada slingbacks.

Standing before the mirror, her appearance was sufficient, stunning even, yet the unmistakable sorrow in her eyes made her pause. Her marriage had issues. Somehow the problems that cropped up had refused to budge. Their communication had gone sideways. They rarely spoke of the dysfunction in their relationship. Walter seemed oblivious to the problem – or perhaps ignoring it was his way of dealing with it.

Today was their first anniversary and although it had been heaven on earth for the first few months, the last part of the year had taxed their love and commitment. She was sure she was still the same person Walter married a year ago. He, on the other hand, had changed a great deal. She still struggled to understand what brought about the transformation.

The more she asked him about it, the angrier he became. He was completely unreasonable. They couldn't seem to communicate their feelings openly without strife. Now he avoided talks about their marriage like the plague. A mixture of terror and anger flooded his eyes whenever she brought up the subject. What was he so afraid of?

The mirror didn't lie. Her forehead was creased in worry. This is what he'd done to her – made her an emotional, nervous wreck and given her premature wrinkles. She rubbed her forehead to ease the tension there. It didn't help.

"We are going to have a good anniversary dinner and I am not going to dwell on the negative tonight. Do you hear me, Sally?

You and Walter are going to have a wonderful time." Taking a deep breath, she exhaled slowly.

If only her words could make it so. She grabbed her coat, purse and keys and exited the apartment.

She drove the nearly hour's drive to Markham through lighter than usual traffic and made her way to her brother's real estate office. Walter didn't usually work full days on Saturdays but he had been swamped the last while and had suggested she meet him here. She parked and headed to the office, scanning the parking lot for sign of Walter's car. It wasn't there. Frustration badgered her but she pushed it down. He knew how important this night was and his effort tonight would be telling.

As she walked into the reception area she was surprised to see Emily seated on one of the chairs. Her sister-in-law was absorbed in a magazine but looked up in surprise when Sally sat down beside her.

"What are you doing here, Sally?"

"I could ask you the same thing."

Closing the magazine, she said, "Robert asked me to meet him here after work. He wants to show me some houses."

"Houses? I didn't know you were planning to move." Her brother and sister-in-law had no need to upgrade. Their house was large and beautiful.

"We're not, but Robert is getting into the rental business. We already own a few rentals. He always asks for my opinion before buying anything."

She nodded. It sounded just like him. "How come he never told me?"

"About his rentals?"

"Yeah."

"He's not one to brag about himself."

"Telling his sister would only be common courtesy. There'd be no bragging involved in that." Sally felt a tinge of hurt. Robert used to confide in her about everything.

"I don't know why he didn't tell you. You'll have to ask him yourself." Emily pointed toward the far side of the room as Robert walked toward them. Sally stood, opened her arms and they embraced.

He pulled away and said, "I haven't seen you in months! I get all my information from Walter these days. You rarely call and never come around."

"I'm here now."

"By the way you're dressed, I can tell you didn't come to visit me!"

She crossed her arms. "Why didn't you tell me about your rental business? Why do I have to find things out through the grapevine?"

"I didn't tell you?" His innocent face didn't fool her.

"You're guilty, Robert. Emily just told me. That's unacceptable! I'm your sister, for crying out loud!"

"Sorry. You know now, so can we call it a truce?" He stuck out his right hand.

She shook her head and glared at him.

"Don't be mad. We see so little of each other. Let's not spoil our rare meetings with anger."

"Brothers! You can't live with them and…yeah, that's about it."

He chuckled. "You need me, sis! Without me, you never would have met Walter." Waving his trump card was becoming a common practice.

The temptation to discredit his matchmaking success was at the forefront of her thoughts but she resisted the temptation with a weak smile.

"It's your anniversary today isn't it, Sally?" Emily said, walking over and wrapping an arm around Robert's waist.

"Yes it is. Can you believe it's already a year?"

"Well, congratulations, sis!" Robert's smile made her feel lighter.

"Walter and I have reservations at a restaurant here in Markham and we'll stay overnight at his parents' for church in the morning."

"You're spending your anniversary night at his parents' house?" Robert asked incredulously.

"I know. That was my initial response too but Walter insisted. His parents are fine and don't get on our case too much. I guess we'll really celebrate when we get home tomorrow night."

"I'll have to have a talk with the guy. It seems his romanticism has taken flight." A look of concern stole from his eyes. "Is he planning to meet you here at the office?"

"That's what he told me last night. Is he around?"

"No. He's out showing a client some houses." He glanced down at his watch. "He left an hour ago and it usually takes a few hours doing a tour of houses. I hope he estimated his time right."

"I can call him on his cell. Can I wait for Walter here?"

"Sure. Emily and I are heading out but I can leave my keys with you as long as you hand them to Walter when he comes. He can bring them back Monday morning."

"Thanks, Robert. I appreciate it." Sally took the keys from his open hand. His sympathetic smile irritated her. There was no way she'd let him know how she was already hurting. "Walter and I are doing fantastic, Robert. He just doesn't understand how important an anniversary is to his wife."

"I'm sure he'll find out tonight." He grinned crookedly.

With a nod, she watched as the two walked out hand in hand.

She dug in her purse for her cell phone. It would be prudent to find out directly from him what the situation was before giving in to anger. She punched speed dial and waited. It eventually switched to his answering system. Talking to a machine only made her more heated. She punched redial and waited. He didn't answer. With every try her fury increased. On the seventh try, he finally picked up.

"Hi honey! What's up?"

"What's up? What do you mean 'what's up'? I'm here at the real estate office waiting for you. It's our anniversary, Walter! You promised you'd be here by seven."

"I'm sorry! Something came up with some clients. I couldn't turn them down. They're from out of town and are flying out tomorrow. I should have called and let you know but I totally forgot. We have one more house to see and then I'll be there, okay?"

"You promised, Walter!" Maybe she sounded selfish but she felt justified.

"Please don't be mad again. I'll be there as soon as I can. Did Robert give you the office key?"

She released a pent up breath. "Yes. How long will you be?"

"No more than an hour."

"An hour? Do you even care about our anniversary? Maybe I'll leave and celebrate on my own."

"Sally, please! I'm with my clients and I can't talk right now. Please wait for me and I'll be there soon."

"I can't promise that." With a snap of the phone she cut him off.

How could he do this to me? It's our anniversary! I'm so upset I feel about to explode!

She stood and headed for the door. Staying here and waiting was out of the question. She was much too agitated to sit still for an hour.

~~~~~

The familiar, small house on the outskirts of Markham brought back a surge of memories. Sally couldn't remember it looking quite so dingy and rundown, though. She hadn't been here for years. Hopefully he still lived here. Perhaps she should have called first.

She parked her car by the curb and studied the unsightly house. Why she was even here, contemplating what she was contemplating, was unnerving; yet she felt vindicated. The exterior paint hung on in strips and many shingles were flapping loose in the cold November breeze. The shutters moved with a clacking sound at the strongest gusts of wind.

The path to the front door was littered with debris and odd pieces of paraphernalia, showing the owner's indifference. An old abandoned washing machine, covered in junk, stood next to the house; four well-worn tires were propped up against it. Scraps of wood were piled up on one side of the yard. Beside them leaned a dented grocery cart, a large roll of electrical wire and a pile of sawhorses. Three old rusted cars sat in the driveway, all of them looking unfit to drive. One sat on blocks, its tires missing. Another had no windshield, the inside open to the elements. The third fared a fraction better but not by much.

Slowly she made her way up the cluttered walk to the front door, sidestepping the rubble and knocked softly. A prolonged wait is what she expected, so when the door flung open immediately, she jumped.

"Ah, I scared ya, didn't I?" His wide grin told her he'd lost a few more teeth since their last encounter. "Well, well, look what the cat dragged here. It's Sally Windsor!"

Buck hadn't changed much. His skinny frame and oily, tousled hair was the same. She couldn't remember feeling so repulsed by him before. His body odor was overwhelming and she backed away a step.

"Hi Buck, but I'm not Sally Windsor." She held up her left hand to display her large diamond. "I'm Sally Tassey now."

"Whew! That's quite the ring there, Sally, and look at ya. You're miss Fifth Avenue with your digs! It looks like ya've done well for yourself, little lady. So what number husband is this one?"

Not only did his words annoy her but she fought down loathing to answer. "My second."

"Well good for ya. I tried it three times but I swear I'll never attempt it again. It's too much hassle for me." He moved back to let her enter and raised his fingernail to pick at his teeth.

Cautiously she entered, feeling entirely uncomfortable. It surprised her. Maybe the years had changed her. Having to deal with his kind again unnerved her. Even Felix had had more class.

Buck closed the door behind her, walked to his filthy couch and plopped down. He pointed to a chair across from him. "Have a seat, 'Miss Fifth Avenue' and tell me what I can do for ya." After finding the thing lodged between his teeth he proceeded to wipe it off on the arm of his chair.

"I think I'd rather stand. I need the usual and then I'll go."

"The usual? How am I supposed to remember? Ya haven't been here in years." By the way, where have ya been buying your stuff?" His look was hard and accusing.

"I haven't been using anything in a long time."

"I don't believe it."

She shrugged. It was almost true.

He looked at her curiously. "So ya thought ya'd go the straight and narrow, did ya? It didn't work? Your marriage is causing ya some pressure, maybe?" Buck smiled grotesquely with an open mouth. His eyes wandered down her frame, stopping and admiring.

She stiffened and forced down the bile in her throat. Perhaps mentioning his long-time rival would divert his attention. "Buck, do you have what I'm looking for or should I try Leonardo?"

As though poked by a red hot iron, he jumped up. "Leonardo? Don't ya dare go to him! His stuff's completely inferior and ya'd be sorry. Cocaine, heroin, meth? You name it, I'll get it."

"Just some cocaine."

Buck hurried down the hall and returned carrying a small wrapped bundle. He stopped before her and she held her breath at the smell of him.

"How much," she asked.

He told her and she paid him.

As he counted, she reluctantly stuffed the package into her purse. After being in his hands there was no way of knowing how many germs came with it.

With a nod, he smiled in satisfaction.

"Thanks! I'll be going now." She spun on her heel and headed for the door.

"Ya can stay, ya know? We have a lot of catching up to do."

"No Buck, I have to go."

"It's a Saturday night and I'm all alone." His intention was all too clear.

"I'm married. I'm sure you could find someone if you tried."

"My beautiful but aloof Sally." There was desire in his eyes as he once again scanned her from head to toe.

Sally was frightened. She shouldn't have come here. "Thanks again but I'm gone." Desperately, she grabbed the door handle, jerked it open and left quickly. Hurrying to her car, she sank gratefully behind the wheel. Buck stood in the doorway looking at her. A quick glance at the clock told her she could get back to the office well before Walter arrived. Without a backward glance, she drove off.

~~~~

Sally and Walter pulled into his parents' driveway in their separate vehicles. Their meal and evening had been tense and artificial. She'd pre-determined not to discuss any contentious issues. It had put Walter's nervousness to rest somewhat and he eventually loosened up, becoming lighthearted toward the end of their meal. Bypassing any type of discord or break in harmony was becoming an art form for her husband.

Emotionally she was dying inside and she felt at a loss of how to stop it. Often she'd tried explaining to Walter how she felt but it never helped to ease the barrier between them. His heart seemed impenetrable. He refused to discuss certain subjects and purposely kept things from her. The more Sally prodded him, the less willing he was to disclose. She didn't know how long she could cope with a relationship that felt increasingly like a dead end.

Sally turned off the engine and slowly exited her vehicle. She popped the trunk and walked to the back to get her suitcase. Walter came up beside her, lifted it out, set it down and closed the trunk. He turned toward her then, wrapped his arms around her and kissed her tenderly.

"I realize this isn't the ideal ending to our anniversary. I'll make it up to you tomorrow night, okay?"

Sally nodded sadly as she stared into her husband's eyes. He was so handsome it took her breath away; yet she felt so distant from him. She couldn't conjure up a smile or a response and felt her tears near the surface.

He gazed at her in concern, pleading with his eyes. "Don't look so sad, Sally. I love you and want to make you happy. I just don't know how. I'm trying my best."

"We need to talk. I need to talk. There can't be secrets any more between us, Walter. I feel like our marriage is dying."

He made a mocking sound with his mouth. "Our marriage is not dying!"

Sally grew silent. It was always this way, him defensive, her pleading. It wearied her beyond words.

However, the look on her face stilled him. "Look, we'll find some time to talk. I promise."

"I need you to be honest with me. We need to communicate if our marriage is going to survive."

A frustrated sound escaped his lips. "You're asking too much. You're asking me to do something I can't do. Things will get better, okay?"

She simply shrugged.

Walter bent over her and placed a kiss on her lips. "Remember, no matter what happens, I love you more than anything else." He wrapped her in a desperate hug. It felt suffocating and claustrophobic.

Something's wrong with him! He never holds me this way. It feels like he's desperate and scared. But why?

Sally pulled away from the far-too-tight embrace and stared at her husband. How things could have changed so drastically in a few months' time was beyond her, but they had. One thing she still knew, looking at him: "I love you too, Walter." But her love was being severely tested.

Walter smiled brightly as if his world was put back in order. He reached down to grab Sally's suitcase then went to pick up his own beside his car. Leading the way to his parents' front door, he rang the doorbell, completely unaware of the turmoil she was struggling with.

The door opened wide and Lynne Tassey welcomed them with open arms. Lynne instructed Walter to take the suitcases to the guest room downstairs. Sally and her mother-in-law waited in the entrance, an awkward silence between them. It seemed odd to wait here. Usually Lynne invited her to the kitchen. Sally never did know what to say to the woman. Lynne was devoid of her own opinions, besides being extremely introverted.

Walter returned soon and Sheffield Tassey appeared seconds later. His commanding presence dominated the atmosphere as he hugged his son in welcome then turned toward Sally and embraced her. His arms were strong and his hug tight.

"Welcome here, both of you!" he said with a booming voice.

"Thank you, sir," Sally said.

He stared at her in irritation. "Sally, you keep forgetting that I'm your father. Call me Dad. I'd prefer it."

"I find it hard to do, Mr. Tassey. I would find it easier calling you Pastor Tassey."

He sighed deeply but his pleasure was clear. "If that works for you, then that's fine with me."

His tall frame and intense demeanor were always overwhelming. Walter got his good looks from his father but Mr. Tassey had a more intimidating presence about him.

"Now come into the living room. I have someone I'd like both of you to meet."

"I thought it was going to be just the four of us tonight, Dad?" said Walter.

"Well, there's been a change in plans. I think you'll approve of our guest and the reason for her visit." Sheffield led the way into the living room.

Sally followed her husband but noticed Lynne slipping away into the kitchen. She let the door close behind her and Sally thought she heard a soft cry. How strange! She stopped and listened for a moment but after hearing nothing more, she followed Sheffield and Walter.

Walter was already shaking the hand of a woman and he said, "Welcome to my parents' home."

Sheffield waved for her to step forward. "Sally, come and meet Tina."

Holding out a hand, she stepped forward. "Hi, Tina. I'm Sally. Nice to meet you."

"I'm so pleased to meet you too. I'm so excited!" gushed Tina.

"Why's that?" To start a conversation this way seemed odd. Why was it so exciting to meet someone you didn't even know?

"I'm going to be saved! Isn't that neat? I never knew getting saved would be this easy and I'm going to join the church, but I need to get saved first." Tina beamed as she took a seat on the large couch.

"So you mean you're going to accept Jesus as Savior?" Not that Sally fully understood those words but they came naturally from years of going to church with her mother.

"I'll do whatever I need to do. Isn't it thrilling?"

The woman was bizarre. Sally couldn't remember anyone with such an exuberant attitude about salvation before actually getting saved. She glanced at Walter for some explanation. His eyes blinked an unusual amount and he struggled to keep eye contact with her.

Something was wrong. She felt it in her gut but couldn't quite place a finger on it. Sally took a seat while Tina and Sheffield chatted. Studying the slight woman, whom she guessed was in her early forties, Sally tried to figure out what was wrong. Although she was pretty enough, she dressed a few years behind in style. Her blue pantsuit and crisp white shirt accented her bleached blond, shoulder-length hair, which was neatly curled under at the ends. She wore gold-framed glasses and tended to smile too much.

The odd woman acted giddy and childlike around Sheffield. It was hard to watch. Sally knew that many women found Sheffield Tassey attractive but it still upset her that this woman was openly flirting with him.

Sally looked at Walter and watched his response. He gave her a discomfited smile. She didn't return it; she couldn't. Discreetly, she shook her head in disgust and pointed at Tina. Walter gave Sally a hard stare and shook his head, a warning no doubt. But a warning about what?

The embarrassing display was too much so Sally stood hastily and left the room. Heading to the kitchen seemed like a safe option. A delicious aroma was wafting from there and she was curious as to what Lynne had made this time. The woman could cook up a storm. And her baking was heavenly. As she stepped through the door, the sight of Lynne stopped her cold.

The older woman was hunched over a counter, sniffling and wiping her eyes.

"Lynne? Are you okay?"

Lynne swung around, a wild look in her eyes at being discovered. She stuffed a tissue into her apron pocket and said, "I'm fine, dear." She tried to smile through her obvious misery and her clearly bloodshot eyes.

Sally couldn't remember seeing Lynne cry before. The woman showed no emotion at all, ever. It was like she was nonexistent, merely someone who lived here and served quietly. To Sally, Lynne was just an appendage of Sheffield Tassey. He was the one who received all the attention and had all the opinions. Sally didn't know what to do. The two of them hardly knew each other. But she stepped toward Lynne regardless. She did feel concern for the woman.

"You've been crying. Why?" Sally placed her hands on Lynne's plump shoulders.

Immediately Lynne lifted Sally's hands and roughly pushed them away. "I told you, I'm fine. Everything is perfectly and absolutely fine. I need to accept God's divine plan and purpose."

"His plan and purpose? I don't understand. I saw you crying. It's obvious you're not perfectly fine and you can tell me what this is about. I'll try to help you."

Lynne turned away and busied herself with dessert preparations, her tears and sorrow stuffed down.

"Please, Lynne, tell me what's going on."

Lynne turned angry eyes to her. "I don't need help and you'll have to ask Walter if you want some answers. He'll be able to tell you."

She already knew Walter would tell her nothing. "What does he need to tell me?"

Lynne turned away and Sally had to strain to catch her words. "Like I said, you'll have to get your answers from him because I can't say any more."

"Walter won't talk to me. He's keeping things from me and I need to know what's going on." She felt terrible for going behind his back but something felt horribly wrong here and she was dying to know.

With eyes full of compassion, Lynne turned back to her. The woman studied her for a few moments without saying a word.

It made Sally feel even more uneasy.

"I promise you this, Sally. It's better for you if you don't know right now. If Walter does tell you, you have to trust it will be the right time for you."

"I don't understand." The woman's guarded answer was infuriating. She should take Lynne by the shoulders and shake the answer out of her.

"You will." With that Lynne turned toward the cupboards, opened a door, took out five plates and set the table.

Sally let her eyes wander to the spread Lynne had prepared. A carrot cake, topped with cream cheese icing stood center on the table. If entered in a contest, Sally was sure Lynne's carrot cake would win. A plateful of peanut butter cookies and another plate of squares sat on either side of the cake. A fruit salad was at one end of the table with bowls and spoons beside it and at the other end a platter of crackers and cheeses.

Sally watched silently as Lynne opened the refrigerator to retrieve a cheesecake.

Wow! This is ridiculous. It looks like she's feeding the whole church. How much does she think we can eat?

It was no surprise that Mrs. Tassey struggled with extra weight. The array of sweets was enough to put a pile of pounds on anyone.

Sally exited the kitchen. She needed a break from the tight-lipped woman and the stuffy air around her. Near the entrance was Mr. Tassey's office, located directly opposite the foyer. It called to her and she entered. She couldn't for the life of her understand Lynne's need for secrecy and she certainly couldn't face the three in the living room right now. Taking a seat in Mr. Tassey's office armchair, she leaned back to rest her head. The mystery seemed to be getting thicker and her understanding of it thinner. This family had seemed fairly normal when she'd first met them. But lately something was going on that put everyone on edge and Sally wracked her mind to imagine what it could be.

A slender binder lay on the desk and with one quick glance toward the doorway; she reached over and flipped the cover over. The inside sheet read, "New Revelations from God."

Now wouldn't this be fascinating, to know what God is saying and be able to write it down!

One more glance at the doorway and she turned the page.

"I'll just take one peek," she whispered quietly. "Maybe this will shed some light on what's been going on around here. And it'll be cool to know God's word before everyone else in the church." Speaking out loud brought a strange sense of companionship, which had been sorely lacking in her life the past few months.

She read a few words but a sound at the door brought her head up. Sheffield's commanding frame filled the doorway and his gaze was stern. She snapped the cover shut and stood, embarrassment warming her cheeks.

"What are you doing in here?" He looked simultaneously surprised and angry. His eyebrows lowered in a grimace when she didn't answer immediately.

Rattled at his unexpected appearance, she replied, "I needed a quiet place for a while and I reasoned that a pastor's office would be the most peaceful place of all." She touched the high back of his chair and said, "This is a very comfortable chair and a very spacious room. It must be a joy to receive your directions from God in this wonderful place. This room has an air of authority and peace all mixed together." Rambling seemed the best way to diffuse the tense situation she'd created.

Mr. Tassey glared at her. "This is my room and I don't want anyone else in here! Do I make myself clear?"

She nodded submissively, feeling like a heel for invading his space. "I'm sorry, sir. I didn't realize my presence in this room would cause such a problem. Forgive me if I've overstepped my bounds."

Mr. Tassey waved her out. "After you."

As she passed him she could feel Sheffield's eyes bore into her but avoided eye contact. He closed the door firmly behind her and locked it. Voices from the kitchen drew her in that direction. Any direction was good as long as she got away from Sheffield's piercing gaze.

Entering, she saw Walter and Tina sitting at the table. Lynne was pouring coffee into mugs.

"Here, I'll help you." Sally took a coffee mug from Lynne's hand, which shook terribly as the cup exchanged hands. Some coffee spilled on Lynne's hand and she cried out in pain.

"Oh no! Let me get something for that." Sally set the cup down and rushed to the refrigerator and got a few pieces of ice. She grabbed a kitchen towel and wrapped the ice in it.

Lynne hadn't moved from her position by the coffee maker. She kept her back turned to the others in the room. From the corner of her eye, Sally could see Sheffield take his seat at the head of the table. She took Lynne's hand and placed the towel-covered ice on the burned area. Lynne's vacant, sad eyes turned to her in grateful thanks.

"It'll be okay. The burn doesn't look too bad. Why don't you take a seat and I'll serve the coffee?"

"I can't stay in this room," she whispered.

The desperation in her voice was odd. Lynne loved to serve. So why not now?

"Are you not feeling well?"

"No. I'm not feeling well at all." With that, Lynne rushed from the room, still holding the ice pack over her hand.

TIME AND HEALING

Mr. Tassey watched his wife leave the room. He turned his stern gaze toward Sally. "Where's she going?"

"She's not feeling well. I think she needed to lie down for a while."

The man suddenly went from pleasant dialogue with his guest to a silent fuming sulk. Walter took over the conversation, attempting to keep Tina engaged in light banter. Sally served the coffee and listened carefully for any more clues.

Tina was as giddy and irritating as ever. Sally couldn't wait to get away from her. The woman seemed oblivious to Mr. Tassey's mood and Sally was sure Tina was attempting to flirt with Walter now. It was completely bizarre.

A few hours later, Tina finally went to bed in a guestroom upstairs. It was such a relief to be rid of her.

Lynne never did make another appearance. Sheffield was in no mood to visit so Sally and Walter headed to their bedroom and the house fell silent.

This home had many guest rooms on the lower level and even a few on the second floor. It was far too big for two people and all the extra rooms seemed a waste. But Sheffield once said it was to help people in need or for visiting ministers. Sally couldn't remember any visiting ministers preaching at Mr. Tassey's church since she had attended there but perhaps they'd had them in the past.

Sally dropped into bed in exhaustion. It had been a long day, a complete roller coaster emotionally. Walter sat down wearily on the edge of the bed and bent over to place a light kiss on her lips. She wrapped her arms around his neck before he could pull away and kissed him again. He released her hold and lay down beside her. Silence stretched between them.

Sally finally asked, "What do you think of Tina? Do you know why she's here and what she meant about getting saved?"

"I don't want to discuss Tina."

"Do you know who she is or where she came from? Your father didn't go into a lot of detail and I was wondering if he confided in you." Maybe pressing the issue would give her some answers.

"No Sally! I don't know her! All I know is that she wants to get saved! That should be enough of an answer, don't you think?"

Curiosity made it impossible for her to let it rest. "Did you notice how Tina acted around your father?"

"No! I don't know what you're implying, but I'd rather we dropped this subject."

"Well, I noticed. It was enough to make any wife upset."

He turned his head and stared at her with a questioning look. "What do you mean by that?"

"Your mother was very upset this evening. She wasn't acting like herself at all. Do you know what was getting to her?"

"Why? What did she say?" He looked concerned.

"It wasn't so much what she said but how she acted."

"You mean, her not feeling well?"

"Well, that's part of it. She was crying earlier in the kitchen and she seemed extremely bothered about something."

"Did she tell you anything?"

"No. She refused to talk about it. Do you have any idea what it could be?"

Walter shook his head and stared at her for a few seconds. Suddenly he sat up and swung his legs out of bed. "I don't, but I believe I should find out." He headed to the door.

"Wait, Walter! I didn't tell you this for you to go and investigate."

He stopped and stared at her.

Sally continued, "I wanted us to discuss it. Don't go prodding your mother about it. Please!"

"My father needs to know."

His father! What? Why?

"Do you think Tina's presence here is what's bothering your mother?"

"I don't know." He opened the door and left.

"Walter, wait!" she shouted in frustration.

This was not the result she'd been looking for. Her quest for answers had only produced another bizarre response. Why was he acting so foolishly? Why would he interfere in his parents' lives like this or disclose what Sally thought she was telling him in confidence? Why was it so difficult for them to have a reasonable discussion without some outlandish response from him? She sat cross-legged and rubbed her scalp. She could feel a headache coming on.

The strange evening left her feeling numb and disoriented. All the secrets and odd behavior were unbearable. This family was twisted and she could make no sense of it. That she was now an intricate part of it made her groan audibly.

She knew their marriage needed open honesty for it to survive and she desperately hoped Walter would realize that before it was too late. This evening was only rapidly decreasing her desire to stay in it.

After twenty minutes, Walter still hadn't returned. She finally crawled beneath the covers and within minutes dozed off.

CHAPTER 20

The air was biting as Sally and Walter made their way to his parents' house after church from his parked car in the driveway. She'd worn her hair up today and placed a hand over her exposed neck for some protection from the bitter cold breeze as they made their way into the main entrance.

Sheffield Tassey's message this morning had been short and to the point and he'd seemed in a cheerful mood, a shift from his normally stern exterior and harsh, condemning word. He'd even resorted to joking occasionally with the congregation, which seemed to place everyone at ease. Toward the end of the service he'd introduced Tina to the congregation as the newest member of Tassey's Sanctuary and informed the people of her salvation. At the eruption of cheering and clapping, Tina had appeared flushed and almost embarrassed. Diverting the congregation's interest back to the business at hand, Sheffield had discussed the meetings and functions that were scheduled for the upcoming week.

Sally tried to remember the point of the message that her father-in-law had so carefully prepared but she had to admit her mind had been too preoccupied to pay much attention. She was keenly aware that over the past year very little scripture was ever read or quoted in his sermons. The lack of depth in his preaching was beginning to baffle her.

Although the man was an eloquent spokesman who was able to capture the attention of his congregation with lively stories or thunderous criticism and accusation, (usually followed by mass repentance), she usually felt beat up after a Sunday morning service. She wondered why this morning's address was different. Sheffield's good mood and his upbeat attitude were refreshing. Scripture reading would have been an added bonus. Something within her felt starved, hungry to hear what God had to say. Why did she feel that way? Shouldn't church service be enough? Why did she always feel so unsatisfied? To share her heart with Walter was out of the question. He'd never understand and was sure to defend his father to the death.

Sally removed her coat at the entrance of the Tassey home and placed it over the chair in the foyer. Sheffield was still at the church, talking to his members. Lynne had stayed home this morning, still sporting a headache and not feeling well.

Walter had insisted they leave right after church, eat out on their way home. He looked in a rush as he raced down the stairs to collect their suitcases. Sally stopped at the edge of the stairway, Lynne on her mind, and wondered how the woman was doing. Turning away from the stairs, she headed down the hall to find her mother-in-law.

At her in-laws' bedroom, she knocked softly. There was no answer so she knocked a little louder. Still no response.

"Lynne, are you there?" she asked.

After a short while a muted voice said, "Who is it?"

"It's Sally. Are you okay in there?"

"Yes, but I want to be left alone. Please go!"

"Walter told me you had a headache." She waited for a response. When none came she said, "We're leaving now. I wanted to say goodbye and check to see how you're feeling."

Lynne didn't appear immediately to say goodbye, which was odd, completely uncharacteristic. Silence echoed back and the door stayed shut.

"I'm doing fine," she finally said with muffled voice. "I can't talk right now. My head is hurting and I need to stay in bed. Please go and I'll see you soon." Her voice cracked and Sally was sure she heard a soft sob.

"Lynne, are you sure you're okay?" Suddenly pain shot up her arm and she turned to face Walter, his hand gripping her and his eyes dark with anger.

"What are you doing?" he demanded.

"I'm checking on your mother!" She glared disbelieving at his hand cinching her arm.

He released his vise-like grip and said, "It's time to go."

Rubbing her arm, she stared at him dumbstruck. "What is wrong with you?"

"I'm sorry, Sally, but we need to go."

"Without checking on your mom and saying goodbye?" She felt completely bewildered at the fear she saw in his eyes.

His jaw clenched in frustration or nervousness, she wasn't sure. "She'll be fine! She wants to be left alone! Didn't you hear her?"

"Yes! I heard her! But I don't understand what's happening. You're upset with me for no reason! Your mother won't even come out to say goodbye? I don't get it!"

Walter visibly reined in his emotions. "Look, I know my mother and when she's not feeling well, she doesn't like being bothered." He pointed down the hall to the front door. "Can we go?"

She couldn't let it drop. "But, she's never acted like this before. She's usually the epitome of hospitality. I really think there's something wrong with her, Walter. I'm not trying to be difficult! I'm very concerned about her!"

Exasperation flooded his eyes. "Listen, she's completely fine. You just don't know my mother well enough."

Maybe he was right. How well did she really know the woman? It's not like they were close or anything. They hardly conversed meaningfully. Lynne merged and harmonized into the woodwork, the plastered walls and the cabinetry of her kitchen. She was notorious for her anonymity.

"Come on, let's go!" His eyes pleaded with her and he reached for her hand and tugged. She pulled her hand free and headed to the front door on her own steam. He followed her.

After slipping into their coats, Walter picked up the suitcases he'd set in the entrance and she opened the door and held it for him. While he placed both suitcases in the trunk of his car, Sally walked over to her vehicle and slipped in behind the wheel.

They'd come in separate vehicles and she was grateful for the solitary ride back to the apartment. She'd suggested skipping eating out and waiting till they arrived home. Glancing over, she saw Walter getting into his car. He looked at her and gave a quick nod before starting his vehicle and pulling out of the driveway.

Following him down the road, her mind was a jumbled mess. He'd never been that forceful with her. Never had he manhandled her before and it infuriated her.

By the time they arrived back at their apartment, Sally couldn't wait to confront him. She waited till he carried the suitcases to their bedroom and returned. She stood behind the couch, her hands resting on the back. He sat down on the couch and picked up the remote without even looking at her. The TV came on and he scurried through the channels like he was in a race. It was surprising the button didn't wear out with his frantic search.

Okay, so that's how it's going to be!

Walking around the couch, she sat down beside him, leaving some distance between them.

"Walter," she started, keeping her voice calm, "we need to talk."

An exasperated sound escaped through his clenched teeth.

Sally swallowed and said, "Does your mother's condition have to do with that Tina lady being there last night?"

His anger was swift. He didn't look at her but his whole countenance and body stiffened and the atmosphere immediately became charged with his fury. "I told you to stop asking me about my mother! I want you to obey now!"

"Obey now?" she asked, incredulous.

His body shook slightly. "Please, stop!"

She did stop but she couldn't stop staring at him. Who was this man beside her? His behavior was steadily growing more deviant. In that moment the horrible truth finally penetrated – she was living with a stranger. The Walter she knew had somehow been abducted and switched into this deplorable version of him.

With his body quivering involuntarily, it was clear he was trying to rein in his frazzled, tense emotions. The TV screen flicked from one channel to the next with lightning speed. She finally headed to the bedroom. Cleaning out suitcases felt more appealing than staying in the same room with him.

The demons he was struggling with were itching to get out. If only she knew what she was dealing with. The future would require some courage from her but she didn't know if she could muster any. She swiped angrily at a tear that trickled down her cheek. Walter would not make her cry, not today!

~~~~~

June 1998

Melody's vegetable garden still needed plenty of work. Sally stood and brushed the dirt off of her knees as she viewed her progress so far. She didn't know if she had the energy to complete it all on her own. She needed to speed up if she ever hoped to get the seeds planted by the end of the day so she picked up the hoe once more and scratched out a shallow trench for another row.

Melody Windsor had experienced a mild stroke a month ago. There were only slight symptoms of the stroke, a limp in her right leg and her right hand wasn't as strong as it used to be. Her mind was still as sharp and strong as ever. Her desire for gardening also hadn't abated.

Since the doctor forbade her any strenuous work, she'd begged Sally to help. The garden was usually planted by the end of May. It was already early June and Melody was frantic to get it done. So here Sally was, digging in dirt, something she'd always hated. Groundhogs surely lived miserable lives.

Her father had been devastated at the initial news. Sally took time off of work to spend time with them, to be there for her father. It brought tangled feelings. To be the caregiver for her parents, a complete reversal of roles, felt unnatural.

Perhaps the news she had to share today would bring some common ground to their relationship. She hoped her parents would respond with the excitement she wished for. A wave of faintness hit her with the intensity of the noon sun beating from above and she felt suddenly parched. Letting the hoe drop, she headed to the deck, up the few stairs and through the patio doors into the kitchen.

The cool air of the house washed over her in refreshing relief. Air conditioning was one of the greatest inventions of the last century, of that she was sure. After pouring a tall glass of ice water, she entered the dining room and, with a relieved sigh, sat down. The cold water went down smooth and revived her. The sound of shuffling feet down the hall made her turn and look. Her father appeared around the corner.

"Oh hi, Dad! I thought you were sleeping."

"No, I was reading but I heard you come in so I came to see how the work is going."

"It's work and it's going! I needed a break though. It's heating up out there."

Mr. Windsor took a seat across from her. He always looked so sad lately. "It doesn't feel right."

"What doesn't feel right?"

"Melody not doing the garden."

"Hey, I bet by next year Mom will be back at it."

"I hope so. I'm worried about her."

Sally was tempted to ask him why he'd treated Melody so badly for most of their marriage if he needed her so desperately, but she resisted the urge. Studying her frail father, she didn't know whether to hate him or feel sorry for him. That he'd changed was clear. She never saw him with a drink any more and his breath never smelled of whiskey. His bad back and weak knees made him look wobbly at times but it wasn't due to being drunk anymore. To adjust to his calm and mellow attitude would take her some time. She was used to keeping up a guard around him, a wall of protection.

"Is Mom resting?"

"Yes. She's on the couch."

"Good! She needs to rest."

"Can I help you with the garden?"

"You help with gardening? You hate to garden."

"I could keep you company."

"Sure, if you want to."

The rest of the afternoon seemed to fly by and her father's company proved to be a needed asset. Vern mostly sat in a chair beneath a large maple tree and gave his opinion and encouragement. They chatted about trivial things and her father actually opened up more than she could ever remember. He revealed things about his life she'd never before cared to know. It was eye-opening and by the time the last seed was in the ground and the last flower planted, Sally's side ached from laughter. She'd never known him to be this much fun. Vern kept the jokes coming and the silly banter felt wonderful. It relieved the tension for both of them.

They headed to the deck together, her father pouring two glasses of ice water for them. They sat at the patio table, beneath the canopy and drank the cold liquid. A slight breeze cooled the perspiration dotted across her face and neck.

Sitting still made her realize how exhausted she really was. Every fiber of her body ached and groaned with the unfamiliar exertion. The day's work had been more taxing than she'd anticipated and she gratefully allowed her muscles to unwind. Silence surrounded them and it was an added balm.

The yard looked good; maybe not as good as if her mother had done at it, but it was fair enough. She'd accomplished a lot and it brought a wave of satisfaction. A butterfly floated gracefully toward her, flitting up and down and finally moving on to a flowering shrub. How carefree and peaceful it looked.

She was reminded of the tranquil state of her marriage. The memories of their anniversary debacle six months ago seemed faint. She only hoped this peaceful trend would continue. Not that he'd opened up any. Perhaps she'd reconciled the fact that he was a private person. She could understand that to some degree.

"Thank you for doing the garden, Sally."

She gave him a smile. "You're welcome. I actually enjoyed it. I'm totally exhausted, but it was rewarding."

"Melody's an amazing woman. I've often felt unworthy of her love and devotion." His eyes misted and the guilt on his face made Sally look away.

It was true that he was unworthy of her. He didn't deserve any of them. He'd been a lousy father. Sally couldn't look at him right now, concerned she'd say something she'd regret.

"I've done very little to deserve her love and yet she's stayed with me all these years. I'm a blessed man, Sally."

She looked at him then. "No. She's a stupid woman. She has a complete martyr mindset."

It made him laugh and lightened the mood. And it didn't stop him from talking like Sally had hoped.

"Your mother always believed in me even when I had given up on myself. I owe your mother my very life. I wish there was some way I could repay her."

"You already have, my dear husband."

Sally and Vern both turned at the familiar voice. Melody stood at the patio door looking out. She slid the screen door open and walked toward them. Vern stood and pulled out a chair for her and helped as she slowly lowered herself into the seat.

After she had settled into the chair comfortably, she gazed at her husband with a satisfied smile. "My dear Vern, I believe you know where I got the courage and my faith to stay with you."

Vern pointed a finger up at the clear blue sky in response. "The guy upstairs?"

"He's my Heavenly Father and without him I'd have become a basket case."

"It was that bad?"

"We went through a lot of difficult years but they are nothing for a great God to handle. He can turn any person around and head them in a new direction. I kept holding onto that hope all through the years. And look at you, Vern! You've changed right before my eyes and how I thank God for that!"

"So you're not ashamed to call me your husband anymore?"

She gazed at him lovingly. "I've never been ashamed to call you my husband! I was disappointed in you for many years but I never stopped loving you."

"I thank my lucky stars for that!" He chuckled to release some of the strain.

Never had Sally heard such honesty from her father before.

"I believe it's God you need to thank and not lucky stars." Melody looked youthful and flirtatious while bating her husband. She still looked amazingly good for her age, even with the stroke.

"Yeah, that's what I meant."

"Thanks, Sally, for doing my garden and all the flowers. Everything looks so beautiful! I don't know how to thank you enough."

Sally shrugged. "It was no big deal. I actually enjoyed it and I had an opportunity to spend some time with Dad."

With a quizzical look, Melody said, "You enjoyed it? We're talking gardening here, right?"

Sally chuckled. "It's true. It always looked boring and monotonous but I actually liked digging in the dirt."

Her parents' laughter sounded light and bubbly. To be here, seeing them in love and at peace, laughing with her, brought a tinge of regret. She couldn't remember a single time they'd ever done this before. Her parents had always lived separate lives; they'd never been a team, together, supporting, listening to their kids.

"I have news." said Sally, suddenly.

Melody looked at her curiously and Vern glanced at her sideways but his expression remained relaxed.

"Walter and I are expecting a baby."

Melody stared in stunned silence, while Vern let out a walloping howl.

"I've been waiting years to be a grandfather and my Sally will be the one to do it. I always thought Robert would have one first but you beat him to it!" He turned to Melody. "What do you think of this? This is what you've always wanted, a little one running around again. Won't it be wonderful?" Vern reached for her hand across the table and she took his willingly.

Melody smiled in pleasure but there was also concern in her eyes. "I'm thrilled that I'll finally be a grandmother. I've been waiting for this many years."

It's what she didn't say that bothered Sally. "But…" She could feel her guard going up.

"But what?" Melody retorted.

"What is it you're not saying?"

Melody took a deep breath and released it slowly. "You know."

"No I don't. I have no clue what you're thinking."

"You must have some idea if you suspected something."

Sally shrugged. It was simply commonplace to have her mother disapprove of her life.

Melody said, "I have some concern about the stability of your marriage, Sally, but if this is what you want then I'll support you."

"You don't have to worry about our marriage. We're doing great. We've both settled into married life."

Melody leaned forward. "Sally, you've often looked so sad and unhappy the last few months. I'm only saying that I have some concerns."

"Mom, we're happy! Walter is thrilled about the baby and I believe he'll make a terrific father. Please, for once just be happy for me."

"I want to be. When will the baby be born?"

Sally was grateful for the shift in conversation. "My due date is December 10th."

"A Christmas baby!" Vern said.

"It'll be the best Christmas present I've ever received. I can't tell you how excited I am about this pregnancy." Sally rubbed her abdomen.

Melody made a sound deep in her throat. "Oh no! You did all that gardening work and we didn't know you were pregnant! You should have told us! I feel so awful! What if you overstrained yourself?"

"Mother, I'm fine! I work hard all the time. I'm a little tired but I just need to rest."

"Why don't you stay here for the night?" offered Vern. "We have the quest room and I don't want you driving back to Toronto after all that gardening."

Their concern was way over the top. "Thanks for the offer but I want to get back to Walter."

Melody said, "Why don't you call Walter and ask him to swing by? He's welcome to stay overnight too. That way we could spend time with the both of you. We hardly ever see him."

Sally found it hard to come up with any good excuses. "All right, I'll call him but I can't imagine him wanting to drive out this time of night." She glanced at her watch. "It's seven o'clock? I didn't know it was that late!"

"Go on, call him," said Vern, turning to Melody and winking.

They were scheming together! Sally shook her head in wonder and went inside to make the call.

When she returned, both her parents stared at her in anticipation.

"So, what did he say?" asked Melody.

"He's coming. He has a meeting tonight, here in Markham, which we both forgot about. He'll drop my luggage here, go to his meeting and then be back later to spend the night. Is that okay?"

Vern said, "That's wonderful! You'll be able to rest and that's the main thing. Spending time with Walter tonight would have been a bonus but maybe there'll be time tomorrow."

"Tomorrow is Sunday and Walter and I will be at church."

"Your mother and I will be at church too but why don't you come back and join us for lunch?"

It would be a nice break from dining with the Tasseys. She couldn't help smile as she stared at her father. "Are you offering to cook?"

"I can make a mean meat loaf!"

"Meat loaf? I hate meat loaf!"

"Well then, I'm also pretty good at barbequed pork chops."

"Okay, pork chops will do. Walter and I will pick up some dessert and bread."

"Then it's planned. Perfect!" Vern rubbed his hands together as if in triumph.

Sally stood and headed inside. She was ready for a shower and a rest as well. The churning of her empty stomach would need some attention first. There's no way she could rest with it growling in protest.

CHAPTER 21

March 2004

Tessa scanned over her weekly planner, checking the schedule for the day. A glance out the window revealed the snowfall hadn't let up yet. A deluge of white, large flakes filled the air and the snow was steadily rising in drifts from the bulging clouds and wind. It was early March and winter still hung on with icy fingers.

How she longed for spring. The baby was due in August, which meant she'd have to brave the heat during the last months of her pregnancy. But even that didn't smother her desire for summer to come soon.

She rubbed her small baby bump. Curiosity was a funny thing. To know the sex of her child felt overwhelming at times. Whom would the child resemble? And what about the personality of the child?

She often felt impatient lately. Organized, practical and rational were terms she'd usually use to describe herself. Now those terms didn't fit. This baby hidden inside, this gift from heaven, was always on her mind. Now she needed to jot down every meeting and appointment right away or else she'd forget. It was like she had some strange baby fever and nothing else seemed to matter. But yes, other things did matter, a lot!

Grabbing her weekly planner, she double-checked to be sure. A young girl was scheduled to arrive within the hour. Tessa needed to prepare a new file folder and print off the forms she'd require for the interview.

Tessa's office had moved to another room. Their new receptionist, Leona Hilt, now occupied her old office. Leona worked part-time so Tessa still spent some time helping out with the receptionist position.

Her new office was located at the back of the mansion, in the former sitting room, which looked out on the vast back yard. She could see the gazebo from here, the snow-covered walkway leading to it and large trees covering the stone-fenced yard. The gazebo was surrounded by shrubs, new snow covering everything with a crisp whiteness.

The office she now occupied was much too large for its purpose but she did enjoy the rich feel to the place and the spectacular view. Windows graced three sides, allowing a visual feast of the yard, making it feel more like a sunroom than an office. Two chandeliers hung from the high ceiling, beautiful artwork graced the walls, well-defined upholstered chairs gave the room a comfortable feel and potted plants maintained the sunroom quality. Although she loved the opulence of the space, she did feel guilty for having one of the nicest rooms as her office.

She turned to her keyboard and punched in a few notes from the interview from the day before. Then she prayed for wisdom for her next appointment.

"Hey there, preggy!"

Tessa looked up in surprise to see Richelle standing in the doorway and said, "I didn't know you were working today!"

"Some of the women asked if I'd come in today because, as you know, my due date is tomorrow. I thought I'd finish up some loose ends before I take my leave." She sauntered into the room and gratefully lowered her large but attractive frame into a chair across from Tessa.

"Richelle, do you know how beautiful you look?"

"Don't flatter me! I'm huge and ugly and I waddle when I walk! I can't wait till this baby comes!"

"I'm serious, Richelle! You look amazing! You've looked gorgeous through your whole pregnancy! I only hope I'll look as good at nine months."

"Honestly, when you get this big..." Richelle pointed to her ballooned abdomen, "you won't feel one bit attractive. I can assure you of that! I feel awkward, clumsy and like the Goodyear blimp."

"Well, I still say you look gorgeous and that's that."

Her eyebrows rose quizzically. "You obviously haven't heard Luke's opinion."

Tessa nodded. "I've heard it. He's just trying to get a rise out of you." She smiled and then asked, "How's Charlie handling your big tummy?"

Her eyes grew round with wonder and she raised her hands in incredulity. "It's a complete shock! He loves it! He talks to the baby all the time and rubs my tummy anytime he has a chance. He can't wait till the baby comes and is so encouraging with constant compliments. I don't believe him, though."

"Why not?"

"He's my husband. I'm his wife."

"From the way he looks at you, I know he means it!"

"Do you really think so?"

"I know so!"

Richelle waved her hand and said, "Well, that's enough about me. How are you doing?"

"I'm feeling pretty good. My emotions are a little out of whack but I'm doing well."

"And how's your new job?"

"I'm a little nervous but I'm sure I'll adjust to it and hopefully be able to manage on my own without yelping for help all the time. I'm sure Deborah is getting tired of leaving her busy schedule to help me."

"Well, once you're more confident it should take some of the workload off of Deborah and Patricia. I'm sure that's what they're hoping for."

Tessa nodded. She was sure it was true. It would just take time. A change of subject would be good. "Have you had any contractions yet?"

Richelle shook her head uncertainly. "I feel different lately. My tummy has dropped some and I think I've been having Braxton Hicks for a few weeks now. I feel sorry for Charlie! I've been so miserable lately and I take it out on him. He doesn't know what he's doing wrong. His hurt puppy dog face makes me feel like a terrible wench! I don't mean to be cruel but I can't help myself. I'm never in the mood for you know what and Charlie has been out of sorts lately."

"So, this is what I have to look forward to?"

"Oh, don't let it bother you," Richelle said with a flamboyant wave of her hand. "I know I'm almost through this so there's definitely an end in sight. You might breeze right through with no drama at all. You're more level-headed than I am."

With her emotions so on edge lately, Tessa wasn't so sure. "Here's for wishing, right?"

"Anyway, I don't want to hold you up. I have to get back to the beauty salon and get my work done." Richelle stood slowly, gripping the armrests of the chair to support her weight. She waddled out of the room, turned with a small wave and closed the door behind her.

Tessa had to admit that Richelle's once sexy swing of her hips had been replaced by a duck's waddle. Richelle had mentioned more than once lately that she no longer received the attention she once did and freely admitted that she missed it.

Luke had let go of his pet name for Richelle. Barbie Doll had changed to Barney for a time but lately his favorite name for her was Daffy Duck. Richelle had been furious but Luke had only reveled in the charged response it brought. Tessa felt sorry for Richelle.

At least they didn't need as much refereeing as they once did and Tessa was grateful to let go of that position. It was a sign that perhaps her friends had matured a slight degree.

Tessa placed the new file folder on her desk and began to print off the forms that she would need for the coming interview. A light knock on her door brought her head around. The door swung open and Deborah Elliot poked her head inside.

"I don't need help yet, do I?"

Deb walked in and closed the door behind her. "No, dear, and hopefully you won't have to." She sat down in the chair Richelle had just vacated. "I just need to inform you about this girl that's coming. Her mother called after hours last night and explained a few things to me. I thought you should know before she arrives."

"Okay."

Linking her fingers together in her lap, Deb said, "Bridget Howard's mother informed me that Bridget tried to commit suicide a few days ago."

"No!"

"She overdosed on pain medication and her mother rushed her to the emergency room to have her stomach pumped. She survived but she's still in a sensitive state of mind."

"Wouldn't that make the fifth time she's tried it?"

Deborah nodded, her face pinched with concern. "We've had similar cases to hers before but we've been able to help them. I want to encourage you that there's no case too hard for God. Try to convey this hope to Bridget in any form you can think of. She won't have much optimism when she comes. Try to instill a strong confirmation that she's not doomed to failure. If she can be encouraged to find any hope at all, her recovery will be faster because she will choose to become proactive in her treatment."

"I understand. I don't exactly know what words need to be said but I'll be praying for wisdom."

"All right, I'll leave and let you get your stuff done. Call if you need anything." Deborah stood.

Tessa nodded. "Thanks, Deborah!"

Deb smiled, turned and left the room.

Within half an hour Tessa had all her paperwork in order. She had a few minutes left so hurried to the staff lounge to prepare a cup of hot tea. With mug in hand she entered the foyer and noticed two ladies seated in the waiting area, mother and daughter. The young girl looked on edge, her eyes downcast and her hands moving in nervous tension. The mother caught Tessa's eye with a pleading, desperate look.

Tessa walked toward them and smiled. "Hello. Could I have your names, please?"

The older woman spoke. "I'm Louise Howard and this is my daughter, Bridget."

With a nod, Tessa said, "I've been expecting you. Won't you follow me to my office?"

Tessa led the way. Louise Howard took her daughter by the arm and guided her to stand. Bridget pulled away angrily and followed. Louise gave Tessa an apologetic smile as she entered the office. Tessa waited by the door as Bridget, with slow and defiant steps, followed her mother.

Bridget looked a few years older than what the report had listed. According to the file, she was only sixteen and yet her lifestyle had obviously robbed her of some of her youth. She had deep circles beneath her eyes and sunken cheeks, which made her face look hollow. She appeared but a wisp of a thing.

Tessa's heart broke for the girl. It was always a shock to see firsthand what a destructive addiction could accomplish in someone so young. The many suicide attempts had only added to the mix. Tessa shut the door and took her seat behind her desk.

Opening her carefully-organized file, she prepared to ask the many questions necessary and explain the procedures and requirements of this home. She gave Louise an encouraging smile. Bridget still refused to make eye contact and stubbornly studied the floor. After a quick heart-prayer to her Heavenly Father, Tessa turned her attention toward Louise to begin.

"My name is Tessa Fields and I'll ask some questions, go over some procedures and do a basic interview. I'll not make a final decision on the exact program that will be right for Bridget but I will have a big influence on that decision. I want to assure you that we want to work with you, as opposed to working independently of you, in reaching complete freedom for Bridget. I also want to let you know that we have seen cases like Bridget's before and know that recovery is completely possible and continued freedom from substance abuse is also absolutely doable."

A look of relief passed through Louise's eyes and she nodded.

"I want to make it clear right from the outset that this home is Christian-based and we do implement Christian principles and teachings. The Bible is our main textbook in bringing freedom to the women who come to us and we believe that is why we have experienced so much success. If you are opposed to our methods, please tell us immediately so that we can find a home that is more suited to your needs." Tessa waited a few moments for any objection.

Louise nodded in approval.

"How did you come to hear about Mansion of Hope?"

Louise cleared her throat. "Well, I have a nephew who has been through a similar program at the Manor of Peace. I called them and asked them if there was any home like that for girls and they directed me here."

"What was your nephew's experience at the Manor of Peace?"

"Well, Neal was addicted to cocaine and it was slowly killing him. He was eighteen when he finally agreed to go for help. He knew he was destroying himself and was desperate to live a normal life. After nine months of treatment, he was a completely different person. It's been two years now and he is still doing well." Louise looked at her daughter then back to Tessa. Her eyes misted. "I want those same results for my daughter."

Tessa nodded. "I can assure you that our staff is of the highest caliber and they're here because they want to see women set free of addictions. Our goal is to place each client back into normal life situations but with the tools they need to resist the temptation of returning to old habits. We also supply our residents with training for developing coping skills. We believe very strongly that without God in the picture, there would be very little hope of permanent recovery. Our premise is that with God all things are possible and He cares more about these women's freedom than what we ever could. And we care a lot!" Tessa smiled.

Louise looked somewhat nervous but nodded again.

"I want to ask you another question and our decision to admit your daughter is not hinged on your answer. This is something we ask all of our applicants and helps us to help them. What is your religion?"

Louise said, "We're non-religious. My husband was raised Catholic but doesn't practice. I wasn't raised with any religion and hence, our daughter has no beliefs. I do want you to know that if this program works for my daughter and if God will set her free from this evil thing then I would be willing to give him a try. Nothing else has worked so far. Honestly, I'm skeptical of your methods but if you say they work then I'm willing to give it a go. I mean, it worked for Neal so maybe it will work for Bridget too."

"Well, Louise, even though you don't feel you have a lot of faith, God still hears everyone's cries for help." Tessa scribbled down the answers before continuing.

"Bridget is sixteen, is that correct?"

"Yes. She'll be seventeen in two months."

"Was she willing to come with you to this interview?"

Louise Howard glanced at her daughter for any sign of response. She turned back to Tessa and said, "Not exactly, but she knows she needs help. She knows she's killing herself with the drugs and there are also the suicide attempts. She needs help desperately!"

"Where is her father?"

"He had to work today."

"Do Bridget and her father get along?"

Louise looked uncomfortable. "Not exactly."

"Could you elaborate on that, please?"

With a pained expression, she said, "They fight a lot."

A choked grunt came from Bridget's mouth.

"They've never seen eye to eye and there's always been a wedge in their relationship. It's better if I'm here with her."

Tessa studied Bridget's response. Her eyes drifted from the floor to the expansive windows, where the snow was still falling heavily.

"Has there been any abuse that you are aware of?" Tessa aimed the question at Louise Howard.

Anger flashed in Louise's eyes. "Yes! We're here because of the drug abuse!"

It was a typically defensive response. Tessa had seen it before and yet she knew she had to plow on. "That's not what I'm referring to. Has Bridget's father ever abused her physically or sexually?"

"I don't see how that's any of your business. You're hardly any older than Bridget and you're asking us all these personal questions that have nothing to do with her situation."

"I'm sorry that this is difficult for you, Louise, but this line of questioning has a lot to do with the predicament Bridget is in. Something has triggered her desire to escape reality. Drug use is one way of escaping the difficult circumstances of one's life and finding some solace in the 'high' that drugs can give. We try to determine through this interview what the root cause has been so that we are able to help your daughter experience complete freedom. Your cooperation is vitally important in this process. This initial interview is one of the most difficult things to overcome. No one wants to admit to problems in their homes but it is the first step in overcoming the cause of substance abuse."

Louise still looked angry and immovable after Tessa's carefully worded explanation. Tessa didn't know if she'd have to ask for Deborah's help once again. She often felt stuck when people refused to respond to the questions on the form she was supposed to follow.

"Why don't we move onto another question and we can always come back to that one later."

"My dad loves to beat on me. He thinks I'm a punching bag." The voice was quiet, almost indiscernible but flowed with bitterness. Bridget slowly turned her face from the window and locked her tortured eyes on Tessa. "My dad hates me and he always has."

"Bridget, stop this. That's not true and you know it. Your father loves you a great deal."

With icy eyes, Bridget said, "Is that why he never came to see me in the hospital? And is that why he's not here today? Is that why he hits me every time I make a wrong move? Because he loves me so much?"

"I don't know." Louise looked dejected, angry and frustrated that the secret was out. She glanced from Tessa to her daughter and back again, not sure of what to say. With an indignant gaze, she said, "So, now you know our family problems. What will that help?"

The gravity of their hurt filled the space of her office. Silence hung in the air and Tessa waited a few moments to continue. "It helps the staff here a great deal to know the root of the problem. It would do very little good to chop away at the branches of the tree if the root is never dealt with. If the root issue is left covered and hidden, the branches and fruit will grow back and you'll be left with the same situation to deal with over and over again. I promise you that the more willing you are to uncover details and work with us, the greater chance Bridget will have of getting and staying free of substance abuse. It will also help the staff assist Bridget to overcome her desire to kill herself."

"Life isn't worth living anymore," Bridget mumbled.

Tessa sucked in a tight breath of air. The girl's lack of optimism was glaring but her honesty was commendable. "There's always something worth living for, Bridget. God will give you a reason to live," she said softly.

The girl's sunken eyes stared at Tessa sullenly but she remained quiet.

Tessa turned her attention to Louise once more. "How is your relationship with your husband?" She scanned her notes for his name. "His name is Roger; is that correct?"

Louise nodded. The firm set of her jaw showed her resistance but her features then softened and she released a deep breath. She said, "Bridget will end up telling you about it anyway so I may as well tell you. We've never been a very happily married couple."

A cynical grunt escaped Bridget's lips as she kept busily studying the floor.

Louise ignored her and said, "We fight a lot and I don't like the way Roger treats Bridget so I nag him about that all the time. We've never agreed on how to discipline our children so that has caused a lot of fights. Roger has a mean streak which he's taken out on me as well. I've learned to stick up for myself, though, so he doesn't bother with me much any more."

"What about the black and blue arm you had last month, Mom?" Bridget asked without looking up.

Louise scowled at her daughter. "I fell on the steps! My arm bruised from the fall!"

"I don't believe it," she said, her eyes glued to the tiles below her feet.

"Bridget thinks she knows everything about me but she doesn't."

Tessa nodded. "Children have a tendency of coming to their own conclusions, based on how they view their world. If their window on the world is negative, they'll view every situation through that colored glass."

Bridget looked up with disdain.

Tessa decided it was time to move on to less intrusive questions. Bridget was stiff and slow with her answers at first but the interview began to run more smoothly.

How long had she used cocaine? Five years. Where did she get the cocaine? A supplier at school provided everything she needed and more. Why had she started in the first place? Her friends had told her it would make her feel good and she needed something – anything to make her feel good. Did she realize how addicting and dangerous it was? No. Her parents threatened to beat the "you know what out of her" if she ever tried it. Her dad beat her all the time anyway so why shouldn't she? Did it help her cope with what was going on at home? Yes. How much cocaine did she need each week?

With that question, Bridget's eyes hardened and she said, "I don't know. I need some right now." She jumped up and turned to her mother. "Can we go? I need to get out of here."

Tessa needed to stop her. "Not quite yet. I have just a few more things to go over."

Louise turned pleading eyes to her daughter. "Please, just a few more minutes.

Bridget looked to Tessa to verify this.

Tessa nodded. "It won't take long."

Bridget grudgingly sat back down.

Tessa reviewed their policies and procedures as quickly as she could. As the interview ended, Tessa gave Louise her card. "We'll call within twenty-four hours to let you know our recommendation and availability at the home." She then held out a hand to Louise.

Louise shook Tessa's hand. "Thank you."

Bridget was already standing at the door, her hand on the knob, ready to bolt.

"It's been wonderful to meet the two of you and we look forward to what we know God will do in Bridget's life."

Louise looked uncertain. "I hope you can help her somehow."

Her hesitation would change in time. It always did.

The two left and Tessa's office fell silent. She didn't know if she'd ever adjust to the heartbreaking stories she heard here in this room. She closed her eyes and sent up a prayer for Bridget and her family. Bridget wasn't the only one who needed help and counseling. The whole family was dysfunctional and needed a great deal of direction and healing. But Tessa had seen so many helped through this home. The path toward freedom was rough, yes, but she was fully convinced that Bridget could receive complete deliverance.

Tessa transferred the information from her paper file into her computer, checked her schedule for the afternoon, grabbed her lunch and headed for the staff room. She decided to peek into the salon before having her lunch. Richelle was cutting Lily's hair as she walked through the door.

"Hi Richelle. Hi Lily." Tessa sat down in a chair by the door. She turned to Lily and asked, "I hear that you're about to leave us. Is that true?"

Her faced beamed. "Yes! I'm about done. This has been like home to me the past eight months. I can't believe it's taken me this long."

"You haven't been full-time the past few months, though, have you?"

"No. I've been coming in a day a week for a while and doing the evening sessions. I really believe that I can stay free now. I'm back at work and staying away from my old friends. Veronica and I became good friends here at the home and we stay in touch. She seems so strong and is a real encouragement to me."

"I'm so happy for you. You look wonderful!"

"With my hair wet and all over the place?"

"Yes, even with that. I see hope and anticipation in your eyes. That's always the giveaway. It's sure a change from when you first came here."

"I was a mess, wasn't I?"

"Things have a way of transitioning around here. You come in one way and you leave different."

"You two! I hate to break up this 'happy talk' but I think I'm transitioning too!" Richelle looked shocked as she pointed down to the floor. A puddle on the tile was growing under her feet and her inner pant legs were soaked.

"What?" gasped Lily.

Tessa knew immediately. "Your water broke!"

CHAPTER 22

Richelle looked terrified. "Ahh...! Well I certainly didn't pee my pants, I promise!"

"You're going to have your baby right here?" cried Lily in panic.

"No, I don't want to have it here! What do I do?" Richelle made a startling sight, holding a comb in one hand and scissors in the other, her arms raised, water beneath her and shock filling her eyes.

Tessa said the first thing that came to mind. "Ah... I can take you to the hospital."

"But I'm not done Lily's haircut," Richelle insisted.

If the situation wasn't so serious, Tessa would have laughed at the absurdity. "You want to finish the haircut in your condition? I'm sure Lily understands the situation."

"I can get my hair done somewhere else. This baby is coming, haircut or not."

"I'm sorry, Lily!" Richelle looked beside herself. "Here, let me just get your ends a little more even. I hate sending you off with a crooked style." She stepped up to Lily and resumed the cut, water sloshing beneath her.

Tessa couldn't believe her eyes. "Richelle, what are you doing? What if your baby comes fast? You need to get to the hospital!"

Richelle turned to face her. "Please call Charlie and tell him to come pick me up. By the time he gets here, I'll be done."

Tessa had to protest. "I think this is stupid! What if..."

Richelle cut her off. "Just do it! This is what I want."

"Okay, I'll call him."

"Yes!" Richelle didn't even look up, so focused was she on getting the cut done.

Tessa ran from the room, shaking her head at her friend's obsessive ways. That girl would not let anyone out of her chair looking anything short of perfect. Tessa had left her cell phone sitting on her desk. She grabbed it and punched in Charlie's number. He didn't answer. She tried three more times. Then she called the Manor of Peace. He wasn't there either. She rushed back to the salon to talk some sense into Richelle.

Lily was looking increasingly nervous, while Richelle floated around her, her feet mixing water and slips of hair into a brown goop on the floor.

The sight stopped Tessa cold. When Richelle looked up, Tessa blurted out, "Charlie's not at the Manor of Peace. They told me he went out to buy some supplies for the office and he didn't take his cell. I told them it's an emergency and to have him call my cell as soon as he gets in. Richelle, come with me. You have to go to the hospital right now! It's serious when your water breaks.!"

Richelle didn't stop snipping at Lily's hair as she listened. "I'm not done. First let me finish."

"Richelle!"

She looked up with a condescending look. "This is my first baby. It won't come that fast." Turning back, she made one last cut and laid the scissors down. Her feet made sloshing sounds with every move she made. Picking up the blow dryer, she started to dry Lily's hair.

I don't believe this! She's going to dry Lily's hair too! She could slip on that water and then what? I have to say something to snap her out of her moronic state!

"Are you having contractions?"

"No."

Frustration gnawed at Tessa. Richelle could be so incredibly stubborn. There was nothing else to do but wait until Lily looked runway-model ready. Tessa sat down by the door, crossed her legs and swung one nervously.

Ten minutes later the dryer stopped, Richelle placed it back in its holder and picked up the iron.

Tessa had had as much as she could take. "Okay already! Enough is enough."

Richelle glared at her. "I'm not done."

Lily squirmed uncomfortably in the chair. She looked ready to bolt. "Really, you don't have to style my hair. I can do it myself."

Tessa waved to Lily. "See, Richelle! You don't have to do this!"

The stubborn mule simply ignored the advice and continued swiping the hot iron through her slight waves. Lily looked like a trapped mouse.

It took all the patience Tessa possessed to calm down and wait.

Five minutes later Richelle finally put the iron down and announced, "I'm done."

Lily bolted out of the chair like a prisoner set free. She pulled the cape off and threw it on the hydraulic chair.

"I got it done," Richelle announced in triumph.

Lily glanced into the mirror. "It's very nice. Thank you."

"No problem." And with that Richelle suddenly doubled over and cried out, "Ohhh!"

Tessa jumped up and ran to her side. "Are you okay?"

She slowly straightened. "I think that was a contraction, but boy was it ever intense! I think we better rush to the hospital now."

"I told you we should have gone right away!"

"Ohhh!" Another contraction hit and Richelle folded in half again.

Tessa grabbed Richelle's coat and draped it over her shoulders, wrapped a hand around her arm and helped her down the hall. Lily took hold of Richelle's other arm as they made their way to the back entrance and out to the parking lot. A few hard contractions racked her frame during their short walk.

Tessa was about to unlock her car door but Richelle stopped her.

"I'm not going to make it to the hospital. It feels like this baby is ready to come very soon." She stopped to catch her breath. "Take me back inside and call 911."

Tessa almost shrieked, "Richelle! You're not serious, are you?"

"Please, Tessa, take me back inside!" Richelle's breathing sounded labored.

Richelle wasn't kidding. This was actually happening. They turned Richelle around and helped her back into the building and settled her into the staff room. It seemed the only logical place to have a baby.

What am I thinking? Richelle can't have her baby here! This is outrageous! I have to get a hold of Charlie. But first I have to take care of Richelle.

After settling Richelle into a chair, Tessa turned to Lily and spoke rapidly, "Please go find a rollaway bed somewhere. Ask for Deborah and she'll help you. Also, get some towels or linens or something."

Lily ran from the room and Tessa grabbed her cell phone to make the 911 call. She explained the situation and gave them the address. She barely clicked her phone off, when it began to ring. Charlie's number flashed on the screen. Flicking her phone open again, she answered.

He sounded frantic. "Tessa, what's happening? They told me it was an emergency!"

"Richelle's water broke and she went into a fast and hard labor soon after. I was going to take her to the hospital but she said she'd never make it. She's here at Mansion of Hope and an ambulance is on its way. You need to get down here as fast as you can." Charlie yelled something before she even finished and clicked his phone off. He was on his way.

Richelle's face scrunched in unfamiliar pain. Tessa went over to her, lowered to her haunches and took Richelle's hand. She didn't know what else to do. She heard footsteps hurrying down the hall and looked at the door. It opened and Lily and Deborah wheeled in the rollaway bed. There were towels and linens stacked on top and a big metal bowl rested beside them. At least they were prepared for the worst. Lily grabbed the linens and bowl and placed them on the counter beside the sink while Deborah and Tessa opened the bed. Soon Richelle was lying flat on her back but not happy about it.

"I hurt so bad! I can't stand this position! Ohhh...!" That's all she could say as her body convulsed under a contraction.

Deborah grabbed a stack of towels and placed them beneath Richelle's head and shoulders to elevate her and give her some back support.

With a look of astonishment, Deborah said, "It's quite the situation we find ourselves in, isn't it?"

"You can say that again."

Deb shook her head. "I know how to deal with addictions but I've never delivered a baby. Richelle, you just have to wait until a doctor gets here, okay?"

Richelle panted frantically, trying to control the pain. As the contraction subsided she spoke with a scared voice. "I can't promise. This baby wants to come now!"

"Now?" Tessa felt fear pounding against her ribs and make its way to her throat. She almost gagged and swallowed hard.

"Yes!" Richelle looked over at Lily. "Lily, I hate to say this, but could you leave the room? This is embarrassing enough without my salon customer seeing me like this."

Lily nodded graciously, promised to pray and gratefully fled the room.

"Lily, wait!" said Tessa. "Would you stand guard outside the door and make sure we don't have any unwelcome intruders?"

"Okay!"

"Oh, and please direct the ambulance workers our way when they arrive," added Deb.

"Yes, I'll do that."

Deborah and Tessa prepared things the best they knew how. They didn't know much. Tessa only hoped the ambulance would make it in time.

"Tessa, come here!" Richelle's forehead was beaded with perspiration and her eyes told the rest. She was afraid.

Taking Richelle's hand, she squeezed and asked, "What?"

"Stay with me, okay?"

"You mean till the ambulance guys get here?"

"No. I mean till the baby is born."

Tessa didn't know if she could endure watching her friend go through the whole ordeal. Seeing her fear now was unnerving. Besides, it would be too vivid of a memory for when she herself would give birth. "I don't know, Richelle. Charlie will be here soon and he'll be with you."

"I want you here too. Promise me! Don't leave me!"

Although she felt conflicted and uncertain, she couldn't say no, not to Richelle. They were best friends. If her presence would make the ordeal easier, she was willing to do it.

"All right, I'll stay."

"Pray for me," Richelle commanded as another contraction wracked her frame.

Tessa watched her friend and prayed. "Dear Father, give Richelle the strength she needs to deliver her baby and I ask that you'd bring this baby out easily and as pain-free as possible. I ask that your peace would rest on her right now and command all fear to go. I also ask that the ambulance and Charlie will get here in time, in Jesus's name, amen." She gave Richelle's hand another squeeze as the contraction subsided.

Tessa grabbed a towel and wiped the moisture off her friend's forehead.

Richelle turned pain-filled eyes to her and smiled. "This is really happening."

Tessa returned the smile. "It sure is."

"I was going to have an epidural and everything. This is not going as planned."

"It'll be okay."

Richelle didn't look so sure.

Tessa glanced over at Deborah, who was filling the sink with water. Deb was a take-charge person and her leadership skills were a tremendous blessing at this moment. Deb then filled the large metal bowl with water too. She proceeded to prepare a small table against the wall as a makeshift basinet for the soon-to-arrive baby. Relief flooded Tessa that Deb was here.

A loud knock on the door made them both turn around.

Charlie poked his head in, stepped inside, closed the door and hurried to Richelle.

Anger was Richelle's first response. "Look what you've done to me!" She punched Charlie soundly on the arm. He seemed to take it in stride.

Tessa was surprised Richelle had the strength to do it.

"I know, sweetheart! It'll be over soon and we'll have our baby in our arms."

"That's easy for you to say! You're not the one lying on this bed!"

"How are you doing, gorgeous?"

"How do you think I'm doing? I'm in agony and there's no doctor in sight!"

Charlie looked up at Tessa on the other side of the bed. "Okay, I believe she's actually in labor."

"What's that supposed to mean?" Richelle barked.

He had no time to answer. Richelle's body once again convulsed with a strong contraction. When Richelle could breathe normally again, she said, "Please help me, Charlie, please! I need some pain killers."

"I don't have anything."

Richelle groaned loudly and started crying.

"Oh, baby, don't cry." Charlie smoothed her hair back and kissed her forehead.

That man's a saint. He treats her so well! And she's turned into an absolute tyrant now that she's in labor!

That those thoughts even came made Tessa smile. Charlie was a different man from when she first met him. She couldn't stand the earlier version of him. But this changed, caring man had been radically transformed by God.

"I'll pray, okay?" he asked.

Richelle nodded.

Charlie grabbed her hands and began to pray. "Father, thank you for this baby that's coming. I pray for Richelle as she gives birth. Help her not to have too much pain and give your peace to flood over her. All fear has to go, in the name of Jesus. I ask that you protect our baby as it's born. Thank you for your angels surrounding Richelle and our little one, to protect them. In Jesus' name I pray, amen!"

His strong faith and confident words brought calm to the room. Charlie had always had a demanding presence and before he was saved he thrived on intimidating people. Now he commanded respect by his simple trust in God's promises and his childlike faith. He was as gentle as a lamb but as bold as a lion when it came to spiritual warfare.

Commotion in the hall drew Tessa's attention and she headed to the door and opened it. Two paramedics hurried down the hall with their equipment. Lily stood just outside the door, relief flooding her face.

"She's in here," Tessa informed them, holding the door for them and closing it after they entered. She stood back and watched as the paramedics went straight to work.

"Tessa, I need you!" Richelle called out.

There was no way to avoid this. Tessa stepped beside the rollaway and patted Richelle's shoulder. "I'm here."

Richelle reached for and clung to Tessa's hand. After a few minutes Tessa wished she could pull away. Richelle's vise-like grip was making her fingers numb.

The paramedics tried to lighten the mood by making small talk and joking about Richelle's predicament.

She was furious that they weren't loading her into the ambulance and rushing her to the hospital. She demanded an epidural but they insisted she was too far along and too dilated for it to make any difference. They assured her the baby would be out within minutes and her pain would be over. From the look on her face, she wasn't convinced.

As her pains came and went, her language was a shock to everyone in the room and Charlie kept apologizing for her. That made her even more irritable and she kept hitting him, telling him to shut up.

In between all that commotion and excitement, Richelle's contractions kept coming, one nearly right after the other. That she had any energy to pound on Charlie in between was amazing. With her increased pain, her civility came undone, her tongue uncouth and her Christian principles flew out the window.

The paramedics took the situation in stride, focusing instead on getting things ready for the imminent arrival of the baby.

When everything was prepared, the man who introduced himself as Stone Reynolds sat at the end of the rollaway and said, "You're fully dilated so when I say, you start to push, okay?"

Richelle groaned and nodded as another contraction squeezed her abdomen.

The other man, Brett Felder, stood beside him, ready to assist.

Stone gave the word and Richelle went to work. She was brave as the pushing started. Her grip grew tighter with every effort.

Tessa was tempted to extract her aching hand but she held steady.

Ten minutes later the baby slipped out into the bright lights of the staff room. Tessa held her breath at the blue-tinged, bloody baby that lay in Stone's hands. He suctioned the nose and mouth and the baby let out a lusty cry in protest. Brett clamped off the umbilical cord and handed Charlie the scissors to cut his baby loose. Charlie looked both excited and nervous as he cut through the thick cord.

"It looks like you just got yourselves a brand new boy." Stone held up the bluish baby boy, who wailed in protest, for inspection.

Richelle finally let go of Tessa's hand. She was now completely engrossed in what she'd delivered. Tessa rubbed her hand to bring feeling back, but her heart was full of emotion. She'd just witnessed a miracle.

Deborah stood by with a waiting towel and Stone handed the baby to her. She speedily wrapped him and carried him to the waiting table to clean him before handing him to Richelle, who was now beaming with relief and joy. Deb approached with the small bundle and he no longer looked blue. His cries had turned to limp whimpers with the blanket now warming him. A slight pink tint colored his skin.

With watery eyes, Richelle reached for him and held him close. Tears flowed easily then and moistened her cheeks.

Charlie looked confused. "Why are you crying? He's beautiful!

She looked up at him. "I'm so happy! He is beautiful and it's finally over!" She turned back to her son and gently stroked his cheek.

Beaming from ear to ear, Charlie leaned over Richelle and his new son to get a better look. He moved a piece of Richelle's hair from her wet cheek and placed a kiss on her forehead. "I'm so proud of you, Richelle!"

She lifted her face to his and they kissed tenderly.

It was a sacred moment. Tessa moved back to give the new family some space. Relief flooded her. This ordeal was over and the result of all Richelle's hard work lay in her hands. In only five months Tessa would be going through this too. It seemed overwhelming but exciting. Part of her couldn't wait for that day. Another part could wait forever.

Tessa checked her watch. Her next appointment was coming in half an hour. She really needed to get ready. Reaching over, she touched Richelle's shoulder. "I have to go now."

Accusation filled her eyes. "Where are you going?"

"I have an appointment in half an hour and I haven't prepared at all."

"I just gave birth to my son and all you can think about is work?"

Tessa smiled apologetically. "I can spare a few more minutes."

Richelle looked at her son and said, "Isn't he beautiful, Tessa?"

"He's adorable!"

"What should we name him?"

"What are the options?" Tessa was surprised they hadn't decided on that sooner.

A sheepish look crossed Richelle's face. "I was so sure that my baby would be a girl that I didn't pick out any boy names."

Tessa looked at Charlie. "What name do you like for a boy?"

"Well...., I like Bruno or Duke or Rocky."

Tessa stared at him. *You've got to be kidding! Okay, some common sense is direly needed right now!* "I can see why you both need some help."

Richelle pleaded with her eyes. "I told you!"

"What's wrong with my suggestions?"

He didn't deserve to be hurt, even if his name ideas were stupid.

Richelle rubbed his arm and said, "I'm sorry, honey. You're good at many things. Names just aren't your specialty. That's all."

Stone and Brett chuckled in the background as they cleaned up.

"Stone's a good name," Stone said.

"I've always liked Brett," said Brett.

Charlie said, "Yeah, I like Stone."

"You would," said Tessa. "You liked Rocky."

Richelle sighed and said, "Nice names, but not my style."

Deborah had cleaned up many of the towels and rinsed out the sink and metal bowl. Now she came over to take another look at the little fellow. After studying him for a while, she said, "How about Jadon? My daughter considered that as a boy's name when she was pregnant but she had a girl. I have a granddaughter named Lindsay. Jadon means Jehovah has heard."

"Jadon," Richelle said contemplatively.

"Jadon Kendal," Charlie said, trying it out.

Richelle looked at him. "What do you think?"

"I like it."

She looked at Charlie again. "What about a second name?"

He shrugged, looking nervous even to suggest anything.

Richelle said, "I like the name Royce. How does Jadon Royce Kendal sound?"

Charlie nodded. "Not bad."

She smiled and turned to look at her son in her arms. "Welcome to the world, Jadon Royce Kendal!"

Charlie gave a wide grin and reached down to rub his son's head. He looked pleased with the choice. Richelle reached for Charlie's hand and they became absorbed in studying the small bundle in her arms. It made a beautiful picture.

Tessa took that moment to slip out quietly. They didn't need her anymore. Stone and Brett were getting things ready to transfer Richelle and baby to the hospital. Tessa was needed elsewhere.

CHAPTER 23

October 1998

Sally made her way out of the apartment complex and hit the sidewalk. Leaves floated down around her, adding to the accumulation on the ground and crunched beneath her feet. The fall air was cool but she didn't mind. She was always hot lately, eight months pregnant and feeling big and uncomfortable. Just to go for this walk had been like an exercise in acrobatics. Doing up her running shoes was a trying experience. She could barely reach her shoes, never mind accomplish the task of tying the laces. It left her winded and spent.

The bright colors of fall always managed to cheer her spirits. The trees lining the streets were bursting with color and vibrant. It gave her a spring in her step, if that were even possible in her state. Maybe a lively waddle was more accurate.

She had the day off and exercise seemed the wise thing to do. She got so little of that lately and if she cared at all about keeping in shape, she really had no choice. With a brisk, but somewhat awkward gait, she headed downtown.

Leaves fell with the slight breeze and drifted around her feet. She turned her face toward the sky, wishing for one to brush against her cheek, forehead, anything to connect with the beauty showering around her.

In one yard, a man tried to corral the leaves in his yard with a rake. The wind scattered them as fast as he could trap them; all his effort looked futile. The trees rustled and creaked in the breeze, mocking the man's attempts below. A dichotomy existed between human desire for order and nature's carefree exuberance. If anyone should know that, Sally did.

She walked on, enjoying the sound of the dry leaves beneath her feet and the warmth of the October sun shifting through the branches above, making dappled shadows on the sidewalk. The cool, fresh air calmed her tense emotions.

Maybe shopping for new maternity clothes would help to distract her. She really had enough clothes but shopping usually cheered her. Fashion was her obsession and she freely admitted it.

Thoughts of her husband came uninvited, although she'd vowed not to think of him today. The familiar heaviness barged in, crowding out the picture-perfect world she was walking through. Walter was excited about the coming baby but his agitation was also increasing. About what, she had no idea. His extreme preoccupation puzzled her. He refused to discuss it with her. The excuse he always used was that he didn't want to hurt her and that he'd deal with it.

So that was the issue. What was going on that could hurt her? She'd asked him if he was unfaithful. No. He vehemently swore he'd never do that to her. So what could it be? She'd hoped their marriage would improve with the anticipation of a baby. It had at first. They finally had a common interest. But instead things had steadily deteriorated during her pregnancy. Now the icy silence between them was back. They couldn't talk without getting angry.

If having a baby couldn't help their marriage, what could? She felt at the end of her rope. She'd made a terrible mistake and it couldn't be undone. In a month they'd be a family. A child would join the mix. Walter was merely a stranger who refused to let her into his world. What was his secret? Secrets were made to uncover and that's exactly what she planned to do, whether the truth would destroy her or not.

Three hours later, Sally returned to the apartment carrying bags of new clothes. Exhausted, she set the things down beside the door. The exercise had been good for her but her head hurt from too many thoughts of Walter filling her day. Shopping hadn't been a sedative after all.

Sally wandered into her bedroom and sprawled across the bed. When she opened her eyes and glanced at the time she was shocked. Two hours had passed. Sitting up, she arranged her pillows as a backrest and relaxed, rubbing the sleep from her eyes.

Her mother's face paraded before her and the words she'd spoken months earlier heralded in her ears: "Sally, only God can give you the peace and joy that you long for. No man can give you that. Men will fail you, but God will never fail you. Pick up your Bible and read. That's the first step in getting to know the awesome God that I know. He'll be more than enough for you."

Sally reached over to her nightstand and pulled out the Bible that she'd placed there a few days before. She didn't have the nerve to read it then. To get it from her storage box in the hall closet and place it in her nightstand took all the courage she'd been able to muster. The black, leather-bound book felt soft and comforting in her hands. Could it really be the answer for her?

She brushed the golden edges of its pages, flipping through the book aimlessly. Could she really understand what it said? She'd always relied on Sheffield's wisdom to understand God. Not that he read from the Bible much.

Allowing it to fall open, it spread wide at the book of John, chapters fourteen through sixteen. Not knowing where to start, she closed her eyes and pointed with her index finger to mark a spot. She opened her eyes and looked.

Her finger rested on chapter fourteen, verse twenty-seven. "Humph!" she grunted. It seemed as good a place to start as any.

"Peace I leave with you; my peace I give to you. I do not give as the world gives. Do not let your hearts be troubled and do not be afraid."

Peace. That sounds good! And he just gives it? Why do I have so little of it then?

Sally looked up at the ceiling, wondering where exactly God was. Why was it so hard feeling close to him? Did he even exist? She wondered that lately. Wouldn't his peace be more tangible if he were the giver of peace? Why was it that she felt only turmoil? Marrying Walter hadn't brought her any closer to God. If anything, God felt more distant than ever.

After reading a few more verses and understanding nothing, she slammed the book shut and placed it back in the nightstand.

She got up and hung her new clothes in the closet. Maybe God's plan for her didn't include happiness. Perhaps hurt, pain and disillusionment was her lot. Walter was a Christian but if that's what defined Christianity, did she even want it? The only thing she'd reaped from their relationship was confusion. And it weighed on her like an anchor, ready to pull her into the depths.

TIME AND HEALING

~~~~~

November 1998

Robert walked Sally back to the apartment. He'd taken her for dinner, made a special trip to Toronto just to spend time with her. Walter was busy doing something. She was never sure what he was busy with. She appreciated Robert's effort but now he was acting like a dweeb.

"Why don't you come in for a while?"

"I really need to get going."

"I'd like you to come in." She needed some positive interaction. She felt starved for meaningful communication.

He smiled. "You look exhausted."

"I'm always tired. I only have a few weeks left." Walking up the stairs had winded her.

"It's gone fast. And you're still working?"

She nodded.

"You should take some time off before the baby comes."

"I'd go stir-crazy sitting around this apartment with nothing to do. I have to work!"

"Well, try to rest as much as you can then before the baby comes."

Sally shook her head. "You worry too much."

"I'm your brother. I have a right to worry." He grinned.

She missed him. She saw so little of him and his crooked grin made her feel sad. It reminded her of simpler days when they were both young and carefree.

Robert stepped forward and placed a kiss on her cheek, then said, "I really have to run. Emily invited our neighbors over for the evening. I promised her I'd be home in time."

Promises. Aren't promises made to break? Walter seldom keeps his.

"Are you okay?" Concern showed in his eyes.

Sally nodded.

"You don't look okay."

"I'm just tired."

"How are you and Walter doing?"

Sally shrugged her shoulders in reply. "I thought you had to go."

"Don't want to talk about it, huh?"

"Don't want to talk about what?"

The voice brought both of their heads around.

Walter appeared from down the hall and stepped toward them. "What are you doing here, Robert?" He clapped Robert on the back.

"Sally and I went out for dinner. It was a spur-of-the-moment thing. I called this morning and we planned it. She told me you were busy anyway so it worked out. We just got back."

"That was nice of you."

"And what were you up to?" asked Robert.

"I had meetings at the church."

Sally was surprised he was home so early. It was unusual. "I didn't expect you back until later." He spent every Saturday with his father, going over church details and schedules and who knew what else?

"We finished up early so I thought I'd spend some time with my beautiful, pregnant wife for a change." Walter grinned boyishly. He turned toward Robert. "Why don't you stay for a while? We don't get the pleasure of your company very often."

"We invited our neighbors over tonight. They'll be arriving at seven and I'll barely make it as it is."

Walter looked at his watch and nodded.

"Look, why don't we make plans for the four of us to go out before the baby comes?" Robert looked from one to the other.

"I'd love that!" Sally said.

Walter said, "We'll hold you to that."

"I completely expect you to. I'll talk it over with Emily and we'll call you."

Sally smiled. "Wonderful."

Robert headed to the stairwell.

Walter walked into the apartment; Sally followed him and closed the door.

Walter gathered her into his arms and kissed her long and tenderly. He finally pulled back and looked into her eyes.

It made Sally feel safe when he took the time to hold her close but it was a rare happening. She didn't want him to pull away. She stepped closer, as close as she could with her protruding belly, and laid her head on his chest. He wrapped his arms around her and rested his chin on her head. The warmth of his breath on her hair felt wonderful. If only they could stay this close, this loving.

"What do you think you're having?"

"A baby."

"Boy or girl?"

She shrugged. "I don't know. It doesn't really matter to me."

"I want a boy."

"And if it's a girl?"

He pulled away then and said, "My father and I prayed for a boy, to carry on the Tassey name."

She stared at him. Where did he come up with these dingers? "We'll love our child whether it's a boy or a girl!"

He raised his hand and rubbed his neck. "I've had a long day. It's time for a little TV time." With that he turned and headed to the bedroom.

Sally stared after him, her mouth ajar and her heart tired. It was clear he didn't want to talk and she didn't want to start another fight. But he had used combative words and by that very fact was begging for an altercation even though he hated confrontation. Did he do it just to aggravate her?

He doesn't want a girl? Why has he never mentioned this to me before? And what if this baby is a girl? What then?

She rubbed her tummy and wondered. A stiff coffee is what she needed. She headed to the kitchen and made a strong brew in the coffee maker. She sat at the table and drank her coffee alone. It was becoming habit for her, sitting in the kitchen alone, thinking things through. No matter how much time she sat trying to unsnarl the knots in their relationship, she always ended up with a bigger ball of tangled matter.

Angrily, she swiped at the tears trickling down her cheeks. She was tired of crying. It didn't help anyway.

Was leaving Walter an option? She'd thought about it a lot. But there was a baby involved, another life to consider. This little one deserved to grow up conventionally with two parents that loved it. She'd determined long ago to do things differently than what her parents had done to her. Their child deserved a normal upbringing, whatever "normal" was. Sticking it out might be challenging but she was resolute in her decision. She had to stay.

CHAPTER 24

One week later, Sally stepped into the apartment feeling exhausted. Helping her parents was rewarding but it wore her out at this stage of her pregnancy. She wanted nothing more than to fill the large tub with hot water and soak her aching bones.

Heading down the hall to the bedroom, she heard commotion in the nursery. Walter had been working on it for months and she'd reminded him only yesterday that not much time remained. As she stepped into the room she could see that he'd finished the wallpaper and border. He was cleaning up his mess.

"Walter, you finished it! It looks great! I love it!"

He turned toward her and grinned. He seemed happy and relaxed. She couldn't remember the last time she'd seen him this way. It lifted her spirits.

The top half of the wall was painted a light yellow. The bottom half was covered with teddy bear wallpaper with a matching teddy bear border separating it from the painted wall above. The simple pattern and muted colors suited her and would be fitting for either a boy or a girl. A deep-stained maple crib stood in the middle of the room, the bedding for it bought and waiting. The matching change table and three-drawer dresser snuggled up beside the crib in the middle of the room and a matching rocker sat in the hall.

She toddled over to Walter, wrapped her arms around his neck and kissed him. "Thank you, Walter."

"You're welcome. I think the baby will be impressed, don't you?"

"I think it's perfect."

"Now I just need to clean up and rearrange the room."

She smiled up at him. He could be so good to her when he tried. He bent down and gave her a light kiss on the lips.

"You look tired."

"I feel exhausted!" she admitted.

"How are your parents?"

"Mom's doing well and getting stronger all the time. Dad is still weepy but doing okay. They are so funny to watch. I never knew Dad was so dependent on Mom. He wants to be with her all the time. It's really quite bizarre."

Walter nodded distractedly.

"I'd like to have a long, hot bath," Sally said.

"Go on then. I'll fix up this room."

She headed to the bathroom.

Later, dried and with her robe wrapped around her, she entered the bedroom, scrunching her hair with one hand to bring out some natural curl. The TV was on and Walter sat on the bed, flicking through channels. She looked at him and smiled. It wasn't often he was home on a Saturday and she hoped his good mood would hold.

He didn't return her smile but fished beside him for something and held up a book. "What's this doing here?"

She wasn't sure what it was at first. Then recognition came. "That's my Bible."

"Where'd you get it?" His voice had a hard edge to it, an accusing tone.

Sally felt her heart constrict and her nerves tighten. "My mother gave it to me years ago, before you and I ever met. It was a gift for my thirteenth birthday. Flip it open to the front page and you'll see what she wrote and the date." To assimilate why she had to explain this to him, a pastor's son, was baffling.

"Have you been reading it?" There was warning in his eyes.

"A few verses, yes."

"Why?"

"I felt confused and thought reading the Bible might help me sort things out."

Sally could see that Walter was visibly controlling his rising anger.

"And why did you think such a thing?"

"What? That the Bible might have an answer?"

He nodded, his lips quivering with restrained frustration.

Shrugging, she said, "Well, your father's sermons don't contain much scripture. I wanted to know what the Bible said. I felt I needed to know."

Sally was sure a shudder went through his body.

"So you chose to disobey?"

This conversation was getting bizarre and she knew she had to diffuse his weirdness somehow. "Disobey who?"

"God!"

She stared at him with open mouth.

He took a steadying breath and walked toward her. Holding the Bible up to her face, he said, "My father has clearly forbidden the congregation to read this book. It has been stated in the membership agreement, an agreement that you signed when you joined the church."

Really? It said that in there? I obviously didn't read it very carefully.

Her confusion must have shown.

With disdain, he said, "You didn't read it, did you?"

"What?"

"The membership agreement."

She shook her head. The blackness of his eyes scared her. Anger was changing his color, from the throat up, to a bright crimson.

"I'm sure he's also spoken this requirement from the pulpit," Walter spat out. "Why have you rebelled against the church?"

His reasoning seemed flawed. She couldn't just stand here and have him accuse her this way. "Why would God go to the bother of having a book written if he didn't want us to read it? It doesn't make any sense."

"Do you have to understand everything before you obey?"

"No, but honestly, I've never once heard your father tell us we couldn't read the Bible on our own. And why is it a bad thing?"

"Because..." he said between clenched teeth, "my father hears from God and this is the instruction God gave. My father is God's voice to us, the congregation. That should be enough for you!"

"What if it's not enough?"

He lifted the Bible and threw it to the floor at her feet. "Get rid of it! If Sheffield finds out about this, he'll discipline both of us!"

Sally's mind whirled with the craziness of it. "Your father would discipline us for having a Bible? How? I mean, we're not children! Don't we have a right to read whatever we want?"

"No, we do not! We must obey God!" His hands closed into fists.

Sally backed up a step. To pursue the reasoning behind the cockamamie demand felt perilous. His control looked ready to snap.

She tried once more. "I just don't get it! You're afraid of your father? I grew up reading the Bible! My mother has read the Bible for years. Almost every church encourages their members to read the Bible. So why can't we read it?"

Stepping forward, Walter took hold of her shoulders and shook hard, the darkness in his eyes growing darker, if that were possible. Her shoulders stung with his fierce grip. "You need to follow my spiritual leadership in this home! I am the head of this home! You will destroy this Bible or else I will!"

When the giggle started, Sally wasn't sure, but it filled the space around them. She couldn't stop.

Pushing her hard, he demanded, "Stop!"

She hit the wall behind her but it didn't hurt. Laughter washed away the tension and left her feeling so much better.

Walter turned on his heel and stormed out of the room. Seconds later the door to their apartment slammed shut.

Sally's giggles faded away. The situation had been so surreal; she couldn't stop herself from laughing. There was no way she'd destroy the Bible, not now. Walking over to it, she picked it up and stared at it. Walter's threats only fueled her desire to read it.

His behavior was steadily growing more eccentric. The church she once admired was becoming a huge point of contention between them. The anger she saw in his eyes today frightened her. What if he let himself go? What if his carefully guarded control let loose and he lost all reserve? Would he hurt her? And what about the baby? Was he capable of harming their child? Maybe she should leave for a while. Let things cool off. Let Walter cool off. Her decision was made.

~~~~~

Sitting behind her desk in her small cubicle, Sally gratefully dove into her work. It was her lifeline right now.

The last few nights she'd stayed in a hotel, shut off her cell phone and refused to contact Walter. If he wanted, he could drop by her work but she hadn't seen him and she was relieved. Although she struggled to focus, as the days went on, it was becoming easier to block out her husband's face and focus on her new deadline. She had to get her finishing touches on her spring line of designs.

A dull ache in her chest had settled in shortly after Walter left their apartment that night. She placed a hand over her heart and wished for the pain to go. It devastated her to realize that their tenuous bond was almost gone. If she dwelt on it, it brought her to tears. Ignoring the whole thing seemed best to her and made it easier to cope.

The bruises on her shoulder and back were slowly disappearing. She'd hit the wall harder than she'd thought. With the cool November weather, it was easy to keep it covered, hidden with long-sleeved blouses and sweaters.

Sally clicked at her computer and brought up a file of designs that needed editing.

Jason's voice brought her head around. "Hey there! I hear your spring line is awesome. Can I take a peek?" He leaned up against her cubby partition with his arms crossed.

She turned away from him and focused on her computer screen. "Not now. I have a lot of work to do and my line is none of your business anyway."

"Aw! Come on. Why are you suddenly being so secretive? You sure haven't minded bragging about it the last few weeks. I just want to see what all the boasting's been about." He lifted his eyebrows. "Or maybe it's not quite as impressive as you've let on."

Turning in her chair, she looked at him. "Jason, please, I'm in no mood to talk right now!" She turned back to her computer.

"What's wrong? Did you have a fight with your husband?"

"None of your business." His nosiness was aggravating.

"Oh, don't tell me. You're in labor, right?"

"No, I'm not in labor! Just go away!" Working with him standing and yapping was impossible.

"If you let me have a peek at one of your designs, I'll leave you alone."

"No!"

Without looking, she assumed he'd left. She opened one of her files to edit.

"Aha! So that's one of them?"

Sally clicked it off her screen, spun around and yelled, "Jason, get out of here!"

He grinned like a school boy. It irritated her even more.

"Jason, please!" she begged.

A look of concern passed through his eyes.

Sally looked down at the floor.

Jason lowered himself to his haunches and looked up into her face. "I can tell something's bugging you. You're not yourself at all this week. You're way more introverted than usual."

"Why would that concern you?" She still had a hard time looking at him. He could read her like a book some days and it unnerved her.

"I care about you. You're my main contender and I have to take care of you. If you're not in top form, the whole designing thing loses its competitive edge. Without rivalry, my job becomes monotonous."

His philosophy made her smile. "I'll be okay."

"In other words, you're telling me you haven't been okay?"

"I'm fine!"

He stared at her and she stared back, anger nipping the back of her neck.

"No, you're not okay. I can see it in your eyes."

How can he tell that by simply looking into my eyes? Am I that readable? Is my pain that obvious?

She looked away.

"What is it?"

"Why are you bothering me?"

He shrugged. "I think something's going on and I want to know what it is. You're not in top form and it makes me wonder."

Sally released a pent-up sigh. "I'm almost ready to pop out this baby. Don't you think that's enough of a reason not to be in top form?"

Shrugging again, he stood and said, "Have it your way. I was willing to lend my shoulder, my ear, whatever you needed to get through. But I suppose your stubbornness won out again."

Yes it did, Jason. Now go away!

She didn't have to say it. He left of his own accord and she was grateful.

Opening her file, she started editing. Feet in the hall coming toward her cubby made her cringe.

Jennifer peaked inside and said, "Hi, Sally! It looks like you have a secret admirer." In her hand she held a large arrangement of flowers.

"Just leave them on the counter."

Jennifer set them down and looked at her. "Well, aren't you going to read the note?"

"I'm in the middle of something and I'll get to it soon." Sally turned back to her computer and hoped Jennifer would make herself scarce.

"You have to promise to tell me later who they're from."

"I'm sure they're from my husband."

Jennifer's brow furrowed. "Is it your anniversary or birthday or something? It's a very large arrangement." The woman was efficient and like a mother to the staff but her desire to stay up to date on everything could be annoying.

Sally tried to be polite but she was in no mood for this today. "Jennifer, please!"

"Okay, okay. I'll leave you alone. The flowers are beautiful, Sally. You haven't even looked at them yet! And they smell heavenly."

Jennifer's footsteps faded away and Sally slowly turned to look. The arrangement was massive.

Roses, irises, carnations, lilies, baby's breath, mixed with various green sprays filled her work cubicle with a sweet fragrance. The bright, beautiful blooms mocked her. How could something so gorgeous remind her of something so utterly ugly? How could Walter think this could make up for their farce of a marriage?

A card was tucked on a stand in the center of the blooms. She picked it out, opened the envelope and steeled herself for what it would say. Her eyes reluctantly scanned the words scribbled across the crisp white paper. The writing was familiar and the words were expected.

"Sally, please forgive me for treating you so roughly. I was upset but shouldn't have pushed you. I love you with all my heart and can't live without you. Please come back to me! With all my love, Walter."

The paper crunched easily in one hand and landed nicely in the trash beside her. She wasn't in a forgiving mood. Living without him was peaceful. Her hotel room wasn't filled with anxious thoughts of what mood Walter would be in. She'd forgotten how tranquil life could be living alone. To go back now caused her unease.

She dove into her work, pushing Walter to the background. Late in the day her phone rang and she picked it up absently.

"Sally Windsor." To omit her husband's last name felt empowering.

It was Jennifer. "Sally, your husband is waiting for you in the foyer." Her voice was lilting and cheery. "I'm positive he's waiting for a response to that flower arrangement he sent you, but I'm sure you've already thanked him for it."

Jennifer could think what she wanted. Sally wasn't admitting anything. "Thank you, Jennifer. I'll be right out."

Walter's appearance didn't really surprise her. She'd left five days ago and they hadn't spoken since. That he'd want to see her made sense but she wasn't ready. She didn't know what to say. The idea of going back scared her. Perhaps an extended break would be best for both of them. With shaky hands, she shut down her computer and cleared her desk.

She put on her coat and slipped her purse over her shoulder. After a deep breath and steadying exhale, she headed for the entrance.

Jennifer noticed her, smiled big and said, "He decided to wait for you in the hall. See you tomorrow. Have a great night!"

"Thanks," Sally managed before exiting.

CHAPTER 25

Sally's heart beat in an uneasy cadence when she saw him standing with his back to the wall close to the elevator. He spotted her, pushed away from the wall and walked toward her. It suddenly felt hard to breathe and her knees started to shake. She stopped and waited for him.

His eyes were filled with regret as he stopped before her. "I'm sorry, Sally."

His steady gaze forced her to avert her eyes and study her fidgeting hands instead.

He reached for her chin and lifted it till their eyes met.

"I want you to come back to me, Sally. I can't live without you. I'm sorry for the way I treated you. I'm sorry for being so forceful. I don't know what comes over me sometimes."

Uncertainty gnawed at her as she looked at him. "I don't know. I'm just not happy anymore. Our relationship has too many problems."

He reached for her then, gripping her shoulders and pulling her close. "Please come back to me." Wrapping his arms around her, he held her tightly.

His heart thudded against her chest and the warmth of his body soothed her ragged emotions. How was it possible? Why was it that her heart melted whenever he did this? How could he have so much power over her? She needed him. She knew that then. Living without this man was impossible. His simple embrace caused her heart to flutter. All her resolve to be firm was slipping away and she hated herself for it.

With all her strength she pulled away and removed his hands from around her. "How can I trust you? You were angry enough to hurt me. I saw it in your eyes."

He moved closer again but she held up a hand to halt him. Tears formed in his eyes. "I promise I will never get that angry again."

She scrunched up her eyebrows. "But what if you do? What if you hurt me or the baby? What then?"

"I promise that I will never hurt you or the baby! I could never do that!"

"But you did."

"I pushed you, yes."

"You bruised me!"

A startled and pained look filled his eyes. "I'm sorry."

She stared at him, not knowing whether to believe him. His moods were as unpredictable as the wind. Did she even want to give him another try? For the baby, the answer was of course yes. The baby hadn't done anything wrong. Why make it suffer? The child needed two parents. But for herself, she wasn't at all sure.

"I'll die if you leave me, Sally! I can't live without you, even for a day. This week has been torture, not knowing where you were or if you were planning to come home. I love you! You mean everything to me!"

Although she tried to stay immovable and angry, the desperation on his face was starting to soften her stiff resolve. His handsome, mesmerizing eyes always hypnotized her. He held a magic over her that made it almost impossible to think straight.

He lowered himself to his knees and reached for her hands. She pulled away.

"Please, Sally, give me a chance."

It was too much. Tears slipped from her eyes and trailed down her cheeks. He stood and took her in his arms. With soft kisses he caressed her lips, face and neck. She melted into his embrace and clung to him like a lifeline. Although her emotions still felt shattered and frayed, Walter's warm embrace felt like the safest place to be.

She knew it was madness to trust him again. He was still the same Walter. But to live without him seemed like agony.

Walter looked into her eyes. "Come on, sweetheart, I'll take you home."

Pulling away again, she said, "I have my car here and I need to get my things from the hotel."

"I'll come with you."

"No!" She needed some time to think first. Being around him turned her mind to mush. "I'll meet you at the apartment."

Worry lined his eyes. "Do you promise you'll come home?"

She nodded.

"Tonight?"

She rubbed her forehead. "Yes, I think so. If I don't show tonight, I promise I'll be back tomorrow."

Walter looked uncertain and afraid. "I need you, Sally."

Nodding, she said, "I know." To admit she needed him would only give him the upper hand. She didn't want to give in to his need for control this time.

Raising his arms, palms toward her, he said, "Okay, no more pressure. You go and do what you need to do…but I'll be waiting for you." He walked her to her car, kissed her and left.

~~~~~

After work the next day, Sally walked into the apartment feeling both dread and excitement. How could she love Walter so much and yet hate him at the same time?

He came out from the kitchen, smiling. "Welcome home."

"Thanks."

Walter walked toward her, kissed her with desire and then picked up her suitcase and carried it to their bedroom. When he came back, he said, "I made dinner for us."

Raising her eyebrows, she said, "Really?"

"I guess an old dog can learn new tricks." He grinned impishly.

It felt like their dating days. He was being completely charming.

"I made meat sauce. I'll go cook the spaghetti."

She followed him to the kitchen. He never cooked. Taking her out to a restaurant was his way of treating her. It touched her that he'd go to this effort for her. Hopefully she'd survive the meal.

Taking a seat at the table, she watched as he worked. He kept turning to her and smiling. It was clear he was pleased she was back.

The meal wasn't too bad. He'd used the correct spices and it actually had some flavor. After eating, Walter served them both a coffee.

As they sipped it, he looked at her and asked, "You got rid of it, right?"

Setting her mug down on the table and wrapping her hands around it, she wondered what he was talking about. "What?"

"The Bible."

Oh! Its back to that, is it? What is wrong with him? Why doesn't he just drop his stupid issues already?

"I'm sorry. I just need to know." Although he looked apologetic, his jaw started to look stiff.

He was a master of secrets. Well, two could play at that game.

Looking him straight in the eye, she said, "Yes, I got rid of it." He'd never have to know the truth.

His shoulders relaxed and he released a pent up breath. "Good." Leaning forward, he reached for her hands.

She unlocked them from around her cup and placed them in his.

"I know the book meant a lot to you, especially since it was a gift from your mother." He reached down to the seat beside him and lifted a box to the tabletop. "I bought you these books to replace that one. I thought you'd like them."

The ridiculous box sat between them on the table and all Sally could think of was throwing the whole thing against the wall and screaming. But instead she would open it, say thanks and pretend that everything was fine. Tearing away at the wrapping, she opened the lid, looked inside and lifted out one book at a time, stacking them up beside the box. It was full of teaching books, commentaries on the Bible, books she recognized from Sheffield's library.

Looking up at him, she asked, "Your father was willing to part with these?"

He nodded and smiled. "I think you'll like them."

Picking up the last one, she leafed through it. It looked old, boring and hard to read. But then again, the Bible had been hard to read too. Stuffing down a barrage of mixed emotions, she looked up at him and said, "Thank you."

The grin on his face told her his world was on track once more. Then why did she feel so disconnected and floundering?

CHAPTER 26

April 2004

Tessa swept patches of snow off their small deck. A cloudless blue sky, the sun reigning supreme, warmed the south-facing back yard. It had turned unseasonably warm for early April and the bushels of snow that had accumulated during the winter were nearly gone. Sweeping small amounts left on the deck to the grass below didn't take much effort. The bright sunshine would help dry the deck in no time. The lawn chair she'd washed down earlier was almost dry.

She stepped inside and made a mug of hot chocolate before retreating back to the deck. She'd positioned the chair so that the afternoon sun shone down to bathe her in warmth. It felt wonderful and she could feel her body relax. Saturdays were her favorite days, especially when she didn't have to work. To have a warm, sunny day was like hitting the jackpot.

Cody was out doing the grocery shopping. He'd be home soon and maybe he'd come join her out here. She'd cleared a chair for him too and it was dry and waiting for him.

Any extra time together was a bonus. Life was so busy lately. After she finished her hot chocolate, she set her cup by her feet and leaned back in the chair. Reclining it, she turned her face up to the sun and closed her eyes, hoping to get some color on her skin. It wasn't long till she felt herself dozing off. She gave in to the heaviness that weighted her eyes.

Tessa awoke with a start and sat up as if poked with a red-hot iron. "No!" Instinctively, her hand went to her round abdomen and the baby fluttered within. She lifted her eyes to the blue sky and asked, "God, why am I having this dream again?" Perspiration dotted her forehead and she reached up to wipe it away. Her heart was beating a crazy cadence.

Noise in the house alerted her and she looked to the screen door. Cody's face appeared and, as his smile disappeared and concern took its place, he opened the door and stepped out on the deck.

"What's wrong?"

She shrugged. "We can talk about it later. Do you need help with the groceries?"

"I noticed you were sleeping so I put them away." He kissed her lips before taking the other chair. "So what's up?"

"I had the dream again." She fidgeted with her wedding ring and tried to force the fear down.

"Remember, Tessa, the dream is from God and he's obviously trying to tell you something."

That was hard to accept. Would something from God make her so afraid? She looked at him. "I'm scared."

He scooted closer, took her hands, bowed his head and prayed. Mostly, he took authority over the fear and told it to go, in Jesus' name. But he also asked that the meaning of the dream would become clear.

She felt a bit better. At least the fear was gone but the confusion remained.

"Was there any more detail to your dream? Anything you haven't told me?"

She sighed and thought it over. To dwell on it seemed pointless for it would only stir up the fear again. But she would do it for his sake. He really did want to help.

"There was something different about this dream, something that truly surprised me. This time I think I recognized the woman who took the baby from my arms."

"Who was it?"

"My mother." It didn't compute. Why would her mother take her baby from her?

Cody shook his head. "I don't get it."

"Neither do I."

He smiled and said, "We'll wait. God will show us what it means."

"I'm not so sure. What if it means nothing at all?"

"Either way, we'll know eventually."

While Tessa changed from her Sunday outfit to sweats and a large t-shirt, Cody started the grill on the deck. Since they were having a warm weekend, burgers seemed like the perfect lunch.

After the meal they retreated to the living room. Cody's sipped on a cup of coffee and Tessa savored a cup of Chai tea. After flicking through a few channels, Cody found a sports station where a hockey game was in progress.

Tessa didn't mind too much. It was nice just to spend the day together.

The doorbell rang and Cody turned to her. "Were you expecting someone?"

"No. Were you?"

"No." Cody stood and walked to the door.

She recognized his voice immediately. Luke walked into the living room and she stood to embrace him. Cody was right behind him.

"I haven't seen you in a while," Tessa said.

After a firm hug, Luke pulled back and asked, "How's Mrs. Prego doing today?" He grinned mischievously.

She punched him for that. "You and your pet names. I'm doing fine and welcome here."

"Thanks!" Luke let himself drop onto the couch beside Cody as if exhausted.

"Where's Janaye?" She was surprised he came without her.

"She's in her church choir and they have this big production tonight so they're practicing this afternoon. I thought I'd drop in here for a while."

"I'm glad you came," said Tessa.

Cody said, "I don't see my bro very often."

"I know. Life is busy." Luke focused on the hockey game as the action intensified.

Luke and Cody were half-brothers, raised by different mothers, both abandoned by their father. God had miraculously brought them together as adults. They hadn't known about each other till just a few years ago during their time travel experience. Tessa and Luke had met in high school and became fast friends. God had amazingly connected the dots and brought the two brothers together.

She looked at him and wondered how he was doing. He and Janaye were still dating and it surprised her. Janaye being a Christian hadn't scared him off yet. By the sound of things, she was quite involved with her church. That Luke could tolerate it was remarkable. Maybe he was softening.

Luke looked at her, saw her eyes on him and a question flitted across his face. "What?"

She shrugged. "Just wondering how you're doing."

"Good."

"That's it?"

"What else were you fishing for?"

She shrugged again and turned to the TV.

"Look at that play," yelled Cody. "How amazing was that?"

"They're walking away with the game," Luke said.

"They're definitely dominating." With his arms resting on his knees and sitting on the edge of the couch, Cody was really into the game.

"Do you watch much hockey?" asked Luke.

Cody shook his head. "Not enough time. I read the stats, though, and try to keep abreast of what's happening." He turned toward Luke. "How about you?"

"I don't miss too many games."

The room grew silent except for the cheering, skates scraping and rushing over ice and sticks slapping the puck.

Luke broke the silence. "I was wondering," he said to no one in particular.

Tessa and Cody waited.

Luke took a deep breath and released it. "Do you think I missed my chance?" He turned and looked at Tessa.

"Your chance at what?"

He lifted his shoulders and held. "God?" He slowly lowered his shoulders and focused on the TV.

Tessa wasn't sure what he was getting at. "What do you mean?"

"Well, you know how we had that time travel experience. That angel kept showing up and showing us stuff. I didn't exactly accept what he said."

It was true. The angel had been very blunt. Luke had been faced with an eternal decision but he'd walked away, scorning and rejecting it. But why was he questioning it now? Was being in relationship with Janaye the reason?

"Does Janaye have something to do with this?" asked Tessa.

"Maybe." He looked at her. "It was more what the pastor at church said this morning."

"What did he say?" asked Cody.

"He said if a person continues to reject God, eventually God will leave him be. But he also talked about prayer. He said praying for the 'lost'" (he made quotations marks with his fingers) "would open the door for God to continue working in a person's life." He rubbed the palms of his hands together. "Do you think God's given up on me? Have I rejected him too many times?"

Cody gave Tessa a sweet look before returning his attention to Luke. "I don't believe God ever gives up on anyone. He's very patient and has been waiting for you. He'll continue to wait till you're ready. The fact that you're questioning shows that you care. I'd encourage you to make the decision now. If you'd like, we'll pray with you and you can become a child of God. It's that simple."

He raised his hands. "Whoa! I'm not ready yet. If God's so patient, he'll wait for me, right?"

What could she say? Cody had already admitted to God's patience. Tessa felt the disappointment like a punch to her gut. Why was Luke so stubborn? He was clearly feeling the pull toward God, so why not go ahead and accept Christ? Was it his pride? Was he afraid of losing control?

With a roguish grin, Luke pulled something out of his sports coat pocket. It was a small box. He opened it slowly and displayed it for the two of them to see.

A large, diamond ring sat within a dark blue, felt-lined box. The size of it made Tessa gasp. "You're going to propose to Janaye?"

"Yes. I thought I'd let you know before I do. I'll propose tonight but I feel so excited and nervous that I couldn't keep it quiet any longer." He looked boyish and giddy at what was coming later.

"What if she says no?" asked Cody.

It probably wasn't the response Luke wanted to hear but Tessa knew it could be a very real possibility.

"Why would she say no? I'm the most eligible and wealthy bachelor around. With my looks and her sweetness, we'd make quite a team." He grinned crookedly.

Tessa couldn't help but chuckle. His blend of charm and cockiness actually worked for him.

With a lively jingle, the doorbell chimed again.

"Now, who could that be?" asked Cody.

"This is turning out to be an interesting day," Tessa said, heading to the door. Swinging it wide, she said, "Richelle and Charlie! Come on in!"

"Is it okay that we just dropped by?" asked Richelle, looking awkward. "We took Charlie's dad out for lunch and were on our way home when we decided to drop in here for a quick visit."

"Of course it's okay. How many times have I asked you to bring Jadon over so we can see him?"

"Too many times."

"Exactly."

The two stepped inside, Charlie carrying the car seat with the sleeping baby. He set it down in the small entrance.

Tessa hunched down beside it and lifted the blanket to get a peek. She hadn't seen him in weeks. He was sleeping soundly so she left him in his car seat. The tyke had grown and was absolutely adorable.

She stood and asked, "How's he been?"

"He's sleeping better but I still feel exhausted."

Tessa nodded.

"Is that Luke's car out there?" asked Richelle.

Tessa nodded again.

That's all Richelle needed. She rushed into the living room and screamed in excitement. Charlie grabbed the car seat and followed. Tessa took up the rear.

Luke stood and held Richelle in a tight hug, twirled her around and set her down.

"How come you're here?" Richelle asked.

"I could ask you the same thing."

"You just dropped by?"

"Yep."

"Well, isn't this cool?" Richelle plopped down on the couch and Charlie took the floor beside her.

They didn't have enough chairs for so many people. Cody got up and grabbed some more chairs from the kitchen table and brought them into the room. Charlie stood to take one.

Richelle looked around and asked, "Where's Janaye?"

"She had something up this afternoon but I'll meet her later."

"Oh, that's too bad that she can't be here too." Suddenly Richelle jumped up and did a small catwalk across the tight room. Her post-pregnancy look was fabulous! She was as slim and gorgeous as ever.

To Tessa it was clear whom this was for. Richelle's new slim look couldn't be denied. Not even Luke could find fault with her figure now.

With hands on hips, she said to Luke, "You can't call me 'Barney' or 'Daffy Duck' anymore! Ha!"

He laughed. "Just wait till after number three or four. Then we'll see what shape you'll be in."

She looked scornful at the suggestion. "Three or four? Give me a break. Two kids, at the most, that's it! It's only in your dreams that I'd be big and fat."

"That would be more like a nightmare!" Luke stated.

Richelle shook her head.

Charlie's deep voice interrupted. "No one's asked me how many children I want!"

Tessa looked at him, chuckled and asked. "How many?"

Richelle crossed her arms and waited for his answer.

"I've actually always envisioned a house full of kids. I was thinking more in the line of five or six." He smiled comically, already anticipating his wife's reaction.

"Go ahead and have those babies by yourself then. I won't be helping you out."

"I can't do it without you."

"My point exactly!"

A barrage of laughter filled the room, Charlie laughing the loudest.

Charlie looked at Cody. "How about you two? How many kids are you planning to have?"

Cody caught her eye before answering. "Two or three."

"That's plenty for me," agreed Tessa.

Richelle turned to Luke and said, "Just think of all the nephews and nieces you'll be able to babysit for."

"Huh-uh! I don't do babies!"

Tessa said, "You'll be an uncle. That title comes with certain responsibilities."

"Hey, hold it. I never signed up for this."

"Ah, poor baby," said Richelle condescendingly.

Luke ignored her and asked, "What kind of responsibilities?"

Tessa started listing them, lifting a finger for each item. "Spending time with our kids, showering them with gifts, babysitting." He groaned at that one. "And all the basic uncle stuff."

Richelle added, "And that includes changing diapers."

Luke lifted his hands in protest. "I don't babysit and I absolutely do not do diapers!"

Everyone laughed.

It felt good to be together like this. Tessa loved having her favorite people all together.

Cries from the car seat got everyone's attention. Richelle reached over and unbuckled Jadon. "He's hungry."

Charlie stood. "I'll get the diaper bag."

When he returned from the entrance, Richelle asked him. "Would you grab the bottle and warm it up?"

Charlie agreed while Richelle went ahead and changed little Jadon's diaper. Luke looked away in disgust and focused on the game, which was about to end.

Charlie returned and handed Richelle the bottle.

Luke watched the scene with a smirk on his face but thankfully he didn't say anything derogatory. He could come up with real dingers, hurtful things if he wanted to. He'd never liked Charlie and to goad him was a pastime for Luke. Tessa was relieved he controlled his tongue today.

Tessa watched as Richelle lifted her son into her arms, placed the bottle in his mouth and cuddled him in close. It was such a tender picture. Tessa could feel tears threatening. She chided herself for being so emotional. It was because she was pregnant, she was sure.

Luke left after an hour's visit. Janaye was expecting him. Charlie and Richelle stayed longer.

Cody and Tessa took the time to fill them in on Luke's situation. Cody suggested they pray for him and the two readily agreed. Cody led and the rest of them joined in. Tessa was sure it wouldn't be long till Luke accepted Christ. He was surrounded by Christians and was dating a Christian. How could he resist the pull of all the prayers going up for him?

CHAPTER 27

May 1999

A brisk wind blew Sally's hair in a frenzied pattern as she pushed the stroller toward her apartment building. The chilly May air made summer seem like a distant wish. Bare branches on the trees lining the street, creaked in protest. The faintest sign of buds was showing but there'd be no advance today. It was much too cool for that.

How she longed for warmer weather. Walks would be so much more enjoyable and she was tired of the drab, brown landscape. The grass in front of her apartment complex was struggling to turn green. Rain and somewhat warmer temperatures were being forecast for next week. Maybe there'd be something green to look at before long.

After her two-mile trek, she stopped the stroller in front of her apartment. Her baby was crying. She'd obviously had enough, was hungry or needed changing.

Sally headed home. Once in the apartment, it didn't take long to change her daughter, warm the bottle and settle into the rocking chair to feed her. With Isabella snuggled into the crook of her arm, everything felt right. The intensity of her love for this child still astounded her. Isabella Rae Tassey was beautiful and perfect, belonged to her, and Sally felt so much pride. Whenever she gazed at her daughter, her heart swelled with love and joy. A miracle lay in her lap. The day she first held her daughter in the hospital was the most amazing moment of her life.

She'd told her mother right after Isabella was born how she thanked her lucky stars for this gift. That had been a mistake. Her mother told her, in no uncertain terms, that lucky stars didn't deserve the credit for this child. God was Isabella's creator and deserved all the praise.

Sally grinned at the memory. Leave it to her mother to spiritualize everything. Such talk still made her squirm.

With one finger Sally traced little Isabella's chin as she lustily sucked at the bottle. Isabella had a head full of curly hair. She'd be able to blame Sally for that later on. Hopefully she wouldn't hate her curls too much. Looking at her was like looking at Walter. The same shimmering, blue, mesmerizing quality shone from her daughter's eyes. This girl would be beautiful. She already was.

The bond she felt with Isabella surprised her. The strength of it sometimes took her breath away. That Walter acted so indifferent toward this child bothered her terribly.

He'd rarely held Isabella and barely looked at her. He claimed he was too busy. How could one man have that many meetings, that many house showings? She'd called him on it, raged at him, demanded that he take interest in Isabella but so far the confrontations had helped nothing.

Her frustration was mounting and Sally didn't know what to do. They'd both agreed to start a family. Why was he now pushing all the responsibility of raising Isabella onto her?

When she'd moved back in, he'd tried hard. He'd seemed excited when Isabella was born and even held her at the hospital. It was only when Sally and Isabella came home that his true feelings began to show. He gradually withdrew more and more. Sally had hoped Walter would develop some affection for his daughter over time. But since he spent so little time with her, how could he?

The bottle was empty and Sally pulled it out of Isabella's mouth. She cried the moment it left. Sally found the pacifier and inserted that. Isabella stilled and Sally settled her down on a blanket on the floor, placing the infant play gym over her to keep her occupied.

How could he not love her? Just looking at Isabella warmed Sally's heart. Their baby was already five months old but she still hoped he'd take interest, stop his frantic schedule and spend time with them. She longed for him to fall in love with their daughter.

The front door opened and Sally turned to watch Walter step inside. She felt furious at the sight of his cheerful face. He was always happy lately and she was miserable. The difference only fueled her resentment.

Placing his coat in the closet, he turned to her and said, "How was your day?"

"Great," she said, unsmiling. She didn't feel great.

"Mine was amazing."

She didn't answer. His enthusiasm lately was odd. It certainly had nothing to do with coming home and seeing his wife and daughter, of that she was sure. She'd questioned him but he insisted he loved his job and his work at the church, that's all.

He stopped and took in a deep breath. "Is dinner started?"

"No." She waited a moment and then asked, "How was your meeting with your father?"

"Very productive."

She nodded. Just thinking about Sheffield made her angry. The man was so full of himself and his church. What he'd said about Isabella right after her birth sat like a weight of bitterness in the pit of her stomach. He'd looked at her and said, "Too bad it wasn't a boy." That's it! That's all he'd ever said about her. As if to be born a girl was a curse. The man had a lot of nerve. She suspected Walter thought the same but at least he'd never voiced it. His actions said enough.

Walter was speaking. Sally struggled to pay attention. "We have some new converts to the faith and they will be introduced in tomorrow's service. My father and I discussed some business and went over the week's schedule as usual and that's about it." He rubbed his hands together. "But I'm starved. Why don't we order in?"

"Sure, go ahead."

"Chinese?"

"That's fine."

She watched him walk off to the kitchen phone, wondering what secrets he was keeping. But then again, didn't everyone have secrets?

~~~~~

December 1999

Isabella toddled around the apartment while Sally put the finishing touches on the decorations. The year since her birth had flown by in a whirl. She was convinced that parenting made time speed up.

Sally stepped back to view the overall effect. Bright, pink, yellow and white streamers hung above the table and draped the room on three sides. Balloons were taped to the walls, chairs and light fixture above the table. Even the highchair was decorated. Isabella couldn't quite reach the lowest balloon but she sure put in a good effort. She finally gave up and wandered to her pile of toys in the corner.

It had been a month since Isabella had started walking and she was doing great. She hardly ever fell anymore.

A glance at the clock told Sally the party guests would arrive soon. Walter promised he'd be home in time. Hopefully he'd keep his word. This day was important. He should know how significant this day was to her, to both of them. She tried his cell but he didn't answer. That was typical so she left a message.

Her hand shook as she put the phone back in its holder. She needed something before the apartment filled with people. Just a little something would tide her over. Making a quick trip to the bathroom, she dug out a small box hidden on the bottom shelf of the linen closet, beneath a layer of rags and cleaning cloths. She'd gotten a prescription of anti-depressants from her doctor months ago. A good dose should help calm her nerves. Lately she was dipping into her prescription more than usual. A stash of cocaine sat next to the anti-depressants in the small box. Tonight it would assist in the hosting role, an act she was dreading. After taking some of both, she carefully placed them back in their hidden spots.

She could hear the intercom buzzer from here. After closing the closet door firmly, she went to answer it. Depressing the button and hearing their voices on the speaker, she pushed the knob to open the door from the lobby. A few minutes later there was a knock at the door. Opening it revealed her smiling parents.

"Hi, Sally," said Melody, stepping inside to hug her daughter.

"Hi."

Her father followed suit, wrapping Sally in his arms and squeezing hard.

"Welcome," she said.

"Bama," Isabella said, waddling toward them and pointing to Melody. "Bapa." She included Vern, turning her hand in his direction.

That was all the encouragement he needed. He held out his hands and she nearly jumped into them. Isabella giggled as Vern threw her into the air and caught her. The game was set and Vern looked as though in heaven. He loved his granddaughter.

Sally smiled at the scene.

Melody shook her head in concern. "Be careful, Vern. She's just little."

Vern held Isabella out at arm's length and looked at her. "No, you're not little. You're a one-year-old now. You're a big girl."

Isabella giggled at that. "One."

"Yes, you are," he said, laughing with her. "Big girl."

She just stared at him.

"Say, 'Big girl.'"

"ig irl," she tried.

That made him laugh again. He held her close then and sat down, placing her on his lap. She sat still for a bit but then wiggled till she was on the floor and free. Her toys held too much fascination.

Melody still stood, holding a gift bag. She looked at Sally and asked, "Where should I put Isabella's gift?"

"We'll be celebrating in the kitchen so why don't we put it in there?" Sally led the way and her mother followed.

"Oh my, the decorations are beautiful, Sally!" she exclaimed as they entered. "You went to a lot of work! Look at all the pink and yellow! This is so cute!" Her eyes scanned the counter. "And did you make this cake?" Melody walked over to it to get a better look.

"Yes, I did."

"It's so nicely done. I didn't know you could decorate cakes."

"Thanks. I tried my best."

Melody turned and looked at Sally. Her smile slowly disappeared and concern caused lines to form on her forehead. "Are you okay, dear?"

"Of course! Why wouldn't I be okay?" She had no intention of sharing her worries or her mother would just start in on her again.

"Your eyes look strange. Glazed or something."

Sally turned away then and fussed with the wrapping on the paper plates. "I look like me, Mom."

"Maybe you're getting sick. Do you feel well?" Melody walked toward her and lifted a hand to Sally's forehead.

Sally raised her hand in protest and backed up a step. "Mom, stop! I'm fine. I'm just a little tired and maybe a trite upset. That's all."

"What are you upset about?" Melody stood with arms at her sides, concern in her eyes.

She released a frustrated breath. "Walter isn't here yet. He promised he'd be home before the party started."

"I'm sure he'll be home soon. It is his daughter's birthday."

Sally looked at her mother. "Yes." She couldn't say more. All she could do was seethe. The wrapper over the plastic cups was being difficult. Sally got a scissor and cut the package open.

Melody stood leaning against the counter and watched.

The appetizers should go into the oven soon. Sally pulled a few boxes of frozen appetizers from the fridge freezer and laid out cookie sheets for them.

Robert and Emily would arrive shortly, as well as her uncle and aunt, Tommy and Clara Parker. Her cousin, their son, Benny, who was now twenty-five was living in Vancouver.

Sally had invited a few others, some of her closest friends.

"Has Walter held Isabella since the hospital?"

Sally tensed immediately. She never should have told her. It had been a mistake, a blunder at a weak moment. The question pierced her bruised heart and she couldn't speak. Fussing with the appetizers was easier than looking at her mother.

"Sally, I didn't ask that to hurt you. I'm only concerned for you and Isabella. She needs her father and it makes me sad to think that he doesn't spend any time with her. He's not acting like a father. It's just not natural."

"I didn't have a good father either and I survived." They were the only words that came to salvage the hurt and anger she felt.

Melody said, "I thought by now you'd have forgiven your father."

Sally looked at her then. Melody was upset. "I think I have forgiven Dad but memories are hard to forget."

"If you truly forgive someone then God will give you the grace to love them too."

Sally laughed cynically. "Mom, in my own way I love Dad, but I can't let go of the things he did. He was an awful father."

"Is he still an awful father?"

"Well, I have to admit that he does try hard now. Being a grandfather has changed him."

Melody nodded. "People can change, but only by the power of God. Your father has changed a great deal."

The conversation stalled and Sally was thankful. She busied herself with the party preparations. Melody stepped in beside her and helped.

The evening was more difficult than Sally had ever anticipated. With all the questions about Walter's whereabouts and the sympathetic looks from family and friends, Sally felt overcome with relief when the last birthday guest finally left. After changing Isabella into pajamas and tucking her into the crib, Sally headed for the bathroom. Isabella would be asleep in no time. The little thing was exhausted from all the action tonight.

In the bathroom, Sally withdrew the hidden box from the closet and took more than usual. The drug would numb her pain, at least for a while. Every hour or so, she went back for more. The need to cover the disappointment of the night overwhelmed her.

~~~~~

In the distance she heard a soft echo calling her. "Sally, Sally wake up."

Everything felt light and airy like she was floating, flying or drifting through space. The lethargic, carefree feeling was wonderful. Peace and tranquility ruled here and she had no desire to leave. Whoever was calling her would just have to wait. Rushing back to reality held no appeal. But then again, what was reality? She couldn't remember why she wouldn't want to go back. What was it that held such revulsion there?

Her mind felt foggy. To think straight was impossible. But why would she want to? This is the result she'd been after. Wasn't it?

The echo started again. "Sally, what's wrong with you? Wake up."

There was shuffling in the distance and she felt herself jerked in an uncomfortable manner. That was unusual. To open her eyes was pointless. There was no way she could do it. Maybe someone had taped her eyes shut. That made her laugh and yet she couldn't hear any laughter. Her mind was really playing tricks on her.

The floating feeling shimmied with some strange jolting motion again. She didn't want to stop flying. Her mind whirled in disjointed thoughts. It felt like her head was spinning out of control as if caught on a carousel, with no way to get off and it wasn't a sensation she was eager to release. The tranquility of this place was heavenly. The only negative was the soft voice urging her to wake up. Where was that coming from anyway? If only it would go away, leave her in peace.

"Sally, wake up right now!"

The intensity of the command brought some clarity to her dull senses. She tried to pry her eyes open but they closed just as quickly. It was way too bright out there so she folded back into the stillness, the darkness, back to the peace.

The shaking started then and rattled her head. A dull pain started in her shoulders and slowly grew stronger. The fog over her mind gradually lifted and she opened her eyes a crack.

His face looked familiar. She strained to focus.

"Come on, Sally, wake up."

Walter! It was Walter. The realization made her eyes open a bit further. She looked up and saw fear in his eyes. Why? Why would he be afraid? Of her? That was silly.

He tugged on her arms till she was sitting. The drug was still strong in her veins. She felt herself fall even as she sat up. He righted her and held her up. Sitting beside her he cushioned her, his arm around her waist to steady her.

She felt like a rag doll, flopping around helplessly. Walter finally laid her down, arranged some pillows behind her head to elevate her and sat beside her, waiting.

Darkness swallowed her and she drifted off. When she finally did open her eyes again, he was gone. Had she only imagined it? She reached back and felt the stack of pillows beneath her head. No, he had been here. Looking down, she noticed a blanket covering her, which was odd. The time on her nightstand clock showed just after eight.

That made her sit up. Isabella wasn't awake yet? Sally's head spun crazily. Already the downward spiral of depression started hitting her, common after such a dose of anti-depressants. She couldn't dwell on that now. Isabella needed her. Slipping into a pair of slippers, she steadied herself and headed to the door.

Isabella was curled up in her crib, thumb in her mouth, still sleeping peacefully. What an angel she was. Sally smiled. Isabella was the one great joy of her life. No one could take that away.

Sally wandered toward the kitchen and, as she did, she suddenly realized that it was Sunday morning. Walter would be at church. It was much too late for her to make it.

She could only imagine how angry he'd be. They were not allowed to miss church for any reason. Sheffield's rules ruled.

A note beside the coffee maker got her attention. It was Walter's writing. It said they'd talk when he got home.

Uttering a deep sound in her throat, she scoffed at it. A talk to him was telling her how to act, what to do and how to live. She was fed up with it. The probability of them discussing anything of importance rationally was slim. The despondency she felt over the upcoming "talk" didn't help her mood as she fixed a pot of coffee.

Hours later, Isabella was fed and playing quietly in the corner with her toys. Sally sat on the couch reading a magazine and drinking coffee when Walter walked in. Her nerves grew taut immediately. He closed the door quietly, took off his coat, hung it up, turned and looked at her. His eyes were hard to read.

After taking a seat opposite her, he asked, "So, how did Isabella's party go?"

She glared at him. Hurt and anger marched in quickly. "Why would you care? You certainly didn't make any effort to be a part of it!"

"I'm sorry, Sally. I truly am."

"Sorry doesn't cut it anymore, Walter!"

He breathed deeply and sighed. "Some important business came up at the church and I couldn't get away."

"So important that you couldn't even call to let me know where you were?"

"It was an awkward time for us at the church. It just wasn't convenient." He said it with a hint of a smile.

"So you find this whole situation amusing? You think it's a big joke that you hurt me terribly, embarrassed me in front of our guests yesterday and refuse to be a part of Isabella's life? Do you think I want to go on with a marriage like this?"

The smile disappeared. "Sally, I said I was sorry and I mean that. I never intended to miss her party. I had full intentions of being here and I bought her a gift too. I have it wrapped and it's waiting for her in the closet." He pointed in that direction. "I would never hurt you intentionally, Sally. You have to know that." He didn't look as repentant as his words implied.

"You have to make more effort with our daughter."

"I'm doing my best."

She chuckled cynically. "It's not nearly enough."

He released an exasperated breath. "I'm just not good at parenting. I don't know how to be the father you want me to be."

"You don't even try!" She pointed to Isabella, who had turned to watch them. "Look at the beautiful daughter God has given us. She needs you to love her. She needs both of us!"

He shook his head. "I don't know how."

"Is it because you wanted a son? Is that why you refuse to love her?" To express those words hurt her but she had to know.

"No!"

"You should thank God for this gift he's given you before you expect him to give you any more." Her words surprised even herself. They came without forethought.

His face changed from defensive to accusing within a second, making Sally suck in a tight breath.

With stony face he asked, "What was going on last night? You were on some drug, weren't you?"

Preservation was her only strategy plan. "It's one way to survive this marriage."

He looked shocked for a moment before his face hardened again. "Find a different way, Sally! I want you to stop taking drugs! That is no way for a church member to live and I am commanding you to stop!"

"And, if I don't?" She had no intention of allowing him to control and manipulate her any longer.

"I'll have to bring it to the attention of my father." The threat hung between them.

Sally laughed. "Oh, so you'll let your daddy take care of all your problems? Can't we work through our marriage without your daddy helping you?"

That she'd stepped too far was instantaneously clear. Walter flew from his chair and sailed toward her. His hand drew back and hit her hard across her cheek. Her head snapped back and her hand flew to her injured face. His eyes blazed with anger.

Although he looked furious, his voice was calm as he said, "You are going to stop taking whatever drug you've been using! I will leave my father out of it for now. It's only because I love you that I won't involve him. But don't you ever mock me again for the respect I show him!"

But he doesn't deserve any respect!

Although Sally thought it, she stayed silent. There was no point in arguing. Walter feared his father and Sally had grown to despise him. They were at polar ends of opinion concerning Sheffield Tassey.

"I need to leave for a while."

"Yeah, sure. Run off like usual." Sally shouldn't have said it.

His eyes immediately flared with anger.

She raised both hands in surrender. "Just go."

Isabella started to cry. He was scaring her.

He turned to leave but reiterated, "Get rid of all the drugs! I'll search the place when I get back." With that, he grabbed his coat, opened the door and left. The door smacked shut behind him.

Sally stood, picked up her daughter and held her close. Isabella's cries stopped and she stared into her mother's eyes.

"I'm sorry, baby. Daddy doesn't know what he's doing."

"Dada?"

Sally nodded.

Isabella pulled away so Sally set her back down. Isabella toddled back to her toys. If she let herself go she could cry but she was so weary of crying. This burning anger inside was destroying her. She determined to find a better hiding spot for the cocaine and anti-depressants, one he'd never find.

CHAPTER 28

July 2000

Perhaps her growing addiction was a problem, but Sally didn't perceive it that way. It was a coping mechanism and accommodated saneness. In her opinion, she managed life capably despite her escalating need for prescription meds and cocaine. Keeping it hidden it from Walter amused her.

Her merriment of the game was only tainted by his lack of love. Their marriage was now totally a charade. Proceeding from one day to the next was a task.

She'd found a supplier close to her work. The bank where he worked had no idea their employee was dabbling in an alternate enterprise. His suit and tie and smart looks made it a pleasure doing business. Negotiating with him felt respectable. They met at a convenient coffee shop between their offices and exchanged envelopes. Anyone observing would swear they were honest business people just going about their everyday jobs. He always brought his laptop and was tapping at those keys every time she entered the coffee joint. It made things look so legit and him so devoted to his work. The thought made her smile.

Even though her dependence had grown, as long as it didn't interfere with her work, she didn't mind. Fashion design was one love she refused to give up or sacrifice. She'd put way too much time into it to abandon it now. Her reputation had grown in the industry and there was no way she was willing to toss that. It had gotten to the point where there was talk that she could easily launch out on her own. She'd heard the grapevine gossip second-hand from Jason. He'd even told her without any sign of jealousy or animosity. However, she felt too spent emotionally lately to pursue any sort of entrepreneurial venture.

Her thoughts turned to Walter. Sally became morose as she contemplated the heights from which their former, sweet love had fallen. To leave, to call it quits, forced her to admit defeat once again.

Sally forced her attention back to the computer screen. After staring at it blankly for a full five minutes, she finally delved into what needed doing.

Two hours later, she sat back in the chair, her elbows resting on the armrests and her chin on her folded hands. She'd accomplished a lot in a few hours.

Her mind was swimming with the repercussions of what she was planning to do but she was ready. She dug the phone number out of her pocket and stared at it. It was during Jason's difficulties that he'd dropped the name of the law firm. As far as she knew, they had been satisfactory to his liking.

She still wasn't sure she was doing the right thing but she didn't know what else to do. Walter had not turned out to be the dream she'd hoped for. He no longer seemed to love her. They rarely saw each other. He came home late every night. Even on Sundays their time together was minimal. They'd go to church together but then Walter had meetings with his father and she and Isabella would spend the remainder of the day alone. They always drove to church at different times now, making it easy to live separate lives.

Walter almost never looked at his daughter. He never held her or spent any meaningful time with her. Isabella cried if he got too close and he seemed fine with that. Sally didn't bother bringing up his façade of a relationship with Isabella anymore. Furthermore, Walter refused to discuss it.

Sally had had enough and it was time to make a change. She picked up the phone and dialed the number to Rhineland, Griffith and Crichton Law Office.

When she lowered the phone back into its base, she felt serene. They had been more than helpful and a date had been set to discuss her options. It finally felt like she was getting somewhere, moving on with her life, taking charge. To feel like she was back in control was liberating. Relief flooded her.

Sally glanced at the clock. Oh dear, it was a few minutes past lunch time. Her moment of relief vanished and dread returned. Mary had talked her into joining her down at the corner deli, insisting they needed to talk. It was hard to believe. Although they'd worked together for many years, they'd never socialized. Mary accessorized the outfits Sally made for the shows. Designers and the after-effects crew rarely mingled. Why Mary was now making an effort to connect was a mystery.

Sally gathered her things and headed to the door. Mary was probably at the restaurant already.

Outside, the hot July sun beat down on her as she traversed the busy sidewalk. Stepping into the restaurant, the air conditioning cooled the perspiration that had accumulated on her neck and face. It felt heavenly to get out of the sun. She spotted Mary sitting at a booth along the side. Sally said hi and slipped in opposite her.

Mary smiled warmly. She was a few years older and had worked for Gregory Taylor faithfully for years. Gregory viewed Mary as indispensable to his business and Sally had to admit that the woman was confident, smart and extremely creative in accessorizing every outfit produced by Taylor Design. Her ideas were legendary. She once admitted having been courted by other design companies offering lucrative salaries but her devotion to Gregory made her turn down the proposals.

After eating, they both ordered coffee. Mary indulged in an apple crumble with ice cream. Sally stayed with her black coffee.

After wiping the crumbs from her mouth with a napkin, Mary laid it down and looked at Sally. A sudden, inexplicable tension filled the air between them and Sally wondered what Mary had in mind.

"I'm sure you're wondering what this is all about."

Sally leaned back and laid her hands in her lap. "Yes. I have been wondering."

Mary took a more aggressive approach, leaning forward with her arms folded on the table. "I've heard rumors – changes that are coming for Taylor Fashion Design and I don't like it. It hasn't been that long since the last upheaval and I'm not ready for another one."

There'd been talk but Sally hadn't paid much attention. Problems of her own had occupied her attention.

Mary continued, "I heard that Gregory is planning to move more people to the States, but this time to Minneapolis. The office there has experienced a lot of staff turnover and their productivity has been less than stellar. Gregory is losing patience. I've heard he's planning to fire the office manager and replace him."

The gossip grapevine was in full bloom. That was far more than Sally had heard. Her forehead creased in bewilderment. "And who did you hear all this from?"

"It doesn't matter. What does matter is that our office can't sustain more major changes like this. A number of people left in the last transition to New York. The new people we hired have come along but how can this fashion division keep hiring new designers without feeling the effects? At the last transition I started to see a decline in valuable and consumable designs. With the coming changes, it could degenerate again. It's causing me great alarm. This can't go on. If Gregory wants me to continue accessorizing his designs he will have to give me progressively superior designs to commission. My reputation is on the line."

"I can understand your concerns, but how does this relate to me? Why not go straight to Gregory and discuss your apprehensions with him?"

"For one thing, he doesn't know I know about the changes." Mary hesitated.

"And? What else?"

"And...I have an issue with your designs as well." She let out a pent up breath. "There I finally said it!"

A sudden defensiveness rose up. "There's nothing wrong with my designs!" If only Mary knew how hard she had worked lately, she would never say such a thing.

"I don't mean to insult or to degrade your work, but there has been an obvious decline in creativity, vision and on-the-edge design work from you in the past year."

Sally wracked her mind to find some variance or fault in her work ethic, creativity or relevancy in her designs. Nothing came to mind. She worked just as hard, ideas flowed seamlessly like usual and Gregory was as pleased as always. Her eyes narrowed as she studied the woman across from her and wondered about her motives.

Mary asked, "Is something going on in your life that's producing this deterioration in quality work?"

Two could play this game. With an edge, Sally answered, "I work harder than all the other designers in this office. I have consistently produced quality blueprints, designs that Gregory has fully endorsed. What right do you have to criticize something you don't know anything about? What does someone in accessories know about designs anyway? Your accusations are totally biased and unfounded."

Mary raised her hands in surrender. "Whoa, Sally. You need to know that I have a lot of confidence in your ability and I respect your creativity. Your past record shows that you are a top-notch designer."

Her words calmed Sally's agitation slightly.

"I obviously need to take a different approach." Mary smiled.

Sally saw no need to respond.

"I've seen this kind of thing before."

Warily, Sally asked, "What are you talking about?"

"I've seen very successful, promising people with great aptitude and awesome savvy, slowly begin to decline and become non-influential in their fields of expertise. I've seen it happen almost overnight."

Sally's skin crawled at the implications.

"From where I sit, it's either an addiction to alcohol or drugs."

"How dare you?" There was no way she'd admit to anything, especially not to someone in accessories!

"You can't keep it a secret forever. If I've noticed, others in the office will notice soon too."

Sally stared at her with what she hoped looked like fury and indignation.

Mary didn't flinch. "I've had friends who've been through addictions. Your glassy-looking eyes are the giveaway."

Sally blinked a few times, realized what she was doing and stopped. "You're barking up the wrong tree, girl!"

The putdown didn't faze Mary a bit. "Some of my friends sought help and others didn't. The ones who pursued guidance are back at their professions and are doing what they once did with great success. The ones who refused to accept advice are now either dead or on skid row. You need help and I know of some good clinics that can help you get off whatever you're on."

Does she ever have a lot of nerve! Why doesn't she find a high cliff somewhere and take a flying leap?

Sally looked around to see if she recognized anyone she knew. If anyone was listening in, this kind of conversation could be disastrous to her future.

Mary smiled again from across the table. "Don't worry. There's no one you know here, except me."

Leaning forward, Sally spoke very clearly. "I am not addicted to anything! Work means everything to me! My greatest problem right now is you! You need to mind your own business and leave me alone! You're meddling in stuff you know nothing about."

"I know enough just to look at you. You have the classic signs of substance abuse. If your husband doesn't see it, I certainly do. You might be able to fool everyone else but you're not fooling me. I've had too many people around me destroyed by drugs and booze and I don't want to see you dismantling your future by using them. You're too good of a designer just to let it slip away."

Sitting back, anger riding up her spine, her gaze locked on Mary, Sally shook her head. "Why are you doing this? My work is none of your concern. I answer to Gregory, not to you."

"It's not that simple. If you can't do your work effectively then I refuse to have my work associated and sabotaged because of your sloppy designs."

The insult was too much. She stood up abruptly and said, "I don't need to listen to this garbage." Digging in her purse for a twenty, she threw it on the table.

"It's part of the business, Sally. If you can't compete, then get out."

She stared at Mary wide-eyed. The woman had a lot of guts.

Mary stared back. "I'd rather see you get your life straightened out and progress as the innovative designer I know you are. I'm trying to be a friend here, let you know that you need to stay competitive and avant-garde or else you'll be left behind. I'm trying to help you."

With a sarcastic edge, Sally said, "Thanks for your help!" She turned and left the restaurant. She felt badly shaken. If Gregory ever got wind of Mary's suspicions she could lose everything she'd achieved to date. To have her work taken from her would destroy her.

After work, Sally picked up Isabella at the daycare and placed her in the stroller. Each morning she left the wheeled contraption at the daycare, storing it for her till she got back for pickup. They headed to the Go Train station and got on. It was the most economical way to travel the downtown core and it serviced her neighborhood. From their exit point, Sally only needed to walk a few blocks to reach her apartment.

Waiting for her exit, Sally gazed at Isabella and marveled again at the little beauty she was becoming. Even at twenty months, her looks foretold the gorgeous woman she would one day be. If only Walter could see that Isabella resembled him; maybe then he'd fall in love with her. Sally brushed the thought away. It was too late for wishful thinking.

The Go Train came to a halt. Sally pushed the stroller out, crossed the street and headed up the sidewalk.

She stopped in the foyer of her apartment building to get her mail before heading up. Once in the apartment she extracted Isabella from her stroller. She hurried over to her toys and started playing. Sally watched her daughter rub her tired eyes. The little thing would need to eat dinner soon then head to bed. Sally had so little time with Isabella. It was a poignant thought. At times like this she wished she were a stay-at-home mom.

Sally sat on the couch and scanned through the stack of mail. A brown, sturdy envelope caught her attention. The return address in the corner told her what it would contain. She tore it open and read every word to make sure it was exactly as she had specified. Laying the divorce papers on her lap, she knew her decision was for the best. Once she approved the draft, they'd send Walter a copy of his own. She should tell him tonight. It was only fair that he knew what was coming.

After putting the document with the rest of the mail, she glanced at her watch. It was getting late and she wasn't expecting Walter till later. Isabella was always asleep when he got home. Sally no longer mentioned his late hours. It only caused arguments and she didn't care about his so-called packed schedule. His agenda rarely included her. Well, if he no longer wanted her in his life then she was ready to let him go.

She prepared dinner for the two of them and put Isabella to bed. Stroking her daughter's cheek affectionately, she watched her fall asleep. The poor thing was exhausted!

While clearing the table, she heard a loud knock at her door. How could anyone get up to her apartment without her activating the security door downstairs in the foyer? Unless a resident had let them sneak in with them.

Nervously, she walked to the door and looked through the view hole. A policeman's uniform came into view. She stepped back in surprise, her mind racing with the possibilities. The first thing that came to mind was Walter. *He's been in an accident.* Her throat tightened with emotion. Although she was done with their marriage, she never willed any harm toward him.

They knocked again. Apprehensively, she released the lock and opened the door. "Yes? How can I help you?"

One officer took the lead, the sternness in his eyes intimidating. "Are you Mrs. Tassey?"

"Yes, I'm Sally Tassey."

"And your husband's name is Walter Tassey?"

"Yes, that's correct."

"Is he home?"

"Home?"

Now, why would they ask that? He's not hurt after all?

"No, he hasn't arrived home yet. Do you need to talk with him?"

"We have a warrant for his arrest."

Shock reverberated through her. "His arrest? But why?"

"We can't go into detail until we speak with him. When do you expect him?"

With one hand she rubbed her forehead. "I don't know. He usually gets home quite late."

"We'll wait for him downstairs. We have his identification with us so we should have no problem recognizing him." The officer nodded and turned.

"Wait!"

He turned back to her.

"Please, would you mind if I had a chance to speak with him first? Let him come up to the apartment, give us some time to talk and then you can come arrest him. Please?" Sally could see the hesitation on his face. "I need to hear it from him first, please!"

Her plea must have touched the younger officer beside him. He said, "It wouldn't hurt. We'll stay close and she could call us when they're done."

The other officer turned a fierce look in her direction. "Well, considering the tender nature of the offense, it might be for the best. We'll be at the coffee shop down the street. I'll leave my number with you. You'll need to call us as soon as you're ready. If you don't call within the hour, we'll be back here. Is that understood?"

"But he won't be back in an hour." Sally looked at her watch and then met the officer's eyes again. "It'll be more like two hours."

He released a frustrated breath. "All right, we'll give you two hours, no longer."

"Thank you."

The men turned away and headed down the hall. Sally closed the door and leaned against it.

For an hour she paced her apartment, worry and fear gnawing at her. No matter how she tried, she couldn't for the life of her figure out what this was about. What could Walter have gotten into that was illegal? All he did was work at the real estate office and help out at his father's church. At least that's what she'd thought till now.

She considered her Bible hidden away beneath her clothes in her bottom dresser drawer. Maybe she should get it out and read again. But what would it solve? Walter was in a pickle and mere words weren't enough to help.

It was still much too early for Walter to be home. She switched on the TV and watched some news, a reality show and a comedy. Nothing held her attention. Finally, a sound at the door brought her head around. His whistling gave him away. The clock on the wall showed they had twenty minutes to spare till the officers came back.

Walter stepped through the door, set down his briefcase, looked at her and smiled. His cheerfulness instantly disappeared when he saw the look on her.

"What's wrong? How are you doing?"

"Not very well."

"Why?"

"Because our marriage is over."

His smile vanished. "What? What are you talking about?"

"It's over, Walter. I want out."

After studying her face for a minute, with a firm voice he said, "No. It's not over. Our marriage is vitally important to me. It's God-ordained and it's meant to last for a lifetime."

"Are those your words or church words?" Sally was in no mood for his pat answers, especially not tonight.

"Come on, Sally, let's not argue. We hardly have time together as it is and we need to make the most of the few moments we have."

He was right on that point. There were only a few moments to say what she had to say. "I want to know what you do all these late nights and on the weekends with your father."

Taking a deep breath of air, he released it tiredly. "Not this again!"

She felt just as tired as he sounded. "If you don't tell me, I'm about to find out anyway. I'd prefer hearing it from you."

"What in the world are you talking about?" He shook his head in confusion, turned away from her and picked up the stack of mail on the coffee table.

The brown envelope sat in Walter's hands. The realization caused perspiration to moisten Sally's hands. Maybe hitting it square on was the best way to deal with the issue.

Walter lifted it and asked, "What's this about? It's addressed to you."

"Those are divorce papers sent from my lawyer." She watched him.

A dumbstruck look spread across his face and his mouth stood ajar.

"I'm serious, Walter. We're through."

His mouth closed and he shook his head. "No, we're not."

His denial was expected. She would have to divert his attention to another matter first. There wasn't much time left. "There's something else you need to know."

"You're not leaving me, Sally. We belong together."

She felt sorry for him. He was so disillusioned, it was truly sad.

"When I said, 'I do,' I meant it for a lifetime."

"No you didn't, Walter. I don't matter to you anymore. Isabella doesn't matter to you."

"Of course you do." The reality was starting to hit home. He looked lost.

She had to refocus him on what was about to walk through their front door. "Walter, listen to me. In a few minutes two police officers are coming here to arrest you."

It took a bit for the information to register. "What?"

"Two officers came to our door earlier this evening."

Confusion clouded his eyes. "Two officers?"

She nodded.

"But why?"

"I don't know. You tell me. They were planning to arrest you down in the lobby when you arrived home but I asked if I could speak with you first."

"I've done nothing wrong!"

"If you're innocent then why would they want to arrest you?"

"None of this makes sense." He did look worried, though.

She glanced down at her watch. "They'll be back here in ten minutes."

He sprang from his chair and paced. "I have to get out of here."

His response stunned her. She stood and went to him. "Walter, you can't run from the police! Tell me what's going on!"

"I can't." Frantically, he rushed toward the door, grabbed his brief case, coat and keys and flung the door wide. He turned back and said, "I promise I'll come back and then I'll explain everything."

"Walter, you can't run! You have to face up to whatever this is."

"I can't stay." With that the door closed and he was gone.

It felt surreal, like she was dreaming. After a moment's thought, she took her key, left her apartment, locked it and took the elevator down. Before the doors even opened on the main floor, she could hear the commotion.

The sight that greeted her was astonishing. Walter was face down on the lobby floor with one police officer's knee on his back, slapping handcuffs around his wrists. The other officer was pointing a gun at his head. Walter pleaded for mercy. The officers ignored his petition.

Sally's heart was in her throat as she watched the implausible scene. As if her life wasn't enough to deal with, now she had another dose of impossible to cope with. To see the man she once loved in such a humiliating situation brought tears to her eyes. How could this be happening?

The officers pulled Walter to his feet and that's when he saw her.

"Sally! Tell them I haven't done anything wrong. Tell them, Sally!"

Her cheeks felt wet as tears spilled from her eyes.

The officers turned apologetic glances her way but kept a firm grip on Walter's arms.

"Tell them I'm an innocent man, a good husband and father! Tell them, Sally!" His voice was desperate and growing louder.

No words came. She was too choked up to speak. What could she say? She didn't know who he was anymore. A good husband he was not and he was an ever worse father.

The two officers turned Walter firmly and led him to the front doors. A few residents had stopped to watch the action. Thankfully, at this time at night, there weren't a lot of people coming and going.

Walter screamed, "Sally, Sally? Say something, Sally!"

Her tears came harder then.

As the doors closed behind the three leaving, Walter's voice became muffled but she could still hear his agitated words.

"I'm a good Christian man! I'm a church-going man! I don't deserve this!"

She watched them open the squad car and push him inside.

"Sally, please, come with me! Sal…"

That was the last she heard as the car door slammed shut. Soon the lights flared and the police car pulled away.

Angrily, she swiped at her wet face and forced the tide of anxiety down. A tinge of gratitude surfaced. Walter's secrets were about to be exposed and for that she was grateful. Even though it wrenched her insides to see him in such a state, everything hidden would finally be brought into the open.

As she walked back to her apartment, she was greeted with a ringing phone. She ignored it as she paced the floor, hoping it wouldn't wake Isabella. There was no way she could speak to anyone right now. She was an emotional wreck!

She cried, she punched pillows, the couch, anything available and she wondered. The phone rang a few more times.

"If it's important, leave a message!" she yelled to the unknown caller.

And then, that's exactly what happened.

Lynne Tassey's shaky voice said, "Sally, if you're there, please pick up."

Sally stared at the phone, wondering. Finally, she grabbed the headset, put it to her ear and said, "I'm here."

"Sally."

Sally waited but Lynne remained silent. Was she crying?

Yes, Lynne was definitely crying. "Did…they arrest…Walter too?"

"Lynne, what's going on?"

Sobs filled the earpiece. She settled somewhat and said, "The police came and arrested Sheffield. It's so horrible. I don't know what to do. Can I please speak to Walter?"

"They took Walter away."

"Who?"

"The police."

"No!" Lynne broke down on the other end, crying hysterically.

Sally waited a few moments. She needed information. Lynne was the one to give it. "Lynne, please tell me what you know."

"I can't tell you, Sally."

"Look, I'm going to find out anyway! Sheffield and Walter have both been arrested. Soon, whatever this is about will be in every newspaper in this city and on every newscast. I'm going to find out."

"No." Her sobs filled the earpiece again.

"It would be easier for me if I knew before the whole world knows. Please, Lynne, tell me what's going on?"

For a while, there was silence on the other end. Lynne sniffled and wiped her nose. Sally waited and hoped the woman would have sense enough to come clean.

Lynne then finally broke her silence and her solemn vow of secrecy and told Sally everything.

CHAPTER 29

December 2000

Five months after Walter's arrest and incarceration, Sally moved to Minneapolis/St. Paul, the twin cities in Minnesota. It was right after Christmas. Gregory Taylor had talked her into it and she was thankful. It gave her a fresh start. He needed her at the Minneapolis branch and had full confidence in her. So much for Mary's misgivings.

A new manager had been hired in Minneapolis and Gregory had flown him to Toronto in November so the two of them could meet. Sally had liked him from the start. Fritz Lecanto was in his fifties, pudgy around the middle and balding, but his attitude was full of confidence and his vision for the Minneapolis branch was inspiring.

When she told her parents of her move, they were understandably upset. They balked at it, saying they'd miss her and Isabella. Sally assured them she'd come back for visits and insisted they come to see her often. Melody said they were getting older and it was harder to travel. Vern dismissed that statement by promising to come as often as they could.

Robert, when he heard, understood but the sorrow in his eyes was clear. He said he'd miss her terribly and promised to come see her when he could.

Although the move gave Sally a new lease on life, moving away was harder than she'd imagined. There were so many changes within such a short period. It rocked her for a time. Isabella became cranky and moody for months. Eventually things settled into a regular routine. The Minneapolis office gradually settled as well and the new staff slowly gelled and began working as a team. Despite all this, Sally's emotions remained raw, oozing pain. It was impossible to forget the rejection and heartache Walter had caused. Cocaine helped numb her feelings. A new dealer had been easy to find.

~~~~~

May 2004

The waiting room seemed stifling and the chair uncomfortable as Sally waited for her appointment. The drug she'd taken before she came helped curb her nervousness.

How could she have messed up so big time? Her move four years earlier had seemed like the perfect opportunity at the right time. Gregory Taylor had offered her the greatest gift possible.

If only she'd kicked her habit when she'd moved, she wouldn't be in this place. She hadn't really wanted to quit back then; the stuff helped her get from one day to the next. Now cocaine had a tight grip on her body. She'd tried to stop a few times but she couldn't do it.

In the last year, drugs had eaten away at her pocket book and even with a large salary, benefits and perks, she was struggling to survive. To keep up with her rent payment and utilities wasn't doable anymore. Her ability to concentrate and benefit the design company had diminished rapidly the last six months.

She rubbed her hands together nervously. First, Fritz Lecanto had called her on it. He suspected she was a user and demanded an explanation of her shoddy workmanship. She finally broke down and admitted it. It was obvious, even to her, that she was barely capable of artistic designs. Even in her own estimation, her work the last months was horrible. She struggled to think or create. Her once cutting-edge vision in the fashion industry had nosedived into oblivion.

It wasn't long till Gregory was informed. He'd been furious at first. She couldn't blame him. There'd been a lot of money and shuffling involved to make her transition to Minneapolis possible. A lot had been invested moving her here and he'd lauded her praises to Fritz. Guilt and depression had barraged her since she'd been found out.

Gregory Taylor had flown down numerous times to discuss solutions to the problem and he finally laid out an ultimatum. After checking out the options, and since Sally had been with the company many years, he made it as painless as possible for her.

His requirements had seemed reasonable and that was why she was here, waiting in this office for her appointment to begin. Gregory didn't want to let her go, but agreed to bring in a replacement for the time being. After doing some research, he'd found this rehabilitation home in Chelsey for her and insisted on paying. If she completed the rehab successfully, he was willing to take her back. His kindness brought tears to her eyes. He was a good man.

Breaking the news to her mother was the worst. Melody had taken it well. Years of dealing with Vern's alcohol addiction had helped to harden her. Melody had agreed to fly out to Minneapolis to take care of Isabella. There was no way Sally could do this without her mother's help. Vern would come later. He'd gotten a part-time job and didn't want to give it up.

Isabella was attending first grade at a private school close to their apartment in Minneapolis. Melody would have to drive her there and back but other than that, there wasn't much she would need to do except cook meals. Thinking of Isabella caused Sally's guilt to soar anew. She'd failed as a mother. Isabella had so many questions and she didn't know how to answer them.

"Why are you going away? Why are you sick, Mommy? Can I come too? Why can't you stay home with me? Why does Grandma have to take care of me? Won't you miss me? Who will take me to school?"

Moisture filled Sally's eyes and a tear trickled down her cheek. She swiped it away. Crying wouldn't help and it wouldn't reunite her with Isabella any sooner.

Why couldn't Gregory have found a drug rehab in Minneapolis? Weren't there any credible places there? Why in Chelsey? What did this small, out-of-the-way place have that a big city like Minneapolis didn't? It frustrated her to be so far away from Isabella. She didn't know when she'd be able to see her daughter again.

Posters on the walls caught her attention. Her eyes darted from one to the next. Every one of them contained a Bible verse in bold lettering. Her heart constricted at the sight. This place was a religious organization? She hadn't been told. She'd had enough religion to last her a lifetime. Why hadn't she known before? Why hadn't she asked Gregory more questions? She'd simply trusted him to make a wise choice for her.

Her stomach churned with anxiety and revulsion. The desire to get up and run out was overwhelming. She tried to focus on something else, anything to get her mind off the posters.

The foyer where she sat was huge, the high ceiling above her dwarfing her. It was an impressive place. A large crystal chandelier hung from the high ceiling, the lights making patterned designs everywhere. Identical curved stairways swooped up to the top floor, which overlooked the expansive foyer below. In the center of the foyer stood a circular, ornate table holding a massive floral arrangement. The place looked far more like an elaborate hotel entrance than a rehabilitation home.

Even with the beauty all around her, Sally couldn't evade the scriptures posted on the walls. They were hung everywhere.

She reached for a magazine and leafed through it. What had Gregory told her about this place? He'd said their success rate was phenomenal and that they used innovative ideas to free their residents of drug addiction. He said they had cutting-edge techniques. She glanced at one of the posters. Was this what he meant? As far as she knew, he wasn't religious at all. Curse words poured freely when he was frazzled. She read the words on the poster directly across from her.

"Then you will know the truth and the truth will set you free. John 8:32"

Sally grunted in disgust. "Yeah, right! Like that'll work."

The longer she studied those words, the more it felt like fear would swallow her whole. The last thing she needed was more pat answers and simple-minded Bible verses. Avoiding any religious institution had become a talent of hers. To find herself here, surrounded by all these Bible sayings was nauseating.

Sally thought of her own Bible. She didn't know where it was anymore. It was probably still packed in one of the boxes in storage. She hadn't read it since Walter forbade it. She'd intended to read it just to spite him but it was hard to understand and didn't seem to help anyway.

"Hello, Sally?"

The voice made her jump.

"I'm sorry. I didn't mean to startle you." The young woman stepped forward and held out her hand. "I'm Tessa Fields. Are you Sally Tassey?"

Sally brushed her long, stringy hair out of her eyes, nodded and shook the girl's hand. The drugs had done that, made her hair nasty and unmanageable. The look in the young woman's eyes was like a magnet. They were full of concern and compassion but Sally determined to keep her guard up. There was no way she'd give in to some sweet young thing with no life experience.

Swallowing her fear, Sally said, "Actually, I go by Sally Windsor. I haven't used the name Tassey in years."

"Oh, okay." Tessa opened the file folder in her hands, wrote down the information and looked up. "Will you please follow me to my office?" She smiled sweetly and walked toward a hallway, past a row of offices.

Sally stood on wobbly legs and followed the young thing into an office. She was struck by the grandeur and splendor of the archways, French doors and tall, ornately-carved window frames all around her, not to mention the gardens outside the windows. She took the seat opposite Tessa's desk, trying not to stare, and placed her folded hands in her lap.

The young woman glanced at the information in the file and looked up. "I want to welcome you to the Mansion of Hope, Sally. This truly is a place of hope. So many women who enter our program feel complete despair. I want to assure you that you won't leave feeling that way. We have helped so many women overcome and fight addiction to drugs and substances and have been able to lead them into a spiritual experience that has brought them tremendous peace."

"Okay, that's the place to start then." Sally couldn't let another moment go by without setting things straight.

"What place is that?"

"I want to know what kind of spiritual experience you're talking about."

"Well, as you know from our advertising and mission statement, we are a Christian organization. We base our program on John 8:32 where Jesus says, 'You will know the truth, and the truth will set you free.' We believe that the only way to real freedom is through the truth written in God's Word. We implement scriptures in our methods and have had tremendous success."

Sally couldn't hide her disdain. She could feel her face twisting in revulsion.

"Is this something you object to?"

"Religion and I don't get along too well. Let's just say I've had my issues." She knew she had to get out of here soon. This was the wrong place for her. Sitting still took great effort.

"We have had other women who were opposed to scriptures being read over them and the Christian foundation of this home. However, if you've read some of the testimonials online, you'll see that all of them reveal dramatic changes experienced through our program. We as counselors and those on staff can only do so much to help you. We're human like you are and on our own we can do very little. The God who created us wrote the Bible and he knows what we need and how to bring us deliverance. At the Mansion of Hope we simply take God's Word, which is a detailed description of his will, and read and declare it over the lives of the women he sends us. God's Word, his promises, has his power within them to bring them to pass."

The long description sounded too religious and yet Tessa's explanation hit a chord. Was there really power in words? Did God's words have power to deliver her? It seemed like wishful thinking. Is this what Gregory meant by innovative techniques?

Tessa smiled. "You're welcome to speak to any of the women that have been through our program and ask them about our effectiveness. I know they will be completely upfront and honest with you."

Sally shook her head. She just wanted to get out of here.

"Once you agree to enter our program, if at any point you feel this is not for you and insist on leaving, we will honor your request and let you go. But I absolutely believe in our program and its ability to help you."

"I'm so tired of religion." Sally rubbed her forehead with the fingers of her right hand. Weariness was increasing with this young woman's long-winded talk. What was her name again? She'd already forgotten. A glance at the nameplate sitting on the desk refreshed her memory.

"We're not here to push religion or Christianity down your throat. A relationship with Jesus Christ is your own decision. What we do insist on is our proven method of bringing you to freedom from drugs. It has been extremely effective for many women."

Sally nodded tentatively. Their method scared her but she knew she needed to get free. She owed it to Gregory.

"When women see the power of God begin to work in their lives, setting them free, they become eager to know this God better. God's plan for you is good."

Whoa! I don't believe this crap!

"You've been hurt by religion."

Tessa's statement only infuriated Sally. "So what?"

"A true encounter with God would liberate you, not enslave you."

Sally didn't know how to answer. The statement was bold and daring. A slave she was. She couldn't deny that. Cocaine held her tightly by the throat and refused to loosen its grip. The last church she'd been involved with had been like a prison and it certainly hadn't liberated anyone.

"God is love. Experiencing the love of God will melt you from the inside out. It won't turn you into a fortress of steel."

Is that how she sees me? An impenetrable fortress?

She'd vowed not to allow anyone in to hurt her again. So it was working.

Tessa said, "You see, a fortress is only good if you want to live a solitary life."

Sally could feel her defenses going up. It sounded like the young thing was about to trash her life dogma.

Tessa continued, "It not only keeps you safe from hurt, but it keeps everyone else at a full arm's length. You'll never be close to anyone again, not even your daughter. And you won't let God get anywhere near you."

"That's right."

Tessa stared at her, compassion flowing from her eyes.

Sally looked at her hands in her lap, wanting to focus on anything to get away from the pity in the young woman's eyes.

"Why don't you tell me how religion hurt you?"

Sally's head snapped up. "Why?" She'd never shared it with anyone and didn't want to start now. Only her family knew and they were far enough away not to remind her. The whole wretched ordeal was best left forgotten and buried.

"It'll help us understand you better and will assist us in helping you."

"You don't want to know about my garbage."

"Yes, I do."

Sally stared at her. *Why? Why does she want to know? And what would it help to dredge it up?*

"It's vitally important that we know as much about your past experiences as possible. The drugs that you are addicted to are a cover-up for something much deeper. Drugs only help to numb pain and trauma and getting rid of the drugs is just part of the program. We want to bring healing to the pain so that drugs will no longer be needed. If the pain remains, the lure of drugs will remain strong."

"So you want me to air all my dirty laundry so you can look at it, and then what?" Sally wasn't sure this was such a good idea.

"Sally, if you're not willing to share your past with us, we can't bring you to complete freedom or deliverance. Being truthful about your issues and problems is the only way we can truly help you. If you continue to hide your hurtful past and cover it all up with substance abuse, it will eventually kill you."

"I died years ago. My love for my daughter is the only thing still alive."

"There's something in your past that took hope and life from you. I know a God who loves you, wants to heal those broken areas and give you a renewed hope."

Tears unexpectedly threatened just below the surface. Sally felt her carefully-guarded, stony heart begin to crumble. She'd caught a glimpse of hope. She wanted to live, to laugh and to feel again. Was this really possible? It seemed so risky. She looked at Tessa. "What do I do?"

"Start wherever you want."

Sally couldn't believe it! Suddenly she wanted to talk. It was uncanny and unnatural. What was with this room that moved her this way? She looked around but saw no clue. Maybe there was hidden incense burning somewhere that was affecting her senses. Perhaps it was spiked with something strong to get people's tongues flapping. There was no sign of trickery in the room. It was an office with file cabinets, desk, chairs, a few plants scattered about and a coat rack – an overly-ornate-looking room, yes, but still an office – and it didn't give off any bad vibes. Why was she feeling this way? She had an overwhelming urge finally to open up and spill her guts.

Sally looked at Tessa and studied her.

Tessa gave her an encouraging smile.

After a deep breath and heavy sigh, Sally began to talk. She shared it all, her childhood, dysfunctional upbringing, failed relationships, divorces and disappointments. Only when she came to Walter and his father's church did she choke up. Tears slipped down her cheeks and she batted at them angrily.

"He must have hurt you very much."

"He's not worth crying over."

"What happened?"

After getting her emotions in check, she shared how they fell in love and how Walter seemed like the perfect husband. His religion is what drew her to him. He was a strong spiritual leader and offered stability. She shared the downward spiral. She shared it all.

When she got to the arrests, her tears started again. Rummaging in her purse for tissue, she found only wet, used ones.

Tessa reached for the tissue box sitting on her desk and handed it over. Sally grabbed it, took two and wiped her cheeks.

Tessa asked, "Why were they arrested?"

Sally met the young woman's eyes, wondering what she thought. The story was embarrassing. How could anyone be sucked in to a cult like she was? Had she been that blind?

"It's okay. I've heard many stories that are hard to believe."

Can she read my thoughts?

Sally swallowed hard and continued, "Sheffield Tassey had this revelation from heaven. They had a new way to offer salvation." She grimaced and then continued. "By having sex with women, they guaranteed them a free pass to heaven."

The look on Tessa's face made Sally stop. She had shocked the young thing.

Tessa finally said, "Go on."

"I guess they didn't use their brains. They got involved with minors and when the girls' fathers found out, that was the end of it.

Charges were laid and Sheffield and Walter were arrested." Sally's tears had dried up with the telling. "Now they're sitting in a jail cell where they belong."

Tessa nodded. "And what about your daughter? Does she miss her father?"

"No. He was never a father to her. I married him because I thought he'd be a good role model for our children and I ended up marrying a devil in disguise."

"And when did you move to Minneapolis?"

"As soon as I could get away."

The young woman nodded, closed the file and folded her hands on her desk. "Thank you. I know it took courage to open up and tell me all of this and I appreciate it."

Sally nodded. Where the bravery came from, she had no idea. That she'd opened up at all was a shock. She felt completely drained and so very tired.

CHAPTER 30

July 2004

The July wind was wicked. It whipped Tessa's hair around in a frantic pattern. She grabbed her hair with one hand, held the gift bag with the other and headed to the door of Richelle and Charlie's new house. They'd had it built, a three-bedroom bungalow with an unfinished basement. They were able to make all the finishing selections according to their tastes and moved in two weeks ago. Tessa and Cody had helped them move but this was her first official visit.

The neighborhood was brand new. Houses were going up all around and the clamor of construction filled the air. There was only one home with completed landscaping. It stood across the street, surrounded by green sod against a backdrop of mounds of dirt banked up everywhere. It would be a while for the neighborhood to take shape and it made Tessa thankful for the mature trees and greenery in her well-established neighborhood.

Walking across wooden planks, which served as a path to the door, kept her flip flops clean but it did take some concentration. She rang the doorbell and waited.

The door opened and Richelle smiled brightly. "Hi Tessa, come on in."

Tessa held out the gift. "Here, this is for you."

"What's this?"

"A house-warming gift."

"Oh! That's so thoughtful!" She grabbed it, left Tessa standing by the door and went to sit down in the living room to open it. Tessa shook her head, stepped inside, closed the door, slipped out of her flip flops and followed her

After ripping out the sparkly teal tissue paper from the gift bag, Richelle lifted out the rectangular box and opened it. She held up the metal wall hanging. "I love it!" Three trees were connected by a metal strip of grass. It was different, funky.

"I'm glad. I thought it would go well in your dining room."

Richelle held it up and nodded. "Yeah, it might. Or our bedroom.

Tessa would leave the decision to her. She glanced around. "Where's Jadon?"

Richelle pointed down the hall. "He's sleeping. He does a lot of that lately."

"He must be having a growing spurt."

"He's always growing!"

Tessa chuckled and asked, "So, do you feel settled yet?"

"Somewhat. I need to decorate the place. I want to sew some valances and window coverings and I have some great ideas for our bedroom and the kitchen."

"I'm sure you'll have the place looking amazing in no time."

After placing the wall hanging back in the gift bag and leaning back, Richelle asked. "So how are things at Mansion of Hope? I sure do miss that place!"

"Are you planning to come back soon?"

"I've discussed it with Charlie. We've agreed to wait till Jadon is six months. I started back at the salon two weeks ago but I'm only working Saturdays for now. That's the only day Charlie can watch Jadon."

"Do you miss the Mansion of Hope?"

"I do! I miss the ladies. I'm sure there's been a big turn-over by now."

"Yes, but that's a good thing."

Richelle nodded. "Whatever happened with Bridget? Did she come back?"

Tessa's heart fell at the question. Bridget left the home early, insisting she couldn't bear it one more day. Her mother obliged her wishes, backed her request. "No. She won't be coming back. She went to this all-out party, got high as a kite and overdosed."

"No!"

Tessa waited a moment and then said, "She died."

Richelle placed both hands over her mouth and made a squeaking sound.

"Her mother is suing us."

Richelle lowered her hands. "What?"

Tessa nodded. "I know. She's the one who came to pick Bridget up from the home, despite our misgivings. We clearly told her it was the wrong thing to do, that it was completely counterproductive."

"Oh my!"

"Did you ever meet Bridget?"

"No, I never did."

"I wish we could have helped her. It tears me up inside."

"You've helped many, many women, Tessa. Don't let this get to you."

Tessa nodded, but she couldn't help it. Every time she thought of Bridget, she wanted to cry.

"How's it going with that new woman you told me about?"

"Sally?"

"Yeah."

"Actually, it's frustrating. She's been at the Home for two and half months and we've hit a brick wall. We're following the normal format and yet we're at an impasse. The initial detoxification process was difficult for her but she made it through okay. Her cravings are still pretty intense. She's also quite depressed. She misses her daughter a lot. Isabella's about five years old and her grandmother is caring for her right now. I don't know what to try next. Sally's a hard nut to crack."

"Has she accepted the Lord?"

"No, she hasn't. That's one of those brick wall issues. She's extremely resistant to letting down her guard. Religion has made her very gun shy. She barely puts up with the scriptures we read over her and I mean that literally!" Tessa rolled her eyes. "But she has no interest in taking it any further. I know there's something we're missing but I can't put my finger on it. Progress has really stalled with her."

With palms up and hands held out, Richelle said, "But she's seen results. And I'm sure she's been exposed to the other women's stories, how God's working in their lives. How can she resist the pull?"

"Religion has hurt her. She's so stubborn and determined to do it on her own. I'm at the end of my rope. I don't know what to do or how to get through to her. It's my age, I think. When I ask her questions during our counseling sessions, she gets this look of disdain, like she's talking to a juvenile."

"That's just plumb stupid!"

Richelle's shocked face made Tessa giggle.

Richelle shook her head. "Do you think she's still hiding something?"

"I've been wondering that. What else could be holding her back?"

"It could be the blockage you're looking for."

Tessa nodded. "I sense she's keeping a secret, something that's hurt her and she won't let it go."

"Besides the religion and husband thing?"

Tessa nodded.

"Hmm..."

"Could you pray about this? I need wisdom."

"Of course."

A small cry came from the other room. Tessa looked at Richelle.

"He'll be fine. He'll probably fall back asleep."

Tessa wished Jadon would wake up. She was anxious to hold him. It'd been too long since she'd seen him last.

"Have you heard from Luke lately?" asked Richelle.

"Actually I called him a few days ago."

"How's he doing?"

"Not well. He's very down and admitted feeling awful."

"Well, can you blame him?"

"No."

"With Janaye refusing his proposal, any guy would be bummed."

Tessa nodded. "I understand why she did it though. He still isn't a Christian and refuses to become one just to please her."

"That's good, isn't it? I mean, he should do it because it means something to him, not just to get the girl."

"That's what Luke said. If he does accept Christ, it will be because he knows it's right. He just isn't sure yet."

"He's scared of losing control." Richelle crossed her arms and nodded knowingly.

"Maybe." Tessa wasn't sure. Luke hated pretense. His honest, upfront way made her certain he wouldn't put on a masquerade just to get Janaye. She respected him tremendously for that.

Richelle's forehead furrowed. "So is he okay with her rejection?"

"No, of course not! He's heartbroken. I told you he was depressed."

"Is he still seeing her, pursuing her, calling her, what?"

"He's giving them both some space right now. He's not sure what to do."

"But he knows why she said no, right?"

"He knows it's because he's not a Christian. But Janaye loves him. She's said as much. It confuses him and he's hurt."

"I can relate to that. When Charlie became a Christian I was so angry and hurt. I thought he had ditched me for God and it infuriated me. I wanted him to abandon it and come back to me, but he wouldn't." She rubbed her forehead with her fingers. "That was such a trying time for me. I did so much soul searching."

"I think Luke's going through that right now."

Richelle nodded. "If only he'd realize how much peace a relationship with God will bring."

"He's consumed with the rebuff right now and angry at her. He feels betrayed."

Richelle nodded.

"Janaye is hurt too. She loves Luke. It took a lot of courage to do what she did, to obey God instead of giving in to her wants. We'll just have to keep praying for both of them."

Looking at Richelle warmed Tessa's heart. God had answered her prayers for Richelle. She'd accepted Christ. Luke was a tad more stubborn but she had full confidence that God would answer this prayer too.

~~~~

Tessa fanned her face with the folder as she waited for Sally to arrive. The air conditioning had gone on the fritz and it was blazing hot. Being nearly eight months pregnant didn't help the situation. Perspiration trickled down her neck and glistened on her face. The small fan she'd set up on the floor near her didn't do much to cool the air.

At their last session together, Sally had insisted she was substantially complete with the program and was looking forward to leaving. Tessa had made it quite clear that she was still in the inception stages and that she needed to extend her plans. Sally's stubborn refusal to open up during the sharing classes was one of the warning signs. She was definitely hiding something. Tessa silently prayed for God's help.

The woman had disclosed so many things, divulged so much. What could she still be harboring?

If Sally demanded they release her, they would. Tessa had full assurance that Sally would eventually be back, dependent on drugs again and needing help to get free again. Hopefully she'd be able to convince her to stay, to give the program a full go.

Deborah Elliot had been informed of the lack of headway with Sally. She'd agreed to help out with the next session and Tessa was looking forward to the older woman's wisdom.

~~~~~

Sally sat on the edge of her bed, knowing that she should be on her way to her appointment but she didn't see much rationale for it. The counseling sessions hadn't done her any good so far. Every time she went, pressure was applied to compel her to talk. To place her past on exhibit for everyone to view twisted her insides into a knot. There was nothing about her life to boast about, save Isabella. What did it matter anyway? She was drug-free now. Why keep her here longer? Okay, yes, she still craved the stuff. Was that a crime? Didn't they say that once a drug addict, always a drug addict? But she'd never go back to it. She knew that and was committed.

They didn't believe her. She could see it in their eyes. She ground her teeth in frustration at the thought.

Sally missed Isabella terribly. Her arms ached to hold her. This was all about her daughter anyway – and her job of course.

The past few months had been pure hell. To leave today sounded heavenly. If only they could see that she was ready.

The young, smooth-faced thing, Tessa something or other, thought she was so smart. Her superior attitude infuriated her. Thinking that a few Bible verses would help her stay off of drugs was ridiculous! Did they have their heads in the clouds? So they had a few success stories with some other women but she wouldn't be one of them. She'd gotten free of her cocaine addiction without the Bible. And she'd stay free without it too.

Sally glanced into the mirror attached to the small dresser that stood opposite her bed. Her gaunt, emaciated look was a telltale sign of the torment she'd been through. The drugs had taken their toll and the rehabilitation had been like hell on earth. She was as thin now as when she first came through those doors. Dark circles hung below her eyes, her cheeks looked sunken and her hair was lifeless and limp.

She ran a hand through her shoulder-length hair. To have her full-bodied texture back again would be so nice. Her once-curly hair only hung in limp waves.

"I look horrible!" She said to no one but herself.

Slowly she stood and tightened the string around her pants. They looked like hospital garb, big, baggy and hanging low in the crotch. None of her designer clothes would fit and they weren't allowed here. The home had assigned her a uniform and the oversized, light green uniform made her thin frame appear even more wasted.

The food they dished up here at the home was good and tasty enough but she didn't have much appetite these days. Her ordeal had sucked pounds from her body and left her looking like a third-world, starving child.

Her reflection in the mirror didn't look like a woman ready to face the world. A long, extended vacation somewhere hot, tropical and all-inclusive would be more fitting. She'd aged. At thirty-nine she looked more like fifty. Looking at her image in the mirror was disheartening. Turning away, she headed to the door.

Walking down the stairs was physically draining but there was no way she'd broadcast that to any of the staff. She held tightly to the rail as she descended. Catching her breath at the bottom, she walked down the hall to the counseling room, dread dogging her steps.

Sitting in front of the hugely pregnant woman, who knew nothing of the hardships of life, didn't bring her any visions of joy. All she felt for Tessa was contempt. What did this young girl know of unfaithfulness and divorce? The innocence on her face was a mockery to Sally's load of pain. The girl's rosy view of things was stifling and having to sit through another session was unbearable.

Sally placed her hand on the door handle and released a labored breath.

"Are things that bad, Sally?"

She jumped at the voice and turned to see Deborah Elliot walk up to her. "I didn't see you."

"Tessa asked me to join the two of you for this session."

Two of them! Great! Just what I need! Double the agony!

"Don't look so discouraged, Sally. I believe your breakthrough is just around the corner." Deborah pointed to the door. "Shall we go on in?"

Sally's face scrunched in unbelief. "Breakthrough from what?"

Deborah didn't answer but opened the door and held it for her.

Although greatly aggravated, Sally walked in. She'd already found breakthrough. The drug habit had been kicked. What other breakthrough was there?

She reached the chair and gratefully sank into it. Somehow she had to convince these two that she was ready to leave.

Deborah sat down opposite her. Tessa was already in the room and seated, her large belly jutting out awkwardly, with a folder in one hand and a pen in the other. Sally grimaced at the young thing, green behind the ears and naive as a child. Just the sight of her made her cringe. She was so tired of this ridiculous game.

The only reason she didn't get up right now and demand to be released was out of respect for Gregory Taylor. She owed him a great deal. It was because of him that she still had a job to go back to. If she left before she was ready, butchered this opportunity and regressed, she wasn't sure he'd give her another chance. She ground her teeth and prepared for the onslaught.

Tessa squirmed to get comfortable.

Sally couldn't help but smile in cynicism.

"Well, here we are," said Tessa.

That's as obvious as your protruding stomach.

Tessa smiled and said, "I asked Deborah Elliot to join us for this session."

Deborah said, "I already told her."

"Would you start us off with prayer?" asked Tessa.

Deborah nodded, bowed her head, folded her hands and prayed.

Sally watched the two women with bowed heads, praying to someone they couldn't see and who wouldn't answer anyway.

They are so deluded!

"Heavenly Father, I thank you that you're here with us and that you know what Sally needs today. We ask that your Holy Spirit would uncover what needs to be revealed and that Tessa and I will say the words that need to be said. We ask for complete emotional, physical and mental healing for Sally. She needs you so desperately and I ask that you would reveal to her how much you want to help her. You are the healer, deliverer, provider and comforter. You are more than enough to meet every one of Sally's needs. Show her your desire to heal and set her free, not only from drug use but also from the forces that led her into it. We have grown to love her and care so much about her. You love her far more than we ever could. We ask for your help now, in Jesus' name, amen."

They both looked up and locked eyes on her. Sally diverted her focus to her hands on her lap. She was resigned to trudge through this session but her emotions felt a million miles away.

After a moment of silence, Deborah asked, "Why don't tell us how you feel about your drug treatment so far?"

Sally looked at Deborah with surprise. To have such an early opportunity to convince these women to let her leave was providential.

She cleared her throat and said, "Well, I feel I've done remarkably well during the time I've been here. It hasn't exactly been a vacation but I've stayed off drugs and I know I won't ever go back on them. The Mansion of Hope has really helped me, given me the strength to go on." *Laying it on thick seems the best technique.* "I'm determined to stay free. The staff here has been tremendous. They've really helped me see the light. I'll never forget what you've all done for me. I'm ready to try life back on my own now."

By the look on their faces, they weren't falling for it.

With an amusing smile, Deborah said, "Yes, you've made tremendous strides during your time here. But there are some issues that we feel need to be addressed before you leave and we're hoping for your cooperation."

Defiance reared up in her heart. "I don't know of any issues remaining."

Deb looked down at her notes. "Could you tell me why your upbringing was so difficult?"

She couldn't keep anger from putting an edge to her words. "I've already gone over all of that with Tessa. I don't want to talk about it again!"

"All right. Then I'll just go over the items already listed in your file." Deborah gave Sally no chance to object. "It says here that your father was an alcoholic and that your mother was the spiritual leader of the home. It also says that there was a great deal of strife during your formative years. Your father didn't take an active role in your upbringing and he left everything to your mother. When you began to rebel, your father didn't try to curb it or seem to care. This caused you to feel unloved by him. He was a non-existent mentor in your life, but he did influence you to such a degree that you've never been able to have a successful relationship with any man."

"Stop! How dare you say that my father was responsible for all the deadbeats I was involved with? That's completely unfair!"

"Oh, is it? You've been angry with your father for a lifetime and that anger has transferred to all the men in your life. Even though you don't want to marry deadbeats, as you put it, you have sought to replace your father in every one of them."

Sally stiffened in anger. "What you're saying is way off base!" She'd never known Deborah to be this blunt and cruel.

"It's very well documented and easily confirmable that women that have had fathers caught in substance abuse will marry men of the same caliber, or abuse substances themselves. Your case is classic in that regard. You have clearly been in many dysfunctional relationships which mirror your parents' difficult marriage. You've relied on substances to get you through those relationships. Sally, if this pattern isn't dealt with and you don't receive some closure of the past, your young daughter will face the same statistics. Is that what you want for her?"

The room felt stifling and claustrophobic. "It won't happen to her. That's why I'm here to get help and that's why I want to leave and be with her so that I can protect her from this."

"Was your mother able to protect you from the painful relationships you went through?"

Leave my mother out of this!

"Sally?" said Deborah.

Sally looked up. "No, but she wasn't much of a mother, now, was she?" She bit her lip in frustration. She hadn't meant to say a derogatory word about her mother and here she was blabbing her big mouth off.

Deborah looked confounded for a moment before continuing. "I thought your mother was the spiritual leader of the home." Deborah scanned the notes resting on her lap. "You said she was a strong Christian woman, that she showed great concern when you rebelled as a teenager and longed for you to live right. You also said that she was quite nagging and controlling but that she did that because she loved you and wanted better for you. It's also listed here that she is a wonderful grandmother to your daughter, Isabella. You mentioned that she determined to stay with your father, no matter what, and that she prayed him into changing. In your file I see that that it's because of the prayers of your mother that you're still alive and here today." Deborah looked up and met Sally's gaze. "So what has changed? Why would you say your mother wasn't much of a mother?"

Sally could feel Tessa's eyes on her and it made her furious. Why didn't the innocent, inexperienced youth wait in the hall? She studied her thin, bony hands for a while. "It's just that we never got along that well. We had our run-ins and I guess that's what I was thinking about." Hopefully the ploy would work.

Deborah removed her eyeglasses, laid them in her lap and with a hint of a smile, said, "There's more, isn't there, Sally? She did something that you just can't forgive. Tell us the truth."

Sally squirmed uncomfortably. "I told you the truth."

"You haven't convinced me. You look too nervous."

Deborah's stare was uncanny and Sally tried to avoid it. Her eyes were like lasers, blazing into her soul. There was no way of knowing how much the woman could see into her. How much did she know? And how could she tell?

"Why can't you just leave me alone?" She felt cornered and wanted some space, some peace. Not that she'd ever known peace but the idea sounded wonderful.

"Because we care about you and want to help you."

The woman's eyes could change on a dime. One minute they were boring into her like a beam of light, exposing her heart, and the next they were pools of concern that warmed her insides. It freaked Sally out.

"Don't you know enough already? You've been digging around in my past long enough! Frankly, I'm tired of it! I'm off of drugs and I've stayed clean! Isn't that enough for the two of you?"

Deborah breathed deeply and released it slowly. "You've been angry for a long, long time. Sharing what happened between you and your mother will help you deal with all that anger. Forgiving those who hurt you is the only way you can truly live free."

Sally grunted mockingly. "Forgive?"

"So, is there something you could forgive your mother for?"

Sally stared at Deborah. The woman was persistent. "No!"

"Why is it so hard to tell us?"

"You don't know her."

"But you said she was a good mother."

"She was."

"Can you forgive her for her mistakes?"

"Never!"

Deborah's gaze became laser-like again. Sally looked away.

Why am I giving myself away? Why can't I keep my mouth shut?

"She's taking care of Isabella right now, isn't she?"

Sally nodded. She didn't trust her voice. Her insides were shaking, quivering. She didn't know why but the words were so close to the surface it terrified her.

"Do you trust her with Isabella?"

Sally couldn't speak. Keeping from breaking down was taking all her energy. Deborah needed to stop but Sally didn't know how to make her. She nodded again.

"Has she ever hurt Isabella?"

"No," Sally managed to whisper.

"But she's hurt you?"
Sally stayed quiet.
"How did she hurt you?"
Sally swore.

It didn't stop Deborah. "If she didn't hurt you and there's nothing to forgive, why did you move so far away from her?"

"I needed space."

"From her?"

Sally finally lifted her eyes to Deborah's. "Yes."

"Why?"

Okay, I'll tell them! Maybe then they'll stop hounding me!

Completely exasperated, she said, "She took my baby away!" Tears threatened but she swallowed hard and pushed her raw emotions down.

"What do you mean?"

Sally gathered her courage and said, "I got pregnant when I was fourteen. When my mother found out, she was furious. She was very involved in the church. Her reputation was at stake." Bitterness oozed from her but suddenly she didn't care. "To her, giving the baby away seemed the perfect solution. She didn't care how I felt about it. I knew I had made a mistake, but I wanted to keep my baby. I was fifteen when I gave birth to my daughter. She was beautiful." A tear escaped and trickled down Sally's cheek. "My mother said she wasn't raising my baby and neither was I. I needed to finish high school and that didn't fit with being a teen mother. I begged, screamed and cried but she refused to budge. She contacted an adoption agency and they came to the hospital. My baby girl was two days old when they took her from me. I had no say and I've never forgiven my mother for that."

The room became deathly quiet. Tears flowed down Tessa's face and she wiped at them with a tissue. Deborah's eyes were moist and shiny. Looking at the two of them was torture so Sally kept her eyes glued to the floor. She'd never felt so drained and spent. Deborah talked some more but Sally didn't hear it. She needed time to process what just happened. For some reason she felt different. Something had shifted but she wasn't sure what nor why. She needed to get to her room and away from these two.

CHAPTER 31

Tessa finished putting the groceries away, poured herself a tall glass of lemonade and sat down on the couch. It had been a busy week and she felt exhausted. Her feet were swollen again. Resting them on the ottoman should help take the swelling down somewhat. Cooking supper was beyond her at this point. Maybe they'd order in pizza once Cody got home.

Her thoughts wandered to the Mansion of Hope and Sally's inner turmoil. Since Sally had shared about her baby, she'd seemed different. Lines of worry filled her forehead and her desire to be alone had increased dramatically. She lived like a hermit these past few days. Unless Tessa went to Sally's room to check on her, she hardly ever saw her.

It was abundantly clear Sally was dealing with deep heart issues but as yet she still balked at giving her cares to God and allowing him heal her. Tessa had encouraged her a few times in the last few days to do just that. Each time, Sally's sullen face grimaced at the idea. All she could do was keep praying for the woman.

Tessa couldn't get Sally's confession out of her mind and kept thinking how uncanny it was the way her story lined up with her dreams. Initially it had really upset her. She'd questioned whether there was a connection but it seemed implausible. She finally came to the conclusion that God was preparing her for her work with Sally and she was at peace with it.

The front door opened and she craned her neck around till Cody appeared in the doorway.

He grinned and said, "Don't feel like cooking?"

"How can you tell?"

"I don't smell dinner."

"How does ordering pizza sound?"

"Great. I'll go order it." He disappeared into the kitchen to grab the phone.

In a few minutes he was back, carrying a glass of water and the mail in his other hand. After setting the stack of mail on the coffee table, he leaned over Tessa, gave her a kiss then sat down opposite her. He lifted a large, brown envelope from the pile and handed it to her.

"It came," he said.

Tessa sat up and stared at it. "It did?"

Cody gazed lovingly at her. "Are you scared?"

She locked eyes with him and nodded.

"You want me to open it?"

"Please." Pinpricks of nervousness raced across her skin. Whether she felt ready or not, she was about to find out.

He tore the envelope open and pulled out the contents.

Tessa patted the spot beside her on the couch. He stood, came over and sat down next to her. After scanning the papers, he started with the front page and read out loud.

~~~~~

Sally didn't know what was happening to her. Ever since she'd opened her big mouth and divulged about her mother and giving up her daughter, she'd felt undone. Her insides were like mush, she had this uncontrollable desire to cry and any contact with people seemed unbearable. If only she could get a grip on herself! But days had passed since then and still she felt bombarded with grief and anger, as though her heart was experiencing a continual earthquake and she didn't know how to make it stop.

Why would going back and visiting that part of her life rattle her so? All she did was talk about it to two women who were far too nosy for their own good. So why this? What she needed was some crack cocaine. That would calm her nerves in a jiffy.

What was she thinking! She'd determined to never go back to that. Is this what Deborah and Tessa were up to? They wanted to shake her to the point of showing her weakest link? Okay, so she was an addict. Why go to such extremes to prove it to her? So she'd see she wasn't ready to leave? Is that why they pushed her to the edge? So she'd finally get it?

Sorrow filled her heart, threatening to suffocate her. She smiled sullenly, amused that she didn't feel angry. Usually anger was her first method of defense. The smile died on her lips.

To think that getting off cocaine and staying off wasn't enough rattled her to the core. Would she go back to it as soon as life got to her again? Stress was bound to come eventually. Her instability screamed failure to her right now. It was thoroughly demoralizing.

Isabella's face flitted over her consciousness.

Tears pooled in her eyes, slid down her face and dripped onto her drab uniform. All these months and she still wasn't ready. Disappointment sapped her of all hope.

~~~~~

It had been a week since their last counseling session with Sally. Tessa had requested another get-together with her, just the two of them. Sally had eventually conceded but she hadn't looked thrilled about it.

To admit she was nervous was the understatement of the century. Tessa fidgeted with her hands in her lap while she waited, praying with all her heart for God to give her the right words.

A sound at the door got her attention. Sally's thin frame was morphed by the doorway and her weary face spoke volumes. It had been a tough week for her.

"Come on in, Sally."

Sally shuffled over and slowly sat down opposite Tessa. She averted her eyes, studying the floor tile in earnest.

Tessa sent up one more quick prayer and said, "I've noticed you've been very anti-social this last week."

Sally refused to look at her.

Tessa pushed on. "Do you want to tell me what it's about?"

No answer and still no eye contact.

After a steadying breath, Tessa said, "It's necessary for you to forgive your mother. She only did what she felt was best for you and best for your baby. Her goal was to make your life easier. It would have been very challenging being a mother at fifteen. She did what she did because she loved you."

Finally, Sally raised her eyes. "She had a funny way of showing it. I wanted to keep my baby!" There was torture in her eyes.

Tessa looked away. It was hard to look at such despair. "Have you ever wondered where your daughter is right now?"

"Often."

Tessa reached for the envelope she'd placed on the floor earlier.

Sally's eyes followed her movements. "What's that?"

She held up the large package for Sally to see. The return address in the corner was in large print, easy to read.

Her response was immediate. "You contacted an adoption agency? How dare you meddle in my business? You had no right!" She stood and turned to the door.

"Sally, wait! It's not what you think." Tessa stood and waited.

Sally's hand was already on the doorknob when she turned tentatively to look back.

"Please, let me explain."

Sally paused and slowly made her way back. No one was created to carry that much anger and bitterness; it would wear anyone down. Tessa's heart broke for her.

"So what did you do? Contact my daughter and arrange for the two of us to meet? Try to fix me? Snap me out of my depression?"

Tessa shook her head.

"I never said I wanted to meet her!" Anger and sorrow exuded from her eyes simultaneously.

"So, you're saying you never want to meet her?"

"Stop putting words in my mouth!"

"I was just wondering." Fear pounded in Tessa's heart.

"I certainly don't want you to manipulate my life. You've done enough harm already."

Tessa was sure Sally meant all the sharing she'd encouraged her to do. Opening up was never easy for those caught in addiction. Sally was angry and holding a grudge. It was a well-entrenched habit of hers.

Sally shook her head despondently. "I can't handle any more rejection. If she rejects me, it would destroy me."

The truth was out. Sally was terrified of meeting her daughter. There was too much risk involved. This only bolstered Tessa's determination to forge ahead.

With the envelope resting on her lap, Tessa pulled out the contents and held them. She glanced at Sally and said, "I sent away for these papers long before I ever met you."

Confusion clouded Sally's face.

"These are my adoption papers. They tell me who my birth mother is."

Anger replaced the confusion quickly. "So you think telling me about your little story will somehow snap me out of this and make me all better."

The mockery in her voice made Tessa cringe but she couldn't stop now. "I don't know. What I do know is that it will answer some questions."

Sally sneered at her.

Tessa focused on the papers in her hands. "My adoption was done through an international agency. It says here that my birth mother gave birth to me in Toronto, Canada at Mount Sinai Hospital."

The sneer dissipated from Sally's face.

"It says the father is unknown and that my mother gave me up willingly." Tessa looked up, deep into Sally's eyes. "It lists my mother's name as Sally Windsor."

Sally's deep brown eyes mirrored Tessa's brown eyes. They filled with shock then quickly clouded and filled with tears. They spilled over and doused her cheeks with moisture. Her broken sobs filled the small room.

Tessa saw raw fear in Sally and knew she needed to do something. She scooted her chair close to Sally's and placed an arm around her shoulders.

"I grew to love you, Sally, before I ever knew you were my birth mother. These papers only came in the mail two days ago." She felt on the verge of tears with the telling. "I'm so proud of what you've accomplished here and so proud to call you my mother."

Sally pulled away, took her arms, wrapped them around Tessa's neck and held tightly. "I'm so sorry! I never wanted to give you away!" She wailed again, gut-wrenching sobs flowing from deep within her soul. "I'm so sorry, baby!"

"It's okay. I forgive you." Tessa couldn't stop her own tears then. They flowed freely.

They clung to each other desperately, weeping. A healing balm was released from above that covered both of them with the warmth of heaven.

CHAPTER 32

The road had been long and difficult. Even now, Sally wasn't sure she was ready to leave. But they'd given her the okay, the virtual thumbs up. Essentially, they were kicking her out and it felt good. All the tools she needed to stay clean they'd imparted to her, taught her and role-played for her. She'd be forever grateful.

Since Tessa's revelation, her heart had done a one-eighty. Sally didn't recognize herself. She'd changed dramatically, not only emotionally, but physically. Her frame no longer resembled a holocaust survivor. She was beginning to put on weight. Her hair now gave off a shiny glow and her curls were full. Looking in the mirror was no longer painful. Sally was beginning to like herself again.

The biggest change, however, took place inside. Her once-locked-and-sealed heart had finally begun to open. Being reunited with her eldest daughter had caused her soul to begin to mend. Forgiving her mother was easier now. Maybe if God was capable of restoring a daughter, he could restore other areas of her past. For the first time ever, she felt at peace with herself. As unaccustomed as she was to it, she quite enjoyed the novel tranquil state.

Sally packed the last of her belongings into the small suitcase she'd brought and zipped it shut. Deborah had called a taxi for her. It would be here any minute.

The goodbyes were already said. The Home had had a celebration dinner for her a few days ago, along with two other women. It had been a magical, surreal evening, filled with festivity and joy. The staff at the beautiful Mansion of Hope knew how to throw a party.

For a moment she felt anxiety at having to leave the safety of this place. She'd come to rely on the staff and their support. Others like her were here who could understand and relate to her, women who knew the struggles out in the real world. They'd become friends over the months and leaving seemed like a handicapped person leaving the safety of a wheelchair to try to walk unsupported.

And yet the thought of seeing Isabella dwarfed all the unknowns. Only twice had she been able to see her during her stay here. Her mother had driven to Chelsey those times, bringing Isabella with her. It wasn't nearly enough for Sally. Her arms ached for her daughter and to be a mother again. It was the incentive she needed to stay clean out there.

With determination she grabbed her suitcase and set it by the door. She slipped into her coat, slung her purse handle over her shoulder and scanned her sparse room. Soon another woman would occupy this space. She sent up a short prayer for whomever it would be. The woman would need it; of that she was sure.

Slowly she opened the door, stepped into the hall and descended the elegant, curved stairway down to the massive foyer. She would miss this beautiful place. The Mansion of Hope would forever be a reminder of the reversal of the course of her life. This was where her heart began to melt and heal. This was where she'd been reunited with her long-lost daughter and that thought brought an automatic smile. God had divinely led her here. He had orchestrated the whole thing and she was thankful.

Deborah Elliot met her at the door and hugged her tightly. They said their final goodbyes and Sally made the giant step to the outdoors. The taxi was already waiting at the curb. The driver stepped out and placed her suitcase in the trunk. With one more wave to Deb, standing at the large, double doors of the home, Sally slipped into the back seat and closed the door. The taxi pulled away and Sally craned her neck and watched as the Mansion of Hope grew smaller behind them.

They turned the corner and Sally swiveled back to the front. Before she headed to Minneapolis, there was one stop she wanted to make first. She handed the driver a slip of paper with the address.

Tessa opened the door and smiled brightly. She'd come! "Welcome here."

Sally walked in, opened her arms and Tessa went to her. The hug was firm and intense. Sally finally released her hold and, looking around, said, "I love your place!"

"Thank you."

Smiling shyly, Sally said, "Is she awake?"

"Yes."

"Wonderful!" Sally handed over a gift.

Tessa took it from her hands and led the way to the living room. The basinet sat in the corner with a pink, knit blanket draped over the side.

Walking right to it, Sally gazed inside. She reached in and lifted the small bundle into her arms.

Tears threatened as Tessa watched her birth mother hold her daughter. It was a surreal moment, one she never thought she'd see.

"She's beautiful." The pride in Sally's eyes was undeniable.

"I'm sorry I wasn't at your celebration dinner."

Sally looked at her. "You had the baby early. There was no way you could have planned that differently."

They both sat down on the couch. Tessa set the gift from Sally at her feet; she'd open it later. Nothing could compare to the gift of having her birth mother visit her home. What an unexpected gift from above. She now understood the puzzling dreams. God prepared her, warned her of what was coming. Tessa realized she was the baby in the dream and Sally the mother of the child. God showed her what her birth mother had gone through before she ever met her.

Sally tucked the baby up close to her chest and gazed at her with awestruck eyes. "I still can't believe it. I'm a grandmother."

It brought a smile. Tessa said, "And I'm doubly blessed. I have two mothers now, and Faith Grace has another grandmother."

Sally looked up. "I love the name. It reminds me of my journey. I've found a new faith and have experienced God's grace."

Tessa nodded. God had worked a miracle in Sally and divinely brought them together.

Now that Sally was leaving, heading back to Minneapolis, it brought mixed feelings. Having been reunited with her mother for such a short time, it was hard to let her go.

"I've been thinking," said Sally.

Tessa waited for her to go on.

"I need support. I won't have that in Minneapolis."

"I know. That's what Deborah and I have tried to tell you."

Sally nodded. "So I've been debating the pros and cons of moving here."

Tessa wanted to clap her hands in delight as her heart fluttered in anticipation.

"I'll look into it and see if I can work from here and send my designs in via email. I can always drive there if I need to for meetings and so on. I'll talk to Gregory Taylor and see what can be arranged." Sally smiled. "It can't hurt to try."

"Oh, I'd love that!" exclaimed Tessa.

"Would you?" she asked uncertainly. "I wasn't sure."

"Of course! To have you close would be a dream come true."

Sally's eyes misted. "It would be a dream come true for me too."

It really was uncanny how much she knew about her birth mother. Sally had shared the most difficult moments of her life, the down-and-dirty details. And yet Tessa didn't see that when she looked at her. She'd grown to love her. It took great courage to face one's fears, pain and heartache and determinedly move forward to something more positive. Sally's courage was an inspiration.

Sally had told her about Isabella. Tessa would love to meet her. They were sisters and the only sister Tessa had. It made her heart smile.

As if Sally could read her thoughts, she said, "I'd like to bring Isabella with me the next time I come to visit."

"Will you? I'm so excited about meeting her!"

Sally's face lit up. "She's thrilled to have a sister."

"She knows?"

"Yes, we talked on the phone and I told her."

Looking at Sally astounded her. The resemblance between the two of them was amazing. Tessa was surprised that she hadn't noticed it right from the first day she met Sally. But then again,

Sally looked different then. At their first meeting she had looked old and sickly, her eyes drab and lifeless. Looking at her now, Tessa could easily see where she got her curly, dark hair from and her deep, brown eyes. They had nearly identical profiles. The only difference Tessa could see was in their lips. Sally's were thinner, while hers were full.

"She'll know right away."

"Know what?" asked Tessa.

"That you're my daughter."

"You noticed the resemblance too, huh?"

"It's uncanny." Sally shook her head in wonder. "I was too irritated with you at first to take note, you know, when I first got to Mansion of Hope. But now," she grew pensive for a moment, "it's so obvious."

Sally turned to study her granddaughter, pure joy written on her face.

Tessa watched with a thankful heart.

Sally looked up and said, "I don't know if I ever told you about the supernatural things that happened when I was in my early twenties."

"I think you did at one of our sessions. Was it about using the name of Jesus and having people come back to life?"

"I shared that?"

Tessa nodded as Sally became thoughtful.

"Way back then, God was trying to woo me to himself. But even though those were unexpected and astounding miracles, the greatest miracle of all happened here in Chelsey. God used you to make me whole again. It's because of you that I allowed God into my life again. You're the greatest miracle I've ever experienced."

Tessa choked up to hear her mother say it. That was why she started working at the Mansion of Hope. She wanted to make a difference, do something for eternity. To bring healing to wounded people was her passion, but to think that God gave her the privilege of ministering to her own mother astounded her. She felt blessed beyond words.

"Hope. That's what you've given me, Tessa. And it's what God's given me."

"That's what the Mansion of Hope is in the business of doing."

"And you do it well."

Joy and hope shone from Sally's eyes and Tessa was thankful beyond words.

###

THANK YOU

Thank you for reading *Time And Healing*. If you enjoyed it, won't you please take a moment to leave me a review at your favorite retailer?

Also, if you'd like to know more of Tessa's and Sally's stories, check out the third book of the trilogy - *Time and Restoration*. The third book follows Isabella, Sally's younger daughter, as she searches for answers to her past. Sally is determined to keep certain aspects of her history hidden. Will Isabella find a way to unravel the past and finally be at peace?

OTHER NOVELS BY AUTHOR

HEAVEN ON EARTH SERIES:

Assignment Code 110
Assignment Code 123
Assignment Code 321

TIME TRILOGY:

Time and Destiny – Book 1 of Trilogy
Time and Restoration – Book 3 of Trilogy

SHORT STORIES:

The author's short stories are on her blog, located on her website - colleenreimer.ca or colleenreimer.com.

For more information about these books or short stories go to www.colleenreimer.ca or www.colleenreimer.com. To sign up to receive her short story notifications, go to her web site and enter your email information.

ABOUT THE AUTHOR

Colleen Reimer lives near Calgary, Canada with her husband and four children, although only the youngest two still live at home. She has lived in multiple places over the years, in many different Canadian cities and also spent seven years in North Carolina.

Besides writing, Colleen also enjoys gardening, travelling, chatting with friends, a hot cup of Chai tea and chocolate.

Manufactured by Amazon.ca
Bolton, ON